Cricket in a Fist

Cricket in a Fist

NAOMI K. LEWIS

GOOSE LANE

The epigraph is an excerpt from "Liberation" by Abraham Sutzkever, translated by Barbara and Benjamin Harshav and published in *A. Sutzkever: Selected Poetry and Prose* (Berkeley: University of California Press: 1990).

Edited by Laurel Boone.
Cover photograph copyright © Andy Dean, Dreamstime.com.
Cover and interior design by Julie Scriver.
Printed in Canada on 100% PCW paper.
10 9 8 7 6 5 4 3 2 1

Library and Archives Canada Cataloguing in Publication

Lewis, Naomi K., 1976-

    Cricket in a fist / Naomi K. Lewis

ISBN 978-0-86492-495-7

Title.

PS8623.E967C75 2008   C813'.6   C2007-906409-4

Goose Lane Editions acknowledges the financial support of the Canada Council for the Arts, the Government of Canada through the Book Publishing Industry Development Program (BPIDP), and the New Brunswick Department of Wellness, Culture and Sport for its publishing activities.

Goose Lane Editions
Suite 330, 500 Beaverbrook Court
Fredericton, New Brunswick
CANADA E3B 5X4
www.gooselane.com

For my family

You will look for a key to fit
Your jammed locks.
Like bread you will bite the streets
And think: better the past.
And time will drill you quietly
Like a cricket caught in a fist.

— Abraham Sutzkever, "Liberation"

Cricket in a Fist

I woke into a white room full of cut flowers, and my whole life slipped away like some epic, complex dream that leaves a formless uneasiness in the wake of its details. People gathered round me — people I recognized but couldn't place. A woman spoke to me, said a name that was clearly mine. I grasped at my few remaining threads of memory, but they receded, leaving me empty-minded. All I could recall was a rush of red, a multi-hued fluttering. When I tried to remember more, this redness barricaded the past, leaving me with nothing but the present moment. The younger of the two girls, who I realized later were my daughters, began to cry. Days and weeks passed in a blur. There were always people around my bed, and I was certain they wanted to stop looking at me, but, smiling bravely, they took me home instead.

For the first few months I was very quiet. I had broken my ankle at the same time as injuring my head, and it was in a cast, so I sat at the kitchen table, where I could see out the window, and waited. When people spoke to me, I couldn't think of a response. I began to read my old journals and books, and soon I realized that I remembered things. I knew about my childhood, how I'd grown up with my mother and grandmother. I remembered my father's death and my grandmother's, remembered marrying and having children. I kept waiting for the accompanying feelings to return, but they never did. I remembered loving my husband, remembered the torment at the times when I didn't love him. But I felt — nothing. Not even loss; not even guilt.

As my therapist recommended, I began to write daily, whatever came into my head. My handwriting kept changing. In my house, in the hospital, limping down the street on my crutches, I was disoriented and lost, like a recent arrival on an alien planet. What's more, I felt pursued. I often perceived a presence just behind me, and when I turned, no one was there. I'd wake in the night panicking, sure that someone was standing beside my bed; but when I opened my eyes the room was empty. My husband, a neurobiologist, was very much involved in my treatment. He and the doctors told me that sensed presences are common after certain kinds of head trauma, but I still believe I was haunted at that time. My lurking pursuer was not a physiological phenomenon or a metaphor — she was the ghost of my former self, armed with all the miserable memories and cynical beliefs that made her the way she was, trying to scare me out of moving forward.

In The Willing Amnesiac *I will tell stories about the figures that haunted the shadowy dream-life I led before waking up and taking control. All names have been changed for the protection and privacy of those still living. I do not wish to slander or misrepresent anyone, and I acknowledge that, ultimately, this story is only about me. It is worth mentioning that I have changed my own name as well, and though I was called by many names throughout my former life, the one I have now is unique because I chose it myself.*

J. Virginia Morgan
The Willing Amnesiac: Reappearing into the Present

One

I spent the day sitting on my dirty white sofa, sewing a scarlet A across the chest of a thrift-store cocktail dress. I'd cut the letter from a large piece of felt, and I leaned close, smoothing the fabric, making each even stitch tiny and tight. Each time I pushed the needle through, I remembered that it was Halloween; it had been nine years.

And when I sat back, my task complete, I noticed that my neck ached, my fingers were cramped, and the sun had risen high and then set. I hadn't eaten all day. I prepared spaghetti and tomato sauce and ate at my desk, then showered and dressed and put in my contacts. With my hair up, eyes dark and lipstick lurid, I turned in front of the mirror, running a finger along my letter's edge, the perfect seam. I pulled on my shoes and jacket, turned back to answer the phone, and thought of that one misstep. The first cancerous cell in my family's now unrecognizable body.

I brought the phone to the mirror. "I'm just going out to a party," I said, rubbing concealer under my eyes. I lived in a huge, square room with a small, separate kitchen and a bathroom too tiny for a tub. The building had once housed offices, and my apartment still had grey industrial carpet from wall to white wall, even in the kitchen. Lamps in every corner meant I never had to use the acoustic-tiled ceiling's flat, fluorescent lights.

"I did it," Minnie said. "I'm not bullshitting you. I'm in the terminal. The Toronto bus terminal. I told you, I told you I was going to do it."

I suspected she was calling from Ottawa, sitting comfortably on her bed, hoping to shake me up. It had been nine years today, and she knew it. But I could hear that she was in a large, open space, with strangers walking past her. My little sister was in the wrong city. My city. "But," I said, "how did you get there?"

"On the bus. What do you think? Didn't you get my e-mail? So can you come and get me, or what?"

I looked at the two long, backless bookcases that served as a wall between my bedroom and living room; Minnie would look outside and see my view of the adult video store, a billboard featuring a cowgirl drinking beer and a streetlight that shone on my pillow all night, impossible to block out completely. I loved my apartment; no one I was related to had ever seen it.

"Agatha!" she said. "Hurry, okay? I'm about to get kidnapped or something. Don't tell Dad," she added, and hung up.

Thinking of Dad and Lara's hardwood-floored house with its stainless steel appliances, diagonally folded napkins and avocado-coloured dining room walls, the kind of house Min was used to, I hurried to straighten my dusty lampshades. I rearranged my great-grandmother's old green and brown shawl to hide the frayed upholstery on my yard-sale armchair. I stopped halfway to the bed and hesitated, looking back toward the door. I didn't have time — I settled for shaking out my duvet and letting it fall over the crumpled sheet, still crooked, then shoved a pile of clothes from the floor into the laundry hamper. And my bookcases — I wondered if she'd notice the shelves of women's autobiographies organized chronologically, beginning with *The Life of Teresa of Jesus*. I took a cardigan from the back of a chair and tucked it over the slew of celebrity memoirs and self-help books that concluded the collection.

I couldn't leave Minnie alone or bring her to the party; I'd made the costume for nothing. In the bathroom, I unzipped my jacket and looked at the dress, short, tight and lettered, and stared at my reflection, willing it to change. I looked sallow. I knew it was just the light, but my red lipstick seemed garish, my skin jaundiced, and my hair so yellow it was greenish, the shadows under my eyes like bruises. I'd barely thought about my sister's latest e-mail, now several days old. She'd written something about not being able to take it anymore. *Any tips?* she'd written. *I'll e-mail again when I can. Don't tell Dad.* She rode the bus away from Ottawa, toward Toronto and toward me, alone, down the 401, and I had forgotten about her. I was stitching around the edge of my scarlet letter, dressing by the bathroom's gruesome light, and pulling on my fishnets. I was examining it again — the scene I had replayed in my head until it incorporated itself into my breathing and my heartbeat to become as constant and essential as any bodily rhythm.

She was walking downstairs fast, pointy-heeled black pumps clicking on the salon's grey-tiled stairs, and I was standing hand in hand with my four-year-old sister. Minnie was disguised as Fireman Jeff, a character of her own devising, and my hair was bright red. From the top step, I watched my mother's descent. Below me and Minnie, the back of Mama's trench coat swished, her stiff-sprayed hair bounced; we watched her hurry down the stairs, one hand skimming the orange handrail. I saw where Mama's left foot was headed, saw the roof of Minnie's beloved plastic fire truck. I don't know what I heard first — my sister's shriek, the audible crack of ankle bone or the fire truck clattering down the stairs. Mama's ankle buckled and her body twisted as she struggled for balance. She spun around, arms thrown up as if in surrender, and she was facing us when she fell. Ankles bent unnaturally, arms raised inelegantly, she looked right at me like a diver who'd already leapt. She seemed to hover there before her fists clutched air, knees gave way, head bent back. The smells in the stairwell were faint and chemical: perm solution, hair dye, nail polish remover. The wallpaper was brown and beige paisley with little orange leaves that matched the handrail and the door.

Our grandmother, Tam-Tam, heard the crash from behind the front desk of the salon; she pushed past us down the stairs, held

Mama's hand and sent us outside to wait in the rain. We heard the siren a minute before we saw the ambulance hurtling toward us down the block, traffic parting for our mother's rescuers. Two paramedics carried a stretcher through the rust-coloured door. Beside the curb, a fire truck's lights were flashing. Minnie sucked her bottom lip hopefully.

In the hospital waiting room, Tam-Tam, in her cashmere sweater, sipped tea, leaving lipstick prints on the white Styrofoam. My sister rested on Dad's lap, staring at a baseball-capped man with a huge piece of gauze taped to his bony shin; later, when it was dark outside and she'd irrevocably missed trick-or-treating, Minnie curled up on a chair under Dad's jacket. The first thing he said to me, running his finger gently down my forehead: "What did those imbeciles do to your hair?"

I pulled away from his hand. "It's just semi-permanent. It was supposed to be for my Halloween costume."

"Take a look in the mirror."

The hair dye had dripped in the rain, and long streaks had run down my forehead and around my eyebrows to pool and dry under the frames of my glasses. My Halloween makeup was ruined, sparkly dark eyeliner smudged under my eyes, and there was a wine-like stain around the neck of my T-shirt. After putting my hair in a ponytail, I folded my glasses onto the sink top and peeled off the red false lashes, painfully removing a few of my real lashes in the process. I scrubbed my face with hand soap, dried my skin with paper towels.

The nurse moved us to another waiting room, through a set of doors and less crowded, and kept calling Dad aside, talking in a way that made him stoop to hear, nod as if he understood. He told us that Mama had hit her head hard, that we couldn't leave until we knew how badly she was hurt. I wasn't eager to go home and change into my red dress and the matching wings I'd made from a coat hanger and pantyhose. If anything, I was glad I'd be missing the Halloween dance. The television in the waiting room played sitcoms, the evening news, eventually *Saturday Night Live*. I was fifteen. I was touching my sore lips with the tips of my fingers, thinking about the blond, cigarette-smelling boy I'd kissed under the stairs at school the day before.

One evening, just months earlier, Mama had left our house by taxi, tea towel wrapped tight around the hand she'd cut along with the carrots for our dinner. At regular intervals, Dad drove her away in the night, Mama wheezing or limping or retching. She was accident-and-illness-prone, but she always recovered, and she'd been hospitalized so many times we'd come to believe she was invincible. Dad and Tam-Tam would say later that my sister sensed before anyone else that this time was different. "She cried through the whole taxi ride to the hospital," Tam-Tam said. She described Minnie's snuffling, restrained and sorrowful — "not like one of her tantrums." I didn't correct them, didn't argue that she was only crying out of disappointment over not getting to ride in the fire truck, the first real one she'd ever seen up close.

"The bus?" said Dad, when I called him from the streetcar. "They let a thirteen-year-old on the bus, alone?" I heard him move the phone away from his mouth to tell Lara what my sister had done, and then Lara's muffled, panicked reply. Lara was practically Minnie's mother; I barely knew her.

"Agatha," Dad said. "Go to the terminal and find her, then get back on the next bus with her and bring her home. I'll pay for both tickets."

"I can't do that," I said. "I have to go to work tomorrow. I have shifts every day this week."

"Can't you tell them it's a family emergency?"

"No!" I said. "I can't. They're depending on me. Not to mention it's my *job*. It's my income. I have a life here."

"You know that I'm happy to help you out financially until you find something better. Did you apply for the job in Gerry's office?"

"Steven," I said. "I'm not moving back to Ottawa to be your cousin's receptionist. I can't believe you're bringing this up right now. I have to go. I'm going into the subway station."

The terminal was two trains away, and I knew that if Minnie changed her mind she could leave, walk down Bay Street and dissolve into the city, and I might never find her. I'd lived with Dad and Lara for only three months when I ran away, but Dad found me two days later in the food court of the mall, drinking rum and Coke out of a cardboard cup with my twenty-one-year-old drug-dealer boyfriend. Running away to Toronto is different; my sister had really left home. Two people could live in Toronto for years and never cross paths. That's why I always checked. In restaurants, streetcars and stores. I walked the length of subway cars, scanning each face. I saw other people staring down at newspapers or gazing intently at dark windows that offered only reflections. Any two people could be long lost to each other, could sit one orange vinyl seat away and never realize how close they'd come.

I had never found J. Virginia Morgan, and we'd lived in the same city for over four years. It said on her latest book jacket that she divided her time between Toronto and Spain and also toured a lot, giving seminars mostly in American cities. It was unlikely that someone her age, with such a lucrative career, would take the subway, but more and more frequently I thought I caught a glimpse of her across the subway tracks, waiting for a train heading in the other direction. Behind me, I'd catch a flash of business suit, a waft of perfume, but when I turned, it was never her. Didn't even look like her. My hands would shake with adrenalin for minutes, and I would tell myself I should move to a different city. I reminded myself why I moved to Toronto, that it was my best option, the best university. It wasn't because of what her book jacket said *About the Author*, wasn't so that, in every crowd, movie, grocery store, I'd feel the possibility of her breath on my neck.

Since arriving in Toronto, I'd found a thrill in the underground connection between subway station, mall and bus terminal. It was no coincidence that I'd met two boyfriends on the bus; I found people with giant packs strapped to their backs, entering the city from afar or heading for another destination, irresistibly alluring. Usually I entered the terminal because I was leaving town, and it felt strange to walk in with no bag, no intention to take a bus out of the city and onto the highway. Minnie was exactly where I'd told her to stay, sitting on a grey chair with a big red backpack on her lap. She stood when she saw me, and it was plain that she was almost fourteen, poor Minnie, possessed by adolescence at its worst. Since I'd last seen her in Ottawa, six months earlier, her reddish hair had grown longer and she'd put on weight. She'd grown breasts — she had a woman's body — and was wearing so much dark eye makeup it was visible from across the room. I saw her struggle not to smile as she stood and squared her shoulders. She came towards me past the rows of chairs and the pay phones, chin up, swinging her hips and pouting, catwalking in her yellow platform sneakers. I'd never seen her walk that way before. I recognized the blue and grey Adidas jacket that Dad used to wear.

"Min." I grabbed her and held on tight. She was bigger than me, more solid, and the shoes made her even taller. "What were you thinking?" She shifted uncomfortably in my arms, but relief made it difficult to let go. I released the back of her jacket from my fists and stepped away.

"You took out your nose ring," she said. "You're shorter than me. Why are you dressed like that?"

"It's a Halloween costume." I opened my jacket and showed her the dress. "The scarlet letter. You know? I'm a character from a book."

"Oh." She must have applied a fresh coat of lipstick while waiting, because her lips were dark, shiny purple. Her breath smelled like gum. It didn't occur to her that I must be dressed up for a party, that I had cancelled my plans for her. Of course it didn't; she was thirteen.

I led Minnie down the escalator and looked up to see our reflection; behind me, she leaned on one foot as if she was trying to disappear into the escalator railing. She'd inherited Mama's full features and Dad's bulky height. Her nose and lips were fleshy, breasts full, lips full, limbs long. Away from the light of my apartment, I was pleased to see how good I looked in my costume. My hair was a vampish approximation of Victorian, my lips bright, shiny red. My skin looked pink and healthy and I was satisfyingly slight.

My sister followed my gaze up to the mirrored ceiling and scowled. No one would have guessed that we were related.

"I'm starving," Minnie said, as we walked through the food court under Bay Street. After considering her options, she ordered Chinese food served from large metal tubs and waited for me to pay and choose a table. She used the disposable chopsticks easily and thoughtlessly, and I watched her eat half the food and drink a whole cup of pop. There was an amoebic blob of purplish red polish in the centre of each of her fingernails, and she still sucked her lips between bites — she would have been humiliated to know how childlike it made her look. Finally I asked, "So, what the hell happened?"

"Are you going to rat me out?"

"I don't know," I told her. "I don't even know what you're doing here."

"Didn't you think I'd come? Did you get my e-mail?" She'd been writing me daily, sending articles about J. Virginia Morgan and interviews with her. I had stopped reading her messages carefully, since they mostly consisted of rants about Lara's mother, Bev, who'd moved in with them. "I guess you weren't paying too much attention," she said. "I wasn't going to call you, by the way. But the person who was supposed to meet me at the bus station didn't show up."

"What? Minnie? Who do you know in Toronto?"

"You know no one calls me that anymore. Jasmine." Our mother had been six months pregnant when she had her ultrasound and decided on the name Emily Jasmine. As soon as she was born, my sister became Minnie. Mini she was: three pounds when she came into the world, and though for the first four years of her life she grew softly round and tall for her age, she was still miniature to us, and her full name was reserved for reprimands. When she started kindergarten, she was Jasmine at school, still Minnie at home. The first time a little girl phoned and asked sweetly for Jasmine Winter, I saw my sister's personality splitting: she was a child who turned into a different person when her parents were out of mind. She looked at me evenly, elbow on the table, chopsticks between her fingers.

J. Virginia Morgan writes in all her books that your past, and your family's past, are just stories. They are no more important and have no more claim on you than any other story. You feel shackled, she claims, but you're really just afraid to let go. And I was wondering already, as Minnie pushed chow mein around her plate, why she'd really run away. It was Halloween, the day the worst had happened, the day everything always came back to haunt us. Surely she had come looking for an explanation, the details that would make everything clear. I was the only other person who'd seen it happen; I was the one who was supposed to have protected her, and my sister had come with some matters to settle.

I was ten when Minnie was born. Mama and Dad had prepared me, and I had pictured the scene many times. It would two weeks before Christmas, and I would stay at Granny and Grandpa Winter's house. We lived in Aylmer, Quebec, and I went to the anglophone school in Hull. But when my sister came, I wouldn't take the bus home with my best friend, Helena, like I usually did; Grandpa Winter would be waiting for me in his car, clad in sweater vest and tweed tie, pipe between his friendly yellow teeth, to take me to Ottawa's west end. When I returned home at the end of a week of grandparently indulgence, I would have a sister. But Minnie arrived over a month early, before the world was ready for her, purple and gold wallpaper for her nursery still rolled up in the closet, cradle bought but unassembled, Granny and Grandpa Winter at an auction out of town, buying aged objects for their antique store.

Mama had been immobile for two months, swelling and reclining, reading and watching TV. She told all her piano students she was taking a break from teaching. "I'm not putting my feet up," she told Dad. "I'm just putting them aside until after the baby's born." When Mama put her feet aside, she fell limp onto the brown corduroy sofa and stayed there all day with a book in her hand and the television on. When I came home from school, she'd be watching

Three's Company, looking resignedly sardonic, running her fingertips over cushions, over the coffee table, over her thighs in silent scales and sonatas.

"Hey, little Agamemnon," she'd say, as I settled on the floor with my homework. She was always inventing new nicknames for me; she had only recently stopped calling me *Agmire*. "My inescapable Agmire," she used to cry as I walked in the door.

During her pregnancy, Mama's hair had lost all its lustre and hung, scraggly and perpetually greasy, down to her shoulders. Then she had it all cut off, and I hated the way it looked, bristly and red like a hedgehog. The three freckles on her sweat-shiny nose stood out like stains, and the shape of her face had changed, once-high cheekbones rounded. Her hands were bumpy and rough with warts and eczema. My fingers were spotted with little round bandages where Mama had dabbed my own warts with drugstore medication, but she wasn't allowed to use it herself because of the pregnancy.

One morning in late autumn instead of mid-winter, Mama insisted something was wrong, and by late afternoon she was lying on the sofa, a towel under her hips. I waited with her in the living room, watching her grimace, while Dad did the unthinkable: he phoned Tam-Tam and Oma Esther and asked them to come over and watch me. I expected Mama to put up a fight, but she only looked dismayed, then sighed and didn't even argue. Dad took me into the kitchen and motioned for me to jump up and sit on the counter so our eyes were level. He said quietly, as if he was telling me a secret, "Agatha, the baby's coming early. I need you to be a big girl and take good care of your guests, all right?" I knew it was the other way round and Dad was trying to trick me into being good, but I nodded.

My grandmother and great-grandmother hadn't come out to Aylmer for at least a year. Neither of them drove, so Tam-Tam and Oma Esther had to take a taxi all the way from downtown Ottawa. When it pulled up in front of the house, Dad left Mama lying on her back, rushed outside and grabbed the overnight bags from the trunk. I followed him to the door and watched from among our boots while Mama complained from the couch that I was letting all our heat out the open door. Dad helped Oma Esther from the far side of the taxi. White head, red coat, black pants, she looked like a ladybug and stood barely higher than Dad's elbow, and the breeze blew his dark hair around into his face so it was indistinguishable from his beard. My great-grandmother safely transported to the sidewalk, Dad looked around as though he'd lost something. Quickly recovering, he opened the car door on the side closest to him and released Tam-Tam. Hand in the crook of his sweatered arm, she stood straight-backed, gracefully blond and vaguely offended, smoothing her pants as if she were brushing off dirt.

Two minutes later, Dad and Mama were in the car and gone. I stood in the foyer while Oma Esther settled onto the brown corduroy couch. There she would remain for most of the evening, slowly moving her jaw from side to side in an eternal struggle with her dentures. Tam-Tam walked around the living room, into the kitchen and back again. She paused by the piano and pressed down one of the yellowed ivory keys, so slowly it didn't make a sound. Mama usually taught piano lessons a few times a week, and I, reluctantly, was one of her students. She even had me booked into her schedule: my lessons were after school on Tuesdays. The piano used to be in Tam-Tam's house — it had been her husband's, and he was Mama's first teacher. My grandfather died long before I was born, hit by a bus while riding his bike, back when my mother was just a little girl. I knew a few things about him — that he was Irish, that he used to eat Marmite, a knife-scrape of pungent tar on toast. His parents had died before he met Tam-Tam, which was why he left Tam-Tam all the money she eventually used to start her salon. I knew that he used to play the piano and sing loud enough to wake the dead, otherwise known as Oma Esther. Mama said that her father never realized what he was letting himself in for, taking Tam-Tam and Oma Esther into his home, that he could never understand or abide by their rules and rituals. She said that when the bus hit her father's bicycle, the force of impact threw Mama-as-a-little-girl off the handlebars and out of harm's way. She only broke her elbow. I wondered if she'd seen his body.

Once I heard Dad ask Mama why Tam-Tam had never dated or

remarried since her husband's death. Mama laughed in surprise. "Oh, she's had a few chances," she said. Dad's question disappointed me with its cluelessness. Even at the age of ten, I knew Tam-Tam's attention to grooming had nothing to do with attracting men. She lived with Oma Esther and loved me and my mother. She liked the girls who worked in her salon, liked to dress them up and tweeze unsightly hairs from their faces. Men were far too brutish for her. I only wondered how and why she had ever married one in the first place.

"Shall I follow you to the guest room?" Tam-Tam turned to me, hands on hips. Her accent was exaggerated inside our house, which seemed too small for her voice and the way she moved. Tam-Tam had trouble pronouncing "the"; it often came out *dah*. Because, as Mama explained, her first language was Dutch. She avoided the *th* in my name by always calling me *Aga*. Oma Esther's accent was different because she'd grown up speaking Yiddish as well. The bright blond of Tam-Tam's hair, the soft red of her lipstick and the smells of her perfume and powder all seemed too vivid for such a humble house, with its standard suburban design. I looked over at Oma Esther, who was fumbling intently with the buttons on her cardigan. I longed to sit on the floor by her legs and let her braid my hair while I thought the whole situation through, but Tam-Tam said, "Come along," pausing by the overnight bags she'd left near me, at the bottom of the stairs. "Will you show me where to put these?" She handed me Oma Esther's big purse that opened on top like a mouth and snapped shut with two twists of shiny metal.

"You don't remember where the guest room is?" I said, not wanting to lose the autumn smell near the door, the warmth of Mama and Dad's coats against my back. I'd said the wrong thing; I slipped past Tam-Tam's horror-stricken face and started up the stairs with the purse, neck burning with disappointment that I had somehow hurt her feelings already, confirming her well-known suspicion that Mama wasn't raising me right. We didn't speak while she unpacked, and I watched in disgrace from one of the guest room's twin beds.

Tam-Tam's golden hair curled at the ends where it touched her slim shoulders; it was a completely different blond from my own, which was darker on top and almost white at the tips, sun-bleached from a summer of reading in the backyard hammock. Tam-Tam was not, I had come to realize, a normal grandmother. When I was ten, she was elegant and striking; when she was younger, she had been movie-star beautiful. Her clothes placed neatly in one drawer and Oma Esther's in another, Tam-Tam set her cotton makeup bag on top of the dresser. Sitting in the rocking chair, she removed her warm black socks and pulled a pair of shiny gold slippers over the sheer stockings underneath. "Your shoulder's ripped," said Tam-Tam, eyeing the seam of my favourite blue sweater. "You change your top, then come along downstairs and show me what Steven left us to eat." I wondered what she would say if she saw the thick wool work socks that Mama wore around the house all winter.

Mama was in a hospital bed and Minnie on her way by the time Tam-Tam reheated Dad's vegetable stew from the night before. I set the dining room table with the special-occasion dishes, each wide bowl dark blue with a big green flower in the middle. Mama, Dad and I often ate in the living room, plates on our laps, watching *Jeopardy*. This habit was as comforting and snug as Mama's wool socks with the white toes and red stripes around the tops. Tam-Tam and Oma Esther would think we ate this way every night, and I was proud of myself for protecting my parents' precious and unrespect-able habits, their unbreakable thick glass plates.

Oma Esther examined her stew, pushing the carrots and potatoes aside. She turned to me. "Where is my handbag, *Vlinderkind*?" That was her special nickname for me; Mama said it meant butterfly-child, which was the most flattering thing anyone had ever called me.

"Butt, for short," Mama had pointed out.

"Please get her handbag from upstairs," Tam-Tam told me; I was already standing.

When I returned, Oma Esther patted my cheek before clicking her huge purse open. She snapped her fingers against the twists of metal at the top, and, like an adventurer with a bottomless bag of provisions, retrieved three fist-sized packages wrapped individually in napkins. She handed one to Tam-Tam, who accepted it without reaction, and held another out to me, nodding for me to take it. She unwrapped the third. "Sticky buns with sweet ground beef," said Oma Esther. We didn't eat meat in our house, though Mama and I ate anything we could get our hands on when we were at restaurants or other people's houses. Dad would have been upset if he'd known meat had touched his dishes, so I placed my bun on the napkin and ate it from there.

"These are so good," I said, wondering what other treats were hidden away in the pockets of Oma Esther's overnight bag. She and Tam-Tam ate over their bowls, little bits of the delicious, spicy beef tumbling and tainting Dad's stew below. Two more secrets. Dad mustn't know that his dishes had touched beef; I told myself I'd put some extra soap in the dishwasher. I also knew that Oma Esther's habit of keeping food in her purse was one of Mama's most hated things.

After dinner, I sat on the floor in the living room making paper snowflakes for the Christmas play we were rehearsing at school. Tam-Tam flipped through a fashion magazine, and Oma Esther studied a book she'd found in the kitchen, running her finger slowly along the pages as though concentrating her attention on each word before moving on to the next. A bright, glossy garlic bulb filled the front cover. The book had been on the kitchen's bookshelf, unopened, for as long as I could remember. Someone, likely Oma Esther herself, must have given it to Mama as a gift. My grandmother and great-grandmother were out of place and odd, and I was beginning to feel sorry for them almost as much as I felt sorry for myself. Tam-Tam looked silly sitting on the brown corduroy couch in her stylish out-fit, shiny white-tipped nails against glossy, perfumed magazine pages. Tam-Tam kept herself and Oma Esther immaculately put together. Oma Esther had stopped dying her hair brown now that she was in her early eighties, and it was pure white but permed into shape. She wore only a tiny amount of makeup, and her skin was a mass of wrinkles. The cookbook in her lap was a small but reassuring reminder that this silent, denture-adjusting Oma Esther was the same person I knew from Saturday mornings at Inner Beauty.

Mama and I had lived with Tam-Tam and Oma Esther until I was three, when Mama married Dad, but I remembered almost nothing of those years. Seemingly all my life, my mother and I had seen Tam-Tam and Oma Esther every Saturday morning when we crossed the Ottawa River to Ontario to shop in the Byward Market and visit Inner Beauty, my grandmother's hair salon and beauty spa. For as long as I could remember, Tam-Tam had seen me and my mother only in our visiting clothes. Mama wore skirts and stockings, her eyelashes dark and lumpy with mascara, and I was forced to wear a dress with patent leather shoes that squashed my feet. The way we usually looked — my well-loved sneakers with the hole in the toe and Mama's plaid shirts with socks under sandals — was a well-kept secret.

Inner Beauty occupied the top floor of the house, and Tam-Tam and Oma Esther lived underneath. They belonged in the apartment and salon — Tam-Tam directing hair snipping and lipstick selling, leg sugaring and eyebrow waxing. Oma Esther sat in one of the royal blue chairs, her head a mass of pink curlers, then went downstairs to the kitchen, to her pots and pans and blenders and cookbooks. Her racks and racks of spices. The apartment and Inner Beauty had separate entrances from the street; a brown door opened to Tam-Tam and Oma Esther's front hallway, and a narrower rust-coloured door led upstairs. The salon's front stairwell matched our kitchen because Tam-Tam had given Mama and Dad her leftover paisley wallpaper. There hadn't been quite enough paper left for us, so there were two exposed squares of yellow-painted drywall beside our kitchen cupboards. It was always strange to see our wallpaper as we ascended to the salon, the familiar pattern under fluorescent light. The narrow door and wooden handrail were painted the same deep orangey-rust as the tiny leaves on the wall.

Each Saturday, Oma Esther had her hair set by one of the stylists and then went back downstairs until it was time to set her tightened curls free. She never said anything to me on her way out of the salon, just walked out past the cash, down towards the rust door. I would wait a few minutes and then go quietly down the hallway past the cosmetics counter. Tam-Tam's office was accessible through a pink door beside the washroom; it had a grey-blue carpet and was spotlessly clean, decorated with framed photographs on the walls, the desk and the top of the binder-filled bookcase. One of them showed Tam-Tam as a little girl, reaching up to hold hands with her parents. She had blond braids and was smiling. The girl in the photo was pretty and held herself as if she was used to posing. Oma Esther had short, straight, light brown hair with bangs and looked happy and tired, and her husband was almost a foot taller than she was. He had a smouldering cigarette between the fingers of his other hand and a mischievous look in his eyes. Mama told me that he went missing after the war, and that she was named after him: his name was Jozef. No one had ever called Mama by her first name, Josephine. I liked the idea that my mother had a hidden first name and wished I had one myself — it made her seem like a spy with a secret identity. There was also a picture of Tam-Tam with Margaret Trudeau, whose makeup she'd done a few times.

My interest in Tam-Tam's office lay in the door across from her desk. It looked as though it would open to a closet, but it led to a steep, dark, wood-smelling staircase so narrow I could reach out and press my arms against the walls on either side. For years, our weekly visits had been redeemed for me by this secret passageway that descended from Tam-Tam's private office into the kitchen of the apartment below. The stairs were old and unfinished but somehow clean and never dusty. The Saturday before Jasmine was born, I'd crept down, brave and adventurous, holding a make-believe candle in my fist. There was no light, so I had to leave the door upstairs slightly ajar and keep my hand on the rough handrail. I'd learned not to lean on it too hard after Mama had to gouge a series of splinters from my palm with a needle. I walked slowly, trying not to make the stairs creak; the stair treads were narrow, and there was a perilously steep drop from each to the next.

When my fingers bumped against the cigarette pack lodged between handrail and wall, I stopped to check. Each time I looked there were a different number of cigarettes. I thought with a thrill about the ghost of Tam-Tam's father visiting regularly and sitting on the stairs with a smoke, listening to Oma Esther and Tam-Tam's dinner conversations. I'd considered surreptitiously leaving a note rolled up like a cigarette, imagined starting up a correspondence. Jozef would leave me messages for the family, and though I couldn't quite imagine what these messages might be, my fantasies always involved Mama, Tam-Tam and Oma Esther standing in the meticulous downstairs living room, crying and hugging each other. In the secret staircase, my great-grandfather would be listening, unburdened because the strain on his loved ones was finally lifted. Then his soul would be free. I would see him through the window and he would wave goodbye to me, smiling with love and gratitude before dispersing into a cluster of snowflakes and floating away. The others would be too distracted to notice him.

I'd written many drafts of letters to Jozef. It didn't worry me that he never knew English, since death must surely free a person from all limits imposed by the human brain. But I could never maintain the exalted tone required to initiate contact with my haunted, haunting great-grandfather. *Dear Jozef,* I'd write. *My name is Agatha and I am your great-granddaughter. I'm the girl with straight blond hair and glasses who goes up and down these stairs every Saturday. You're probably wondering how I know about you. I don't know why, but I have a special way of knowing about magical things.* My letters invariably devolved into a plea for help instead of an offering. *Mama's a fat cow. I don't know why Steven ever married her. Helena says I take her forgrantid. I wish she wouldn't always do whatever I say, she's so gullable. I wish she was smarter instead of so nice and pretty. Did you ever feel like this when you were alive?* What kind of person, I reprimanded myself, dumps her problems on a disembodied soul stuck haunting his wife and daughter instead of going to heaven — as if Jozef didn't have enough to worry about already. I satisfied myself by checking the cigarette pack each week. I'd lean over to smell the eternally fresh tobacco, eyes closed, and conjure my great-grandfather's clever black-and-white face.

I knocked on the door at the bottom of the stairs before pushing it open. It didn't have a doorknob but swung out like the door you'd find on a pantry, and anyone looking at it from the outside would have thought that's what it was. Mama had told me that, when her father died, most of his money went to Tam-Tam, but he'd left some to Oma Esther, too. Oma Esther invested her inheritance and never spent a penny of it until they moved into this home; then she spent all her savings to create the kitchen she'd always dreamed of. "My father always loved her cooking," Mama said. "He probably left her that money hoping she'd use it to become a world-famous chef."

Two large bookcases stood at right angles in the corner, separated from the stove, sink and cupboards by a wide, polished wooden counter. The counter was low, built to accommodate Oma Esther's barely five-foot frame, and the bookcases were neatly filled with her hundreds of cookbooks, organized in alphabetical order. Shiny pots and pans hung from racks over the cooking area, perilously low for the average adult. On the wall beside the counter were three spice racks, each jar labelled bilingually in Oma Esther's surprisingly girlish handwriting. According to Mama, Oma Esther's culinary expertise and her meticulously organized kitchen were manifestations of a creepy and unhealthy obsession. Mama always looked tense and unsettled when we ate with Tam-Tam and Oma Esther, helping herself to tiny portions of the perfect meals and pushing them around her plate like a child with a plateful of boiled vegetables. The kitchen table was at the other side of the room, in a corner near the door to the living room. Tam-Tam had assumed ownership of that portion of the room and decorated the walls with white porcelain plates, a glossy peach or strawberry in the centre of each one. A white china bowl full of pears and apples sat in the middle of the yellow tablecloth. I had learned the hard way that the flawless fruit was made of plaster.

The Saturday before Minnie was born, I found Oma Esther sitting behind her counter on one of the two art deco bar stools my parents had given her one birthday. They were chrome with blue and green vinyl upholstery. She was refilling spice jars, carefully spooning the contents of a small plastic bag into a jar marked *notemuskaat/nutmeg*. She greeted me with a nod as I came through the door, and I walked over to let her brush imaginary spiderwebs from my face. Instead of speaking, she grabbed my face between her plump, spice-smelling hands and squeezed affectionately, smoothing my hair. When she climbed down from her stool, I was almost as tall as she was, and standing at eye level with an adult made me feel as disproportionately huge as Alice in Wonderland.

Oma Esther's English was much worse than Tam-Tam's, though they'd moved to Canada at the same time. She often pronounced my name in a distorted way that made it sound like *Anchor*. Mama complained during one Saturday afternoon drive back to Aylmer that Oma Esther refused to speak English properly because she couldn't let go of the past. Mama shook her head, her Saturday hairdo moving with it, stiff as a helmet. "She clings to that accent like bees to a bonnet."

"That's wrong," I said. "It's, She has a bee *in* her bonnet."

"Oh," said Mama, "she has a bee in her bonnet all right. She's always adored you, though. She took care of you all the time when you were small — you'd have thought she'd never seen a baby before." I knew I was Oma Esther's favourite: every time we visited, she told anyone who'd listen that she had fed me my first solid food, a spoonful of Hungarian goulash. "She loved it," Oma Esther claimed, describing me slurping down the tomato sauce, arms and legs flailing with joy.

"First thing," Oma Esther said, releasing my face and putting the spice jar aside, "we pray." Every week, she gave me two quarters to climb onto the bar stool beside her, look solemn and say "Amen" when she did. No one in my family ever prayed except for Oma Esther, and it was our secret. She could display her religious tendencies only in front of me, her born-and-bred atheist great-granddaughter. Mama would have been mortified if she knew, but she never came across us praying and I never told her. Bribed into piety, I sat uncomprehending — partly because I didn't understand Hebrew, but partly because Oma Esther's praying was a toothless, run-on mutter, her dentures resting in a glass on the counter.

After pocketing my earnings, I opened the cupboard under the sink to retrieve the mixture Oma Esther made earlier in the morning, now risen to fill its bowl. I loved to help her punch down the bloated dough, squeezing it, soft and buttery, in my hands. The good bread smell countered the beauty-salon stench emanating from Oma

Esther's curlered head. After forming two balls, she climbed off her stool and threw a small chunk of dough into the oven, muttering a prayer. She divided the remaining dough into six balls, stretched them into long cylinders, and braided two perfect loaves.

Oma Esther's Saturday-morning ritual drove Mama to distraction. She avoided going downstairs, she said, because the absurdity of it made her skin crawl. "Jewish people traditionally prepare that bread on Friday, before sunset, for the Sabbath. It doesn't mean anything if you do it on Saturday." When Mama was a child, Oma Esther at least used to cook the bread on the right day. "I don't know what this Saturday thing is about," Mama complained. "It's just an excuse for her to be eccentric." I didn't understand why any of this should distress my mother and quietly ignored her incomprehensible disapproval of everything Oma Esther ever did. Still, I knew not to let her catch me during the week trying to imitate Oma Esther's toothless, throaty muttering and flicking bits of torn paper into my Barbie oven.

With the challah safely baking, Oma Esther put on her jacket and walked through the apartment, outside to the street, and back up the paisley-walled staircase. She didn't like small spaces and never used the former servants' stairs. I slipped back through the door beside the pantry and tiptoed up to Tam-Tam's office. When Oma Esther reappeared upstairs in a royal blue swivel chair to have her curlers removed and her hair combed out and sprayed, we exchanged sly smiles. She always gave me a challah to take home for Saturday dinner, pushing it, still warm, into my hands when we went downstairs to say goodbye. "So tiny," she'd sigh, wrapping her thumb and pointer finger around my wrist. "Just a tiny *Vlinderkind*. Still only vegetables? Proper food she needs." My mother rolled her eyes.

Mama wouldn't eat Oma Esther's challah, but Dad and I always finished the whole thing by the end of the weekend. "Your grandmother really is a wonderful cook," Dad would tell Mama. "Come on, Ginny, it's just food. Just really good bread. It's nice, reminds me of my grandparents."

"It's *not just*," Mama said, uniting me with Dad against her. "You know it, Steven. You know it's all part of her neurosis."

"Sometimes," said Dad, a piece of challah emerging from his mouth cigar-style, sesame seeds clinging to his beard, "a loaf of bread is just a loaf of bread."

The night Mama went to the hospital sitting on a towel, I watched Oma Esther sitting on our couch and tried to ignore how old and helpless she seemed. I anticipated my next visit to her kitchen, when I'd be reassured of her competence and invincibility. That next visit was never to be — my mother was in the hospital overnight, and by the following Saturday, Oma Esther was in the hospital herself. Minnie came into my life just as Oma Esther left it; my great-grandmother suffered a massive stroke and died two days later. She only saw my sister once, through the glass wall of an incubator. When my mother spoke at the funeral, she said she was going to change Minnie's other name to Esther; afterwards, she told Dad and me that she thought of the name change on the spot, just for something to say, and that she didn't really want to give up Minnie's intended first name, Emily.

"It was a lovely gesture," Dad said. They had her birth certificate changed and even gave a copy to Tam-Tam, for proof.

My new sister was a small, insistent creature, producing gurgles, shouts and farts of impressive potency, and she changed everything. The house was ever more messy, Mama and Dad tired and ragged-looking. By the time we regained our old routines and returned one Saturday to Inner Beauty, Mama looked like her old self, hair shiny and warts gone. The baby was still tiny, with a streak of orange hair down the middle of her head and round cheeks that the salon ladies all had to touch. Tam-Tam took us downstairs for tea, and I saw she'd packed most of her mother's cookbooks away, along with all but one spice rack. My grandmother had never been one for cooking. I realized then that Oma Esther was really gone, that I'd let her death pass by unnoticed.

*

I took Jasmine home on the subway and the streetcar. Sitting beside her reminded me, strangely, of spending time with my last boyfriend, whom I'd dated for two months. I kept looking at her face, checking to see if she was noticing her surroundings, wondering what she was thinking; but she just gazed straight ahead, seemingly uninterested in the people around her, myself included. I wouldn't have been surprised if my sister had caught me staring and said, What? What, *what?*

"This is where you live?" she said, finally showing some reaction to her environment as I unlocked the steel door to the square brick building.

After Mama's accident, Minnie had slept in my bed all the time. She was so tiny then, and so trusting. There was no way, now, that she'd cuddle against me for comfort. She changed into her pyjamas in the bathroom and then I did the same, guessing she'd be horrified if I changed in front of her. I turned off the lamp by the bed and Jasmine pulled the duvet up to her chin as I climbed in beside her.

Just as I thought she had fallen asleep and was beginning to doze off myself, Minnie said, "Do you have a boyfriend?"

"No," I told her. "Not right now. Do you?"

I braced myself for a confession, but she said, "No," and rolled onto her back. The streetlight outside the window cast a sliver of brightness across her body's shape. "Who was the first person you ever kissed?" she asked.

I sliced the light with my hand. "Well," I told her, "you won't believe this, but the first guy I ever kissed was this European guy with a name no one could pronounce. He wore track pants, you know? Everyone called him Indigo Blackman. I never even told Helena about him — she would have thought I was crazy."

"Ugh," said Minnie. "Really?"

"Yeah. He was a weird guy, too. A terrible kisser. I ate lunch with him one day and then kissed him by the trees outside the school."

"How old were you?"

"Fifteen or so."

"What was his real name?"

"I don't know," I said. "I don't remember."

"Oh," said Minnie. Then she added, "Did you love him?"

"Oh. No, I guess not. I guess I would have cared less about what Helena thought, if I loved him." I waited, then asked, "What about you? Have you kissed someone?" She didn't say anything, just rolled onto her side, facing away from me. Finally she said she hadn't.

"Agatha," said Jasmine, startling me again out of near slumber. "What would you do if you met her?"

"Helena?"

Jasmine sighed loudly, as though I were being purposely dense. "Our mother." I stared at the back of my sister's head, her thick, reddish hair exactly like Mama's used to be.

Jasmine, I thought, my heart pounding, willing me to speak. *It was me.* I would confess at last. *I was the last one to speak with her. I'm to blame.*

Jasmine said, "I would kill her."

Minnie was born at three in the morning. Long after I'd been sent to bed, I was woken by the phone. I lay still with my eyes open for several minutes, until Tam-Tam stepped into the room. Eyes un-accustomed to the glow of my night light, she walked slowly, arms outstretched at her sides, a dainty zombie in beige silk pyjamas. I silently watched her progress towards a pile of books in the middle of the floor until she finally kicked it over with one gold-slippered foot.

"My God," she gasped. "What a mess. Aga?" She stepped around the books and sat on the side of my bed. I watched her through squinted eyes so she wouldn't know I was awake. Even without my glasses I could see there was something unfamiliar and unearthly about her face; she looked ghostly pale, skin white and shiny.

"Aga." She tried again to wake me, squeezing my ankle.

"Tam-Tam?" I blinked and opened my eyes. "What time is it?"

"Just after three. I thought you'd like to know right away that you have a little sister. She's very small, but she'll be fine, and so will your mother." She shifted her weight and wrapped her arms around her body. The posture was unlike her and, along with her pallid skin and colourless lips, made me recoil from her body as though it were radiating cold. I closed my eyes and concentrated on her voice, still unable to shake the feeling that the woman on the bed wasn't Tam-Tam but an impostor.

"I had a sister once," said my grandmother. I flinched at this revelation, telling myself I might well be dreaming. "Not related by blood, of course," she added quickly. "A girl I thought of like a sister." I relaxed slightly. I wanted my feeble family tree intact.

"I lived with Femke and her parents for almost two years," Tam-Tam went on. "We had to sleep in the same bed. Can you imagine? She had a little room, a single bed. And she had to share it with me. I wasn't allowed to go outside. I had to stay in the bedroom all day long with the blinds drawn while she went to school. She hated to share with me." Tam-Tam wasn't looking in my direction. I suspected she was dreaming out loud; her story made no sense.

"I waited each day for her to come home" — Tam-Tam glanced my way, as though confessing to a crime — "and she'd bring me things, tell me about the day at school. She was a year older than me. Church-going Christian. She had the thickest dark hair."

Tam-Tam reached up and touched her own coiffure, which was squashed on the side but still retained something of its shape; her eyes were deep shadows. "After the war, of course, my mother came back and we came to Canada. We didn't hear about the van Daams anymore, Femke's family." Tam-Tam was apparently trying to tell a parable about sisterhood, but I couldn't imagine what it meant. The tone of the story, the warning it held, seemed connected to Tam-Tam's sickly appearance.

"Do you know," said Tam-Tam, "even after we came to Canada, my mother believed for years that my father was still alive. That he was living somewhere and had lost his memory. She used to tell tales of his new life, imagine that he had become an engineer. A man who drives trains." She laughed. I'd never heard her talk about Jozef before, even in passing. "Steven's a good father," she concluded. "Isn't he?"

I nodded, surprised that she had drawn me into her monologue. "He's kind to your mother," she said. "Poor thing."

It was a year and a half after Mama's accident when Dad found me in the food court of the Rideau Centre. I'd bleached my short hair white-blond and pierced my nose during the two days I'd been gone; I hadn't done much else. I was leaning back against plastic, my head aching from the rum-spiked Coke that was serving as breakfast and lunch. Diesel, the guy whose apartment I'd moved into, was selling acid to a thirteen-year-old girl he was obviously hoping to deflower. His blond dreadlocks were so thick I hadn't realized how much dandruff they housed until the night I'd gone to his basement apartment with my backpack and, straddling him, looked down at the top of his head.

I was just wondering what I'd missed in school and was considering going to the public library for the day to sleep when I looked up to see my father standing five feet away, eyebrows raised, hands in the pockets of his Adidas jacket. His hair was getting shaggy and his beard was bushy. He was wearing old sneakers and jeans worn to threads. I was so grateful he hadn't worn his professor clothes. I wished he'd pick me up and sling me over his shoulder like he used to; I'd fall asleep before we got to the car.

"You can either come with me," Dad said, "or resign yourself to being a lifelong loser and victim. You're letting this moron take advantage of your need for affection." I caught up with him at the escalator, my already forgotten boyfriend not bothering to call after me. As he pulled out of the parking lot, Dad offered me a Tylenol and informed me I wouldn't be living with him and Lara anymore. "If you can't stand living with people who don't share your DNA," he said, referring to my tantrum the day before I left, "you don't have to."

"I'm sorry, Dad," I said, wondering where he was planning to send me — reform school came to mind. "I didn't mean you weren't really my father. Dr. Steinberg said it's perfectly understandable for me to be acting out, abandoned by both my biological parents. You don't know what it's like, not being related to anyone."

"All right," said Dad. "Acting out. Perfectly understandable." He informed me that I would move in with Tam-Tam and go back to high school. "Your grandmother," he said, "is undeniably related to you. Lucky girl." My clothes were already packed into the trunk. Dad carried my things into Tam-Tam's front hallway, my grandmother taking a break from the salon to supervise. He kissed me on the forehead, told me he loved me and said, "Incidentally, your sister's related to you, too, and she misses you — please phone her tonight. She'll be spending weekends with you here. Now have a sandwich and a good nap."

Although I suspected that Lara was only too glad to be rid of me and resented her more than ever, Dad's was an ingenious strategy. Once in Tam-Tam's care, I realized that good grades and university were the best and only sure escape route and devoted myself single-mindedly to school work. I didn't dare run away, skip school or even play loud music. With her air of brittle determination and restrained melancholy, Tam-Tam wielded an irresistible power without having to say a word. Finally, too late, I imagined what it must have been like having her as a mother.

One night, shortly after I'd moved into Oma Esther's old room, I was doing my homework at the kitchen table when Tam-Tam emerged from the stairway beside the pantry; she still went up to her office each night to settle the salon's accounts. She wore a pale blue robe and had a silk scarf tied around her head so her silver-white hairline showed. It was uncanny that this washed-out version of my grandmother should haunt the salon after it closed, replacing the rosy-cheeked, shiny-lipped Tamar all her customers knew. I remembered the night Minnie was born, how strange Tam-Tam had appeared, and realized I had simply seen my grandmother for the first time without makeup.

That night when I was ten, she had stayed on the edge of my bed after I closed my eyes. I felt the mattress shift when she eventually rose, and she remained standing there for so long I thought maybe she had left after all, so silently I hadn't heard her footsteps. I didn't dare open my eyes. At last she announced her continued presence by sighing loudly, "She needs so very much protection." I pretended not to hear, kept my eyes tightly closed and breathed deeply.

Lying in bed beside Jasmine, I thought about the night she was born and wondered who Tam-Tam thought needed protection and who was supposed to supply it. I'd often thought she must have meant Mama, or maybe Oma Esther. But when Tam-Tam delivered her cryptic message, I received it as the ominous imperative of an oracle following birth. I understood that my new sister was a being of the most precarious kind, and that Tam-Tam had somehow placed this fragile life squarely in my hands.

Ask any adult to describe the worst feeling in the world, and most will say betrayal. The worst thing: to discover the one you love most is a stranger. The person you've been so close to, known inside out, turns out not to exist. Every cherished moment spent with the betrayer is contaminated by your new knowledge. It's no joke, this shattering of your own self-story; if you don't revise fast enough, it can be lethal. The truth is you can never know a person and you can never hold on to a person. You can only know how someone makes you feel at a particular time; and trying to hold on to a person is like trying to hold sand in a sieve. If your love object refuses to be who he seemed to be, don't make his inauthenticity your albatross. The unreliable live with their eyes half closed, and their fists clutch desperately at anything shiny and new. You need not feel anything for them but pity. You, the open-eyed amnesiac, are whole and real, and no revisionist can make you doubt yourself. You know that remembering is revision, love is revision, laughter is revision. You know that all is revision, so you have learned to revise better than anyone else.

J. Virginia Morgan
The Maternal Return: An Anti-Memoir

Two

It was morning, the sun's first, thin light overflowing her off-white curtains, when Tamar heard the lock rattle. Minutes later, the bathroom door scraped its ill-fitting frame, and then water ran through pipes, drumming against tile. It was her husband, Robert, all over again, home beyond late on Friday night. Half awake, she would hear him through the floor, coughing, clearing his throat; even his sighs were amplified by the echo chamber of running water. The sounds were Robert expelling the whole night, whatever he did when he was gone, water easing it all down the drain. In the morning he was untainted. Clean and even-tempered, he'd erased all traces, and he would hum as he ate, dropping breakfast crumbs on the newspaper.

When she heard the crash, Tamar was out of bed and running for the bathroom door, pulling the shower curtain open, nine-one-one on the tips of her fingers. Robert was a decade gone, bus-crushed and buried, the house they'd lived in together sold long ago. And Ginny was twenty-two, studying this and that on university scholarships. Throughout the winter she'd been coming home progressively later; and now, six in the morning, she was sitting on the floor of the tub with her head in both hands, dark reddish hair twisted into a soaked and fraying knot. Before Ginny seized the flowered curtain from her mother's hand and pulled it closed again, Tamar saw that she had a bruise on one shoulder. Robert's shoulders, too, had been bone white and flushed with freckles; Tamar would never have entered the bathroom while Robert was in there. She would never have known if his shoulders were bruised.

"I slipped, Mother," Ginny said through the curtain. "I'm fine. Go back to bed. I'm having a private moment of angst here. I'm contemplating my near-death experience."

"Did you hit your head? You might have a concussion again — you sound slurred." She looked at the closed curtain uncertainly. "Do you need help?"

Ginny's body was a shadow through the curtain. Standing, she held one hand against the side of her head. "That really hurt. Steven said that I should wash my feet with soap, and it made them slippery." Ginny giggled, then laughed loudly. "He said that most people wash their feet with soap. Is that true?" Tamar turned to see her mother in the hallway behind her, cardigan wrapped tight around her small chest.

"Her feet?" said Esther. She stepped into the bathroom and spoke over the sound of the shower. "In the bath, this doesn't happen."

"There's nothing inherently evil about showers, for godsake, Oma!"

"It's hopeless." Esther turned back down the hall, and Tamar stepped into the doorway to watch her retreat and ease her bedroom door to just a crack from closed, in case its knob got red-hot if the house caught on fire.

"Do you wash between your piggies, Mother?" Ginny's voice rose above the drumming of the shower. "Tell me the truth, please tell me truth. I need to know if I've been duped."

"You know how your grandmother struggles to get her sleep." When it was clear that Ginny had no intention of responding, Tamar wiped her palm across the steam-clouded mirror and pressed her fingertips under her eyes, smoothing out the skin.

"Tamar," said Ginny. "Are you still in here?"

"No."

"I'm sorry I woke Oma Esther. Please go back to bed. I don't have a concussion. Everything is peachy."

Tamar lay in bed for another half hour, though she knew she wouldn't get any more sleep, and later she'd wonder if Ginny, in the bedroom across the hall, had any inkling of what was transpiring inside her own body. "The grand miracle of life," as Robert had called it. He'd drawn Tamar a diagram right after proposing, or, rather, declaring that they would marry. "Imagine, my little sperm wiggling its way into your ovum. Right about now, our future child consists of approximately ten cells." And twenty-two years later, Asher's little sperm wiggled its way. Because that was the night Ginny, for some unfathomable reason, had offered her body, dirty feet and all, to Asher Acker.

Two days later, she'd force a confession on Tamar and Esther while they sat in the living room after dinner, listening to the CBC. In their apartment, they'd recreated, almost exactly, the sitting room they once occupied in Robert's house. Esther was crocheting and Tamar sorting lipstick samples from work. Around her shoulders, Esther wore a green and blue crocheted shawl identical to the one she was now making in beige and brown. She could never get warm enough, and she wrapped herself in woollen layers each evening. "*Zij heft geen waardigheid*," she said to Tamar. "No dignity. Like her father, coming home at all hours. I tried to tell him, too, do you remember? That civilized people take baths. And now look what's happened: shower slipped her up and cracked her head." She tapped her temple. "You never know what a person might do after a crush on the head. The mishigas that girl brings into this house will be the end of us."

"The new bath mat will prevent slipping," said Tamar. "I should have bought one years ago. I don't know why I wasn't thinking straight."

"Crooked thinking runs in this family. Some kind of family."

"I can hear you talking about me, you turkeys." Ginny strode into the room, bell-bottoms flapping around her ankles. She stood by the big radio in the living room, grabbed a ball of orange wool from Esther's basket and squeezed it hard. It matched the wide belt cinched tight around her waist. "You think slipping in the shower made me crazy?" Ginny put her free hand on the radio as though considering pushing it off its stand, then pulled away as if she'd touched something hot.

"What is she saying?" said Esther. "I don't understand."

"I'm crazy. Deranged! It must have been the shower that did it! Why did you think I'd take a shower after a date in the first place? Earlier that very night Asher and I committed an act of flagrant lust. What do you think of that? We did it in his car and it wasn't at all romantic. And do you suppose he was my first lover? Until two days ago, was I an unplucked flower?" Ginny paused as though giving her audience a chance to decide on their answer.

"Please don't yell," said Esther. "My headache. Where are my pills?"

Ginny tossed the wool back into Esther's basket and retrieved the pill bottle from under a pair of knitting needles. With her fist closed around it, she stood with her legs apart, clenched hands at her sides, a boxer poised to pummel the soft furniture, the cushions and the walls, all swathed in Esther's crocheted covers, blankets and shawls. Esther stared at the red lid visible through Ginny's fingers. "I'm moving in with Asher. Not getting married. Moving in. He wants me to, and I'm going to, so." She took a deep breath and crossed her arms. With swift and jarring composure, as though speaking to a pair of slow-witted children, she said, "I won't be going with you to the new place, so you needn't worry about building that extra bedroom. You can move into your fancy new apartment together and meld into one person, just like you've always wanted. Free of me. I'm an adult now. Asher and I are going to be having a baby."

"You're not an adult," said Tamar. "You're a hysterical child. Look at you, my God. She's not having a baby," she told her mother, despite a knot of dismay in her stomach so painful it made her head light. "Ginia, don't be ridiculous. What about Steven?"

"What do you mean, I'm not having a baby? And what about Steven? What about him?"

"Of course there's no baby. Your theatrics are a bit much. You didn't really — did you?" But before Ginny had a chance to flood the room with unbearable details, Tamar added quickly, "In any case, you can't know you're pregnant after two days."

Ginny set down Esther's pill bottle, turned and fled, shoulder bumping the door frame. Minutes later, Tamar heard the girl's voice, her words indecipherable, pleading with someone on the phone. And it occurred to Tamar, as she stood to retrieve the red-lidded bottle and place two tablets into her mother's hand, that maybe it was true after all. Despite Ginny's beads and polyester shifts and free-bouncing breasts, despite the way she talked, she was fundamentally a throwback, an heiress to folly, credulous enough to get herself in trouble in this most old-fashioned of ways.

The next morning, in the vise-grip of a dare gone too far, Ginny bundled her clothes into two suitcases and several enormous macramé purses, carried them down two flights of narrow stairs and dumped them in Asher's rusty Ford. The trunk was full of clothes, the back seat loaded with books. Already dressed for her afternoon — evening shift at the cosmetics counter, Tamar followed Ginny downstairs and stood on the front steps in her camel-hair coat and high heels. Asher ignored her and stood smoking on the sidewalk, his dark blond hair shaggier than ever, while Ginny pushed two more bags into the trunk and slammed it shut. Asher was gaunt and tired, the shadows under his eyes like bruises; surely he hadn't always been quite so pallid. Tamar looked away.

Ginny wore a fitted, cherry-coloured leather jacket that clashed with her scarlet platform clogs, a bulky white scarf and one of the matching gloves. She stomped in the puddles along the sidewalk, melted snow splashing muddy streaks along her shoes and soaking the cuffs of her jeans. In her bare hand, she held a cigarette. Tamar had never seen Ginny smoke before; she watched her daughter struggle for elegance, her weight on one foot, smoking hand-on-hip until she doubled over to cough. With a violent wrist-flick, Ginny tossed the cigarette into a depleted snowbank. Asher shook his head and climbed in the driver's side of the car as Ginny fished the second glove out of her pocket and pulled it on. She turned and ran back to the building to take the six concrete steps two at a time. Bracing herself for the collision, Tamar barely resisted taking a step backward; Ginny stopped just short of hurtling herself into her mother's arms. Taking Ginny's gloved hands firmly in her own, Tamar said, "You should never wear white." The gloves were stained a shade or two darker than the scarf and streaked with dust and dirt. Ginny sighed.

"I see you up there, Oma Esther," she yelled at the corner third-floor window. "No point hiding. Goodbye, goodbye. Don't quit your day job to be a spy!"

"I'm not going to hear the end of this," said Tamar. "Please phone us when you get there. You know how worried she gets."

Ginny's cheeks were rosy, her eyes fever-bright, and Tamar was reminded vividly of the moment, many years earlier, before Ginny had pirouetted across the crochet-lined living room to collide with solid wood and glass. It must have been relatively soon after Robert died. Ginny had been lying on her stomach on the living room floor, a loop of yellow wool around both hands. Humming tunelessly, she wove the wool into a series of elaborate shapes with her fingers. They were alone in the room because Esther had gone to bed early with a backache.

"When I'm a doctor," said Ginny, "I'm going to invent a new medicine that will make Oma Esther's pains go away without making her sad." Ginny had been obsessed for several months with the notion of following her father's medical career. "I think it will involve sending the medicine straight to her back instead of through her brain first, relaxing the vertebrae." She hooked her pointer fingers together, looked at Tamar, pale eyebrows raised, and wiggled her fingers against each other in an eerie impersonation of Robert explaining the workings of the human body. Yes, Ginny was speaking gibberish, but she spoke it with Robert's mannerisms, even his facial expressions. Tamar watched Ginny create new string-shapes with mechanical quickness, clearly deep in thought. "Don't worry, Mother," she said with conviction. "I'll think of something."

"You're old enough to hear this," said Tamar. "Those pills your father prescribed for your grandmother's backaches are not medicine. They're placebos."

"They're addictive." Ginny nodded wisely. "Oma Esther's a junkie."

"No," said Tamar. "If I tell you a secret, will you promise never to mention it to your grandmother?" Ginny nodded, rapt and worried.

"Those pills are just made of sugar. Do you understand? There's nothing wrong with your grandmother's back. It's more complicated than that. Your father said the pain was all in her head, but she wouldn't believe him. She wanted medicine so he gave her those. No pill is going to make her happy."

Ginny lay in silence, staring at the wool between her hands. Taken aback by this uncommon stillness, Tamar tried to think of the right words — a more thorough and digestible explanation. Too soon, Ginny said, "How is it more complicated, Mother?"

"She's not been herself. She's been a different person since — everyone she ever knew is dead."

The yellow wool was wrapped so tightly around Ginny's pointer fingers that, Tamar saw, they were turning white. Ginny said, "But she knows us."

"Your Oma Esther had a sister," Tamar explained. "My Tante Anke. They were very close. Oma Esther was with Anke when she died of typhus. She had it, too, I think. You mustn't ever say anything about this to her. All right, liefje?"

Half an hour later, Ginny stood up and announced, "I think I should be a ballet dancer. Ballet is my destiny." Freckles burning across her nose, eyes fever-bright, she told Tamar, "Watch this."

Standing with Ginny's hands in hers, Asher's engine running to take her away, Tamar clearly recalled her urge to grab the front of her small daughter's nightgown; she could have reached it easily but instead willed herself to remain stock still and watch. The pirouette was out of control as it began, and Ginny hit the end table spinning. The vase fell and Ginny fell, twisted, on top of it. It took the doctors four hours to pick all the glass slivers out of her side.

Tamar squeezed Ginny's hands tighter. "For godsake. You've made your point. This is going too far." Ginny eased her hands away.

For the next month, Ginny called once a week and didn't answer her phone when Tamar tried to phone more often. She let the telephone ring and ring. Then Asher started calling Tamar. He had a plan. He started showing up by himself again, inviting himself in for tea. It wasn't like before; now he sat on the red sofa instead of in Robert's old mustard and brown chair. He spoke quickly, tapping his long fingers on the upholstered arm. "You and Esther can come, too. What are you doing in Canada? There's a whole country of people like us, Tamar. Where we wouldn't be in exile." People like us. Asher had unkempt dirty-yellow hair that he kept pushing out of his eyes, and he smelled of tobacco and wet wool. He said, "You have to think of me like a son. We're a family now." He was aglow with the drama of what he'd done, just as he trembled with anxiety to be on his way elsewhere.

Leave, she willed.

He had appeared for the first time at Tamar's workplace, beside the makeup counter, picking up crystal perfume bottles and turning them over for inspection the way one might approach a cut of meat. His hair flopped over his forehead, and he looked intently tired, with soft shadows under his wide-set bright grey eyes. It was the kind of face that wore youth unconvincingly, that was made to be old and weather-worn. Tamar reached for the crystal bottle that he was surely about to drop, and he let her take it. He said, "Are you Ginny Reilly's mother?"

And only months later Asher was sitting on the red sofa with its little burgundy flowers, Tamar's pregnant daughter spirited away into some hole of an apartment Tamar had never seen. He said, "Whatever feelings you have about me, you just need to put them aside. I have to concentrate on Ginny. Your daughter is a very intelligent person, but her intelligence is unfocused. She was a precocious child with no structure in her life." He had a habit of opening his hand abruptly to emphasize his words, like a starburst. A frog's foot. He looked at Tamar sadly, wisely. "And now she's a childish, an insecure person."

Tamar willed, *Disappear.*

*

And now Asher was gone, must have landed in Tel Aviv only hours ago. Tamar stood at his sink, scrubbing the last of the dirty dishes he left behind. Mid-August, the humidity at its peak, the apartment sweltering. Asher's dishes, Asher's bedroom, Asher's bathroom. This was Tamar's first visit here, and while she tried to think of it as her daughter's apartment, it only seemed absurd that Ginny would stay here when he had left. Incongruous and invasive. Ginny claimed that if she and Asher were married, Tamar would feel differently. And how grateful Tamar was that there was no marriage to contend with along with everything else. That she was not compelled, as Ginny put it, to take the relationship seriously.

Two foil-covered glass dishes sat on the wooden counter. A dozen chicken croquettes and dish of pad thai — Ginny's favourites. Esther had spent the previous evening preparing the spicy noodles, and just that morning, she'd chopped the leftover chicken she'd been saving and mixed it with a thick, white sauce. Tamar knew there were eggs involved, then bread crumbs and the deep fryer. Esther always cooked and Tamar cleaned up afterwards, and although she frequently resolved to learn some of her mother's recipes, Tamar couldn't retain any memory of the separate steps. She remembered coming home from work, when Robert was alive and Ginny was a little girl, to a fish soup with dumplings. She'd held one of the soft, spongy-white dumplings in her spoon and asked Esther, in English, "How do you make these?"

Esther answered in Dutch, then repeated what she'd said in English for Robert and Ginny's benefit. "You just make. Read in the book. Make so it looks like the picture." But to look in her mother's cookbooks would have been like reading someone's diary. Esther's spidery handwriting filled the margins, sometimes scrawled right on the recipes themselves. Mostly she wrote in Dutch or Yiddish, sometimes in English. Once, sitting down to breakfast, Tamar thought she saw some Hebrew letters pencilled between the lines of a recipe for lemon chicken. Tamar couldn't read Hebrew and hadn't known that Esther could either; she flipped the book shut.

The two dishes, foil tucked perfectly over their contents, could not be put away until Tamar scrubbed Asher's fridge with baking soda. Sitting in front of the open fridge promised relief from the stifling heat, and Tamar was saving the task for last. Long drips of juice had dried onto every surface, and a greenish liquid festered under the vegetable crispers. The room, which served as both kitchen and living room, had seen weeks and months pass since anyone had bothered to clean. Asher and Ginny had the most unfortunate characteristics in common, and this was one of them. Ginny must have learned it from her father, this helplessness in the face of gathering dust and creeping mould.

When Robert hadn't been attending to the frostbitten toes and collapsed arches of his patients, he had been forever in front of the television or at the piano, helping Ginny with her finger exercises, going through sheet music with a pencil. He'd tell his daughter to spread her hands on top of his so she could feel how his fingers moved over the keys. Their backs to the rest of the house, the two of them were united in oblivion to Tamar and Esther's constant war with disorder — with soiled clothing and food-caked dishes. Sometimes Robert clamped a thin cigar between his lips and played Gershwin by ear; one time Tamar saw, with her own eyes, a long cylinder of ash crumble, during a crescendo, from the end of her husband's cigar directly onto Ginny's freshly washed and braided hair.

Tamar had started running a bath. She had already emptied half a dozen bowls of forgotten leftovers from Asher's fridge, each at some stage of decay. At least two were identifiable as pasta. One appeared to have been boiled potatoes, and one was unrecognizable, a pungent mass of multicoloured fuzz. Waiting for the kettle to boil, she wiped her hands on a relatively clean tea towel and glanced around the cluttered room. The bookshelf and coffee table were both overflowing with colourful paper, folded into three-dimensional shapes. There were insects, elephants, frogs. But mostly, Tamar could see, there were birds. Innumerable paper birds, all the same, long necked and sharp beaked. Stepping past the small, curtainless window, she glanced out at Ginny and Esther on the balcony and picked up a purple bird from the bookshelf. Turning it over and spreading the wings, Tamar could see it was a mess of scars inside, white showing through where the dark ink had cracked. Leaning in, she examined another bird. This one was made of white paper and was scrawled with black ink — Ginny's handwriting. The kettle shrieked, and Tamar carefully balanced the purple bird back on top of the psychology textbook where she'd found it. She poured a cup of tea and turned sideways to step outside through the narrow doorway. She was in her stockings because the heels of her shoes would have slipped between the slats of Asher's balcony. Ginny's balcony.

Ginny rocked herself in a rickety chair. Her sprained right ankle was supported on a plant pot, shadowed by green tomatoes. She must have stubbed her big toe when she fell, because the top half of the nail was missing, replaced by an unsanitary-looking scab. Esther played solitaire beside her. Ginny's eyes were closed against the faint sound of running bathwater and the smack and shuffle of cards. Her face was swollen and shiny, her hair limp with sweat. The wrought-iron platform they sat on, what Ginny called a balcony, was actually more like a fire escape. Tamar's pedicured toes were visible through her sheer stocking, their elegance emphasized by unruly surroundings. The potted vegetables and herbs, even the vines, seemed a paltry disguise for a cheap apartment on a rundown centre-town street.

"Your bath should be ready," Tamar told Ginny. She turned to her mother. "Do you want to stay out here? I've made you a cup of tea." Esther looked up from her cards as though surprised to find herself in such an unlikely setting. She waved her hand, seven of spades fluttering. "Three generations and not a man to be seen. All gone. Like this." A butterfly had left Ginny's basil to flutter past the railing. Addressing Ginny's bulge, she concluded, "Such a family you'll be born into." Ginny put her hand protectively over her middle.

Tamar noticed, standing, that Esther's grey roots were clearly visible at the top of her light brown hair, which had been cut and set into a chin-level bob; she would make an appointment for a touch-up the next day. Tamar offered both hands to help Ginny stand, then offered her arm for the limp to the bathroom. Ginny's shift hung down to her ankles at the back, but her belly shortened it to mid-shin at the front. Tamar didn't comment as they shuffled through the cluttered bedroom, past the dresser, desk and floor, all strewn with books, paper and clothes that Asher hadn't bothered to pack or put away. A length of mustard yellow yarn stretched across the room from window to door frame, a flock of crimson, scarlet, rose and russet paper birds dangling from it in loops. Ginny followed Tamar's gaze and said, "I wanted them to look like they were in flight, but instead they look strangled. Isn't it as if their migration was cut short by some kind of trap?"

"Did you fold all of these birds?"

Yes, Ginny had been spending her time folding squares of paper, the same folds every time. "If you make a thousand cranes," she said, "it's supposed to be good luck. Actually," she admitted with a small laugh, "It's supposed to ward off death."

"Well," said Tamar, "it doesn't look that way to me."

"Doesn't look what way?"

"Like the birds are strangled."

"Oh, Mother." They stepped over the red-strapped platform clogs that lay in the doorway to the bathroom, and Tamar resisted the urge to move them. Someone as clumsy as Ginny should never wear shoes like that, especially when eight months pregnant. She had been wearing those shoes, running down the stairs and screaming after Asher, when she sprained her ankle the week before. When Tamar met her at the hospital, Ginny was lying back on an examination table, her ankle already bound in a tensor bandage, infamous red shoes on a table at the side of the tiny room.

Tamar sat on the toilet seat, legs crossed, and didn't stare as Ginny pulled her shift over her head and stepped out of her panties. One hand on either side of the claw-foot tub, Ginny manoeuvred herself into the hot water without wetting her damaged ankle. She let that leg hang over the side. Swollen all over, no wonder she was exhausted. Her breasts looked painfully full, already stretching downward almost to rest on the swell of her belly. Tamar remembered her own pregnancy, how her body barely changed, limbs and face unaffected by the bulge that confined itself to her middle. Ginny was overwhelmed so quickly, impending motherhood touching every part of her. From swollen feet to lacklustre hair, she was strained at the seams.

"Do you think it's funny that I don't have a shower?" said Ginny.

"This isn't right." Tamar clasped her hands. "You can't live here. We'll have room in the new place. We can all move in within the month. In time for the baby."

"He's planning to come back. What am I supposed to do? Throw out his things? Leave him homeless?" Ginny leaned her head against the tub's rolled end. "What about my plants? And anyway, I might go there eventually. After the baby's born and my ankle's healed and all that." She said this as though mustering conviction, but she sounded far from convinced and further from convincing.

"Please, Ginny. This makes no sense. Oma Esther can't understand it at all. It makes her so upset that you're not around to play the piano anymore. It just sits there now, waiting to be dusted."

"Oma Esther thinks I'm a whore and Asher's a lunatic," said Ginny. "And she hates the piano. She thinks it's all just" — Ginny wrapped her arms around her chest and shook her head — "mishigas." Tamar almost had to smile. Ginny had an uncanny gift for imitating mannerisms. Asher had claimed to recognize Tamar, the first time they met, from Ginny's description, but surely he had known her by the girl's performances — impersonations unkind only for their unrelenting accuracy.

"She's not used to all this," Tamar said. "Can you blame her? Frankly, it's a little difficult for everyone."

"You don't say." Ginny filled a green plastic bucket and supported herself with one arm, awkwardly pouring water over her head with the other.

"We're bringing the piano with us when we move," said Tamar, pressing her palms against her thighs. "Despite the expense. Do you have any idea what's involved? It's quite incredible." Ginny didn't respond. "My God," she said. "The expense." Watching Ginny fill the bucket a second time, Tamar took off her bracelet and moved to the edge of the tub. Ginny didn't object to her mother's help, just let her arms fall to her sides. Taking the bucket, Tamar continued to drench her daughter's long hair. Greasy along its centre part, it hung straight, past her shoulder blades. Ginny shut her eyes against the water and scrunched her face, lips reddened by the heat. "Israel is subtropical," she said, as Tamar refilled the bucket. "But it can't be any hotter than here. It'll be dry, won't it, the kind of heat that gives you a nosebleed?" She blinked water out of her eyes and looked up at her mother, waiting for an answer, an explanation. Her long lashes caught beads of water like a spiderweb; at twenty-three, she suddenly looked like herself at six.

Bathing was the only time Ginny had ever chosen Tamar's help over Robert's, the only time she seemed to trust her mother's competence. As a child, she'd let her body sag like a rag doll so Tamar was obliged to do everything for her, even lifting her arms to wash underneath. Ginny's knees and elbows were perpetually scabby and scraped, and every bath day, Tamar found new bruises. Though dressed crisp and neat each morning, hair pulled into two tight braids by Esther, Ginny invariably came home with her outfits skewed, loose hair from her braids standing out in a halo. She stood tall and gangly, one sock crumpled around her ankle. Tamar cringed, watching her daughter walk into chairs and trip over cracks in the sidewalk. Even mosquitoes seemed more attracted to Ginny than to the average person, and from her father she had inherited the pale, faintly freckled skin that often accompanies red hair. Skin that scorches scarlet and raw in the sun, then peels in long strips, fly-wing thin.

At eleven years old, Ginny suffered her first injury serious enough to require doctor-applied bandages and prescribed painkillers. She flew off the front of her father's bicycle, Robert instinctively reaching out to grab her arm. Her sleeve tore in his hand as momentum carried her out of his reach, past the bus's trajectory and into the fatherless rest of her life. Her palms collided with pavement, one elbow fracturing under the force of her own weight. As the doctor prophesied, she would never again be able to straighten that arm completely.

At the hospital, they were led to a private room set aside for grieving families. Esther winced as though from a deep and painful blow when she heard her son-in-law was dead, but Tamar laughed. "No," she said. "How ridiculous. Of course he wasn't killed."

"I'm sorry, Mrs. Reilly." The doctor's manner cut her laugh short, cut her breathing short. Something terrible had happened. She had done something terrible. She was a widow, bereaved; she had a dead man's clothes in her house. She would always remember how this doctor's eyebrows met in the middle, that his eyes were slightly blood-shot. The doctor said, "Robert has passed away. I'm very sorry."

Tamar and Esther sat with Robert's death, waiting for the doctors to set Ginny's broken bones. "There is nothing new for us under the sun," said Esther. Tamar reached and took her mother's hand, and neither of them spoke again until the red-eyed doctor reappeared, some time later, to ask Tamar to identify her husband's body.

Tamar didn't move. She had never felt so incapable of performing a task demanded of her, so simply unable to comply with what was needed.

"I'll do this," said Esther. Tamar looked at her mother, forcing herself to shake her head. "I can do this?" Esther asked the doctor. She touched Tamar's hand and said firmly, "I'll see him." She stood and nodded, followed the doctor from the room.

At her father's funeral, Ginny wore a bandage high on her cheek and a sling to support her cast. Half her lip was swollen and bruised, a lopsided pout. It was a closed-casket funeral, but Tamar knew that Ginny must have seen Robert lifeless on the street beside her. A father with a concrete, bodily death, neat and conclusive. It seemed to confirm that Robert was alien, not one of them. Men in Tamar's family didn't have funerals, didn't leave corpses; they just vanished and faded from memory. The letter from a stranger, confirming her father's death, hadn't extinguished the feeling that he was still out there somewhere, leading some unlikely life. Tamar sat between Esther and Ginny at the funeral, holding their hands tightly. They and a few of Robert's colleagues from the clinic were the only people who attended the funeral.

"This is some family," Esther said. "We touch men, they crumble like dust."

Tamar was the sole beneficiary of Robert's will, except for the piano, which would be Ginny's when she married or turned twenty-one, whichever came first, and a surprisingly large sum that he left to Esther.

Six months after Robert died, Ginny contracted pneumonia and spent a week in the hospital. Then she pirouetted into the end table and fell on the vase, splintered glass wedging into her side. She broke a rib skating on the canal, burnt her foot with the iron and sprained her back dragging a bed away from the wall to check for demons. Tamar hoped Ginny's long, shelf-knocking limbs would give way to a model's figure, but puberty brought Ginny's upward growth to a halt and she swelled outward instead, into a sensual voluptuousness. Esther said, "Trouble." Ginny's lips were full and red, and she stood habitually with one hand pressed against the small of her back, breasts straining her buttons. Esther was always stealing disapproving looks, seeing the girl had become all inefficiency and seduction.

"Don't worry," said Tamar.

Yet the pregnancy seemed like another mishap, another accident that could have been prevented if only Tamar had been vigilant. Once again she had let Ginny out of sight with a man. A man with no sense. Asher opened the door of his rusty red Ford and Ginny climbed inside. A little girl with two new, smooth braids, sitting on the handlebars of a bicycle, skinny legs dangling.

Tamar had shoved a few items into Ginny's bags when the girl moved out, including a bottle of salon-quality shampoo, and now, looking for something to use on her daughter's grease-heavy hair, she found this bottle amid the clutter in a metal basket at the foot of the tub. An ashtray was balanced on top of the basket, encrusted with the sludge of dampened and dried ashes. Putting it on the floor so she could wash it later, Tamar ignored her fleeting desire for a cigarette. Ginny and Esther had never seen her smoke; it usually took her a week to get through a pack, and she only indulged at work, in the department store's employee changing room. It occurred to her for the first time, and with a strangely desperate sense of loss, that when she left her job in a month to start her new business, her smoking days would be over.

Asher had left his shaving cream behind, and dried-up drips of foam glued several blond hairs to the top of the container. Tamar wondered if Asher planned not to shave in Israel, if he planned to grow facial hair and ear locks. She imagined the fair scruff the boy would likely find on his cheeks in lieu of a beard and closed her eyes against the image, immediately aware that she was squeezing her lids together, a habit that had already caused wrinkles to start beside her eyes. She dropped the shaving cream into the trash can — Ginny clearly wasn't using it to shave her legs or armpits — and poured a generous amount of shampoo into her palm. Ginny kept her eyes shut. It was a long time since Tamar had washed hair, even her own. She and Esther had their hair washed and set twice a week. After they moved and Tamar opened her salon over the apartment, Esther would only have to walk upstairs to have her roots touched up. Tamar planned to start with two stylists, a manicurist and a pedicurist. She would sell cosmetics and work the cash herself. She had worked in enough stores that she was confident she could manage the books, at least until she could afford to hire an accountant.

She rubbed the shampoo between her hands and said to Ginny, "Doesn't this smell wonderful?" It did: fruity and musky, the smell of griminess cleared away and beauty released. In Tamar's view, beauty products didn't add to or change a woman's appearance but smoothed out hard edges, revealing her best self. At the vanity table each morning, Tamar watched her real face emerge, features sharpened. According to Asher, she felt the same way about grooming that Esther did about cooking. Asher said that she and Esther were both warding off the spectre that lurks beneath civilization. When she recalled this conversation, Tamar felt ill. It had been not only an act of betrayal, it had also been monstrously silly, an indignity that recalled her second date with Robert, all those years ago, after which she'd lain awake for hours remembering how she squeezed his hand between her legs, gasping, mouth against his. She was tortured by the absurdity of it — how ridiculous that she'd let herself go. And, despite everything, the knowledge that, if given a chance, she would do it again.

Oh, and she did it again. She'd waited for Robert, planned clandestine meetings, and lied so they could be alone. For a little sliver of time, she ached with a desire that demanded all her attention, and she lived to satisfy it. When he had the night shift and she had days off, she took the bus to his house. One time she even met him in his office, and she didn't wait, didn't speak, took the time only to lock the door behind her before tearing into him. When they couldn't meet for several days in a row, she'd find herself motionless at the cosmetics counter, staring at her own reflection in the magnifying mirrors, thinking about his smell, the sound of his voice saying her name; she thought about him while she was working, while she was eating dinner with her mother, as she cleaned the dishes and did the laundry and dyed Esther's hair at the kitchen sink. She was a quiet lover, always aware of the sound of her own breathing and his, and held fistfuls of his thick red hair in her hands.

Robert had shown her something new — he had made her forget about the endless struggle to earn a living and keep her mother's unease at bay; he warded off her panic over the unlikeliness of staying afloat. She believed his claim that this was some sort of love, though it surely in no way resembled the love her parents had shared, which was the kind that led reasonably to marriage. But the kind of love Tamar indulged in three or four times a week led to marriage as well, it turned out, by way of a small, rushed wedding before anything became obvious.

The way Asher coaxed her to speak, conjured confessions — it had all reminded her, in some strange way, of Robert. It was the undivided attention, the look of desire, of wanting something she had and wanting it badly. And she wanted to give it to him. As though he could take her words and leave her free of them. She'd told Asher about her father, that he had been tall and bony, with sharp ribs, cheekbones and shoulders, and had black hair that curled straight up. How he'd swung Tamar into the air with a happiness that was matched in intensity only by his frustration, when his fists slammed against tables and plates smashed against walls. He never directed these brief, fierce rages at Esther, Tamar or any other person but always at inanimate objects, which, however expensively, could be swept up and replaced. And Tamar told Asher that Esther had been small and dainty, with elegant, thin fingers and a girlish, pretty face. Jozef used to pick her up and swing her around, too, singing her name. He touched her face and called her "my sweet love." Tamar's parents had loved each other with a rare and dangerous fierceness; Tamar had not realized this until she watched the van Daams, the brusque and often irritated manner in which they took care of each other and the way they tolerated each other's presence and needs. They used to have dinner parties, Tamar's parents, and she remembered how her father put his arm around Esther's shoulders as he conversed and pulled her close for a moment, protectively, to reinforce that she was dear to him.

After written notification of his death, discussion of Tamar's father stopped abruptly and conclusively, and Esther immediately acquiesced to Tamar's new plan. Tamar sold everything they owned — many of their possessions had been returned by neighbours who'd managed to take them and safeguard them. With the money from her father's furniture, her mother's jewellery, and the art they had bought together, Tamar brought her mother to Canada. They looked in the atlas and were shocked at the size of the country — Tamar had pictured an area approximately the size and location of Alaska. The capital city seemed like a reasonable destination.

Within two months, Tamar was working at a high-end clothing store in downtown Ottawa. She stood in her smart suits and high heels, long hair pulled up and back, hands clasped, in front of rows of Canadian women's clothing. She worried about her mother, home with the doors locked and the radio on, watching the snow-covered sidewalk through a crack in the blinds. Esther organized and reorganized the contents of the fridge, cooked the dishes she knew. Chopped liver and potato kugel, pea soup and chicken croquettes. She'd always harboured a basic contempt for all other races and nationalities, and now she was vehemently convinced of every known stereotype. She disdained her own ethnicity as much as any other; she thought Jews were elitist and superstitious and the Dutch stingy and lazy. Yet at first she prepared Jewish and Dutch dishes with seeming reverence, a care that could easily be mistaken for nostalgia. She often prepared *pannekoeken* with apples for breakfast and challah on Fridays for the weekend.

The first time Tamar brought home a cookbook from the department store, Esther spent the evening poring over pictures of succulent chickens, hams and pies. The next afternoon, she started on the first page, going through the recipes with her English-Dutch dictionary to write translations in pencil beside each ingredient. On her next grocery day, Tamar asked, "Shall I buy you some of those ingredients?"

Esther looked shocked at the suggestion, then nodded. "*Ja.*"

"Which one?" said Tamar. Esther showed her a minced-beef pie, full of potatoes, corn and peas. Tamar copied down the list of ingredients, and two nights later came home to unfamiliar and delicious smells. Her mother had recreated the pie so it looked exactly like the photograph. "This is wonderful," Tamar told her. Esther was utterly absorbed in eating. When they finished, Esther carefully wrapped the leftovers and put them in the fridge.

Tamar bought her mother more cookbooks, all of which Esther studied carefully and translated into Dutch. She wanted to try Italian dishes, French dishes, Asian dishes, and her quest for ingredients finally drew her out of the apartment. Equipped with purse, map and cookbook, Esther took the bus to Little Italy and to the Chinese stores on Somerset Street. She showed store proprietors the English recipes and demonstrated uncharacteristic respect for anyone who sold, cooked, prepared or was in any other way associated with food. The only exceptions were kosher butchers, who she claimed were barbarians. Her grandfather had been a kosher butcher, and she remembered him as a sadistic, unaffectionate man. Her unlikely descriptions had him covered in blood, head to foot, even at family gatherings. "Always, it was black under his nails. I knew it was meat rotting under there." Esther's memories of her childhood had somehow become distorted, warped in strange directions during the two years Tamar had lost her. Tamar knew there was no point in arguing with her mother's beliefs and had long ago given up trying to convince her of anything, even the details of their own lives.

Some of the recipes in Esther's books were too lavish for Tamar's salary, but they were both surprised by how inexpensive it was to eat well. Spices cost only pennies and transformed the most familiar ingredients into unheard-of delight. Over twenty-five years, Esther's arsenal of dishes had grown to the hundreds, but she still refused to diverge from the recipes in her books. Wouldn't replace white flour with whole wheat or habanero peppers with chili. She required exact measurements and penciled them in beside ingredients that could be included "to taste." Once, when Ginny was a little girl, she suggested that Oma Esther add red pepper to her zucchini risotto. Esther didn't respond. Ginny said challah with chocolate chips would be a great dessert, and Esther was appalled. She attributed such suggestions, along with all Ginny's other flaws, to her Irish blood.

As Esther took on more cooking, shopping and housekeeping, Tamar began to work longer hours for increased wages, and her English improved quickly. She had taken English classes as a child, and the conversational requirements of sales came to her easily. Her manager forgave any difficulties, and so did her customers, because her impeccable appearance and manner more than made up for them. Esther, meanwhile, learned the English words for food and its preparation. Within a year, she didn't need to use her dictionary as much and recognized the words for most vegetables, meats and spices. She learned cooking verbs, but only in the imperative voice: whisk, knead, separate, crumble.

Asher tried to convince Tamar that Esther's fixation on food was a common symptom of what he called "survivor syndrome." "Inmates in the camps talked and even dreamed incessantly about food," he told her. "They would spend nights planning the menus for dinner parties. They fantasized about recipes far more than they thought about sex." Asher forced these pictures into Tamar's head: Esther, starving, remembering recipes, dreaming of roast chickens and potatoes.

"My father," Tamar told Asher, "would roll over in his grave, if he had one, to see the way we eat. When I was a child, we weren't allowed to put more than one item on a piece of bread. Either butter or cheese, but not both. It wasn't because we were poor; it was some kind of moral principle."

Asher tapped his finger against his chin. "Is it possible," he said, "that you and your mother feel guilty for accepting your father's death, for leaving him behind — surviving him?"

After washing the length of Ginny's hair, Tamar squeezed more shampoo into her hand. "Once more." This time, she worked up a thick lather and rubbed her daughter's scalp firmly with the tips of her fingers. "Ow," said Ginny. "Nails." She smiled.

"You should see some of the new products they're coming up with," said Tamar. "I know you young girls like to have that straight-down-the-sides-of-your-face look, but you could still use something for shine. Thin eyebrows are in," she added. She ran her finger over Ginny's pale left eyebrow, then used her palm to wipe away a puff of soap she'd left. Tamar's own eyebrows were non-existent, plucked from their follicles and replaced with a brown pencil line. "You could use a facial," she told Ginny. "Betsy can do it. She's wonderful. She'd get rid of all those blackheads, too. The things she does for some of these women. They're like new people." Tamar paused. "Does Steven know Asher has left?" she asked.

"Sure, they're friends."

"Steven's such a nice boy. And he liked you so much."

"Steven still likes me," said Ginny. "And he's n̶ ̶ ̶int, by the way. He's an oddball. He keeps brains in jars of formaldehyde. Asher calls him Doctor Frankenstein."

"That's his area of study, isn't it," said Tamar. "He's a scientist." She winced a little at the thought of the pickled brains. "Anyway, he would never —"

Ginny splashed water up her arms. "Never what?" She shifted her weight, and her ankle bumped against the corner of the soap basket. "Ouch." She regained her balance with an arm on each side of the tub. "This one time, I was at Steven's apartment. There was a dinner party, and I was the last one left." Tamar paused, gripping a handful of hair like a rope before she continued to knead it between her hands. Ginny reached up and touched the top of her head, then let her arm fall back to her side.

"And?" said Tamar.

"And," said Ginny, "we were finishing the last of the wine when he walked over to the window. He told me to come over and look. We could see right into the apartment across the street. The bedroom. Do you want to hear this?"

"If you like."

"Well, there were this man and woman lying side by side, completely naked, holding hands." Ginny paused again, long enough for Tamar to wonder if this was supposed to be the end of the story. Then she added, "They were masturbating."

"They were — goodness, Ginny!"

"Steven said they did that every night. Night after night. And he stands there watching them. He insisted I keep watching until they — were finished." Tamar filled the green bucket and began to rinse the shampoo out of Ginny's hair.

Steven Winter was just a sweet, decent boy. He'd been calling Ginny for months, coming by and taking her to the movies, before Asher got in the way. He'd brought Tamar an assortment of teas in a basket. Terribly tall, he had a ponytail and a thick, bushy beard. But despite the fashion of the day, he had an intelligent face, a gentle face that would someday crinkle around the eyes in a permanent expression of kindness. Tamar was sure that only some strange twist of his sweetness and decency brought him to his window to spy on his neighbours and made him want Ginny to see them, too.

"Well?" said Ginny.

"Well what?"

Tamar pushed Ginny's head forwards to pour a bucketful of water on the back of her hair. She continued to rinse in silence and Ginny sighed, wiped her wet lips with the back of her equally wet wrist. "There," said Tamar at last. "Hair's all clean. Squeaky clean." She squeaked her fingers down one lock to demonstrate.

"Thanks, Mother. I can do the rest." Ginny splashed water on her face. As her mother settled back onto the toilet, drying her arms on an already damp towel, Ginny said, "Honestly. I'll be fine. Maybe you should check on Oma Esther. Can I call you when I need to get out?"

Tamar stood. "Thank you would have been nice."

"I *did* say thank you, Mother." She said it quietly, and Tamar didn't react. Instead, she paused in the doorway and asked, "Where did you get the paper for all those birds?"

"Oh. I buy origami paper at the art supply store. And I cut wrapping paper into squares. You can use anything as long as it's square; sometimes I use old class notes or letters. Junk that comes in the mail. Anything."

Shutting the door behind her so it was open only a crack, Tamar manoeuvred through Asher's clutter to the bed and lifted one end of the balled-up blanket to shake it straight. Asher and Ginny had slept in this bed together for six months. Tamar couldn't picture it. Sleeping bodies, so vulnerable, waking to see each other's faces slack and open.

When Tamar married Robert, she and Esther had packed up the meagre contents of their apartment. Robert put their pots and pans in his bare cupboards, their books beside his own on the many shelves and their furniture in the guest bedrooms and den. He and Tamar slept in the bedroom in his large, furnished basement. The very bedroom where she'd often lain naked, Robert holding her and imagining a future for them, while Esther thought she was working extra shifts at the store. Esther slept upstairs. Tamar hadn't anticipated waking in the night, disoriented, with the panicked conviction that there was a stranger under the covers with her; she had never intended to share a life with him this way, to fall asleep with him. He lay on his back with his wiry, surprisingly robust limbs spread wide. He snored. Sometimes he would roll over and his arm would settle across Tamar's body, heavy and stubborn as an animal. She'd shared a bed once before, but she hadn't predicted waking beside her husband with another name on her lips.

"Who's Femke?" asked Robert. Smiling across the pillow, he said, "You moan in your sleep, love. And you keep saying, *Femke*."

"A girl I knew in Holland." Femke used to curl up against Tamar's back and breathe against her shoulder. Her hair was brown and smelled like soap or like smoke or garlic. Sometimes, after an evening with her friends, she smelled of liquor, and sometimes she passed wind in her sleep. "Don't mention her in front of my mother," said Tamar. Robert was curious, and so she told him, "I stayed with her family when my parents were gone." When she said this, Robert pulled her back against his chest as though to protect her.

One time, Tamar remembered, Femke said, "You better stop making those moaning noises, pervert, or I'll tell them to come and take you away."

"Doesn't your mother want to know what happened to you while she was gone?" said Robert.

Wriggling out from under his arm, Tamar sat up. "You can't mention it to her. Please, you don't understand." She'd told him her mother was interned for a time and that Tamar had stayed with neighbours; she had made it sound like a week or two. She had considered telling Robert the whole story, and considered it again as he sat up in bed beside her and shook his head, perplexed; the urge to confess swelled from her stomach into her throat. But to tell him she hadn't breathed fresh air or been allowed near a window for two years of her life — that the years she was seventeen and eighteen, when most people agonize over first love, worry about exams and dream of extravagant futures, she'd been hidden away like a terrible secret.

She imagined telling Robert about the hours, sometimes entire days, she'd spent lying in the crawl space under the roof, keeping her mind still by conjugating English verbs, thinking of the beach or concentrating on the smell of her mother's rosewater perfume until she could feel the memory in her nose. But she had already vowed, privately, never to tell anyone. How could she, without letting those two years define her? If she described details, admitted to the circumstances of her father's and aunt's deaths and tried to imagine what her mother had witnessed, anything else Tamar said or did or ever achieved would inevitably pale in import beside those twenty-two months' obscenely tragic glow. She would become gruesome in her own eyes and the eyes of others; how could she not?

When she was eight months pregnant, Tamar moved upstairs into the room beside her mother's. Robert said he was disappointed, that he loved her pregnant body, but that he would respect her need for privacy. He thought she was self-conscious about her new shape, and he wasn't completely wrong. When Ginny was born they created a nursery across the hall from Robert's bedroom — his former office — but for the first two months, the baby slept upstairs with Tamar. Robert waited and waited for Tamar to move back to his bedroom, but Ginny started sleeping through the night in her crib, and still Tamar descended the stairs only to use the laundry room and put her daughter to bed.

Robert had walked into Tamar's life through stockings, eyes averted from brassieres, face blushing to match his hair. There were different breeds of men who wandered stocking aisles, but, at first sight, Tamar guessed Robert was the harmless type, love-struck and bewildered. When she asked if he needed a gift for his sweetheart, he said, "My sister." Never, throughout their marriage, did Tamar ask whom he had really been shopping for that day, and he never volunteered the information. Someone had been jilted, quietly shoved aside. Tamar imagined a girl with large breasts, brown curls and a small cross around her neck. The kind of girl Robert had known all his life in the form of aunts, cousins and classmates. He would have known how to be with this girl; it would have been easy, and the restless moments would have passed. They would have slept together in Robert's big bed, and perhaps he would have lived to be an old man, with many children and grandchildren. Tamar knew Robert had fallen into a trap that day in the intimate apparel section. He'd stepped off course and onto a trajectory that would intersect, twelve years later, with the front of an OTC bus. Her straight, small body, her lacquered honey-brown hair, her eyelashes thick and long as brushes. He must have been disappointed to discover those lashes weren't real. They were otherworldly. Her accent, which was much stronger then, had delighted him: he would help her, save her, teach to say *th*. And in return, Tamar would lead him out of mediocrity and into a life of beauty, tragedy and purpose.

"It's my sister's birthday," said Robert, blushing, a large poster of a brassiere over his head. He was twenty-five, two years older than Tamar, fresh out of medical school and interning at the Ottawa General Hospital. He could afford to take Tamar to nice restaurants because, he explained, his parents were both dead and in fact he had no siblings. And he didn't mind that she clearly had no real experience with men. Over their first dinner, he did most of the talking, hands flailing, freckles burning orange across his pale nose. He told her excitedly that, despite his parents' obvious success, his people had suffered. Told her about his great-grandparents coming to Canada as little children during the Irish potato famine. The ships were ill-equipped, and by the time they arrived in Montreal, typhus had broken out. Robert's great-grandparents had survived the makeshift quarantine shacks set up in the Montreal harbour. "Popish and drunk, that's what they think of us. Treated us like animals." Tamar was amazed at his fury about something he had not witnessed, something that happened before his grandparents were born. The immediacy of his great-grandparents' suffering. Tamar's English wasn't perfect, but she noticed that his grammar slipped, vacillating between past and present. Like Asher would, later, he said *us*. Robert was not very close to his remaining family, he said. He said he was a bit of a loner. "Solitary. That's me. I'm not one for much cavorting."

"Cavorting?"

"Socializing. Spending time with groups of people, out and about. I'm alone a lot."

Tamar didn't have friends either, or family, except for Esther. She wasn't one for cavorting. She told Robert that much of her family had "died," including her father, "during the occupation." She admitted quickly, to get it out in the open whatever the consequences, "My parents were Jewish, you know, by birth."

"Jewish? You don't look Jewish. I always saw Jews in Montreal, with the" — he motioned with his hands.

"Hats? No. No. We're not like that at all. It was only that my grandparents were Jewish. But also, not the — hats."

Robert shook his head, perplexed, apparently unable to fathom any connection between blond, peach-skinned Tamar and Jews. "I have renounced Catholicism myself," he offered, spitting out *renounced*. "I don't believe in God. You may as well know that I believe in humanity. And reason. I don't want any children of mine raised to think they're part of the one true religion." Tamar silently watched him across the table, and he blushed. He had almost no eyebrows and brown, fiery eyes.

"You could be a model," he said. "An actress. You're that pretty."

He didn't know. He suspected nothing, Tamar realized. Somehow, the Canadian doctor did not know what it meant that she was Jewish and from Europe and had lived through the war. She was nothing more bizarre than an attractive European with an interesting accent and an exotic religious background.

"You're hardly eating," said Robert, looking at Tamar's fish. Throughout his tirade, Robert had devoured the pork chops and vegetables on his own plate, chewing and swallowing with the same verve as that with which he spoke.

"I am feeling a bit ill," Tamar admitted. "I ought to go home."

Robert looked at her closely. "All right," he said. "I'll drive you. Just let me pay the bill." He signalled to the waiter and looked back at her. "Oh, Tamar," he said. "You're so lovely. But your face is turning green."

When Robert pulled up in front of her house, Tamar slammed the car door and ran inside to huddle over the toilet for half an hour, folded arms pressed against her cramping stomach. She'd never felt so sick, not since moving to Canada. When he phoned a few days later, her stomach rebelled again, and she thought it must be the first sign of love.

"Where's he from?" Esther asked.

"Canada."

"Where is he really from?"

"He was born right here in Ottawa, and his parents were born in Montreal." Esther sighed and put a hand to her head as though Tamar were pummelling her.

Tamar acquiesced. "His family came from Ireland." Esther groaned and shook her head, then launched into a description of well-known Irish vices and failings. Tamar found herself defending Robert as though she'd known him far longer than one week. She told Esther that Robert didn't drink, wouldn't even touch alcohol, in fact. That he was estranged from his family because he refused to go to church. "He's a doctor." She didn't mention that he specialized in disorders of the feet, that he spent many of his waking hours face to face with corns and bunions.

It was that second date that sealed his fate. A movie with Katharine Hepburn, and Tamar's stomach hurt so badly she almost gagged on the few kernels of popcorn that she forced herself to swallow. Robert was worried about appendicitis and, in his car afterwards, put his hand low on her belly. "Does it hurt here?" He pressed firmly. And suddenly it didn't hurt at all. "I'm terribly tired," Tamar said. "Terribly tired." She laid her head against his collarbone.

"Come and see my home," he said.

She had a lover once before that, shortly before moving to Canada. She was working as a seamstress, and he was an older man, an accountant who worked for the same tailor shop. He had bought her several nice dinners and was quite handsome. He didn't think much of her, was clearly convinced he was getting away with something. She hadn't told him she was planning to leave.

Robert occupied the main floor and basement of a three-storey house in Sandy Hill. "You're exhausted," he told her, as he pointed out the bedroom. "Bone-tired. That's the only problem with your health. Please feel free to have a sleep." And though it was strange, undoubtedly, Tamar accepted his diagnosis and his offer, and took a long, deep nap in his bed. She woke late in the night and waited for him to join her.

"Don't worry," said Robert, later, driving her home. "My house is big enough for us and your mother." He had it all planned out, and he smiled at the ceiling, so sure and optimistic. Tamar almost believed him when he stopped in front of her building and said, "The past can be sloughed off like a dried old skin. You'll see."

Within two days, Tamar had a bladder infection, and she thought it was a bad omen, but Robert said "honeymoon cystitis" and prescribed penicillin. Alarmed by the word "honeymoon," Tamar was sure the constant pain in her abdomen was retribution for her own absurd behaviour, but she took the pills and the pain went away again. After she took the last pill, Tamar went straight to Robert's house. She put her hand in his shirt as she stepped close to him in the foyer.

Tamar sat on the edge of the bed, waiting to help Ginny out of the bath. On the floor by her foot lay a used tissue. She looked around for a trash can, but there was none, and she remained sitting.

"Tamar," called Ginny, "are you out there?"

In the dusty mirror across the room, Tamar watched herself mouth the word *no* without saying it aloud. The heat, along with the steam from the bath, had caused her mascara to run, a black smudge under each eye. She heard Ginny splashing, manoeuvring herself into a different position. The gradually recognizable smell of cigarette smoke seeped into the bedroom. Tamar wished she could ask her daughter for a cigarette; longing heightened the tension in her shoulders and up the back of her neck. Just a few puffs to ease her taut nerves.

"I've been an A-plus student all my life," Ginny said loudly. "Do you even realize that? I'm a brilliant bullshitter, name dropper and cocksucker. I bet you didn't even know I was multi-talented. You're not out there listening to me, are you, really, Mother?"

Tamar's reflection blinked at her. She was starting her own business, buying her own house and her own place of work, finally. She was almost fifty years old.

"Steven's in love with me," Ginny said, speaking over her mother's last thought. "Did you know that? I bet you didn't. I tried to seduce him one night but it didn't work. He said he had too much respect for me, that he valued the future of our friendship." Ginny paused. "Asher said he found me fascinating, but do you know what he really found fascinating? That damn scar on Oma Esther's arm. He thinks you two are a real textbook case. He wanted to study the both of you and make his thesis of it. When I told him about Auschwitz he practically had an orgasm." Tamar saw herself cringe, and was grateful Ginny couldn't see her. "I'm surprised he didn't want to talk about it while we were screwing. Not that we've done much of that since I've lived here, though, Mother. My stories about growing up with Oma Esther were a real disappointment. I couldn't come up with anything good. Oh, Mama," said Ginny faintly. "Asher's a real idiot. The real deal. And what am I supposed to do now?"

"I've been trying my best."

"Aha!" Ginny started, but Tamar kept talking.

"It's been my best, *liefje*, and I'm sorry. I'm sorry I didn't Scotch-tape your A-plusses to the fridge like your sainted father would have done. I'm sorry I haven't stopped your bones from breaking every which way." She breathed deeply, calming herself. "But I'm not strong enough to lift you out of that bathtub, Virginia. You're very heavy. You're extremely heavy right now, and you're going to have to help."

Robert had his own bathroom in the basement, and maybe he didn't realize it was right under Tamar's bedroom. Perhaps he didn't know she could hear the shower running, the water surging through the pipes. His nights out: perhaps he really thought they were well hidden. She wondered if it was the woman he'd been shopping for that first time she saw him, or if it was someone else. Maybe it was many women. Nothing seemed impossible; she didn't understand Robert at all. Walking toward her through ladies' apparel, a foreign foot doctor who needed a salesgirl to answer his questions about silk stockings. She could have done that very well, and they both would have kept their dignity. But this grand-miracle-of-life business — it wasn't a business she ever claimed to know anything about.

Ginny's red birds didn't look trapped to Tamar; they were wind-tossed, gliding straight for the window. She wanted to tell her daughter that migration isn't something you can restrain. Not once the will to migrate has set in. The will to seek a place far and foreign, clean and bright and not yet used up. And that's not to say there is such a place; there's not. She could have warned Asher, though it wouldn't have done any good: no place stays that way for long, because winter follows you around the globe. That chill you left behind is always right at your heels.

Amnesia, traditionally understood as a condition imposed by physical or psychological trauma, can also be a way of life, consciously adopted and lived. What is the opposite of amnesia? The opposite of amnesia, as I am using the word, is nostalgia. Nostalgia is a longing for home, a fear that we will never see home again. Nostalgia also tells us that the past is more real, more important, than the present. The past assumes a potency beside which the present is as lacklustre as a dried-out husk. But what if you have no home and no past? Nothing sickly to dredge up, nothing to confess? Then you are free. Amnesia freed me from nostalgia. Technically, my amnesia was temporary — as I recovered from my head injury, memories began to return. First I remembered things from early childhood, and then early adulthood, but I remembered events as though they'd occurred in a book I'd read or a movie I'd seen. I realized I'd wrenched myself free from the chokehold those memories once had on me. The present became and remains luscious and ripe.

Imagine yourself in a train station, dragging everything you've acquired in your life. Not to mention all the clutter you've inherited from your family. All those bags and suitcases — all the anxiety they cause. You're afraid you might lose them, afraid they are becoming too heavy. Afraid they might tumble open and spill your dirty underwear in a humiliating pile around your feet. Put it all down and set it alight — build a pyre and leave it! The train pulls out, leaving that smouldering pile of ashes behind. Yes, it's normal to feel a momentary pang of loss, of regret, just as we grasp at dreams while we wake — even nightmares. But the station is already behind us and there's no need ever to look back. Now you can go wherever you like.

J. Virginia Morgan
The Willing Amnesiac: Reappearing into the Present

Three

It was Benna Hadrick who showed Jasmine the stocky, shiny-faced man in the mall. He had a receding hairline and wore light-coloured jeans and a matching jacket, and he was with four girls, helping them choose clothes in La Boutique. "And those are his hoes," claimed Benna, pushing a small, lacy red shirt into Jasmine's hand. In the changing room, Jasmine took off her father's grey and blue Adidas jacket and dropped it on the floor along with her baggy T-shirt. "Come out and show," said Benna.

A roll of white flesh poked out between the tiny red shirt and Jasmine's jeans, and her chest was squashed, her nipples clearly visible through the fabric. "No," she said. "It doesn't fit."

"Show," said Benna.

"No," said Jasmine, pulling the shirt back over her head. "I ain't your ho."

That was no pimp they saw. There are creatures that slip into this world, that have human faces but that rightly belong to some other order of being. There were more of them when Jasmine was younger; they used to reveal themselves often, in barely perceptible flashes. Angels hovering whitely outside the window; the tooth fairy's quick hand under a pillow; Elijah's split-second sip of wine at Granny and Grandpa Winter's Passover Seders. She didn't believe in many of them anymore, but she was trying with all her might to believe in pimps. Tall men, thin-muscled and silent, with sparkly dark eyes that took everything in, scanning a room in seconds, scavenging for lost girls ripe for sexual slavery.

For years, she had tried to look like a girl whose parents would search for her unremittingly if she was late home from school or swimming; though she was in fact that kind of girl, she was afraid a stranger might mistake her for the other kind. The kind that could slip, like a small animal under a door, into a different life where her parents would never be able to find her. But that was when she was little and afraid to be separated from her father's side, as if the world was trying to drag her away from safety. Now she was older, in grade eight, and she could see that it was the other way round. Her family and her routines and her school — they were traps that she could escape only by violently wrenching herself free.

Lara had recently shown Jasmine an article about pimps — it said an abductor might trail a girl for days waiting for the right moment. "These are calculating, manipulative people," Lara explained over dinner, rubbing her corn over the lopsided, melty butter. "They prey on girls with no social network. Girls who seem lost and insecure."

So, walking in crowds, Jasmine hung back from her parents, trying to look abandoned and astray. When Lara and Dad took her back-to-school shopping at the Bay, they were distracted by a coat sale, and Jasmine wandered across the room into Ladies' Apparel. The underwear section made Jasmine dizzy. Tam-Tam had worked in a ladies' apparel department for years, and no wonder she exuded a superhuman femininity, even now — in the aisles of lacy bras, silky lingerie and black stockings, the air felt electric with womanliness. Trailing after Lara and Dad in the parking lot, Jasmine was ready for a hand to fall on her arm. His fingers would be long and white, his hair black, his cheekbones high. He'd have musky breath with an undercurrent of mint, because pimps always chewed gum. He'd grab her by the hand and pull her into a small, dark place. An alley, a car and finally an apartment and a bed with red sheets. And there she'd wake up, lean and wan, bright-eyed and addicted. She would wear lingerie and live with a lot of other sweet-smelling girls, and none of them would remember where they came from or where they'd been before they were whisked away. Occasionally she thought about the men. There would be men; she understood that. Naked men, maybe ugly. But that part of sex slavery hardly seemed real, hardly even entered her mind.

The first time Jasmine ever skipped swimming after school, she stood outside the bus terminal for a long time before opening the door. Not in hesitation, but out of respect for the last moments of a way of life. It was the end of October, cool and sunny in a bright, brittle way. She watched the carwash next door, the one her father always used. When she was younger, she'd loved going through the carwash, how she couldn't see or hear anything but the big brushes and soapy water battering the windows. The Volvo was a submarine under the ocean — a small pocket of airtight security. She loved the steady, engineless glide and her dad silent beside her; somehow, they both knew not to speak inside the carwash. They passed the massive blow-dryers that made little drops of water scatter, shrink and disappear, and then broke the surface into sunlight, and she was aware of everything at once — the sounds of cars driving by, people laughing and talking, bike bells and birds.

Jasmine thought of never seeing that carwash again and remembered what it said in *The Willing Amnesiac* — that when you're about to leave a place forever, things long taken for granted are suddenly precious. There's always a moment, J. Virginia Morgan wrote, when the small details of the life you're leaving behind seem to shimmer with unprecedented value.

Jasmine stepped through the door and closed it behind her. She could still hear sounds from outside; she had half expected the door, like the one to her father's lab at the university, to shut out all reminders of the outside world. She walked slowly from one end of the room to the other and nothing happened, except that a frizzy-haired middle-aged woman in a blue blazer smiled at her as she passed the Kingston sign.

The seats by the Toronto door were all empty, and they faced the coffee counter with its tiny, round tables — the infamous café Jasmine's whole school had been warned against. At a recent assembly, the principal, Mr. Munro, had talked about the bus terminal lunch counter as though it were teeming with evil. As if its egg salad sandwiches could result only in certain death. Throughout the terminal's condemnation, Jasmine had been sitting on the floor beside Benna, who laughed when Jasmine made a killer sandwich with her hands and made it bite Benna's arm, whispering, "Attack of the baloney on rye." Benna stretched out her legs in their ripped nylons and looked the gym teacher in the eye, giving him an obvious boner.

A middle-aged woman in a blue blouse and a hairnet sat behind the terminal's lunch counter, absorbed in a paperback, and the smell of egg salad made Jasmine think of her grandmother. Tam-Tam, her real grandmother, who had given birth to her biological mother. As far as Jasmine knew, egg salad, tuna and chopped liver were the only sandwich fillings Tam-Tam knew how to make, and that's what she'd always given Jasmine and Agatha for lunch when Jasmine was little. Now Tam-Tam almost always ate restaurant food — the last time Jasmine saw her, they'd spent a Saturday afternoon shopping at the Rideau Centre and then had dinner at the fish restaurant in the market. Although she was usually allowed to take the bus by herself, Dad always dropped Jasmine off and picked her up at the mall when her grandmother was involved. Tam-Tam would be waiting, ladylike, hands clasped in her lap, on a bench near the makeup counters at the Bay. Her makeup was always perfect, and she usually wore a cashmere sweater with a silk scarf arranged perfectly around her neck. And not only did Tam-Tam always buy Jasmine new clothes, she told off salespeople for being too slow and even reprimanded one girl for trying to sell Jasmine a sweater that was clearly two sizes too big. "It certainly doesn't look great," Tam-Tam said. "It looks terrible. Is something not working with your eyes?"

Dad had explained to Jasmine that Tam-Tam sold clothes for years and had taken the job seriously — she had been diligent, tasteful and responsible about it. He asked Jasmine to try to understand how it must feel from Tam-Tam's point of view when other people failed to make the same effort she had. Dad was always suggesting how things must feel from someone else's point of view. It would be great to hear him say, for once, that someone was just a stupid jerk. Like Lara's mother, Bev, for instance.

Jasmine never used to think Tam-Tam was a stupid jerk; only recently had she begun to suspect that Tam-Tam, like everyone else, was keeping things, the most important things, secret. But she still liked how her grandmother always stood up for herself, gazing evenly at a man who tried to push past them on the escalator until he apologized, or asking a waitress for salt and pepper instead of getting the shakers from another table herself. She always walked down the middle of the sidewalk and the middle of the mall, ignoring people's stares. Gorgeous people obviously must get used to being stared at, especially after seventy-something years. Jasmine wasn't ashamed to be seen with Tam-Tam in public — kids from school who saw them together said, "*That*'s your grandmother? How old is she?"

Dad said Tam-Tam was lonely, and that spending time with Jasmine must mean a lot to her. He asked Jasmine to think about it: Tam-Tam had lost a lot of people. And though what Dad said made sense, it was just too hard to picture Tam-Tam being lonely. When she found out Jasmine was gone, she would surely be disgusted. Waiting for her abductor, Jasmine tried not to picture it — Tam-Tam's reaction to the stupidity of being kidnapped.

The grey chairs across from the lunch counter looked disappointingly clean and unthreatening, but Jasmine sat in one of them and looked out the window as if she was waiting for someone coming on a bus. She got her Walkman out of her bag and put on the headphones. She'd found a stash of CDs and tapes in Agatha's old room, now the "study," and had spent two evenings making the best mixed CD ever. Jasmine sat cross-legged, her feet tucked under her thighs, chin in hand, elbow on knee, as though she'd arrived earlier in the day and didn't know where to go, and turned the Agatha CD up loud. She tried to look as if no one cared about her, as if her family was far away and had kicked her out with only ten dollars and a backpack containing a geography textbook and a pencil case, a bathing suit, towel and shampoo. It had been a mistake, she realized, bringing the swimming gear — she should have left it at school. But her posture implied hours of travelling before arriving here in Ottawa, a city she'd never seen before. When she sensed someone watching her from the side, Jasmine didn't look up, just let the sensation sink into her bones and leaned into her hand, rocking a bit in her seat. She was getting uncomfortable and having trouble maintaining the posture.

When Jasmine had paced the living room, hands on her hips, asserting in Mr. Munro's no-nonsense voice that the terminal was "no place for youngsters — one hundred per cent out of bounds," Dad had smiled and Bev even clapped, but Lara said it was no laughing matter.

"It's true, actually," Lara said. "Bus terminals are prime hangouts for pimps. They wait when the buses come, looking for runaways."

"Oh, come now," said Bev.

But Lara said a pimp could spot a runaway girl at a glance. Desperation and confusion created a glowing aura around a young girl that only he could see, and the eyes of a pimp hypnotized like the eyes of a cobra. That's when Jasmine decided to believe Lara, to give it a chance to be true, despite what seemed realistic. Like when she decided at the age of ten to believe in Santa Claus again, even though her parents had admitted two years earlier that it was all made up. The pimp would offer her a place to stay, but it would be a trap; he would buy her nice things and make her take drugs, and then she would be unable to go back. Drugs Jasmine imagined as brightly coloured pills: once they touched her tongue, she would know things she had never imagined, but the drugs would also deliver darkness into her heart and she would forever belong to a different world. She'd pictured the bus terminal as dirty and dark, with nooks and corners perfect for pimps to hide in and girls to disappear into. The place was clean, open and bright. The few people inside seemed so harmless. Pulling the threads at the cuff of her jeans, Jasmine tolerated the sensation of someone staring at her until she couldn't stand it anymore and then glanced over her left shoulder, just with her eyes. She was ready for anything, but it was the woman with the navy blazer, standing right there. Jasmine pulled off her headphones. "Are you all right, dear?" the woman said.

"Yeah. Yes. I'm just about to." She hurried straight to the door without looking back. Half a block down Catherine Street, she spun around in her speed-walk, ready to confront her pursuer. Fists clenched, ready to attack, she faced an empty sidewalk. Half a block away, a teenaged boy glanced up at her and looked away.

She had only been in the terminal for ten minutes. She could still make it to the pool for at least an hour, and though she didn't feel like going through the hassle of changing and showering for just a few laps, she couldn't go straight home. Then she'd have to explain why she wasn't swimming. As she walked towards Bronson Avenue, trying to decide what to do, Jasmine turned to see a city bus coming towards her, and, in a moment, she made her decision, already running for the bus stop. She took the bus past her school and all the way to the Rideau Centre. She only had to wait for ten minutes to catch the bus to Aylmer, and the short wait seemed like a sign — she'd been planning this for weeks, and had looked up the bus number and memorized it, waiting for the right day.

It was rush hour, and the bus was full. Jasmine squeezed into a window seat at the back, grateful that she didn't have to stand. The tightly packed passengers were dressed mostly in business clothes and smelled strongly of perfume and sandwiches. The forty-something, curly-haired woman at Jasmine's side was wearing a lot of blue eyeshadow and had been smoking; Jasmine tried to breathe through the inch of open window.

She'd never been across the bridge to Quebec by herself, only with Dad and Lara for hikes in the Gatineau hills. The embassies along the river's bank and then the island and boats below made her think of picnics and sneakers and the smell of moist leaves, but when the bus turned onto the Boulevard de l'Outaouais, the French signs and the brightly coloured trees at the sides of the highway were as weird as something in another country. It was so easy to leave everything familiar, to insert herself into this crowd of strangers who didn't notice or care that she was out of place. No one was looking at her, concerned; none of these bus people saw her as a lost little girl. She started her CD again from the beginning. The terminal had been nothing but a big, empty room. She should never have gone there; she should have known not to look something magical in the face — that it would only crumble, turn out to be nothing. Like the whole Santa Claus thing. She'd stayed up all night that Christmas, hiding inside the bowl-chair's wooden frame, watching the chimney, waiting to prove everyone wrong. Instead, Dad came down the stairs in his pyjamas, and she hollered as he shoved a new sketchpad and two tangerines into her stocking. He'd felt so bad. Helping her out from under the chair, he looked almost as close to tears as she felt.

Shortly after that Christmas, Jasmine had insisted on going to church one Sunday with her Catholic step-aunt, Hilary. Christians, Dad said, were much too focused on God and godly figures. "They're always looking for something bigger and better than the world we've been given." As far as Jasmine knew, Dad didn't believe in God at all, and she knew he hadn't meant his description of Christianity as a compliment, but bigger and better appealed to Jasmine and she wanted to see it for herself.

The priest at Aunt Hilary's church talked, like a boring teacher, about a woman who found a wallet containing a winning lottery ticket. When she returned the wallet to its owner he gave her half the money. The preacher said the lost wallet with the winning ticket was a test from God, that the woman who found the wallet and the man who shared his winnings were inspired by the Good Book. It was clear to Jasmine, with a heavy, sickening disappointment, that if there was a God, he wouldn't give a damn about lottery tickets. A winning ticket, a lost wallet: those things happened because of chance and luck and even statistical probability, but they were not magical, spiritual or transcendent. Jasmine watched Aunt Hilary and the rest of the congregation take communion as if they were eating a snack. No one's eyes rolled back in their heads when Christ's body touched their tongues and throats and settled into their bellies. She saw no sign of God in the church, felt no goose bumps at the back of her neck, witnessed no miracles of any kind, and she came away from the experience a confirmed non-believer. Dad and Lara had always told her religion was just superstition, and she saw now that it really was made up, tacked onto things in the fakest, most obvious ways.

The bus turned onto a residential street and stopped, and three business people got off. They lived here, in rows of identical houses, steps away from the highway. She tried to imagine it. There was no corner store nearby, even. Most people's lives were so boring, just like J. Virginia Morgan said. Life was so fucking boring. And now the world's latest promise of magic had failed to take effect in the way it was supposed to. Pimps were supposed to be different. They didn't squeeze through chimneys but came into the world through the public washrooms of bus stations and malls. They weren't depicted in stained glass, but in newspaper articles. They didn't leave presents under pillows or in stockings and they didn't care about naughty or nice. They divided children into lost and loved instead and scooped the lost ones into their clutches. They were bad men, a real danger. But what if it was true about that man in the mall? That he really was a pimp and those girls really were what Benna said they were? They hadn't even been pretty and they'd talked loudly, sounding stupid.

Jasmine knew the house was coming a moment before it came into view; she knew it with a physical jolt, like waking a second before the alarm clock goes off. It was a small wooden house on the corner, boarded up with thick, dark planks, out of place on a street featuring mostly aluminum siding. The haunted house. Abruptly, she could see her big sister, hair pulled back in a ponytail, pointing and squealing, "I saw something in there. I saw a ghost, Minnie, did you see it?" Agatha's best friend, Helena, had often been there, too, on the other side of Jasmine, smelling like suntan lotion. There'd often been a smell of chlorine, and always cherry Chap Stick. Cherry Chap Stick was the smell of Jasmine's mother.

And then everything was familiar, in a vague, gut-wrenching way. The corner of a certain light blue house disappearing behind shrubs, the bend of a particular maple tree. Some of the houses seemed new and were a relief to see. An entire development of identical townhouses covered a hill Jasmine was sure had been a vast yellow field of goldenrod that used to make Mama sneeze and sneeze whenever they drove past it. Jasmine remembered the tone and force of her mother's sneezes, and how it had always seemed as if Mama was annoyed with everyone in the car for letting the yellow field exist at all. As if Jasmine, Agatha and Dad had planted it there just to make Mama's life difficult. The distant past had been this close all along, a twenty-minute, two-dollar bus ride. It was the craziest thing, all of a sudden, the vivid memory of Mama turning in the front seat, her long hair falling over her shoulders, her crooked nose perfect on her face. With each stop, the bus crowd thinned out, and Jasmine waited to see her old street. It was called Chemin d'Arthur, she knew that, but she had no idea where it was in relation to other streets. She promised herself she'd e-mail Agatha about it, as soon as she got home, and concentrated on memorizing the name of each *chemin* and *rue* the bus passed, so she could figure out later how close she'd come.

As the route map had promised, the bus stopped in a transit station, turned around, and went back the same way it had come. Back past the eerily familiar streets, back past the Community Centre and the shopping centre, back through Hull. And then she remembered something else. Boulevard des trembles — there was a park coming up. *Parc des trembles*. The tremble park, she'd called it. She'd always thought it was called the tremble park because of the pool and the sprinklers and how, running across the concrete surface, jumping through freezing bursts of water, she'd always reached her mother's deck chair shaking with cold. "Don't touch me," Mama would squeal. "Keep your clammy little hands to yourself." Sometimes Agatha would run through the sprinklers, too, and sometimes she would sit beside Mama, reading a book of her own. Agatha must have been thirteen or fourteen — not much older than Jasmine was now. She had seemed so big and old and acted as if she knew everything. And Jasmine had believed her.

The bus crossed the bridge back to Ottawa, and Jasmine thought of the magazine article she'd found online about J. Virginia Morgan. *The first time I see her in the arrivals lounge of the Tucson airport,* wrote the woman who got to meet her, *she looks like the kind of person who wouldn't forget anything. She is efficiency personified. She glances at me with my cardboard sign and bombards a path straight through the weary-looking travellers. Her hair is long, auburn, perfectly sleek and straight. Her makeup is immaculate, her beige linen suit unwrinkled, and she strides on black high heels, pulling a suitcase carelessly, as though it's light as a feather. Her appearance is next to miraculous considering she's just stepped off a plane.* Jasmine climbed off the bus and bombarded through the people clustered around the shelter, glancing, striding. Her hair didn't have that squashed look that it got from the bathing cap. Lara was smart. She would notice and ask, already knowing the truth, if Jasmine had had a good swim. She would ask why Jasmine was almost an hour late. They would figure it out — that she had been making secret plans, that they didn't know her anymore, that they were on the verge of losing her bodily and had already lost her in every other way.

She didn't even arrive home late enough to get in trouble. Her transgression had made no difference to anyone. Dad wasn't home yet, Bev was watching TV in the den, and Lara was chopping vegetables for dinner, still wearing her work clothes. She had folded her black cardigan over a chair and put her gold rings and bracelets on the table. She stood bare armed in the top that matched the cardigan, and her black hair was sleek against her head, clipped back with a big barrette. Jasmine leaned against the pine counter near the fridge while Lara shredded a head of lettuce into crinkly strips, then cupped her hands to place the food in a white china bowl. She wiped the cutting board with a cloth and picked up a red pepper, examining it from every angle before putting it down in the middle of the board. It matched the colour of her short nails.

"Jas, could you please turn on the light?" Lara had been mad at Jasmine all week for setting a bundle of paper on fire in the bathtub and leaving permanent scorch marks. But now she was being nice. If it was nice not to even care that her child was late. As Jasmine flicked the switch, the kitchen's yellow walls and stainless steel appliances looked even more like a glossy magazine photograph. Lara wiped pepper juice from the cutting board and pushed sizzling tofu slices around the frying pan. She turned and looked at Jasmine leaning against the counter with her jacket on, backpack dangling from one hand. Lara's nose was shiny, makeup softened by the heat of the stove. She smiled briefly, eyes settling on Jasmine's yellow platform shoes. Shoes were forbidden in the kitchen. Lara hesitated, then turned away.

"Dinner in twenty minutes," she said. "The table needs setting."

"I just need to feed Sorbet." Stepping out of her shoes by the back door, Jasmine stopped. Soon she would run away and would never see this house again, would never again take off her shoes and place them on this blue braided rug. Never again pass this bookcase with its cookbooks, photo albums and framed wedding pictures. She examined the photograph of the whole wedding party under a canopy of trees, Dad and Lara in the middle. Jasmine had been six, the flower girl. Her father and Lara married outside at the arboretum in springtime, when all the trees were in bloom, for the benefit of the photos. Lara's cousin, a Unitarian minister, performed the ceremony, and she agreed not to mention God or anything God-related. Jasmine could tell by looking at herself in those photos that she'd believed the party was for her. She looked pleased, as if everyone, her father and Lara included, were there just to see her in that frilly peach dress, carrying her bouquet. Agatha was in the photographs, too, standing off to the side of the kissing couple. At sixteen, she had short blue hair clipped into tufts with plastic children's barrettes, black-framed glasses and a blue dress that matched her hair. She was looking down and off to the side. At least Agatha had known what was happening, hadn't relished the photographer and the guests, hadn't skipped and spun under those carefully placed trees, splashing mud up lacy white socks and chubby bare legs. Dignity: that's what Agatha had at the wedding. What Jasmine lacked.

It wasn't long after the wedding that Agatha ran away. Jasmine had known, somehow, that it was going to happen; she'd felt strongly that her sister was about to disappear and tried to keep a close watch on her, often opening her bedroom door and peeking in to make sure she was still there. One clue was that Agatha never properly unpacked when they moved into Dad and Lara's new house. Her room had been scattered with boxes and half-full suitcases the whole time. That was when her hair had grown back in from being shaved and she was always dying it different colours. She always looked pissed off or sad, and Jasmine was the only one who could cheer her up. She liked that she had the power to make her sister look happy again; but as soon as Jasmine stopped being funny or cute, Agatha looked pissed off or sad again, until one day she was so pissed off she left and didn't come back. Agatha didn't run away for long, but it was the beginning of the end, because she never actually moved back in. She went to live with Tam-Tam and then moved away for university.

Jasmine dumped her backpack in her room, then fed her gerbil, scratching him briefly between the ears. Sorbet was light beige, and Jasmine liked playing with him and training him to do acrobatics. She wasn't mean to him, though, like circus trainers are to their animals. She just played with him, and if he seemed tired or grumpy, she gave him some space. Jasmine needed some space sometimes, too, so she knew how he felt. She bombarded down the stairs, glanced at the unset dining table as she walked past, and pushed open the door to the TV room. "Watcha watching?" Bev didn't understand the concept of giving someone space. She was just *there*. She didn't turn away from the car commercial on the screen as Jasmine sat at the computer desk behind the couch to check her e-mail; on the television, a sleek blue vehicle raced up the side of a mountain. "My soaps," said Bev.

There was nothing from Agatha. Jasmine had written to her

three times since she last heard back, and even though she desperately wanted to ask if her sister remembered the haunted house and the tremble park, if their mother had really sneezed, and where their old street was, she wasn't going to e-mail a fourth time. And Agatha still hadn't even commented about the J. Virginia Morgan website Jasmine had found, or about the interviews and articles. How could she not care — Agatha was the one who'd told Jasmine about J. Virginia Morgan in the first place. Maybe she regretted that now; maybe she wished she'd kept that incredibly important piece of information to herself. What a freak Agatha could be. Every now and then she'd open up and tell Jasmine a whole bunch of stuff about herself, usually when she was home and they stayed up late together, but then she'd clam up again, hardly ever calling and treating Jasmine like a little kid.

After checking J. Virginia Morgan's website, which just had a bunch of crap about upcoming workshops, Jasmine skimmed an e-mail from Mei — something about the book they were reading in English class — and then leaned back to glare at Bev's purplish dye job. It had been neglected for so long there were two inches of white at the top. The way she was sitting, Jasmine could see Bev's profile above her sparkly blue sweater, wrinkles collapsing her face towards her mouth. The room stank of cigarettes — it was so unbelievably disgusting that Dad and Lara let Bev smoke inside. And it was surprising. These were people who ran every morning before work, who did yoga and ate low-fat everything. But Bev was allowed to stink up the house and let herself rot. "It's too late to change her now," Dad said. "She might as well do what she likes."

But if Jasmine found out she was dying, she wouldn't waste her time watching TV and smoking cigarettes. She would make a list of things she wanted to do while there was still time. First she would find J. Virginia Morgan. Virginia would be sorry that Jasmine was dying and would want to get to know her, but Jasmine would tell her she didn't have time. Then she would swim the English Channel. She would go into space, even if it meant dying there. She would do anything it took to get on a rocket and go into orbit. She was determined to be an astronaut, and it filled her with panic to contemplate failing in this goal, to think of spending the rest of her life stuck to the earth. Benna Hadrick, Jasmine knew, didn't believe in her dream. More and more, Jasmine found herself thinking that Benna was surprisingly, dismayingly lacking in imagination.

Jasmine heard her father talking to Lara in the kitchen and left the computer to find him already setting the table. She trailed him, putting napkins beside the forks, straightening the placemats, until he put his arm around her shoulder to kiss the top of her head. "How's my little fish? Did you finish your Halloween costume?" She nodded, sad for him. She hoped he would choose a flattering photo for the milk cartons.

"I used to love Halloween," said Lara, placing dishes of food on the table. She called for Bev. "Remember how I used to love Halloween, Mom?" she said, as they all sat down. Bev nodded non-committally. "Mom," Lara said, "did you see the costume Jas made for tomorrow?"

Bev looked at her blankly. "No," she said after a painfully long pause, "I never did."

"Steven," said Lara, "did I ever tell you about the time my sister and I dressed as the twins from *The Shining*?"

"I think so," said Dad. Lara's laugh, brittle and too loud, faded into a tense smile. Jasmine thought of a quote from Virginia Morgan's website — it was from her new book, *Accidents*. Virginia Morgan's writing always had some embarrassing parts and a lot of incomprehensible parts, but, after reading passages a few times, Jasmine could usually figure out what they were supposed to mean. The quotation said: *Watch closely and you'll begin to see people as actors rehearsing well-learned scenes understood only technically. For so long, I, too, was posed in an exaggerated, pathetically earnest attempt to emulate real life.* Dad reached over to squeeze Lara's hand and kept holding it as Bev said, "I brought my girls to Vegas one year. For Halloween. I had the wildest costume. I was a cigarette girl, and men kept mistaking me for a real cigarette girl. Remember, Lara?"

"Yes," said Lara. "Well, no. Hil and I were too young to go to the party so you left us behind in the hotel room. We got drunk on those little bottles of booze, and Hilary threw up in the bathtub."

"Did she?" Bev frowned. "Well, that was before she started all this God business. I will never understand what happened to that girl." Dad met Jasmine's eyes, smiled sympathetically and winked. He shoved the peas toward her and nodded for her to take some. Jasmine grimaced and, helping herself to half a spoonful, told herself she would never eat peas when she was a sex slave.

"Jas," said Dad, "did I tell you I might get to put some of my guys on a shuttle? To test the effects of weightlessness on spatial memory."

"Really? Would you send Edgar?" Edgar was currently Jasmine's favourite of her father's rats. He was sleek and brown, and he was always bumping into things. She was allowed to hold him sometimes, and she'd run her finger over the scar behind his ears, where no hair grew. She'd had a huge fight with Dad when she was in grade five and figured out that the surgeries he did on his rats weren't performed for the sake of their well-being.

"What's the point of being vegetarian," she'd howled. After a series of long talks, she uneasily accepted his claim that the rats didn't mind, that they had a good life and served the higher good. That he chose to avoid meat "precisely to atone for the necessary sacrifices I make in the course of my work." And, he pointed out, "I'm responsible for far less suffering and death among animals than the average person is." She still had pangs of worry over it, but Dad's arguments were, as always, hard to disagree with.

"Well," Dad said, "it's a long process. Edgar will likely be pretty elderly before the project goes through. What do you think, though? My guys get to be astronauts. Pretty neat, huh, baby?" Jasmine nodded. Sometimes her father seemed so gullible and innocent, so sweet and fascinated by his work, that it made her squirm with frustration, love and guilt. She could see that Lara felt the same way, raising her eyebrows when he talked endlessly about a new neurological study, an outlandish hypothesis posed by a promising student. It was almost Halloween. Why did everyone pretend they didn't remember anything? Did Dad really think that if he didn't bring it up, no one would think about it?

"Edgar's so lucky," said Jasmine.

It was raining the next morning, so Lara drove Jasmine to school. "Why didn't you wear your costume?" she asked, stopping near the gate. The concrete schoolyard was full of kids trying to protect their Halloween makeup under umbrellas.

"I'm in grade eight," said Jasmine. "I'm fourteen, almost."

"So is Mei." There was Mei, in her black cloak and witch hat, huddled under the school's side awning, reading a book.

"Oh God. Mei."

"And Megan." Megan, dressed as a gypsy, was sharing an umbrella near the basketball nets with a tall ghoul. Lara said that everyone was dressed up, and as far as Jasmine could see, she was right. She didn't need Lara to remind her of all the hours she'd spent constructing her papier-mâché astronaut helmet before she realized just how embarrassing and childish it would be to wear it in public.

"That's okay," said Lara. "Maybe you'll use the costume for something else."

"Maybe." Jasmine sighed.

They stayed in the car for another two minutes until the bell rang, then Jasmine kissed Lara on the cheek and ran for the door, down to the basement to her locker, and checked to see if the rain had smudged her eyeliner. She rubbed under each eye with a fingertip. Down the hall, she saw Benna pull off a long, black, stretchy dress, shove it in her locker and secure bunny ears to her head. A cowboy swaggered over and grinned while Benna made bunny paws and hop-hop-hopped, put one hand on her hip and smiled.

Jasmine turned away quickly to hang up her jacket so she could look up in mock surprise when Benna arrived breathlessly at her side. "Oh my God." Benna squeezed herself between Jasmine and the locker mirror. "I'm so embarrassed. This is my cousin's Playboy Bunny T-shirt." Hand on hips, she swivelled to show Jasmine her costume. The short white T-shirt with the bunny logo covered the top half of a black ballet leotard. On her legs, Benna wore only pink stockings, and there was a pink cotton-tail sewn to her leotard's bum. "Ryan said I was sexy," said Benna, glowing with exalted mortification. She was sexy. She was so beautiful and sexy it made Jasmine's stomach hurt.

"I might put on my costume at lunch, Benna," said Jasmine. She always said Benna's name when speaking to her. Sometimes she said the name under her breath when she was lying in bed at night. "Benna. Benna Hadrick." She had recently persuaded Benna to confess her middle name, too, and had been sworn to secrecy.

Benna Caraway Hadrick, mid-September, had been untouchable, unreachable, had been standing beside Jasmine at the sink during recess, circling her eyes with dark liner. This was the closest Jasmine had ever come to the too-old-for-her-age, up-to-no-good queen of grade eight; Benna's sexy underwear was clearly visible above her studded belt. Standing beside Benna at the mirror, Jasmine grimaced at her own reflection. She'd parted her hair on the side because it said in one of Tam-Tam's old-fashioned magazines that a side part distracts attention from a prominent nose. Her grandmother kept baskets full of fashion magazines, the latest ones and the big, matte-paged kind from the sixties and seventies, and Jasmine often read them out of boredom when she visited. The magazine was right. Jasmine's mother used to wear her hair parted in the middle, and it made her nose look huge. Jasmine knew about this because she used to sleep over every weekend when Agatha lived at Tam-Tam's house, and one time they found an old driver's licence of their mother's at the back of a drawer. Jasmine still had it. None of the old albums had photos of their mother; anyone flipping through them would have thought Dad was a single parent until he met Lara.

Putting one hand over the middle of her face, Jasmine looked herself in the eyes. As far as she could see, her eyes and her long hair, both the same reddish brown, were the only attractive features she had left. During the summer, not only had she got her period, which stopped her from swimming for five days every month, but her body had expanded, relentless and itchy, leaving her about a foot taller and her breasts two cup-sizes larger. The bump in the middle of her nose seemed to be getting bumpier. If Lara had been her real mother, Jasmine might have been dark haired and rosy cheeked, with big black eyes. She might have had a small, straight nose. Benna Hadrick was adjusting the safety pin that held the shoulder of her black T-shirt together, and Jasmine felt the unmistakable pre-nosebleed ache under her eyes, the iron taste at the back of her throat.

Benna was known to have made out with Barbara Steele's older brother, who was in high school. Jasmine had seen the older brother and had imagined Benna sitting on his lap in one of her short short skirts, tongue-kissing. The image forced itself back into her head as she stared at her traitorous nose in the mirror, waiting for the inevitable. *Will it thus*, wrote J. Virginia Morgan. The book had a lot of hard quotes from philosophers, and it often wasn't clear how these quotes related to the stories the author told about herself. Waiting for the blood that was welling into her sinuses, Jasmine understood what the book was trying to tell her. It was like what Justin, her swimming coach, said — streamline your body, and you just ease through. *Own the events of your own life.* Don't drag, cannon-balling through life. She put her head back and blew hard through her nostrils, spattered the mirror, scarlet spray. Benna jumped and stepped back.

"Get me toilet paper," said Jasmine.

Benna replaced soggy red wads of paper with fresh white ones for the next twenty minutes. She watched with undivided interest while Jasmine pinched her septum. "That was so gross." Benna was clearly impressed. They left the mirror caked with brownish, drying blood, walked into French class together five minutes late, and sat together near the window. In the weeks that followed, Benna Hadrick changed Jasmine's life. Before she met Benna, Jasmine had often sat and watched the rest of the class glumly. J. Virginia Morgan explained, basically, that it's a mistake to try and fit in with the people that happen to be around. Who cares if they like you or not, or if they think you're weird. But Jasmine couldn't help it — she did want them to like her. After the nosebleed, she and Benna sat together, and Benna giggled all through class at all the jokes Jasmine made. After school, they drank peach schnapps on Benna's fire escape and laughed until Jasmine almost threw up; they drank coffee in cafés; they talked to the punks on Rideau Street; and Jasmine watched Benna get her belly button pierced by a friend of her cousin's, who was covered in tattoos. She'd been sure Benna was too cool to dress up for Halloween.

"Where's your costume?" said Benna.

"Yeah," said Megan, sidling up behind Jasmine. "You said you were working on it all week."

Jasmine promised she'd change at lunchtime, so after history class they all went to her house to eat — Megan, Mei and Benna, with Jasmine leading the way on zigzagging tiptoe because the morning's rainfall had left the sidewalk covered in earthworms. Megan and Benna did the same, stepping gingerly. "This is sick," Benna said, more than once. Her tail looked silly under the clingy black dress, a lopsided bump just below her jean jacket. Megan was dressed as a gypsy, with a long skirt, a kerchief and huge hoop earrings. Mei trailed behind, hands in the front pocket of the YWCA sweatshirt she'd pulled on over her witch costume. The year before, Jasmine and Mei would have picked up worms and helped them to the safety of the grass.

As they turned onto her block, Jasmine bent down, picked up a worm and waved it in Benna's face. "Sick!" squealed Benna, grabbing Megan's arm. Megan hollered, and Jasmine tossed the worm into the street.

"Don't get run over," Jasmine yelled.

"You are seriously damaged," said Benna. Megan laughed, and Mei, watching glumly, fell further back. Jasmine glanced at Benna's hand, still holding Megan's upper arm as they turned up the driveway of her house. Benna and Megan only knew each other because of Jasmine. None of her friends from before liked Benna. Mei had even phoned Jasmine one evening to say, in that painfully serious Mei way, "You think you're cooler now, but I'm telling you as your friend, Benna's changing you for the worse. She's not even a real person, Jas." That Mei was right in a way only made her more annoying. In a way, Jasmine was getting tired of Benna — how she seemed, almost always, to ever-so-slightly miss the point, and the way she ran her hand absent-mindedly up and down her thigh like she was trying to rub something away. How she was always pointing out high school guys with baggy pants and stupid expressions on their faces and wanting Jasmine to get all excited about them. Mostly, though, Jasmine was tired of waking up every day with Benna's face in her head and Benna's name running through her mind like a tune too catchy to shake. Against her will, she memorized Benna's words and agonized over them later; every day, she dressed anticipating Benna's approval and planned funny comments so Benna would laugh and grab Jasmine's arm as though to keep from collapsing. It was not a good feeling. It was just like Virginia's description of "toxic love" — how *one random person glows with a poisonous, greedy light*. Jasmine looked at Benna's hand on Megan's arm, felt sick and thought *poisonous*. But that kind of love, Virginia promised, *ceases quietly and without warning, and the beloved turns out to be just like anyone else*.

The back door was half open and the smell of cigarettes loomed as Jasmine reached for the doorknob. Bev was smoking at the table in the back den with a white-and-silver-clad Elvis impersonator. They had been there for a long time, judging from the density of the smoke. Silver sequinned sunglasses lay neatly folded on the wicker table. "Hi," said Bev. She waved cheerfully at the other three girls and dropped ashes on the floor. "Lara's stepkid," she told Elvis. Jasmine led her friends to the kitchen and then up to her room without looking at any of them. Bev had once invented a board game called "Shake, Rattle and Roll." The game involved cards, dice and a map of Graceland. It turned out she couldn't sell it because of copyright infringement — the greatest tragedy of her life.

Jasmine sat at her desk eating Alphaghetti out of the can while Megan and Mei ate their sandwiches sitting on the bed. Benna stretched out on the floor. She never ate lunch. "What's with that guy's costume?" Megan asked. Jasmine could smell Elvis and Bev's cigarettes. She watched Sorbet flatten himself against the bottom of his cage.

"That's not a Halloween costume," Jasmine said. "He's an Elvis impersonator. You know? Elvis Presley?" Jasmine stood up and gyrated her hips. "Uh huh, uh huh," she grunted. "You know?" Mei giggled.

"That is weird," said Benna. She laughed, "I'm sorry, but seriously. Seriously weird. What *was* that you just did?"

Jasmine tried to lodge a three-hole punch in the window to keep it open.

"Why?" said Megan. "Why is he here?"

"She's just friends with people like that. He probably has a show later or something." The Alphaghetti was balanced on a pile of magazines in the middle of Jasmine's desk. Smoke was creeping in, Jasmine was sure, through the crack under the door. Megan sat cross-legged on the tucked-in bed, apple in hand.

"I can't believe that's your grandmother," she said.

"*Step*-grandmother." Jasmine wished Benna had never seen the man with the glittery belt at the wicker table and that her father would come home soon to see what an idiot Bev was. Dad's parents would never act the way Bev did — Granny and Grandpa Winter, with their tidy house and dark wood furniture. Tam-Tam had never met Bev, and Jasmine couldn't imagine how she would react if she did. Bev was the kind of person who bought a glow-in-the-dark Virgin Mary toothbrush holder at a yard sale and gave it to Jasmine's father for his birthday.

"He's *Jewish*," Lara told Bev.

"As though that were the only problem with the gift," Dad said at a dinner party, when he recounted the story to his friends from the psychology department.

Megan lay back on the bed, talking about a note that had gone around the classroom that morning. At the open window, Jasmine tried to fan fresh air into Sorbet's cage with her hands. The note had listed all the boys in the class in order of cuteness.

"Big deal," said Jasmine, feeling Sorbet for tumours. "They're all losers anyway." She took him out of his cage and held him near the open window. With her back to the room, she couldn't decipher the other girls' silence, didn't know if they were all looking at each other, raising their eyebrows. "Cigarette smoke," said Jasmine, "causes cancer. I happen to know that from personal experience, if you think it's some kind of joke."

"Personal experience means you have it yourself," Mei said quietly.

"I told you she didn't really have a costume," said Megan. Sorbet snuffled fuzzily through his nose. "I'm going back to school. Come on, guys." Megan stood and Jasmine turned to see Mei looking at her uneasily.

"I'll stay with Jas," said Benna. "We'll just stay here if your grandmother won't stop smoking. We can take your gerbil out on the roof." Jasmine knew that sometimes Benna didn't come to school, that her mother didn't care if she went or not. Somehow, with Benna at her side, she was sure she could get away with anything.

"Come on," said Mei. "Come on, Jas. We have to go back."

"I can't," Jasmine told her. "Sorbet can't breathe in here." Mei was standing with her sweatshirt and backpack on, but didn't move. "Bye!" said Jasmine. After Megan and Mei left the room, she handed Sorbet to Benna and hurried to retrieve her astronaut helmet from under a pile of laundry on the closet floor. She'd covered an old bike helmet in papier-mâché and painted it white, with a tiny Canadian flag on its back. The visor was made of an old ski mask she'd found in the basement.

"Wow," said Benna. "Did you make that?" Jasmine climbed through her window onto the roof, and Benna stuck her head out to watch. Breaking the most serious of all rules, Jasmine slid down the slanted roof on her bum, the bottoms of her socks sticking to the asphalt like Velcro, and perched on the perilous edge. When Megan and Mei appeared on the sidewalk, Jasmine dropped the helmet in their path. It didn't smash against the sidewalk, but tumbled gently, turning over in the air. Even its impact was gentle and almost silent as it cracked in front of Megan. Both girls looked up. Mei was hugging herself miserably around the chest. Even Megan seemed defeated, looking back down at the once-perfect helmet with its burgundy fibreglass guts exposed. Jasmine pushed herself up the roof backwards and went back inside to put on warmer clothes and get Sorbet and Benna.

An hour later, the clouds had cleared, but the black asphalt was still damp and cool through Jasmine's jeans. She hadn't been able to fit the whole cage through the window, so Sorbet sat on her lap. Benna sat beside her. Jasmine wore a thick, loose sweater, wool socks under her sneakers and a black and red striped tuque she once found in Agatha's old closet. The possibility that Sorbet would be cold had occurred to her, but this seemed preferable to the inevitable results of second-hand smoke: either a tumour or asphyxiation, whichever set in first. The cuff of her sweater hung over her fingertips and lay on Sorbet's back, serving as a blanket. The little beige body vibrated steadily under her palm, whether from cold or from fear it was hard to tell. Jasmine figured it was a combination of the two: the cool, damp air and the shock of finding stripy-haired Bev reclining in the den across from a reasonable facsimile of Elvis Presley, an old catfood dish full of cigarette butts on the table between them.

Benna was wearing her dress again, and it pulled up when she sat, her pink tights visible to the knee. She reached over to rub Sorbet's head between the ears. "You should sleep over at my place," she said. "You could bring Sorbet if you wanted. We could rent movies and stay up all night."

"Yeah." Jasmine pressed her cheek against Sorbet's back. Mei used to sleep over sometimes last year, and they'd lie in Jasmine's bed looking up at the glow-in-the-dark stars. Jasmine told Mei that if you concentrated really hard, you could convince yourself you were floating in space, weightless, far away from everything, with nothing to see but blackness. You could convince yourself that the stickers were real stars, each one thousands of times bigger than the whole earth. She and Mei had lain side by side in silence for a long time, being astronauts. Sometimes Jasmine moved her hand so it was touching Mei's, and if Mei didn't move away Jasmine felt like every nerve in her body was concentrated into that square inch of skin.

But sleeping over at Benna's was completely different. Benna had her own double waterbed in the attic bedroom and a fire escape at the window, so her mother, who slept downstairs, didn't even know when Benna left and came home. The bedroom was so big there was an extra single bed for guests in a little nook in one corner. Jasmine had never seen a house so messy — there were books, papers and clothes everywhere, dirty dishes piled in the kitchen and dust caked into dried toothpaste around the bathroom sink. And the floor in Benna's own room was entirely covered in clothes; after she did laundry in the basement, Benna just dumped her clean clothes back on the floor. Jasmine had seen her do it. Benna's mother, Lynette, had long brown hair parted in the middle and wore brightly coloured polyester shirts. She was a social worker. One time when Jasmine was there, Lynette said to Benna, "You look a little provocative, don't you think?" Benna was wearing a lacy black top and jeans so low her thong showed.

"You got a problem, cunt-hole?" Benna yelled so loudly Jasmine barely resisted covering her ears.

And Lynette just rolled her eyes, saying, "Really, Benna." She even laughed a little.

Jasmine didn't really want to bring Sorbet to Benna's house. He might get lost in all her piles of clothes, for one thing, or eat something weird from the floor. The phone rang inside the house, and a few minutes later, Bev called her name. Her voice was getting closer. "Jasmine, you in there?" Bev was in the bedroom; Jasmine could picture her standing in the middle of the floor, hands on hips, taking in the empty gerbil cage, open window, piles of clothes on the floor. Maybe she would notice the Alphaghetti can and feel bad for not making lunch. "Are you allowed to play out there?" Stupid Bev, standing there in the middle of the room, cigarette burning between her yellow-stained fingers, scattering ashes everywhere. "Your school called. You have to go back — you're late."

"Benna's sick," Jasmine yelled. "And I'm taking care of her. Diarrhea. The kind that comes out like water." Benna pressed both hands against her mouth, trying not to laugh. They waited in silence, staring at each other. Benna's eyes were light brown.

"I think she's gone," Jasmine whispered, leaning close.

"I don't know," Benna whispered back. "I think I can still hear her walking around. Is she staying here all day?"

"She's living with us," Jasmine said. "Because she's sick. She's dying."

"Dying?" Benna's whisper cracked. Jasmine could smell her musk-and-mint breath.

"Yeah. She's got six months to live." Jasmine leaned forward and rested her forehead against Benna's shoulder. She did it before she realized she was going to, and then she stayed there, scared to move. She felt one of Benna's hands on her back. The way they were sitting, Sorbet was sheltered in the space between the two girls' chests. Jasmine opened her eyes and stared at the white patch of skin beside her face. Benna's neck. "Benna," she said, kissing the patch of skin. She wanted to put both arms around Benna's chest but couldn't because of Sorbet. She kissed her again. Benna didn't move; her hand was still on Jasmine's back and she seemed to be holding her breath. Jasmine sat up, eyes closed, and pressed her lips against Benna's. They were just as soft as she'd expected them to be. The hand moved to the back of her neck. "Benna," whispered Jasmine.

"Jasmine!" Bev. Her face was framed by the window. "Jasmine," she said. "Should I call your father at the university?" And Benna was turning; she was scuttling up the roof like a spider on her hands and feet, shoving past Bev and in through the window. Jasmine turned her back and stared down at Sorbet.

"I'm going back to school!" Jasmine yelled. "Okay? Just give me ten minutes. Don't call Dad, okay?" She rubbed her eyes and glared at the massacred helmet on the sidewalk below, reduced to ruin by her own hands.

Gravity, Jasmine knew, is the enemy. Gravity isn't natural or pure; it's the pull of things bigger and heavier than you are, sucking you in, pinning you down. In space, if you threw something, it would just keep going in a straight line forever, moving effortlessly ahead and away; it would not plummet down and smash. In space, though she knew she'd still be in orbit, or at least within the gravitational fields of the earth and the sun and possibly Mars (where she hoped to live someday in a biosphere), Jasmine would be weightless. That was why she loved swimming and went to the pool three times a week. Not because she wanted to be a competitive swimmer, like Dad and Lara thought. Swimming reminded her of space in a lot of ways. She knew from watching *The Right Stuff* about eight hundred times how much training astronauts have to do. They put you through all these gruelling physical tests to see if you'll throw up or go crazy when you're weightless, and one of the tests is going underwater in a space suit to see if you're afraid of water. So she decided to start her training right away. She trained as much as she could. Obviously, Jasmine wasn't afraid of water, like a lot of people are.

Benna appeared on the sidewalk, speed-walking away, bleached-blond hair bouncing against the collar of her jean jacket, bunny tail visible through the dress. She was practically running. *No mess*, Jasmine quoted to herself, *is irrevocable. Just lift yourself out of it.* She'd had to look up *irrevocable* in the dictionary.

After dumping the contents of her backpack onto her rumpled bed, Jasmine filled it with clothes, just like the day before, again shoving her bathing suit and towel on top. She had one hundred dollars saved and buried in her underwear drawer, and she put it in her wallet. After settling Sorbet in one side of her jacket's front pouch and his food in the other, she moved one of the sketchpads on her nightstand and picked up *The Willing Amnesiac*. She had signed it out of the public library, and it was wrinkly, as if it had been in a flood or snowed on or dropped in the bath. Opening the book for a moment, Jasmine readjusted the bookmark and then looked at the author photo on the back. It was a black-and-white close-up, and one side of J. Virginia Morgan's hair was about to fall into her eyes. When Jasmine first saw the photograph, she'd thought of a popular girl in her class who had hair like that. One side was always flopping down and she would push it back with her hand or by moving her neck quickly to one side — like a horse, Megan said. Virginia looked kind of like Jasmine, only older and pretty. Her face was thin, the high cheekbones almost skeletal, and her nose was straight and narrow.

"Fuck," Jasmine told the photograph. "You're just a person. God damn it." She stared at the serene smile. "Fucking twat." She shoved the book into the bag, down beside the clothes. She took a carefully folded note out of her drawer and wrote the date at the top with her best black pen in her long-rehearsed grown-up writing.

Finally, with a sensation she recognized as true grown-up sadness, Jasmine took Sorbet's food out of her pocket and set it by his cage, then held the gerbil in her hands. "I can't bring you with me," she told him. "I'm sorry." She kissed his face and put him back in the cage, then wrote a note asking Dad to feed and pet him twice a day and carefully taped it to the bars.

Bev stood on the porch, Elvis lurking chubbily behind her in solidarity, and watched Jasmine's progress down the block. Near the corner, Jasmine turned around, yelled, "Wanker!" and ran, backpack bouncing, down the sidewalk, across the street and below the Bronson Avenue overpass. When she reached Central Park, she had to slow to a walk, breathing hard. She blew her nose on a piece of coarse school toilet paper from her jacket pocket.

Why did Dad want to pretend her mother had never existed? Yes, she had only been four, but she knew her mother's accident had happened on Halloween. And Jasmine had been excited the day Mama was coming home from the hospital; she ran to the door and stopped in her tracks, stunned into silence for the first time in her life. When she was little, she'd felt uneasy whenever either of her parents got a haircut. For at least a day, she would be panicky, sure that her mother or father had been replaced by an imposter. It was like that, seeing Dad wheel Mama in the door, her head shaved. For the next year, Jasmine was afraid of this interloper in her house. This strange woman who sat in silence for days, who laughed hysterically like a child, who woke up in the guest room, screaming, in the middle of the night. The woman had not felt like Jasmine's mama, hadn't smelled like her, hadn't talked like her. The longer she stayed, the harder it was for Jasmine to remember what her real mother had been like, and she was relieved the day her father told her the woman had packed her bags and left. Dad held her on his lap and said, "I'm sorry, Minnie, but Mama had to leave," and expected Jasmine to be sad. But that woman was not Mama.

Jasmine entered the bus terminal for the second time without hesitating and found to her relief that there was a bus leaving for

Toronto in fifteen minutes. She tried to look older and sure of herself. "I'm going to visit my mother," she told the man at the ticket counter. "She gave me a note. You can call her if you want, but she's probably at work."

"That's fine," said the man. It was that easy. She bought a ticket and stood with the crowd by the Toronto sign. Over in the arrivals area, she watched a girl her own age put a big backpack on the floor between her feet, breasts stretching the fabric of her faded blue sweatshirt as she bent down to extract a water bottle from the bag. Coatless, the girl pulled the hood of her sweatshirt over her head. She had a particularly blank look on her face, big eyes and slightly parted lips. A real space cadet, Lara would have said — a phrase Jasmine considered insulting to astronauts.

There was one window seat left, near the back, so Jasmine sat and shoved her bag under the seat. She tapped her fingers on her thigh, anxious for the bus to leave before her school called Bev again, and Bev called her father, and the search began. The first thing people do when someone is missing is to phone the airport, the bus terminal and the train station — Jasmine knew that much from books and movies. Through the window, she could see into the terminal; she could see a tall, wiry man speaking to the girl in the sweatshirt; he was wearing a black leather coat and jeans faded to grey, but Jasmine couldn't see his face. The girl looked up, nodding at whatever he was telling her.

Toronto. Jasmine was anxious for the bus to leave before she changed her mind. It said in *The Willing Amnesiac* that it was normal to feel a moment of regret, of doubt. Jasmine had the other two books, *The Maternal Return* and *Accidents* on hold at the library. It had taken her forever to read the first one, with the help of the dictionary, and she had a foreboding that the second, with its weird title, would be even harder to understand. The website said Virginia lived in Toronto. It also listed all her upcoming workshops. They were mainly in American cities, and never in Ottawa, but there would be one at a hotel in Toronto in two days.

Jasmine caught her reflection in the window and experimented with looking vacant. The engine started, the bus eased forward, and it occurred to Jasmine that if Dad called the bus terminal and found out she'd been there, found out where she was headed, there might be rescuers waiting for her in the Toronto terminal. Agents of family togetherness, anti-pimps, with muscles and uniforms, to trap her and send her home. It was too late to turn back. As the bus pulled out, the hooded girl and her tall companion were heading for the exit. It was like watching someone walk toward a disaster, as if Jasmine knew what was about to happen but was paralyzed, unable to stop it. She put her hand against the window as the man led the girl through the terminal and away.

Steven, you piece of shit.

One week ago, I opened my mailbox to your handwriting. I read your letter once, then drove to the middle of the bridge and tossed it in the bay. Three years and five bullshit letters — and then this. You clearly weren't looking for my blessing, since you did it first and told me later.

You must wonder why I decided to respond after all. Was it the suspicion, sneaking into my mind over the course of the week, that I should take some kind of responsibility for skeletons I left in the closet you've chosen to occupy? Or maybe the memory of all those nights we spent drinking at the Laff, debating brain vs. mind? No, Steven, at the risk of causing a rift in your newfound domestic bliss, I'll tell you something you don't know. Two days after your self-congratulatory confession drowned in the Pacific Ocean, I received a postcard with the same news again. It was from Quebec City, a lovely picture of the Chateau Frontenac. Have you ever noticed that Ginny's handwriting looks compulsively neat at first glance but turns out to be practically illegible when you go to read it? I won't bother you with the obvious psychoanalytic implications. But I'll transcribe the postcard for you verbatim.

Dear Asher, I've married Steven Winter. Can't say I'm surprised the Israeli military wasn't your cup of tea. Best, Ginny. PS I'm in

Quebec City right now with Steven and Agatha. Remember how we planned to come here? But then your car broke down so we screwed in the park instead. Afterwards, we ran into Steven at the bookstore. Funny how things turn out. G. PPS Water/Self Service/Please/Self Service. And scrawled sideways up the edge, spanning the whole message: *Steven doesn't know I'm writing to you.*

My initial tantrum had worn off by then, and I didn't have the impetus to get back in the car, drive back to the bridge and send Ginny's epistolary masterpiece to the same watery grave. Instead, I left it on my desk and put it in my pocket the next day. I read it twenty times: on the cable car, in class, while I ate my lunch. I brought it home again and used it as a coaster for my coffee mug. I read it in the bath until the cheap ink ran and then I dropped it in the water to watch it disintegrate. When Ginny and I lived together, she used to stay in the bath for hours every day, reading, soaking the bottom edges of her books and mine. Smoking and dropping ashes on the pages. She told me she hadn't taken a bath since early childhood. Her grandmother insisted that showers were the greatest evil of modern technology, so Ginny had always showered.

The memory of Ginny in my bathtub has a strange and sickly allure. Her stomach sticking up out of the water, cigarette ashes floating around among the bubbles. She marinated herself in tobacco, came out of the bath smelling worse than when she got in. You're so proud of the fact that Ginny quit smoking. Well, I wouldn't be so sure. Being with you has probably pushed parts of her personality into secret places, cigarettes into hidden compartments of her purse. I imagined the baby would be born with a fag in its mouth and a depressed look on its face. To be honest, I always assumed it would be a boy. I don't know why. With all that Nietzsche she read, she was probably hoping to give birth to the Übermensch. Nietzsche and Agatha Christie were her favourite writers at the time, and she didn't seem to think one was any more or less important to the development of human civilization than the other.

And those birds — the paper birds she was always folding.

At first she was hoping for a miscarriage, then just to survive the birth, and she folded a growing a line of defence against the homicidal fetus. I don't know if she ever hit the thousand mark, but she must have come close. When she decided university was a waste of time, Ginny cut all her class notes into perfect squares. Folded them into cranes. Little white birds covered in blue lines and that infuriating handwriting. I'd come home from the university, and there she'd be, folding, bathing, reading, smoking. Swelling up. Sometimes you'd be there, too, sitting with her at the kitchen table, and a hush hung over the room, as if the conversation had ended in mid-sentence when you heard me at the door. Ostensibly, you were waiting for me so we could chat on the balcony. You'd read over drafts of my thesis and give me advice. And I knew you had a thing for her the whole time. I'm an expert on the human psyche. I should at least be able to tell when my friend is infatuated with my girl, hanging on her every neurotic word. Remember, I used to want a crazy girl who had her shit together. You agreed with me. We both thought Ginny was it. And you, despite your claim that it's "completely different now," have yet to come to your senses.

One time, Ginny picked up my plate from the dinner table and threw it across the room like a Frisbee. Greasy tomato sauce sprayed the wall in a morbid trail, and the plate flew right out the window. We heard it break on the sidewalk. It wasn't a satisfying smash like you might expect but more of a distant crunch, like stepping on a baby bird. She said she did it to get a reaction, just so something would happen. We were driving each other nuts with boredom. And you envied me Ginny's body, too. There was that famous time in my car, the culmination of forbidden passion, conception of the looming bastard child — she kept saying "ouch," complaining about the seatbelt buckle digging into her side. When we lived together, sometimes, in bed with her, I'd be looking up at the clock, trying to finish in time to listen to the news. I'm not heartless. I could see she had a spark. But a spark that never catches isn't enough. It's nothing but potential, and you can't love someone indefinitely for potential.

Do you know that, Steven? Do you?

Are you even aware of the emotional complexity of normal human beings? Who see other humans as people, not just brains wrapped in bodies? I'll tell you again, you see people as specimens, experiments, neurons. Yes, I'm accusing you in a letter so you can't defend yourself. I know you think I see people as specimens, too. To you, Ginny may be a collection of neurons, but to me, she was a collection of neuroses and complexes and family secrets. What's the difference, right, Steven? And I retort like I always did: there's more to life than all that. Sometimes a girl's just a piece of ass. You'd better get that through your head. You'd better start seeing your wife as the piece of ass she is, or else she'll leave you. She'll vanish like a brain cell zapped by your chemicals.

Obviously, this isn't the ideal letter from a friend, congratulating you on your recent marriage. But what did you expect? You've married the mother of my child. Well, you're welcome to her.

Can you really be as naïve as you seem? I can't stop picturing how it happened and where it will go. Was that what you were hoping for when you wrote? That I'd be plagued by thoughts of you and Ginny's tender, righteous love, so much better than anything I ever had with her? The first time you kissed her — the most chaste of passionate kisses — you probably told her you loved her truly and deeply for who she really is. You were, no doubt, ecstatic with decency and goodness, thinking you were the first to understand and value her for all that intelligence and potential. And she was touched by your sincerity, tempted by your offer of salvation. She pushed to the back of her mind a sneaking suspicion that you didn't really understand her at all, that your naïveté would never let you see her whole; and I predict that this small suspicion will grow over the years until it pulls her away from you. You won't understand what happened. You'll think, I was so kind to her, so gentle, and I bent myself every which way trying to suit her. How I wish I wasn't so sure I was right. God grant me even a sliver of doubt. You'll hate me for saying this, but someday you'll look back and see that I was right, and you won't be able to say I didn't warn you.

I remember that party at your house, when I met Ginny for the first time. I thought you were ridiculous. She was practically a teenager. Every time I looked in her direction, she smiled and shifted around in her seat. When I left your place, I stopped to have some soup at that Oriental place on Somerset, with the fish tanks in the back. The party had depressed me — I hated the way you acted around those academic types. And all the usual inane chatter about scholarships, theses and drug-induced sexual excess. I was beginning to work on my thesis back then, planning to write about shell shock and Vietnam vets. I had mixed feelings about the whole thing, couldn't shake my nagging envy of those who'd gone to war. I realize now that joining an army wasn't the answer. I left the restaurant just as Ginny came around the corner, balanced precariously on those huge shoes she used to wear. We went back inside, and I watched her eat a bowl of soup. She was still stoned and sucked the stuff in like her life depended on it. She had just spent an hour alone with you, Steven, and she was agitated. Why, I wondered. Wielding the chopsticks expertly, she told me how her grandmother was an obsessive cook, that her family always used chopsticks when they ate this kind of food. I pictured the most genteel family you can imagine. Genteel and gentile, long white candles on the dining room table. There was a sign on the wall:

Water
Self-service
Please
Self-service

and Ginny loved it. Kept reading it aloud: haiku, Shakespeare, beat-poet style. She paid for her meal, and we went to the park across the street and talked for the rest of the night. She was wearing a bulky white scarf thing around her shoulders and faded denim bell-bottoms, and they both looked like she'd never washed them. We sat across from each other at one of those tables with the chessboard tops.

When I told you about my all-nighter with Ginny, you pouted into your beer like a little boy who didn't get his birthday wish. But what I didn't tell you was that she talked about you the whole time, circling around you, trying to dismiss you. I made fun of your lab coat, your formaldehyde specimens. The way you pressed your hands together like a fifty-year-old man when you were explaining something. And she was grateful, relieved to laugh. She told me that for a long time, as a child, she'd wanted to be a nun, covered head to toe in a thick, stiff black habit, a crucifix around her neck. Only eating potatoes, lentils and barley. She'd imagined herself praying in Latin and helping those less fortunate. Her beloved dead father was a lapsed Catholic. Beware girls with beloved dead fathers! She mentioned, casual as can be, that her mother and grandmother moved from Holland to Canada after the war, that of all her family, only those two had survived. I looked for signs of Hebrew blood. That fleshy nose, maybe, but her Irish half had otherwise taken over. "And my mother's blond," she said. "Like you." My parents had lost some distant European cousins in the camps, but in Canada, my family had been safe and sound. My masochistic envy swelled large, the proximity of suffering buzzing like a taut string. I could practically smell the crematoriums of Auschwitz in Ginny's Irish-red hair . . .

Picture a woman in her mid-thirties. Fifteen pounds overweight, dressed in jeans and an oversized sweater. The ever-present wool socks. She opens a bedroom door. She has a headache and her daughters are making a racket — she sees her teenaged daughter tickling the younger one on the bed. They are both shrieking with laughter. The sound makes the mother want to tape the children's mouths closed, sedate them. Anything, as her own mother used to say, for some peace and quiet. She can't believe the children are hers, doesn't know how she came to be in this house, standing in this doorway, feeling this impotent fury. There must have been some kind of mistake. The girls' laughter excludes her and pains her and goes through her head like a knife.

But during my transformation, I laughed all the time. The doctors said my laughter was pathological. They claimed it was only my brain injury, the misfiring and realigning of neurons, that made everything funny. They told me I was defective because I could see absurdity, delicious absurdity, everywhere I looked — in the seriousness, the heaviness of other people. The way they looked at me, pitying, thinking I was someone who had suffered. My husband held my hand and told me earnestly that he was trying to understand what I was going through, that it was hard for everyone — oh, it was enough to make my stomach cramp, the way I laughed. With every convulsion I felt closer to the truth. It was like walking out of quicksand — all I had to do was move my own legs and I could walk out. The philosopher Friedrich Nietzsche tells us, "One does not kill by anger but by laughter." You don't have to sleep until your body rebels and forces you to wake up. Believe me. Laugh. Even if it feels fake at first, even if you don't find anything funny and don't know why you're doing it. Laughing is like praying: you don't have to believe it at first, but if you keep doing it, it will open your eyes and become real. There's plenty of time for peace and quiet after you're dead and buried. I never have headaches anymore. I always know where I am and that I came to be there of my own will.

Nietzsche writes, "I have learned to walk: since then I have learned to run. I have learned to fly: since then I do not have to be pushed to move."

J. Virginia Morgan
The Maternal Return: An Anti-Memoir

Four

The first Halloween after Mama's accident, Dad cut two eye-holes in the middle of an old sheet, secured it over Minnie's head, and told her she was a ghost. He led her through the apartment building, floor by floor, trick-or-treating without going outside. We'd lived on Cooper Street since the beginning of the summer before grade ten, when the rented eleventh-floor apartment was supposed to be temporary, just until Dad and Mama found a house.

I was in the bathroom putting on makeup and washing it off again when my mother emerged from the former guest room, now her bedroom; in the mirror, I watched her walk away down the hall without turning to give me a glance. She was wearing her huge stained track suit and had a full pack on her back, a grocery bag in each hand. Her hair, fluffy from a recent washing, was shapeless, almost shoulder length, and needed a cut badly. I didn't try to get her attention; I'd become almost accustomed to her indifference, her habit of showering twice a day and her steady, alarming weight loss. She hadn't seemed to eat anything at all for the previous two months. All she did was exercise, read and shuffle through boxes in her room with the door closed.

When Dad and Minnie came back with a pillowcase full of candy, I was waiting in the living room, wearing an old slip over a pair of jeans and holding an unlit cigar in my hand. Minnie set to work sorting her loot into categories, and I put on my jacket, telling Dad as I left, "She went somewhere."

I was out until two in the morning. I took off my shoes and jacket as quietly as I could and stepped softly through the living room, only to find Dad standing in the dark hallway. He had the stoic, pale look that comes when anger and shock have exhausted themselves, leaving a calm despair in their wake. "I just went to the diner after the dance," I told him quickly, "with Reiko."

"Agatha," he said. "Can you come with me, please?"

My mother had left her bedroom door wide open. The boxes from her closet, which had contained all her mementos, journals and old clothes, were in the middle of the floor, empty. She hadn't bothered taking my things or Minnie's — a box with all our baby clothes and childhood drawings was undisturbed.

"Look at this," said Dad. All our family photo albums were piled in the corner. He opened the top one. The once-full pages were patchy; it took me only a minute to see that my mother had removed every photograph of herself, leaving me as a baby on Oma Esther's lap; me at three, at the wedding, leaning against Oma Esther's arm; Tam-Tam and Dad; Minnie as a baby. Everything was there, our whole lives, only Mama was completely missing. Dad and I sat on the floor in silence, flipping through the albums, hoping she'd missed something. "She didn't have to do this," Dad said, head in his hands. Then we packed up everything that was left and put the boxes back in the closet. We were both in our own rooms when I heard my mother come back in the early morning, stepping lightly, her bags empty.

A week and a half afterwards, I was late for school, missing math, allegedly because Dad wanted company while his car was cleaned. Long, rubbery strips smacked the soaked windows and smeared the glass with soapy trails while Dad sipped his coffee and I blew steam across the surface of my cup. The carwash was a perfect place for Dad to talk to me; it would be dangerous to open the door. Mama used to do the same thing, save the worst for when we were in transit and I couldn't escape. She'd described sexual intercourse on the way to ballet class when I was eight.

"Don't tell Minnie we came here without her," said Dad. He'd already dropped off my sister at first grade. The carwash always had a uniquely sedative effect on my sister, and Dad used to take her there often, not because the car was dirty, but because she was unmanageably hyper and it was the only way to calm her down. Minnie had changed; her frenetic energy had given way to a pensive shyness, but she still loved the carwash.

The car inched forward. "Your sister still gets so upset when I drop her off in the mornings," Dad said.

"She'll be okay," I told him. "Don't worry, Daddy Longlegs." Dad's limbs looked cramped in any car, even with the seat pushed back, and that's what called up my childhood nickname for him. He smiled and relaxed slightly, grateful for this show of affection. "Nice hair," I said. His usually scruffy hair and beard had been trimmed, so every hair on his head was exactly the same length.

"Well," he said, "you inspired me. I really like it." He pushed my bangs out of my eyes. "I like your hair down." Dad had been surprised when he saw me the night before. He didn't know I visited Tam-Tam at work once a week, usually just for half an hour after school. She was always obsessed with my hair and had finally dragged me upstairs to have it cut.

A set of small pipes blasted the car's windows with hot water, pushing soap-froth to the edges and away. *Kshhhhh*, Minnie would have said. "Well, Agatha," Dad said. "You know I've been talking about adopting you. The papers are ready to go. I'm pretty pleased about that." My glasses were steaming up, but I left them on. "It's quite important that I'm recognized, legally, as your father, because things could get confusing." He had one hand on the steering wheel and was looking straight ahead although the engine wasn't on. "Your mother's never going to be like she was. As Dr. Manning says, we all have to accept that."

Soap and water blasted the windows, brushes closing us in, while Dad talked, backtracked and tried to explain, tapping his hand on the steering wheel, moving things around on the dashboard, and I thought of my mother. I didn't know where she was — working out at whatever gym she frequented or shopping for clothes at newly discovered stores. I knew she'd started swimming; a chlorine-smelling black bathing suit had started appearing in the laundry. When I got home after school, she'd probably be back in her bedroom with the door closed, looking for more possessions to sell, throw in the canal, bury — or whatever she'd done with them.

The car was already spotless, and Dad had to speak up over the hot-air dryers by the time he managed to say, "Her name is Lara." Then we were outside in the sun and I knew. Dad was in love with someone else. That's what he said: "We've fallen in love." We both slumped in our seats until someone banged on the window, startling us, and Dad fumbled in his wallet.

"Here." I pulled a ten from the pocket of my jeans. "The absent-minded professor thing gets a little tired sometimes." Dad ignored me, took a twenty out of his jacket pocket and handed it to the attendant.

I concentrated on cleaning my glasses while Dad drove. When I looked at him with my bare eyes, his face was a blur of beard, eyes, skin. If there were tears in his eyes, I couldn't see them. If his jaw was relaxed in self-assured indifference, I didn't have to know about it.

"Will this ... woman adopt me, too?" I asked. I thought I'd be the first person in the world to be adopted at the age of sixteen, related by blood to neither of my guardians, my real mother set loose, adrift.

"No," said Dad, "of course not. Your mother will still be your mother. And I've always been your father. The adoption is just a legality." I could tell he'd been waiting a long time to tell me all this, dreading it. "I love you and Minnie very much," he added. "I know this is hard. Especially for you."

"Then why are you doing it?"

Before he stopped in front of my school, Dad said, "I understand you're angry right now. We'll talk later when you've had time to think. Lara's an easy person to like. Minnie gets along with her wonderfully."

"You've already introduced her to Minnie?"

"It's okay that you need to yell, I know this is hard to deal with. Yes, they met, but Minnie just thought Lara was a friend of mine. Probably thought she was one of my students."

. The effort to speak in a normal tone made my voice shake. "*Is she one of your students?*" Dad pulled up next to the curb, and there was no one outside the school except one grade ten girl with limp black hair and a lumberjack jacket standing near the curb in the smoker's corner. "No," he said. "She's not my student. She's a lawyer, actually. Works in Gerry's office." Gerry, Dad's cousin.

"Mama gets sick and you just find someone else?" I slammed the door and told him through the window, "Don't drive away, Steven, my foot's in front of your tire."

"We'll talk about this later." Now that Dad had unburdened himself, he was all confidence and composure.

"Does Mama even know?"

"Sweetheart," said Dad, "we'll talk about this as soon as I get home this evening. You're a smart girl and I know you'll be okay. I'm counting on you." He backed away from my foot, pulled past me and away, waving reassuringly. I was surprised to find myself surprised, baffled that I never saw this coming. I'd always thought Mama was the one who didn't love Steven enough. I had evidence. Hard, written evidence that Steven's love for my mother was unyielding and blind. I was standing in the turning circle outside the school, my family crumbling, what was left of its shape finally giving way. The girl in the smoker's corner ground her butt under the heel of one army boot. I knew who she was; she was famous for having fainted during a presentation, collapsing backwards, a half-smoked joint tumbling out of her pocket. She shrugged at me sympathetically.

*

I found everyone packed in the hallways. Every Remembrance Day, the whole school was organized grade by grade, class by class, two by two, and herded to the war memorial, a fifteen-minute walk away. Attendance was taken before and after, absence considered a crime against decency. I was looking for my homeroom half-heartedly when I spotted the back of Helena's head and turned quickly away. I hurried to the pay phone at the end of the hallway; Dad answered his cell phone after three rings.

"How long have you been seeing this person?" I said. I thought of all our therapy sessions with Dr. Manning — Tam-Tam, Dad and I trying to bring Mama back so we could be a family again. "Were you planning this the whole time? Why did you pretend you wanted things to go back to normal if you were just going to dump us anyway? Steven! Hello?"

"I'm not dumping you, Agatha. I'll be your father for the rest of your life. I want you to understand that."

"How many other affairs have you had?" It occurred to me that Mama would no longer even care what he did. "You are the biggest hypocrite I've ever met."

"All right. We'll talk about this later. As much as you need to."

I struggled for words and tried to imagine what Mama, the old Mama, would have said about Dad's mistress. "Fuck you," I said, on Mama's behalf. "Cocksucker." The word sounded idiotic coming out of my mouth. I hung up.

I put another quarter in the phone and dialled the number scrawled on my bus pass. Sundar was there, and barely awake. "You want to skip out on Remembrance Day?" He sounded surprisingly disapproving of my plan.

"I've got to get out of here. Can you come and get me?"

He described his car and said, "Okay, NAC parking lot."

"Ms. Winter," said Mr. Meyers, my history teacher, hand on my shoulder as I hung up. "Get back in line. No, wait." He stepped around in front of me and, in a peculiarly intimate gesture, held me by the front of my fraying brown army jacket to pin a felt poppy in the general area of my heart. His round belly was an inch away from me, his collarbone level with my eyes. I'd been in his Canadian history class the year before and barely passed, though he gave me an A the year before that. I looked up at his face. "If you'd only focus," he said, releasing me, clearly exasperated by the chaos of the day, "you'd be just fine." Smiling noncommittally, I turned away with a strangely pleasurable thrill of paranoia. I'd suspected all year that the teachers discussed me in the staff room, mulling over my mother's bizarre and tragic accident, an injury better suited to a television character than a real person. "Find your homeroom and make sure you're marked present," Mr. Meyers called after me. Instead, I walked to the far end of the hall and stood behind a particularly disorganized swarm of kids. The double-file lines were already dissolving into mayhem.

We walked, fifteen hundred of us, through a misty rain along the canal. I made myself invisible, avoiding teachers and people in my own grade, anyone who would recognize me. I could see my apartment building looming behind the high school. We lived a five-minute walk from school and from the canal. At first, I'd relished the temporary-ness, loved taking an elevator every morning and evening as much as Minnie did. Dad rode his bike to the university, and I could go for walks on Elgin Street in the evenings. My parents had planned to rent only until they found a house in the Glebe, but four months passed and then Mama had her accident. Then another year passed, and I knew that Dad had stopped even looking for another place to live. I'd thought he was waiting until Mama got better — potentially forever.

But now I knew: he was waiting until he could move in with some other woman. Clenching my cold fingers into my sleeves, I thought of the letter I'd found after we moved — the letter my biological father sent after Dad married Mama. As always, I felt sick thinking about that letter. I had no idea where it was, what had happened to it. But I remembered every word of it, and everything it implied. This is what people did; they fell in love and made promises, had children, and then just dropped everything. And then it didn't matter, because there was always someone else.

As the damp teenaged herd approached the National Arts Centre parking lot, I was relieved to see a grey station wagon exactly where we'd agreed, near the stage doors. Sundar was wearing a black tuque, watching the torrent of kids walk by. We'd only met once before, and I realized this was the first time we'd seen each other in normal clothes; he didn't look the way I'd expected. I wondered if I looked as plain and disappointing to him as he did to me, and I considered moving into the midst of the crowd heading to the war memorial. I took one step away from Sundar, then changed my mind. Checking for teachers, I ran to the car and climbed inside. Putting my head down so no one could see me through the windshield, I brushed Sundar's faded-jean hip with my shoulder. "Did anyone see me get in?" I asked.

"I don't think so." He was wearing a thick grey wool sweater. "No one's looking at us. That's Erin." There was a girl stretched out on the back seat. A floppy tuque covered her forehead and most of her eyes, and she had a ring through the middle of her full bottom lip, under which she'd somehow applied lipstick. She was wearing baggy black pants and Converse shoes, and her jacket was open over a thin yellow T-shirt with blue writing on it. I couldn't tell if her eyes were open under the hat's rim, even when she said, "Hey."

"Hey."

"Agatha," said Sundar, starting the engine.

"Agatha," said Erin. "This is fucking weird. It's like we're kidnapping you or something."

"I know," said Sundar. "Like we're harbouring an underage runaway or something."

"Nice hair," said Erin.

"This girl at my grandmother's hair salon does it for free," I told her through the crack between the front seats, my disappointment over not being alone with Sundar fading fast. He had dirt under his nails and smelled like sweaty wool.

Erin stretched in the backseat, plump belly and fully visible breasts replacing her face in my line of vision. A huge plastic wallet chain hung from her pocket. I sat up straight and saw that we'd stopped at a crosswalk on Laurier Street. Helena's homeroom class was crossing the street in front of us and none of the students looked at the car; it was like watching them through a one-way mirror. Helena crossed last, by herself, partnerless. In a yellow rain slicker, she clenched her fists so the sleeves hung over her hands. Her newly short hair was dark and damp against her head. As she passed, she turned as though someone had said her name, looked right at me through the windshield and froze. She looked more like Snow White than ever, pale with black eyes. I ducked down again. "Shit," I said. "Shit, shit, shit." I didn't need to see Helena, damp and duped and prettily wretched. Her face made people imagine a depth that wasn't there; boys fell in love with her at first sight and slipped poems into her locker, slipped hands into her clothes.

"Yeah, that's right," said Sundar, "just move along, stunned missy." Humming to himself, he drove away from the long trail of my classmates, the first of them already at the war memorial. Not one of them or us was thinking about war.

I'd known Sundar for eleven days, since he first appeared as a fairy godmother, transforming me into something beautiful among the plastic food-court tables at the mall. I knew Reiko from math class — she sat beside me and liked to draw cartoon animals with sarcastic speech bubbles between my theorems. She rebelled with rare grace even when buying acid in the food court. She was dressed as a tabby cat, all in tight clothes, with ears on a fuzzy headband and whiskers painted on her cheeks. She'd stuck a Band-Aid on the toe of her black boot. We drank vodka out of a Coke bottle in front of the closed fast-food stands. My fairy godmother was sitting beside Reiko's dreadlocked drug dealer on a yellow plastic seat, army-booted feet on the yellow plastic table.

"This is Diesel," said Reiko, "and Sundar."

Curly black hair full of sparkles, eyelids peacock blue, Sundar pressed his wand's flat, yellow-sparkled star against the middle of my chest and asked me to share my cigar. We smoked it out in the bus shelter while Reiko haggled.

"What's with the costume?" he said.

"I'm a Freudian slip," I admitted. Dad had given me the idea for the costume, and I should have known better. No one knew what I was supposed to be.

"A Freudian slip," repeated Sundar. "When you say one thing but you mean your mother." I laughed. "My parents have a mug with that on it," he said.

Then my tongue was numb and my costume was no longer a costume at all, but Sundar's phone number was inside my bus pass. At the school dance, Reiko, pupils gaping, spun around me in circles, and I thought of Sundar's sparkly star, its tips grazing my breasts like a promise.

During the next ten days, I spoke to Sundar on the phone five times. He told me he'd dropped out of high school, worked as a canvasser for Greenpeace and lived in a boarding house. His parents were rich, he said, but he cared about things more important than money. I didn't tell him anything about my own parents. Instead, I thought of Sundar's body. I couldn't wait for him to see me naked. My lips had not made contact with another human being since I'd started ignoring Ingo Bachmann the year before.

Sitting upright in the passenger seat, I glanced at Sundar's profile. I'd never known a boy with thick, dark stubble before. "Want to dye my hair blue?" I said.

"Let's all dye our hair," said Erin.

"Okay," said Sundar. "I guess."

"We can go to my place." My mother was at therapy, my sister at school and then a friend's house, and my father at the university. None of them would be home for hours.

Sundar parked in the market, uncomfortably close to my grandmother's salon. It felt like a betrayal to take my hair into my own hands instead of acquiescing to Tam-Tam and her hair-styling minions. I glanced down the street in the direction of Inner Beauty as we walked away, afraid Tam-Tam might appear in the doorway and catch me. At the drugstore, Erin selected three boxes of ultra-blond hair bleach. She said there was no point using anything else until we were as blond as we could be. Although I was blond already, she said I wasn't ultra-blond. We chose our future hair colours at a store on Rideau Street: Turquoise for me, Pillar-Box Red for Sundar and Bubblegum Pink for Erin.

Sundar and Erin followed me through the lobby of my apartment building to the elevator. They were quiet all the way up to the eleventh floor and watched with a kind of subservience as I unlocked the door. They dumped their tuques and jackets on the bench beside the closet. Without her hat, Erin's face was something different entirely; she had straight, mousy brown hair, and her eyes and nose looked small in contrast with her lips.

After they'd admired the view of downtown from the living room window and we'd all crowded into the bathroom, Erin took charge. We filled Sundar's hair with bleach first. Erin said it was too dark to turn white, but that it didn't matter because we'd just put the red on top after. He rolled a joint in the living room while Erin and I did each other's hair and secured plastic shopping bags around our heads. My mother's library books were piled on the coffee table, a collection of new-age advice books with "PhD" after the authors' names. My father winced whenever he saw her reading these books, her new passion. I moved them into a tidy pile on the floor before we lit up.

Erin turned on the television and stopped at the first channel. They were replaying the service at the war memorial, which had ended while we were deliberating over hair dye. I watched the pipers playing in the rain and I held smoke in my lungs, trying not to cough. Sundar and Erin smoked pot like experts, letting it settle into their lungs and ooze lazily from their mouths and nostrils. Mama and Dad, I knew, used to smoke pot, too, in the seventies. Mama at parties, quiet and smiling flirtatiously at boys across the room. I looked for people I knew on the TV screen, but the cameras stayed on the veterans. I watched the old men with their incomprehensible expressions until I turned, startled by the piano. Sundar, behind us, was playing out-of-tune Beethoven on Mama's piano: some version of the Fifth Symphony, a sure sign of childhood lessons. Despite the poor condition of the neglected instrument, his proficiency was apparent. I laughed in surprise, and Erin laughed as well. Sundar played it up, the plastic bag on his head bobbing. No one had touched the piano since Mama's accident. Music, once her chief comfort and long-time source of income, was forgotten. She also seemed to have forgotten that the piano had once belonged to her idealized, martyred father, who, she'd always said, gave up his life while saving hers. I had no way of knowing if Mama remembered the hours spent beside me at the piano bench in the futile hope that I'd secretly inherited her talent. Watching my hands mutiny across the keys, she'd lamented, "*Concentrate*, Agatha."

Sundar stopped playing with a crashing finale and rolled onto the floor in front of the sofa by our feet. The sofa was grey-blue and too hard to sink into. "Nice apartment," he said.

"Yeah," I told him, grinning so hard it hurt my cheeks. "We've only lived here for about a year. We used to live in Aylmer. *Vive le Québec libre*, you know?" I stared at them, my eyes watering. "*Vive le Québec*. You know?"

"Fucking right," said Sundar.

Erin grabbed my hand and yanked. "We should hang out again sometime." She took a pen out of her pocket and wrote her phone number on the inside of my arm. "There. Now you can't lose it."

Through the blue-carpeted hallway, I passed every room, tapping my fingertips against doors so they swung slightly open. Kitchen, Dad's room, Minnie's room, my room, Mama's room. Finally, the bathroom. I sat on the toilet for a long time, trying to discern some pattern in the differently shaded green tiles on the wall. *Lara*. I tried saying the name out loud. "Lara." I knew I'd have to say that name again. Many times. But maybe it wouldn't last. And, I told myself again, who could blame Dad, a man whose wife screwed his best friend before marrying him. Surprised by my spastic giggle, I held my palm against my involuntarily grinning mouth. Then my burning, watery eyes. It was one year ago, just over a year ago that Mama had come home. She'd been in the hospital for the first week of November, and Dad brought her home the Saturday afternoon after her accident. He pushed her into the apartment in a wheelchair; her face was wan, and she sat in the entranceway, quiet and curious as a first-time visitor. The break had been bad, and they'd had to screw the bones together with steel. She couldn't use crutches because her left arm had gone completely numb, and she couldn't move it. Dad had explained this — that she had hit the back of her brain, which controls motor functions. She had only been unconscious for a short time, though, and it shouldn't be serious. Even her arm would recover. She lay on the sofa while I helped Dad make spaghetti for dinner, Minnie colouring intently at the kitchen table. Throughout the meal, Mama listened in silence to our forced conversation. Whenever we addressed her, she shook her head apologetically, as though she had been thinking about something else.

According to Dr. Jessup, Mama had retrograde amnesia, a condition that usually resolves itself in hours or days. "Her memory will come back," she assured us. "Surround her with familiar things. Remind her of anything that makes her comfortable and happy. Try to reinstate her old routines." Dr. Jessup said we should remind Mama of happy times, but she would likely never remember the accident itself, and even the hours or days leading up to it could be gone for good.

"But she *might* remember?" I asked. "The hours leading up to it?"

"It's possible. But it's also likely that she won't."

"How likely?"

Dr. Jessup gave me a funny look. "It's very likely that she'll never recover her memory of the accident and the hours leading up to it."

Dad set out to bring Mama back to normal as quickly as possible. On the first night, he cooked her favourite spaghetti sauce, and Mama blinked down at her plate, blinked at Dad. Gave that apologetic little smile, with more than a hint of distress playing around her eyes. Minnie was uncharacteristically silent as well, looking down at her food in shy discomfort, as though there were a stranger in the house. Dad had explained to her about Mama not remembering anything, that we had to act as normal as possible. Later, he would say that he should have left Minnie at his parents' house, at least for the first few days.

The next morning, Tam-Tam came over early to witness Dad wheel Mama down the hall to sit at the kitchen table by the window.

He put a bowl of cereal in front of her, and we watched in silence as she ate all of it, a promising feat. "Your favourite," said Dad, naming the brand. The corners of her lips tightened upwards, eyebrows slightly furrowed — that smile I was coming to know and hate. Tam-Tam offered to help her bathe and Mama looked at her strangely. "No thank you," she said finally, quietly.

For the next three months, Dad regularly took her to the hospital for tests and therapy, prompted her to come to the dining room for dinner and told her when it was time for bed. By the time the cast came off her ankle, she was using her arm again, too, but complaining from time to time of stabbing pains in her bicep, which mystified Dr. Jessup. Tam-Tam came over almost every day for dinner, but we visited her rarely — Mama seemed painfully uncomfortable in Tam-Tam's house, sitting rigidly with her hands clasped as if she was afraid she might break something. "You have a lovely home," she told Tam-Tam politely the first time we took her there. Whenever we came back home, she returned by default to the kitchen, where, chin in hand, she kept watch over the spread of snowy downtown streets visible from eleven floors up. The worst was when I'd find her sitting in there by herself, laughing hysterically and twisting her hands together, short hair standing up in greasy tufts.

I gaped at the green-tiled wall, realizing I was still on the toilet, holding my hand against my jaw but no longer grinning. I had no idea how long I'd spent in the bathroom, Sundar and Erin abandoned in the living room. After flushing the toilet and laboriously washing my hands, I made my way back through the long apartment. The memorial service was still playing on the television, but there was no sound except rain on cameras; soldiers and civilians stood with their heads bowed in reverent silence. Erin was straddling Sundar on the armchair, and I saw them licking each other's tongues, faces an inch apart. As Sundar massaged Erin's ass, I could see one of her nipples threatening to puncture the ancient yellow cotton intended to cover it. Staring at them stupidly, I assured myself they were unlikely to get hair bleach on the furniture if they stayed in that position, then turned and went back past the rooms on either side of the hallway, nudging each door a few inches further open as I passed.

The closet door in my mother's room was mirrored, and I balked at my plastic-bag-headed, red-eyed reflection. My glasses looked like thick, black lines, arranged dorkily outside the grocery bag so they wouldn't be bleached, and the rest of my face receded into an insubstantial blur. I turned on the light in the large closet, stepped in and shut the door behind me. It was roomy now that so many of the boxes were gone. My mother had new clothes hung neatly, clothes hangers all facing in the same direction. She had begun to wear silk blouses and tight, above-the-knee skirts. Some of the clothes in the closet were clearly too small for her. She must have been working towards this new size with her no-fat diet and regular visits to the gym.

I knew I was disappointed about Sundar, but only, I told myself, because it had been a year since I'd had sex with a boy, the only one, and I'd decided that he didn't count. I'd just been hoping for a fuck, for Sundar to become my first-time story, so I could forget about the other one. It had never occurred to me to want a boyfriend or to consider falling in love. I didn't even care very much about the sex itself. I'd only been hoping to acquire a sexual experience, light and lusty, to replace the memory I'd intermittently revisited over the last year in moments of weakness and masochism.

The first person I'd spoken to after my mother's accident who was neither a relative nor a medical professional had not been Helena, who was still supposed to be my best friend. It wasn't any of those girls with magnetized mirrors in their lockers and big, round handwriting that I couldn't for the life of me emulate. It was the Saturday after Mama's accident when I looked up Bachmann in a phone book at the hospital. There was only one listing. A man with an accent just like Ingo Bachmann's, only heavier, answered. "Can I speak to Ingo, please?" I said. The sound of my voice surprised me. It sounded normal. I had never spoken with Ingo Bachmann on the phone before. "It's Agatha," I told him when he said hello. When he didn't respond immediately, I barely resisted adding, Agatha Winter.

"Oh," he said. He sounded like a kid. I didn't think of him as a kid. I had never referred to him out loud before, either, and I had never separated his first name from his last. I asked if I could come over, and he told me which bus to take. He lived north, past the mall, in the dingiest part of downtown. It was a part of the city inhabited by what Tam-Tam called "welfare people." He told me to climb up the fire escape at the back of the house and go in through his bedroom window.

"Don't knock too loud," he told me.

It was early evening but already dark when I found his house, and I was cold in my army jacket and jeans. The rusty stairs wobbled when I put my weight on them, and the paint on the house's outside wall was cracking. It felt wrong to see Ingo Bachmann's home, but I'd made up my mind. I'd been on the bus for forty-five minutes and turning back was not an option. He opened the window and watched, bewildered and bleary-eyed, as I struggled my way through. As my eyes adjusted to the light, he wandered across the room to sit down on a chest by the door and stare at his bare feet. He was wearing jeans and a pyjama top, as though he'd already been ready for bed in the afternoon or was still wearing pyjamas from the night before. I looked around for a place to sit other than on his bed. My only option was an upside-down milk crate by the window. A pile of comic books lay at my feet, along with a few books including his copy of *The Metamorphosis*, which he'd been reading the first time we spoke in the cafeteria. We faced each other from opposite ends of the minimally decorated room. It smelled like a boy's room, the room of a boy without a mother. A small lamp at the foot of his bed was the only source of light, and I could barely see him.

"So," Ingo Bachmann said. "You haven't been at school." I imagined my father's response to this kind of comment: *you have a remarkable grasp of the obvious.*

"I've been at the hospital. My mother was in an accident. She almost died."

He looked up at me. "Your mother almost died?"

"But she's not going to. She's going to be all right, probably." We sat in silence. "My biological father abandoned me before I was born," I said. If my mother didn't get better, I would be like an orphan, alone in the world and dependent on the kindness of strangers. Ingo Bachmann, surely, would be the type to appreciate the tragedy of the situation.

"Agatha," he interrupted me. "I think I should tell you a few things about me. I mean, I'm not sure about, you know, everything we've been doing. I'm not sure I've been acting like I should." Going to his house had been a mistake; I felt stupid for not having realized it. I'd only wanted the comfort of his body, only wanted the heady lust that filled my nose and mouth and pushed everything else away when we groped under the gym-building stairs instead of going to history class. Not knowing how to explain that he'd misunderstood, I hugged myself tightly and leaned forward. I hadn't eaten a proper meal in days — only hospital food and the oven fries Dad had prepared the night before. I had an overwhelming urge to lie down on the bed and go to sleep.

"I'm not sure about anything," Ingo Bachmann said. "My father and I don't get along well. I'm not good at school . . . I don't know. Everything is confusing. There's this girl, her locker is across from mine and I think maybe . . . " His voice was a low murmur, a grumble.

"Could you come and sit over here?" I said, indicating the bed beside my milk crate. We got under the sheets and lay close together. Ingo Bachmann touched my pale pink hair, staring intently at my face. I tried to feel like I did during our make-out sessions on the grass by the canal, despite the dim light and the smell of teenaged boy — unchanged sheets, cigarettes and dusty comic books. He rolled onto his back and stared at the ceiling intensely, his bony shoulder against my cheek. He told me his mother had died after a long illness when he was thirteen. His father had brought him to Canada because they had a few relatives here. He had no idea what to say to his son, not even what to say when they ate dinner together. They kept the television on; that was how Ingo Bachmann learned the English colloquialisms he'd never learned at school. "My mother didn't want to die," he said. "She was remorseful for leaving my father and me alone. You're lucky that your mother will live."

Then he sat up and took off his clothes without looking at me.

He undressed me the way you would a sleeping child, and we lay face to face on our sides. I'd never been naked in front of a boy before. Our bodies were remarkably alike, bony and long limbed. I hoped he didn't mind that my breasts were so small. My face buried against his neck, I squeezed my eyes shut, arms tight around his scrawny, warm, hairless body. I felt close to sleep, sinking into a drowsy well of soft, cigarette-smelling skin and saliva, until he secured me around the waist, grinding his hips into mine. Then, abruptly, he turned me onto my back and lay on top of me. Staring at my face with intense determination, he shoved my legs wide apart and started pushing against me hard, his rib cage weighing painfully on my chest. He never seemed to notice that I had breasts at all. I wriggled under him, trying to get more comfortable without hurting his feelings, and flexed my back so he could push himself inside me.

There, I thought, with a gasp, my eyes watering, *I did it*. I knew it was a moment I was obliged to remember for the rest of my life and took careful note of the details. The way he held his breath, the model planes hanging from the ceiling, and the way he groaned before he rolled off me. We lay with our foreheads pressed together, breathing each other's breath, and I reached down to see if I was bleeding. "I really want you to be my friend, Agatha," Ingo Bachmann murmured. "I really want you to be my friend. Okay?"

"Yeah," I said, touching his greasy pale hair with my other hand. "Of course we're friends. Of course." I knew when I said it that it was a lie. I lay awake for hours watching him sleep, and we kissed awkwardly on the lips after I climbed back out onto the fire escape. I walked home as the sun rose.

Ingo Bachmann faded into the background, too, along with Helena and her volleyball friends. One time, shortly before he dropped out of school, he tried to talk to me in the hallway. He reached out toward my arm and I dodged around him quickly, not looking at his face. After he stopped coming to class I found a note in my locker: *You may think you can take back everything you said, but you can't change the fact that I was inside your body.* I showed it to Reiko, and she said Ingo Bachmann was a misogynist. "Stalker

132

behaviour," she said. But I put him out of my mind easily, focusing on my newly acquired friends, who congregated in the food court of the mall.

My family was not as easy to ignore, especially my sister. Minnie started avoiding our mother after the accident, nervous when they were in the same room and balking at any physical contact, which only ever occurred accidentally, since Mama wasn't eager to touch anyone either. Minnie backed away into corners of our apartment, reminding me of a dog in a werewolf movie who senses before anyone else that she's in the presence of a body without a soul. With Dad and me, Minnie became clingier, always sitting beside Dad on the sofa with a fistful of his sweater sleeve balled in her hand. She was still in morning kindergarten, and Dad often took her to his office at the university for the afternoon. The campus was close to my high school, so I walked there after my classes were over, across the frozen canal, and took my sister home. One afternoon I found her sitting at Dad's desk examining formaldehyde-preserved cross-sections of brain.

"And right down here in the cerebellum, and then up here in the frontal lobe," Dad was saying, tapping the jars with a pencil, "that's where your mother probably incurred her injuries." Minnie insisted on sleeping in my bed almost every night for the first few months. Welcoming the warmth of her little body curled up against me at night, I didn't want to be alone any more than she did.

Minnie's fifth birthday came. Dad bought her a gift and signed the card, *Love Dad and Mama.* That Chanukah, we went to Granny and Grandpa Winter's house for dinner one night, and, on Christmas, Tam-Tam came to our apartment to eat Chinese takeout and exchange small gifts. Dad bought Mama a gift certificate for a day spa and signed the card from all of us; he bought me and Jasmine sweaters and avoided attaching cards at all. By spring, when he took us to Granny and Grandpa's Passover Seder, his face looked tired of smiling. I suggested leaving Mama at home, but he refused. She paid rapt attention to the reading of the Haggadah, and when everyone else joked and laughed she only looked more intent and serious. Dad was still trying to keep the Mama-shaped hole wide open so she could slip back in whenever she was ready, and Mama tolerated all the commotion in her strange, silent way, excluding herself from most conversations by staring at some point on the wall. Sometimes she would blink out of her reverie to stare at whoever was speaking, eyebrows quivering. She shook her head gently as though she'd heard a familiar strain of music and was trying to place it. As though she was trying to solve a riddle.

Late in the spring, Mama left her post at the kitchen table. She cashed in her spa day, came home polished and scrubbed, and then began to bathe regularly again. She washed her hair every day, which she'd never done before, and slicked it down with gel. She easily passed her driving test, and Dad started walking to work so she could take the car to her therapy appointments at the hospital. She joined a gym and started going to exercise classes three times a week. It was a warm day in June when I turned onto our street after school to see a woman in a streamlined track suit walking ahead of me, quick-stepped, straight-backed and decisive. I only realized with a start and after a full minute that it was Mama. I could see that she was breathing hard and guessed she had just been jogging. I waited outside the building for five minutes to avoid taking the elevator with her. She was not becoming more like her old self.

As well as family therapy once every two weeks, Dr. Manning suggested seeing me and Minnie each individually once a month, and it was during one of my sessions that he first told me I should prepare to lose her for good. "We still can't decipher quite how her injury affected her brain," he said. "As you know, I think your mother is suffering from a personality disorder rather than a physical one." Dr. Manning claimed that the pain in Mama's arm was psychosomatic. Conversion disorder, he called it. According to Tam-Tam, Mama's arm hurt at the elbow — the same place where she'd broken it when her father was killed — and Dad was disgusted when Dr. Manning suggested that might not be a coincidence. When Tam-Tam and Dad told Dr. Manning about Mama's long history of accidents, her endless hospital visits and minor surgeries, he suggested that Mama had histrionic personality disorder, which, as far as I could tell, meant she was just trying to get attention.

"But," he told me, "the human brain is fundamentally an enigma, even to those of us who have studied it all our lives. Your father can tell you that even a rat's brain is a thing of great mystery. And the human mind. Well." He nodded, watching my face to see if I felt the force of what he was saying. "I've told your father, and I believe it's important for you to know as well. It seems very possible that your mother, as you know her, is just not going to come back. From my time with her, from what you and your father have told me, it seems as if Ginny is undergoing a profound transformation that still isn't fully complete. Perhaps it's time we stopped trying to trigger her memory and stopped trying to bring her back. And just let her find herself. By herself. I'm sorry, Agatha," he added, maintaining relentless eye contact, hands folded carefully in his lap. "I know this is terribly difficult for all of you. Is there anything on your mind that you'd like to talk about? Confusion about boys? Or social issues? Or about drugs . . ." He waited. Leaned forward. "Agatha, your dad tells me that he's not your biological father. That he married Ginny when you were three. I wonder if you have any feelings about that. That you'd like to explore here. Because Steven is now your primary caregiver and is likely to remain so."

On the floor in front of the skirts, I hugged my legs. This closet had no shelves; Helena and I, when we were children, would have dismissed it as useless. Back in the Aylmer house, long ago, Helena and I used to play in Mama and Dad's closet because it had built-in shelves perfect for playing apartment-building with my dolls. I wasn't allowed in Mama and Dad's room, but we never got caught. I'd known Helena since I was eight, since the first day of grade three, when the whole class sat on the floor for attendance. I was near the back, at the edge of the group. Ms. Connelly said, "Helena Jacob," and the new girl lifted her arm fluidly over her head and back, like a windshield wiper. Flexing the toes of one foot, she flipped her shoe out, leaned back against her hand, and turned to see me staring. She had long, dark hair, sleek and shiny as vinyl, with bangs that stopped just above her eyebrows. My mother hated bangs, so I had always assumed that I hated them, too. There was an iron-on unicorn on the front of Helena's T-shirt, and, smiling at me, she flopped the shoe back with a slap, and turned away again. Her family lived near us, but in a bigger house. The first time I went to play there after school, I heard Helena whisper to her mother, "See, look, her hair is golden." Helena took me down to the basement and we sat inside a huge cardboard box that she had transformed into a fort. There were blankets on the floor, and a flashlight with a wrapping paper lampshade fitted over its head. A photograph of Helena's grey cat, Juniper, that she'd left with her grandmother in Vancouver, hung on one brown-paper wall. Helena had big, black eyes, and she told me the names of all the many cats she'd owned throughout her life.

The muggy August when Mama was pregnant with Minnie, Helena and I had shut ourselves into the big, cool closet when my parents came upstairs to argue about a stack of library books that Dad had returned before Mama finished reading them. "It's not healthy," he told her, bedsprings squeaking as they sat down. This argument had something to do with Oma Esther and concentration camp. I pictured Oma Esther, white perm and all, playing the piano in a camp cabin. Whenever she made mistakes, camp counsellors barked in her ears, "Concentrate!" I guessed that was why Oma Esther was so meticulous with her cooking; surely it took camp-trained concentration to get all those ingredients exactly right. To keep her spice racks so organized, every jar refilled long before it approached empty. I knew there were mysteries surrounding Oma Esther that I didn't fully understand and that were only spoken of guiltily, in hushed tones. I knew she had been married to Jozef, who had not just died, but vanished. That she invented her own versions of religious rituals even though she had never been religious, and that this upset Mama, making her yell at Dad. I knew that Mama's father had, without consulting Tam-Tam, paid for Oma Esther to have a tattoo removed from her arm, but it left a scar. That's why Oma Esther always wore long sleeves, even on the hottest days. I had no idea how all these facts were connected, and they lent Oma Esther an air of mystery; her history was a confusion of events I couldn't begin to understand. I couldn't even picture her as anything but a tiny old woman; I thought of the photograph in Tam-Tam's office of Oma Esther in her thirties and tried to convince myself it was really the same person.

"I don't see how it could be healthy," Mama told Dad, "for me not to think about this stuff. Not to know what happened."

"But why now?" Dad sounded frustrated and sad, strangely angry with Mama. "Whenever you get on this Holocaust kick, you withdraw, do you realize that? You stop eating as much. You lose all your sex drive, too." I looked at Helena, mortified, and made a gagging motion. "It's creepy, if you want to know the truth," said Dad.

"Of course it's creepy," said Mama softly. "It's worse than creepy. Did you see that book about the trains? Did you see the photographs of those people?"

"I've seen other pictures along those lines."

"They were being transported from Westerbork to Auschwitz," said Mama, as though Dad was missing the point. "From *Westerbork* to *Auschwitz*."

"I know, Ginny —"

"Like my grandmother. She was one of those people. Those emaciated, desperate-looking people. And my grandfather," she added. "And my *great-aunt*. Who never even got to *be* my grandfather and my great-aunt. I can't believe I ever wondered how she got to be so fucked up."

"Ginny," said Dad, in his let's-be-reasonable voice. He told Mama about Grandpa Winter, who suffered perpetually from psychosomatic symptoms, who walked with a cane, his limp shifting from one leg to the other. "When I was a kid, my father polished his shoes every week, and more than anything, he dreaded stepping in dog shit. And you know what? He stepped in dog shit almost daily. That's what worrying does." Helena and I covered our mouths in delight each time Dad said *shit*. Mama laughed half-heartedly but stopped when Dad told her, "You are a highly suggestible person. *Highly suggestible*."

I could tell Mama was lying on her side, face against a pillow, from the sound of her voice. She had explained to me two months earlier that she was pregnant, and her belly was now just big enough to get in the way of lying on her front. "If I'm so suggestible," she said, "maybe you should stop telling me how suggestible I am."

Dad paced the room and stopped in front of the closet. Helena's worried face vanished as he flicked off the light. In the sudden darkness, my breathing was loud enough to wake the dead, my heart a machine gun. I held my breath and could still hear Helena. Presumably contemplating his reflection in the full-length mirror, Dad spoke to the closet door. "You know who you're making me think of right now? I can't help being reminded by this fixation on the gory details — the next thing I know you'll be making grandiose statements about *our people* and going off to Israel to shoot an Arab."

"Nice, Steven." Mama had apparently sat up so she could yell. "It's not the same and fuck you for saying so. What are you saying, that there's something sick about wanting to face the past? That I'm some kind of pervert for not wanting to just turn a blind eye? Anyway, you're the one who sounds like him right now — the way he used to analyze me and call me a hysteric."

"Ginny. Why haven't you told Agatha about him?"

Mama didn't say anything. Then she said, dismissively, "Why should I? What would be the point?"

"Well," said Dad. "He was her father. I'm just concerned that eventually she'll realize how long you kept this from her, and she'll hold it against you."

"How long *I* kept it from her."

I could see Helena's eyes, as my own adjusted to the dark. She leaned towards me to whisper and I pressed my palm over her mouth, but what I wanted to do was press my hands against both her ears — stick my fingers in her head and pull out what she'd just heard. My palm was moist from her lips and I wiped it on my T-shirt, staring at her and shaking my head.

"He was your friend, too, Steven. You knew him better than I did, didn't you?"

"He was always a very foolish boy."

"Well, he never cared to have anything to do with Agatha. He

138

never even asked for a photograph, for Christ's sake. So just forget it. Forget it."

"Doesn't change the fact that she's his daughter."

"*Was* his daughter. She's *your* daughter."

"Of course," said Dad. "She is. That's not what I meant. I mean, Ginny, you know how I feel." Mama said something so quiet and muffled, I couldn't hear it, and Dad lowered his voice to match hers. Then they were quiet for a long time.

I avoided looking at Helena and sat silent in the dark until I heard Dad go downstairs to make dinner. I could feel her looking at my face in the darkness but I didn't turn to meet her gaze. Mama was still in the room, but we had no way of knowing if she was awake. I closed my eyes and waited. "Agatha," Helena whispered finally, "your mother's snoring." Pushing the closet door open, I edged through and paused. The snoring continued. I crawled around the bed with Helena at my heels and squeezed through the barely open door. I heard her stand up behind me in the hallway, follow me down the stairs and into the kitchen, where Dad was breaking eggs into a bowl.

"Helena needs to call her parents to come and get her," I said.

"Sure." He turned, surprised. I didn't usually ask for permission to use the phone. I lay on the sofa staring at a magazine while Helena talked quietly in the kitchen, put on her flip-flops and sat in the armchair across from me.

"Agatha?" said Helena, horribly meek. I turned the page. "Why are you mad at me?" I dropped the magazine on the floor and turned onto my side, face against the back of the sofa. I didn't move until Helena went outside to wait on the porch.

Back in the kitchen, Dad was adding grated cheese to the omelettes, mushrooms sizzling in butter and garlic on the stove. "Want to set the table, honey?"

"Sure, Dad." I had never called him that before, always Steven.

He reacted for a split second, holding the cheese still against the grater, then went on as if nothing had happened. He said, "Good girl."

That night, as we all read in front of the TV, Mama noticed a wart on one of her fingers; she held it out toward Dad, saying, "What is *that*?" as though he'd put it there. As her pregnancy went on, the warts multiplied, the skin on her hands bubbling in protest as if some terrible energy was trying to escape. My own skin leapt in sympathy, and I grew three warts on my left hand, two on my right. Mama painted my skin with drugstore remedies, but the warts reappeared only days after diminishing. In the bath, I locked my hands together so that my warts formed a circle and then jabbed my fingers in the air. I was a cartoon superhero, and this hand position promised sudden growth of muscle and a skin-tight outfit. I kicked water all over the floor, fighting off the likes of Skeletor. Because of her pregnancy, Mama was forbidden to use any chemical treatments, and, despite all available natural treatments, her condition worsened until her warts numbered in the hundreds.

Soon after Minnie was born, Mama took me to a man with black hair and a white lab coat. He opened a bucket and white smoke crept along the floor. I howled, terrified, as Mama held my wrists, and the man held an ice-smouldering wand against the five points of my magical constellation. During the next week, my warts swelled and then peeled off. The skin underneath was pink and perfect. There were no marks. Mama's hands were smooth again, too, but a sprinkling of tiny white scars stayed behind to remind her.

I hummed a monotonous note into the backs of my mother's skirts and held it for as long as I could; it vibrated comfortingly through my head. I pulled the new clothes in front of my face like a curtain, an extra barrier between me and whatever was happening on the living room armchair. In the corner, at the back of the closet, was the big cardboard box where Dad and I had put all the papers my mother hadn't taken, and I pulled it towards me. Everything was muddled, out of order: on top, I found Minnie's first attempts at drawing, back when she was obsessed with fire trucks — big red squares with windows and wheels. Underneath, I found my own drawings of stick figures with long hair, triangular skirts modestly covering triangular crotches, and blob-like wings, my name underneath in big crayon writing. Below an identical but wingless figure, I had written "Ariella" and surrounded the name with stars.

I remembered Ariella: she worked at my summer playgroup when I was six and she must have been about eighteen, though she seemed ageless at the time. She had soft hands and a silver smile, braces on every tooth. Ariella of the slender, sandalled toes. My mother didn't approve of my adoration. She said that Ariella was a religious fanatic. As far as Mama was concerned, religious beliefs and behaviour of any kind were tantamount to insanity. "Those Orthodox types," she told me in the car. "The men won't touch their wives when they have their periods. Won't *touch* them. No kisses on the cheek, no backrub, no *nothing*."

"What's have their periods, Mama?"

She concentrated on her driving.

"What's have their periods?"

"It's when a woman wears bandages in her underwear."

I considered this. "Is Ariella's husband mean?" I pictured seeking him out and tying him to a chair, escaping with Ariella out the window. She could move in with us and share my room.

"Ariella is too young to be married. And anyway," Mama added vaguely, "I guess she's not actually Orthodox, exactly. But still."

Whether or not Ariella's future husband would touch her when she had bandages in her underwear, all my fairy pictures and block buildings were created for her approval, just to see her metallic smile and sometimes even get a hug. My clearest memory of Ariella was the day I got sick. When Mama arrived, Mrs. Klein asked, "Was she eating strawberries today?" This must have been a rhetorical question or a reprimand because the evidence was undeniable. I had vomited pink froth dotted with strawberry seeds all over the floor, all over Ariella's flowery cotton skirt. Sitting on her lap, explaining how old I was (six-and-three-quarters), and then, without any warning, bent over and heaving. Mrs. Klein was in charge of the playgroup and I didn't like her. A heavy-set woman who made us ask for a pass when we needed to use the toilet, she had short, greasy-looking brown hair.

"Why didn't you say you were feeling sick, Agatha?" Mrs. Klein couldn't resist asking this question one more time. She asked it while I rinsed my mouth from a plastic cup, again while she wiped my face with damp wads of brown-smelling paper towel, and now once more in front of my mother. Just to emphasize the fact that, with some forethought, I could have deposited my vomit neatly in the toilet instead of out in plain sight. Mama didn't admit to anything, just said, "Oh dear."

Outside, it was much hotter than when my mother had dropped me off. A haze hovered over the tar black parking lot outside the Jewish Community Centre. By the time she had me strapped into the back seat, I was crying quietly and steadily. My mother was rigid, tense and heading back across the river, driving fast, worried about the groceries thawing in the sweltering trunk. She said that once chicken thawed you couldn't freeze it again; "I didn't want to have chicken tonight." She said that if my father had let me go to the francophone Catholic playgroup in our own neighbourhood, instead of the one half a million miles away, "in another *province*," then she wouldn't have to spend half her life driving around. The air conditioning chilled my damp face, and soon the skin under my eyes ached from the cold of it. Mama was still wearing the same jeans and brown plaid shirt that she'd worn earlier, but the sleeves weren't rolled up anymore. She had put her hair in a ponytail that flicked and twitched like a real pony's tail when she turned her head to look past me at the road. I forgot about crying and closed my eyes. Loose strands of my hair blew in the air conditioning and tickled the cold dampness of my face.

That morning, before playgroup, Mama and I had eaten strawberries from a glass bowl. We'd sat at the small table by the kitchen window, the berries between us. The strawberries hadn't come from one of those little cartons at the supermarket. They filled the bowl, a mound of bright red with fine white sugar sprinkled on top. My mother had picked them herself the afternoon before at a farm outside town, and they were so ripe another day would have ruined them. A big pot of strawberry jam bubbled on the stove, but there was still this whole bowlful of leftovers in the middle of the table, and we ate the whole thing. Mama's cooking style was the opposite of Oma Esther's; instead of consulting recipes and using measuring cups, she just chopped and poured haphazardly. Instead of tidy racks, she kept her spices in little plastic bags, all stuffed into an old yogurt container.

Mama told me how much sugar goes in jam, a guilty and gleeful fact of excess: she just dumped sugar right into the pot full of berries, shaking the bag to make it come out faster. That's how much sugar goes in jam. "Because otherwise it won't jell," she explained. We sat at the table and let juice drip down our wrists while we ate. Mama looked pretty when she was still and calm, her face relaxed. She wasn't even thirty then; her hair was long and wavy, reddish brown, and she was wearing it loose instead of in her usual bun or ponytail. She had a bump in the middle of her nose, and her pouty bottom lip was redder than usual from the strawberries. Her cheeks rose when she smiled, as if she had walnuts tucked up there. Mama licked her arm, elbow to wrist, to catch a drip, and I copied her. I knew she should tell me I'd had enough, but she didn't. We kept eating and eating until there were none left.

Inside the garage, I sat with my legs dangling out of the car and Mama crouched in front of me to wipe my face with a wrinkled tissue from her back pocket. She held it around my nose and told me to blow, then folded it and placed it in her shirt pocket. She pushed the hairs that had escaped my barrettes behind my ears and sighed, "We shouldn't have eaten so much fruit." Her hands smelled like dish soap, and I knew she must have washed the glass bowl of all its sugary remnants. I pressed my nose into her palm seeking some hint of sweetness, and she pulled away, a trail of snot hanging between us as she disgustedly brought out the tissue again with her other hand.

"Why are you crying? Do you feel sick again?"

"I'm sorry, Mama," I howled. I didn't want her to regret the morning, eating until there was nothing left in the bowl but juice and seeds and those bitter little green leaves. When everything was strawberries, the big pot on the stove bubbling sweetly towards jam. The way the sun warmed our sticky fingers and cheeks.

Sitting in her closet, I thought of my mother at that same kitchen table, her eyes giving me goose bumps as I scrubbed a burnt pot. It was eerie the way her fingers fell against the wood, two staccato notes before the other three fingers fell together, heavy and dissonant, the rest of the octave left hanging as though she couldn't remember what she'd begun. "Agatha?" The way she said my name, polite and unfamiliar, as if she hadn't chosen it herself, as if she hadn't called across rooms a million times, *Hey Ags*. She asked, "What happened to my skin?"

I turned; she was staring at her hands, palm-down on the brown tablecloth. "Chicken pox," I told her. Frowning, pale eyebrows quivering, she knew I was lying. She was trying to remember chicken pox and knew it was the wrong memory. Dr. Manning said we should talk about significant moments in her life. "Don't you remember? You had chicken pox on Thanksgiving and you noticed the spots on your hands while you were making the cranberry sauce. You thought you were allergic to cranberries." The woman at the table stared at me. "Don't you remember?" She blinked. Her inch-long hair was so dirty it stood out at a ninety-degree angle from her head. I blinked back, imitating her perplexed gaze, and her lips trembled. "Sorry," I started, "it was warts —" and her breath came quicker. She grinned, opened her mouth wide and guffawed, hugged herself around the middle as the shrieking laugh racked her stomach muscles, threatened to break her apart. I slammed the pot down on the counter and left the room.

I heard someone yelling my name, the sound muffled by my mother's clothes and the closet door. For a horrible moment, I thought it was my father, before I stuck my head out and recognized Sundar's voice.

"Agatha." He saw me from the hallway as I stood in the middle of the room. "We have to get this stuff out of our hair, we've left it on way too long."

Erin piped up from behind him, excited and horrified: "It was supposed to stay on for twenty minutes and it's been over an hour."

We took the plastic bags off our heads in the bathroom, and the smell of ammonia scorched my sinuses. Taking turns at the side of the tub with the hand shower, we helped each other rub the frothing, stinking bleach out of our hair. When Erin's hands touched my head, I realized my scalp was tender.

We looked at each other, looked at the mirror, touched our wrecked hair. Mine was white, Erin's light blond, and Sundar's a horribly frizzy brass yellow. The ends of my hair were like straw and broke off when I pulled on them. Sundar ran his hand over his head; clumps of yellow fuzz drifted to the floor. He was helpless, all his charm dissolved.

I found my father's hair clippers in the bathroom drawer. Erin went first: she knelt at the side of the tub and I shaved her head in long, even strips. While she acquainted herself with her remarkably large, round head in the mirror, Sundar knelt in front of me. His back trembled as his ruined locks fell on top of Erin's. Then I handed over the clippers and knelt in front of him.

"I'll do it," said Erin. I understood why Sundar was shaking; my own legs vibrated, knees and elbows unsteady on unrelenting ceramic. My poor Chrissie Hynde bangs, only two days old, fell frizzled and fried into the multicoloured wreckage below.

Erin went down the hall to find her tuque and came back with her shaved head covered. It erased the exaggerated roundness of her head; she looked exactly as she did the first moment I saw her.

"Oh my God," said Sundar, looking me up and down, "you look like *Sophie's Choice* — like a concentration camp person. With the shaved head and that number on your arm" — I looked down at the phone number neatly printed on the inside of my forearm.

"Holy fuck," said Erin.

"You should see yourself in the mirror," said Sundar. He and Erin were staring at me. I grabbed a face cloth from the towel rack and turned on the taps, started rubbing the white hand soap against the numbers on my arm.

"It's permanent marker!" Erin said from the hallway.

They continued to watch me from behind. I wanted them out of my house. "She's freaking," observed Sundar.

"I'm not freaking," I said. "My parents are coming home soon and I'm not even supposed to be here."

As their army boots and sneakers clumped down the hall and out of my life forever, Erin called back to me, "Give me a call sometime." I could still hear them laughing outside the apartment as they headed for the elevator.

Mama came home first and I recognized her footsteps through the kitchen. She even had a new way of walking, nothing like the footsteps I knew before her accident. I didn't stop scrubbing my arm until I heard her stop in the doorway of the bathroom.

"Ha," she said. When I turned and she saw the way my glasses contrasted with my bare head, she laughed out loud. Arms crossed around her chest, in its snug pale blue sweater, she said, "Look at you!"

"Look at you," I answered. Her own hair had been cut and styled, and she was wearing more makeup than I'd ever seen on her face. Even her eyebrows had been plucked into thin, neat arches. "Did Cassandra do that?" Her hands were different, too, nails shiny and smooth, hangnails gone, no rings. I looked closely to see if the manicure had disguised her snowstorm of tiny white scars. She was wearing a slim, knee-length skirt and high black boots.

"No." Her colourful lips grinned at me. "I went somewhere else."

Her nails were too long for a pianist; she was not a pianist. I thought of my last piano lesson, when I was eleven, Minnie jolly-jumping in the doorway. When I turned to look at my sister, Mama put her hand on top of my head, turned my face towards the sheet music. "Concentrate!" she told me.

I answered, "You should work at a concentration camp." I was too stunned by the force of her hand across my cheek to cry. Mama never slapped. She gave up on my piano lessons after that day, and

I could see her hurt, a permanent stain. I'd always thought I'd be overjoyed to be freed from failing to learn music, but her refusal to teach me felt like an almost unbearable punishment. Without understanding what I was being punished for, I tried to make amends by showing how hard I was concentrating. On my home-work, my chores, cutting my fish into even squares and chewing each piece ten times.

I stood with my back to the mirror, bald, one arm soapy. My mother looked in my direction without meeting my eyes, her perfect mascara a barrier between us.

"I'm going to Spain."

"Why?"

"Just somewhere to go. With a friend I met in group. I can't figure out who I am with all these reminders of who I'm not." She waved her tidied hand toward the green tiles of the bathroom wall, the hardwood hallway, the kitchen with its old table and its gleaming new appliances; her hand waved away the hospital and Ottawa and my grandmother's hair salon, Dad's secrets and her own. My blotchy, exposed scalp was nothing to her; the pile of bleach-wrecked hair in the tub was not her concern.

"Well — where did you get the money to go?"

"I sold the piano. Someone will be here to pick it up tomorrow. And I sold my jewellery, too. And I'm changing my name. I don't want to be called Ginny anymore. I'm Virginia. And I'm changing my last name to Morgan." She was glittery-eyed with composed euphoria. "Josephine Virginia Morgan."

"Who *are* you?" I said. "What did you do with Ginny? Where the fuck is my mama?"

"You shouldn't speak that way." She looked superior, amused.

"You used to speak that way all the time. You swore like a motherfucking sailor." I thought I saw a hint of infuriating pity in Virginia's eyes. "You *taught* me to speak that way." My shaved head was starting to make me feel tough.

"I can't really assume responsibility for that right now," she said, surely quoting one of those books she'd been reading; she must have learned her sympathetic but end-of-story voice from Dr. Manning.

She was J. Virginia Morgan, soon-to-be inspirational anti-memoirist, creator of aphorisms, modern-day philosopher. Virginia Morgan had no reason to be angry with me. So many times in the last few years, I'd wished I had a different mother. So many times I'd silently willed Mama to brush her hair, lose ten pounds, buy some new clothes. But now I missed the woman who told me to put my hands over hers at the piano so I could feel how pieces were meant to be played. The woman who let leftovers rot for months at the back of the fridge, shrugging helplessly when Dad called them her science experiments. I wanted to scrub Virginia Morgan's perfectly made-up face until my mother re-emerged. I wanted the woman who'd fed me strawberries, smiling across the table conspiratorially. I didn't know which memories she'd regained and which were gone forever, but I felt sure she knew nothing about pushing that glass bowl into my hands. Mama had said, "Bombs away, pumpkin," and tipped the bowl so I could drink the sugary pink juice left at the bottom, gorging myself on more sweetness than my body could hold.

. . . Steven, the truth is, I didn't throw your letter off any bridge.
A satisfying picture, but I only thought of it the next day, when
it was too late. In fact, I ripped the pages into small pieces and
flushed them down the toilet, where they transformed into an
inky wad. I used the plunger to suck it partway back up, but
finally I had no choice but to stick my hand down and deliver
the papier-mâché cyst from my drain and throw it in the garbage.
Maybe you should follow my example. Stop reading right now,
rip these pages into a thousand pieces and give them the flush.
I recommend doing it one page at a time — that way they'll go
down smoothly. Or ask Ginny to fold each page into a paper
crane and the two of you can fly them off the bridge of your
choice. Bring along a romantic picnic, maybe, make a day of it.

Your letter's true fate exposed, I resolve that the rest of what
I write will be one hundred per cent true as true. Sometimes,
in analysis, it takes a patient quite a while to come around to
the actual facts. I'm in analysis as part of my training here. It's
a strange process, I admit. Threatens to transform us all into
crackpot narcissists before we're turned loose on the wealthy
neurotics of the world. Ginny and the baby, Tamar and Esther,
they've all come up in my sessions, as you can imagine. And
you, too. And now I'm going to tell you another thing you don't
know.

After that first night with Ginny in the park, I went to the
cosmetics counter at the mall and looked for Tamar. I knew it
was her right away, by her accent and from Ginny's description.
Straight-backed, bird-boned, blond. She tried to sell me a little
vial of Chanel for my "sweetheart." Oh Tamar, with her ingenuous

glamour — she was a saleswoman from times long past. Poised to help me win some young virgin's hand with a bottle of smelly chemicals. I could tell I had made an impression, and two days later, I drove to their apartment. When Tamar opened the door, she looked at me strangely, couldn't figure out where she'd seen me before. I asked for Ginny, but I knew she wouldn't be there, that she had a class that night. The third time I dropped by that month, Tamar's curiosity and good manners compelled her to offer me tea. I knew she didn't tell Ginny about all my visits. Especially once she started talking about the war, she needed to keep me secret. And she was my secret, too — I'd go from her apartment to the Chateau Lafayette to drink with you. Sometimes Ginny would be there with you, and neither of you knew a thing about it.

Tamar showed me I was born to be a psychoanalyst. It was almost easy to get her talking about things she'd never said out loud before. I wanted to talk to Esther, too, but she was off limits. If I tried to get into a room with her, Tamar would practically run to block my path. What do you suppose she thought I might do? She was jealous and didn't want to share me. She was afraid I'd initiate the same kind of intimacy with Esther. But Esther wouldn't have been so easy to seduce, even if I'd had the chance. You can tell just by looking at her. She was stuck in her own head in a whole different way.

Tamar told me her husband used to frequent whores. She said she stopped sleeping with him before Ginny was born, so he eventually started sleeping around, a Friday-night ritual. Imagine her telling me these things, the two of us in her living room, sitting as far apart as the furniture arrangement would permit. Her hair was smooth and blond, her eyelids as artful as Brigitte Bardot's. More and more frequently, I saw her looking me up and down. She found me repulsive. Longed for me to scrub my face and trim my hair. When I smiled, she glanced away from the stains on my teeth. I could see she was confused because she longed for me to touch her. Classic transference.

Did you know that she stood across the street, watching,

as the SS took her family? Maybe it's something you should know, if you're going to be part of that family. Maybe you should be equipped with some sort of explanation for that woman's coldness and her daughter's hysteria. Did you know that Tamar was hidden in a neighbour's house for almost two years? She said Esther came back so changed it was like living with a stranger. As she told me this, her mascara ran, a single vertical line down each cheek, like a mime's makeup. Her story was the perfect lead-in for my thesis, which I decided then and there to write about survivor syndrome and survivor guilt — specifically about children who'd been in hiding while their parents were in the camps. Tamar and Esther's relationship was horrible and fascinating to me. I was excited, feeling the key to everything I'd been looking for right in my hands. Was I being exploitative? Don't think I haven't thought of that. But no, I wanted to help her, to use her story to help others. And Esther was in the kitchen as Tamar and I spoke, stuffing tomatoes with smoked oysters and cilantro. I could see her lying emaciated in a crowded bunk, making inventories in her head. Recipes and spices, the potential uses of oysters, smoked and raw.

I told Tamar she was expressing feelings she'd repressed for nearly thiry years. I told her about survivor guilt and explained that her ambivalent feelings toward her mother were perfectly understandable. Abandoning my customary armchair, I crossed the Persian rug and sat on the sofa beside her. She didn't flinch. Her eyelids were painted grey and purple and her eyelashes were black glued-on brushes. If Ginny hadn't mentioned it, I might have thought the lashes were real; they made her look like a beautiful comic-book alien. I leaned in and kissed her. The taste of her lipstick coated my palate like oil; she must have been used to having that taste in her mouth all the time. I asked her to wash off the makeup so I could see her real face. I wanted the real taste of her lips and the real smell from behind her ears. It occurred to me that Tamar's fixation with glamour, with physical flawlessness, wasn't so different from Esther's preoccupation with cooking and eating haute cuisine. When civilization falls apart, food and clothing become purely a matter of survival; the seriousness with which Esther and Tamar approached the aesthetics of food and fashion made perfect sense to me. With my hand in her hair (stiff, impenetrable hair — how I longed for her to wash it!), I told Tamar so. And with that she was gone, as far away as she could get, her arms crossed, ashamed and confused. "You are a silly little boy," she told me. I tried to reason with her, but she kept repeating that I had to leave.

She was so repressed, so irredeemably repressed, and I felt like she'd led me on. All masks on top of masks — I'd peel one off and find another underneath. Just when I thought I'd found some genuine emotion, I found her as opaque as ever. I told her she was frigid to the core. I wasn't a trained analyst, Steven, and I broke down. I was so angry and disappointed with my failure. Maybe if I'd given her more time she would have come round; instead, I went back to her apartment later that night, after the off-limits supper hour. When Tamar came to the door, I asked for Ginny. Told them I was just in the neighbourhood and was wondering if Ginny would like to go for dessert. Dessert, Steven! Ginny was surprised and delighted to see me, if mostly because it annoyed her mother. And what could Tamar do? She let Ginny walk past her, out of the apartment and into my clutches. I went back every evening that week and took Ginny out. And on the seventh day — well, that's when things went too far. A week later, picking up Ginny and all her belongings, I felt like the Pied Piper, luring Tamar's child away as her punishment for cheating me out of my due.

Ginny was obsessed with her childhood, was always talking about the many moments her mother had let her down. She spoke ad nauseam about her grandmother's mental instability, Esther's habit of walking away while someone was speaking to her. Ginny seemed entirely unaware of her own tendency to do just that; the few times we went grocery shopping together, I'd turn in mid-sentence and find she'd wandered off. She remembered, in vivid detail, dinner conversations from when she was seven. What they were eating, what her father was wearing, her mother's hairstyle.

And she seemed to take it as a personal affront that I had no anecdotes, could offer no description of how my mother stood in the kitchen wearing a certain apron.

Abraham Sutzkever was in the Vilna ghetto in 1943 when he wrote "Liberation." Two lines from this poem were going to be the epigraph for my ill-fated thesis: "And time will drill you quietly / Like a cricket caught in a fist." Steven: when we bury memories, they live on in hidden places, and though we're stronger than they are, they're persistent and finally must break free. I hate to think of the four of us — you, me, Ginny and Agatha — bound together forever. I'll try to forget about you, and you'll try to Relegate me to the unfortunate and distant past, but these ties will haunt us all.

By the time I left Ottawa, Ginny couldn't reach her toenails anymore, and they'd grown to absurd lengths. I wished she'd reconnect with her mother; cutting toenails would have been up Tamar's alley. But instead I had to do it. The day before I left, I sat on my bed at Ginny's feet. She'd sprained her ankle chasing me down the fire escape when I showed her my plane ticket. Yelling after me that we'd always be connected because of the baby. I sent her to the hospital in a taxi, then phoned Tamar — I had to reunite them somehow before I left. Ginny's whole foot was swollen, black and blue. I cut the nail too short, and it bled. The pain must have been dulled by whatever they gave her for her ankle, because she didn't seem to notice. I wondered if I should tell her what I'd done. I looked up as she raised her cigarette to her lips; her eyes were closed. In weariness? Pain? I didn't know. I didn't say anything, just blotted the blood away and kept clipping.

I was supposed to meet you at the Laff that last night, and I stood you up. I might as well tell you now that I went downtown and stood outside the bar. I couldn't force myself to go inside, so I watched you through the window. You looked so uncomfortable by yourself, staring down at your drink, glancing up at the door every minute or so. You looked as if you were rehearsing a lecture in your head, as if you were preparing to have the last word.

Watching you alone and waiting, I felt like you must feel, Steven, watching a rat behind a pane of glass. Doesn't the vulnerability ever get to you? The credulity in their faces as you drip neurotransmitter reuptake inhibitors into their water?

The next morning, you insisted on coming over to drive me to the airport. I couldn't talk you out of it. I remember the cabbie pulling away from the curb just as you drove up, the bewildered look on your face. God forgive me, I have to laugh remembering it. I felt guilty as hell, but a grin kept forcing itself onto my face. It was the perfect end to our little melodrama, you standing on the street beside your car, Ginny up on the balcony, the two of you transfixed by my film-worthy exit. I was only thinking about getting away. I was laughing.

And Steven, I didn't want to know what happened next because it had nothing to do with me. You have everything now; I have nothing left to contribute. Please don't write back to me. Don't tell me the sordid details of your love and its eventual decline. I wish the two of you luck sleeping in that bed you've made for yourselves. But it's not my story anymore — just leave me out of it.

Asher Acker

After I burned all my nostalgic relics, I stayed in a hotel for the night. In the morning, I went to the airport and left for Spain. I stayed in a small town for a month, and in this place where I'd never been before, I began to feel nostalgia again, in occasional, unpredictable attacks. But I seemed to be nostalgic for other people's memories: random strains of music I couldn't possibly have heard before, unidentified smells from a neighbour's kitchen, a door with cracked brown paint. I was filled with longing — *fierce, sorrowful and sublime. These experiences were not a backslide in my recovery, not a relapse into memory's propagandistic traps. Rather, they showed me that a sensory experience can be an occasion for pain, but looked at another way, the experience is only a sound, or only food cooking, or only paint peeling on a door. Everywhere is home; everywhere is nowhere in particular.*

Baruch Spinoza writes that "one and the same thing can at the same time be good and bad, and also indifferent. For example, music is good for one who is melancholy, bad for one who is in mourning, and neither good nor bad for the deaf." Memories are just stories, and stories are neither good nor bad for the amnesiac.

J. *Virginia Morgan*
The Willing Amnesiac: Reappearing into the Present

Five

She tried for over a year before she failed. Even on the last day, Tamar was trying. She was trying even as she left the clutter of files on her desk and opened her office door to a slim, strange woman with a shoebox in her hand. Her daughter, her Ginny, stood in the doorway like a friendly acquaintance who has left her engine running while she drops off a few things before leaving town.

A year and a week and four days earlier, Tamar hadn't known she ought to be grief-stricken and afraid. She would have been frightened if she, Steven and the girls had been led to a serene, private room equipped with sofas. Twice she had sat in such a room: once with Esther, when Robert was killed; and once with Ginny, the morning Tamar couldn't wake her mother. But this time the nurse merely led them through a set of doors, down a hallway and through another door into a waiting room Tamar had never seen before. It had cushioned chairs and a television, and the only other person there was a young man with a large bandage on his leg. It was late when the nurse explained that Ginny was conscious but exhausted, heavily medicated for pain, and that they should let her sleep and come back the next day. Steven drove Tamar home. She went straight to bed and had no trouble sleeping. She had wanted a good night's rest before facing Ginny's wrath with the world for tripping her up again.

*

On the day before the last, Aga came by in the afternoon for tea and sat across from Tamar at the kitchen table. Only a rare woman could get away with tying her hair away from her face, and Aga wasn't one of them; the ponytail emphasized her high forehead. Her arms were thin, and she moved her long fingers with unconscious grace. She would have looked wonderful in a nice blouse and skirt, and Tamar was about to tell her so when Aga said, "You look nice. I like your scarf. Are you enjoying your day off?" Tamar examined the question for sarcasm, but there was none. The girl only smiled politely across the table and sipped her tea.

Before the accident, if Ginny had been around, she'd surely have said, "Oh, really, Mother, there was no need to get all dolled up just for me." Ginny would have known that Tamar's outfits and jewellery always complemented each other tastefully, even on days when there was no one to see them at all, and would have expressed her disdain in comments that eluded answers. But now that Ginny was different, was silent, there was no one with the inclination or the gall to batter Tamar so; truth be told, no one knew her well enough to find her weak spots, and no one had any reason to discover where they lay. With a fierce pang of loneliness, Tamar reached across the table to squeeze Aga's wrist, then quickly recovered and turned the hand over to examine its dry cuticles and clean, short nails. "Come upstairs before you go," Tamar said. "I'll get you some skin cream. What do you use?"

Aga didn't pull abruptly away as Ginny might have done, but she didn't answer the question either. Smiling in that mild, somehow secretive way of hers, she leaned back, resting the weight of her arm on Tamar's hand like a princess with her suitor. As though Tamar should lean down and kiss the girl's chapped, lily-white fingers. "Just lotion, I guess," Aga said. "I still have some of that stuff you gave me before."

"Which one?" Tamar let the hand go.

"I'm not sure, Tam-Tam. I don't always remember which product you gave me is which, you know?"

Aga was always polite when she came by, polite on the surface at least, her manner subtly tinged with impatience. Only when Steven was around, when Ginny was around, did Aga become rude and sullen, crossing her arms and looking away from conversations, trying to block them out. During sessions with Dr. Manning, Aga had always looked wearily into her lap or out the window, setting her lips, thinking, presumably, about more important matters. If Aga only knew how her own mother, at that age, used to bite her bottom lip, hold her hand to her throat and furrow her forehead, deep in thought about some perceived injustice. Often, this withdrawal had come over Ginny as she stood by Tamar's side after dinner, holding a tea towel to dry the dishes. As Tamar turned to pass a utensil, she would find the girl still holding the last plate, moving the cloth too slowly and gently to have any effect. Startled out of her reverie, Ginny would finish quickly, with an air of placid compliance. It was only with practised effort that Tamar had resisted grabbing her daughter by the shoulders to shake her. It was so stubborn, so cruel how Ginny looked longingly at some distant point, obviously wishing she had someone worthy of her confidence.

"Will you please focus on the task," Tamar would say, "and put your hair out of your face?"

"And the overbearing mother attempts to correct yet another defect in the slovenly young daughter's comportment," said Ginny, leaning away from Tamar's hand. It was Robert's legacy, this tendency to make bizarre, incomprehensible remarks. She was clever; Tamar was struck by her daughter's cleverness. But instead of trying to "discuss things," as Robert used to do, Ginny would look at Tamar inscrutably, lips pressed together, before she fled to the living room to play Gershwin and Bach on the piano, incessantly and somehow angrily. Ginny had never been like Tamar, nor like anyone Tamar had grown up with or met in Canada. Ginny made herself impossible to know. But, Tamar regretfully admitted to herself, she hadn't wanted Ginny to confide her private thoughts; she had merely longed for the girl to stop thinking them. Ginny's most dreaded weapon, in fact, had always come in the form of confession.

"Don't like my top, do you?" she'd said at the dinner table when she was fifteen. "Well, good news. I didn't spend a cent on it. I ripped it off. Stole it. What are you going to do about that?" Or when she was seventeen and announced that her history teacher had fallen in love with her and bought her an obscene pair of panties, which she flung across the sitting room into Tamar's lap. Surely her claims in that case were invented or at least exaggerated. And then, when Ginny allowed herself to be ensnared by Asher — Tamar could picture her daughter so clearly, standing by Esther's knitting basket, hands on hips, wanting an explosive reaction. And Tamar had only wanted Ginny to stop complaining, confessing; to stop looking so burdened, so suspicious, so often as if she had just come to a realization that changed everything.

"Well," said Aga, startling Tamar as she set her cup down. "I'd better go. I'll see you soon. At the next — well. Whenever."

"Come up just for a minute," Tamar said again, as Aga put on her shoes and jacket and leaned in for a kiss. "I want to give you this new cream for your hands. Please — a gift."

Aga followed Tamar out the front door and up the stairs to the salon. When they reached the reception desk, Tamar linked arms with her lanky granddaughter and held the girl's wrist firmly. Cassandra and Marcy were loitering around the desk, chatting with the new receptionist, the three of them a colourful girlish cluster of red lips and shiny hair.

"Hi, Agatha," Cassandra said, giving the girl a quick hug.

"It's really slow right now," Marcy said.

"Did the new hair potion come?" Tamar asked. She looked behind the desk and saw the unopened box, just as the receptionist pointed it out. Sarah, that was her name. "Do you remember what we talked about, that every stylist needs one at her station?"

"Yes." Sarah stood up.

"You do remember talking about that?"

"Yes, I do." She was already cutting the box open.

"When it's slow," said Tamar, "that's the perfect time for you girls to do these things." The new girl didn't respond, just took a handful of the small, round containers and hurried toward the styling stations.

"Don't you love these long layers?" Tamar fluffed Cassandra's newly dyed hair, with its blond chunks curling chaotically around darker locks. "It frames her face perfectly. Don't you think Aga could have something like that? You know, just some wisps around the forehead. Something softer? Take out your ponytail," she told Agatha.

Within minutes, Cassandra was leading the girl away. "Trust me," Tamar heard Cassandra say. "I know what you'll like. Just trust me." It was true — Cassandra always knew what her clients would like. Tamar was sometimes baffled by the styles Cassandra created, especially for teenagers. But the young women, with mismatched swatches of colour, absurdly short bangs or random long wisps, were always thrilled. And the styles always did somehow flatter their faces.

Tamar sat at the reception desk and looked at Sarah's doodles in the appointment book — all flowers with smiley faces.

"Who hired you?" she said, as the receptionist approached the desk again. She only realized from the girl's expression how nasty the question had sounded.

"You and Cassandra did."

"Oh yes. Of course, of course. Well, good." She stood. "I'm just going to sort out a few things in my office."

Tamar paused beside the sink where Cassandra was washing Aga's hair. "Give her a little makeup, too," Tamar suggested. "A little eye makeup and some lipstick. Some colour in her cheeks."

Aga had removed her glasses and squeezed her eyes shut. It was always telling to see a client leaning back against the sink's neck rest, hair drenched. From this angle, the face looked so different; the view had always reminded Tamar of looking at a familiar house from above, through a crack in the ceiling. Upside down, all the usually hidden nuances appearing out of shadow. And Tamar saw, with new certainty, that Aga would appear old before her time. Her skin wouldn't wrinkle badly, but her face would be world-worn.

Tamar had seen this in Aga even when she was a small child. The night Ginny went into early labour with Minnie, Tamar had sat on Aga's bed and seen it in the pale glow of the night light. She was a pretty little girl, especially without her glasses, elfin and intelligent-looking, but Tamar saw then that this face would come to have the same sickly allure as Asher's: around the eyes, the burden of some terrible wisdom and the suggestion of a monstrously compelling sadness.

Tamar touched Aga's cheek lightly. "Little one," she said, "I'm going to take care of a few things in my office. Don't forget to say goodbye."

The desk in Tamar's office was a shambles, and she sat down with a sigh, slouching for a moment before straightening her back and setting to work. Cassandra's claim terrified her: that they couldn't run the business for much longer without a computer. She wouldn't even know what to do with such a machine, and the more Cassandra tried to convince her, to explain the convenience and the necessity of it, the more helpless Tamar felt. She opened her ledger and flipped through its pencil-smudged pages. She wouldn't be able to run the business much longer at all; that's what it came down to. She would have to hire a manager. She would have to retire, to move behind the scenes. She thought how running a business for fifteen years had changed her, had forced her to be practical and stubborn in ways she hadn't known herself capable of. And she was proud — she had created a business she was truly proud of.

Even after Tamar opened Inner Beauty, Ginny had disparaged her as a "makeup artist," but it had always been more than that, always more than a job, and more than a knack for applying coloured pastes to skin, for teaching others to do the same. "No one spends as much time in front of mirrors as you do. Mirror, mirror on the wall. Oh mirror," Ginny sighed, imitating Tamar's accent. "Please make me the prettiest makeup artist of them all so I can sell my magical wares to the simple-minded townspeople." And Tamar did spend a lot of time looking at mirrors, and not just at mirrors, but at women's faces, a steady stream of them, in all their minutiae. These clients were afraid something was slipping away, and they wanted it back. The changes that alter a face begin so slightly a woman can overlook them for years, but the day comes when she begins to see small signs, and then every new inspection holds the hope that nothing has happened after all, that it was only a trick of the light or a bad night's sleep. It was Tamar's job to smooth these imperfections into oblivion for as long as possible, to ease a face back in its history toward a time before flaws.

Tamar may not have been brilliant and fearless like Robert was, but she had tried to impart to her young daughter the wisdom she possessed, telling her not to distort her forehead so, not to push out her lip, wrinkling her chin. "Elasticity doesn't last forever," she told Ginny, just as she told her clients. "By the age of thirty, everything's going downhill." She brought home the best cleansers, toners and moisturizers for herself and her family, but Ginny would often wash with soap or even just water. Tamar knew this because products in Ginny's shower that should have lasted for two months didn't need replacing for a year.

"Stop scrutinizing me, Mother." Ginny would toss that thick, amazingly lovely hair over her shoulders and roll her eyes. "I'm a human being, not a doll, all right?" It was true that Tamar scrutinized; she couldn't help but notice every stray hair around her daughter's eyebrows, every unsightly reddish blotch on the girl's cheeks and, during the year or two when Ginny ironed her hair, all those frizzy, dry split ends. Very early, Tamar could see Ginny as an old woman, the particular ways that time would ravage her — she could see it in each fine line under the eyes, in the creases that deepened and didn't quite fade after a laugh or a grimace. Just as Tamar had watched the groove between her own mother's eyebrows, which had always appeared at times of intense concentration, such as when she was cooking or pretending to listen to the radio before bed. This line, Tamar foresaw, would engrave itself permanently, visible always, even in sleep, and Esther's worried mouth would shrivel at the edges to fall in on itself.

It never failed, Tamar's uncanny ability to see the future, to predict the face a woman would wear in ten years, the faces she would wear in twenty and fifty years; the way she would come to hold her lips and narrow her eyes; whether she would wear her age with dismay or with dignity. Tamar saw it all, a process lying in wait to unfold, as steady, painful and inevitable as cutting their first teeth. She saw every detail of time's passage, saw each mark and crease, and how each would deepen or lengthen. This was her business. Inner Beauty — Ginny had mocked the name, but Tamar thought it was perfect and not at all ironic. Every woman believes she is meant to be beautiful, and Tamar's gift was the ability to make this beauty actual. That's why Cassandra was her favourite employee — she understood this, too.

Tamar looked around the office at all the photographs and prints she'd mounted, the magazines and books on the shelves. If she hired a manager, she would have to take all her photographs down. This wouldn't be her office anymore. It was a miserable prospect, though she'd tried to convince herself it would just give her more time to help with Ginny. She still half believed this was a reasonable hope, even then, on the second-last day. She picked up the photograph on her desk, which she had removed from the wall days before to study, as though it could tell her something she had never noticed. Once again, she looked at her own sunburnt cheeks — the sunburnt cheeks of a child. And Esther's pale face, framed with a sun-swept bob. Esther, in her early thirties, had looked much younger. People sometimes mistook her in those days for a student, a child. It was something about her skin. It was the combination of Esther's big eyes and her tiny frame, Tamar's father once said, that made women her own age speak to her as if she were a child.

Only once had a face surprised Tamar entirely, had it abandoned its course like a train redirected onto a different track to avoid a wreck. But how, precisely, had her mother changed? Why, a month after the war ended, when Collette van Daam opened the bedroom door, joy and relief visible in her face, had Tamar felt the possibility of her imagined reunion recede forever? Her mother was much thinner than she had been, her hair shorter and no longer smooth or stylish, and it was white at the temples. But what else? Her skin couldn't, surely, have turned grey. Esther smiled falteringly; her eyes were red and swollen, and she held her hand out to Tamar, pulled her close and leaned into her. There was no longed-for whiff of rosewater. Esther smelled stale, like something old. And though, in the months and years that followed, she put on weight and had her hair styled, even dying the white parts brown, though she took her lipstick from a drawer and smeared it on her lips, Esther did not get her old face back.

And Tamar had spoken of these things to Ginny, surely, if only in bursts, in sentences begun and never finished. Perhaps she had described her parents and the day trips they used to take, the three of them, to the beach north of Amsterdam, and the curve of her mother's cheeks, the smoothness of her mouth, dark with the deep red lipstick that was popular at the time. Tamar had told stories, had told Ginny about finding Esther in front of the mirror with that old lipstick in her hand, and how the colour refused to sit on her lips the way it used to, how significant this seemed, though it was only because the makeup was dried out. Had she told Ginny about Esther's nose, how she'd powdered it to cover the pores, and had she described the girlish curve of her mother's nostrils, seen from below? Ginny might well have understood what Tamar meant: between 1943 and 1945, the future of Esther's face was erased and replaced with another. Had Tamar been the one to tell her daughter that a soul can flee this world and leave a living body behind; had she given Ginny the idea to stubbornly insist she'd been knocked out of herself?

Certainly, Dr. Manning thought Ginny had picked this idea up somewhere, that she had mulled it over and held it close, and then, when her head hit the floor, allowed it to overtake her. Tamar hadn't even realized that psychiatrists were considered real doctors, that they had patients with actual injuries and illnesses in their care. She hadn't known hospitals had psychiatrists on staff until Dr. Jessup, the neurologist, introduced them to Dr. Manning, and explained that he, a psychiatrist, would be taking over Ginny's care. Tamar had become accustomed to Dr. Jessup and trusted her, with her tidy, simple hairstyle, enviably long legs and intelligent, plain face.

The pains in Ginny's elbow that had her yelping at night loudly enough to wake Aga and Minnie — the doctors suggested quite clearly that she was making them up. Or, perhaps, was somehow imagining them. Tamar had told Dr. Jessup, privately, about Robert, how he'd grabbed for Ginny, ripping her sweater as she fell and that she'd broken her elbow on impact. She had never spoken of Robert's death, had never spoken of Robert at all, in front of Steven or the girls, but now Dr. Manning knew about it and brought it up.

"Do you remember that, Ginny, your father ripping your sweater?" Dr. Manning asked. Ginny didn't answer. She was sitting between Tamar and Steven, across the desk from the doctors, dressed in the bleach-stained blue track suit she'd adopted as her uniform.

"She was eleven," Tamar said. "And she has never remembered . . . that."

"This is the second serious accident you can't remember?" asked Dr. Manning.

"Ginny," said Dr. Jessup, knowing full well that she wouldn't get an answer. "Would you say you have a history of recklessness and of hypochondria?" Tamar looked at Steven for help. She was betraying her daughter somehow, not explaining properly.

"Wait," Steven said. "There is something wrong with her. We need to get her better. What are you saying? That's she's making the whole thing up? Look at her."

And they all did. Tamar had finally persuaded Ginny to have her hair trimmed, so it was short and tidy and would have looked fine if it wasn't filthy. Her face was pale and slightly bloated. Though Ginny had lost weight with her newly acquired distaste for most foods other than steamed vegetables and rice, she had barely moved a muscle since the accident; she was so lethargic that Tamar felt sleepy just from being near. Ginny looked from face to face. Then she said loudly, in a satirical, sing-song tone, "Doctor, mother, husband, daughter." Tamar braced herself for the hysterical laughter that usually followed moments of tension or absurdity, "pathological laughter," the doctors called it. But Ginny inhaled sharply and then stopped, her face falling as though some terribly serious insight had interrupted whatever had struck her as funny. Aga laughed out loud, briefly, at the comically concerned expression on Ginny's face, and then she, too, stopped abruptly, horrified.

"Sorry," said Aga.

"Ginny," Dr. Manning tried. "Steven tells me you've been writing quite a lot lately. At the kitchen table?"

"Writing quite a lot lately. At the kitchen table? Someone's always looking over my shoulder," she said vaguely.

"Ginny," said Dr. Manning. "Let's start meeting three times a week. Twice alone, and once with the rest of your family, all right?"

"I don't understand," Tamar told Steven as he drove her home that day, down Smythe Road, with Aga and Ginny in the back seat. Minnie must have been with Steven's parents. "Aren't you a neurologist?"

"I'm a neuroscientist."

"You study the brain."

"I study the brain, yes. I observe how rats' brains respond when deprived of sunlight, primarily."

"What a strange topic." Tamar fell silent, watching the tightness in Steven's forehead. She had never truly taken notice of his personality, its nuances, and it came as a surprise to see he was suffering and not behaving altogether reasonably. She'd always thought Steven was entirely dependable. Even when Ginny had first met him at the university and he started phoning, coming by, Steven had struck Tamar as steady and gentle, intelligent and trust-inspiring. Tamar and Esther, calmly ignoring Ginny's insistence that she and Steven were "just friends," wishfully discussed the simple, normal process occurring before them. Ginny had gone to school, attracted a nice man and become the subject of an old-fashioned courtship. Tamar and Esther had a vague and encouraging notion that Steven was a scientist, setting out on an orderly, impressive career that promised wealth and security. Even his parents, it turned out, were exactly the kind of people who would have produced a son like Steven seemed to be. Everything about them — their clothes, their furniture, their belief system — was confidently solid and simple; like Steven, they were almost normal, but too intelligent and scruffy around the edges to bypass eccentricity. Sheila was always slightly overweight, affectionate and motherly, with a baffling inability to keep her greying brown hair from flying around her head like frazzled wire; Fred wore shirts and ties under sweaters, smelled of pipe tobacco and, when he finished a meal, always managed to leave his chair and the floor around it covered in crumbs. Ginny's engagement and marriage had been such a relief, like waking from a bad dream. Steven had won her over after all, despite the rubbish that happened in between. Asher could be put aside as an unfortunate mishap attributable to the folly of youth.

But as Steven drove them home from the hospital that day, Tamar saw that he had changed, that he was sick and tired of the whole thing and could no longer be taken for granted; he was elsewhere, lost in the kind of thoughts that would amount, if he voiced them, to betrayal. Still, she would be shocked, a year later, about his other woman, his engagement. So soon after Ginny left. Tamar would never have thought Steven was complicated enough to have an affair. An affair requires passion, involves heartache and conflict and, surely, the agony of loving, for some period of overlap, two people, and having to choose between them. Tamar hadn't realized Steven was capable of the necessary emotional agitation or the deceit. Robert never had affairs, surely. Whatever he had, they weren't affairs.

When Ginny was long gone, Tamar would learn that Steven had been keeping a mistress all along. Even as they met Dr. Manning, he'd had this woman, this secret. Aga, when she lived with Tamar during the year before she moved to Toronto, would recount the wedding vows, how the new wife described falling in love with Steven in the arboretum in early autumn, and described how she dared to kiss him for the first time. "Early autumn," Aga stressed. "Early autumn, Tam-Tam. Before Mama's accident. How could I live in the same house as them, knowing that?"

And Tamar would wonder if Robert, too, had ever professed love, if another woman had waited, agonized, for him to end his sexless marriage, the details of which he had recounted, and marry her instead. Tamar would wonder if Steven had phoned this mistress, this Lara, after that first session with Dr. Manning, if he had confided in her, admitting, "I don't know how long this will continue." If he said, at the end of the conversation, "I love only you."

The sessions with Dr. Manning had consisted entirely of talking, and Ginny observed the proceedings in a silence that seemed sometimes placid, sometimes obstinate. Tamar, Steven and the girls would review the mundane events of Ginny's week, Dr. Manning asking Ginny how she enjoyed certain meals or events or even what she thought of particular television shows.

"It was fine," Ginny might say, if she was feeling particularly talkative. "It kept my attention, I guess."

"Let's rebuild her life," Dr. Manning told Tamar and Steven. "Rebuild her memories around her and let her walk back into them when she's ready. I think she does remember, but she's turned off her opinions about all these things. This suggests to me that she's been hurt. We need to make her feel safe and cared for."

Steven recounted a family trip to Toronto. When four-year-old Aga got lost in the museum and he found her huddled in a dinosaur display. He described a Christmas party at which one of his professors had collapsed, drunk, across Ginny's lap. He talked about the night Minnie was born. As Steven spoke, Tamar thought of all the things she knew about Steven that he didn't know she knew. She pictured him waiting in a rundown bar the night before Asher Acker left for Israel; she imagined Steven standing at a window with Ginny, late at night, a wine glass in his hand, pointing out his nude neighbours across the alley.

For months, these meetings with Dr. Manning went on. And Ginny changed; she did change. She spoke in longer sentences and was less lethargic. She stopped staring out her kitchen window all day, and she lost weight. So much weight. Aga said Ginny did push-ups and sit-ups in her bedroom and read piles of library books. Aga discovered, by snooping when Ginny was out, that most of these were autobiographies written by the likes of seventeenth-century nuns. Then Ginny got a lock for her bedroom door. And as Ginny showed more signs of life, of sanity and purpose, Dr. Manning had Steven, Tamar and Aga frenziedly narrating her life, trying to steer her back instead of away.

"Do you remember that imaginary friend you had, Ginny?" Tamar said during a session in that winter. "My God, it's been a long time since I thought about that. She insisted she had a sister," Tamar told Dr. Manning. "What was her name — I can't remember." Ginny seemed at least to be listening, if not with particular interest. She was so very thin by then, her collarbone sharply defined above the neckline of her sweatshirt. The whole outfit was ridiculously baggy, several sizes too big, and her hair was raggedy again, growing out into what Aga called a mullet.

"She was very long and very thin, this sister, and could be folded and kept in a pocket. One time, we were crossing Laurier Street during rush hour, Ginny and I. She must have been four or five." Dr. Manning raised his eyebrows meaningfully, and Tamar realized she was doing it again — talking about her daughter in the third person. "You must have been four or five, Ginny," she corrected herself. "The traffic was just terrible, and when we finally got across the road, you started crying and carrying on, insisting that Morgan — that was her name — had fallen from your pocket and was stuck on the other side. You absolutely insisted. This Morgan was a brave soul who'd defeated all manner of enemies, but she was afraid to cross the busy street by herself."

Aga laughed too loudly, as people do when attempting to seem natural around someone insane or very old. "What did you do, Tam-Tam?"

"I took your mother back across. She was throwing a tantrum. A real tantrum. She insisted I take the imaginary character firmly by the hand." Tamar demonstrated, holding out her fist.

"What was she like? Where did the name Morgan come from?" Dr. Manning addressed these questions to Ginny, but Tamar answered.

"Oh, Ginny was so little. Could she remember something from when she was so small?"

"You'd be surprised," Dr. Manning said.

"Morgan was, like I said, very, very thin. She had black hair, right, Ginny? And she was extremely clever. A doctor and a circus performer, Ginny claimed." Aga laughed again, at a more normal volume this time. "Morgan le Fay was Ginny's favourite character in those King Arthur books," Tamar explained. "She loved those books. King Arthur and his knights. You know them? Strange books for a little girl, really." Robert used to read those stories to Ginny, and somehow, Tamar was sure, everyone in the room knew this, was waiting for her to say it. "Oh, and she was an orphan. Morgan was. A wayward waif, Ginny used to say. She must have heard that phrase from — somewhere. She was full of big words. Such a clever girl. Like Aga is."

Dr. Manning had told her that she should try to talk about Ginny's father. Those King Arthur books would be a good memory, surely. That's what Steven was doing — recounting good times, telling stories only of the sparkling moments when everything had seemed perfectly all right. Aga and Steven both seemed to recall long-ago conversations and events in such detail. Aga, especially, claimed to know precisely what was said, the words Ginny had used, for example when she first saw the new apartment downtown, or when Aga had been sick at preschool. Tamar looked at Dr. Manning's narrow face and looked away, a humiliating, infuriating memory seizing her body with the sickening assault of a bad smell. She didn't know how she'd come to be standing in the hallway between her bedroom and her mother's, a laundry basket at her feet, Robert kneeling with his face against her waist, drooling and crying into her clothes. She only remembered the silent struggle as she tried to get his hands out of her skirt, the taste of panic and disgust in her mouth, perspiration under her arms and prickling the palms of her hands. How old had she been? How old was Ginny, and where was she? Esther, certainly, had been in the kitchen nearby, cooking. The smell of marjoram and savory was in the air.

Was it the same day she found Robert reading to Ginny on the sofa in the basement, a football game playing in the background? Esther had made Ginny a monkey out of old socks, and the child always clutched it in her fist as Robert portrayed each of King Arthur's knights with a slightly different accent. Earlier the same day, had Tamar told herself, as she did so often in those days, that soon, perhaps, she would move back to the basement bedroom with her husband? Perhaps, she was forever telling herself, she would soon feel the way a wife should. And truly, it hadn't seemed so unlikely that she might return to work at the department store and that it might make everything better. They didn't need the money, she used to tell herself, but it couldn't hurt. Her mother and Ginny would be fine together for two days or so every week. Just two or three days, for Tamar to go out in the world and talk to people she didn't know, who didn't know her. And then she would be able to love him. They wouldn't necessarily have another baby; they could be careful. He was, after all, a doctor.

As Dr. Manning struggled to engage Ginny in a stilted discussion of nuns and their memoirs, Tamar realized that she did remember. She remembered how she had glanced over to see Robert engrossed in the football game, and how she'd turned from his room to enter Ginny's instead. As she stripped the tiny bed, Tamar heard the television click off, the white noise of the football game happily cut short. She shook the pillow out of its case with unnecessary aggression as Robert stopped in the doorway to watch her but regained control seconds later to drop the white fabric, decorated with tiny strawberries, on top of the pile. She could see, without looking at him directly, that her husband was formulating some infuriating, ironic comment, but he only said, "Ginny's sleeping." He followed Tamar to the laundry room and leaned against the door to watch her separate out the whites. Her husband. How breathtakingly disappointing that the word's meaning had diluted and warped so. *Mijn echtgenoot* — she had expected someone strong, irresistible and slightly mad, who caught you in his arms and kissed your face, whose presence felt comforting and thrilling, domestic with an undercurrent of the erotic.

"And what delight," said Robert, as the washing machine came

172

to life, "does the enigmatic kitchen mistress have in store for the good doctor and his wife tonight?" He waited for Tamar to speak and then added, "I could swear I smell the makings of a pot pie."

"I don't know. Something with carrots and potatoes."

"After me own heart," said Robert in the exaggerated Irish accent he reserved for pithy, self-mocking remarks, but without the joviality he usually reserved for such moments.

Tamar headed upstairs without comment. Robert stepped lightly up behind her and through the kitchen, where Esther was, indeed, rolling pastry while vegetables simmered in a thick white sauce; she was clad in a new blue apron that Tamar had brought home for her. "You're a genius," Robert remarked as he passed, as though to a moody child who could be tickled into cheeriness; as always, his manner with Esther made Tamar cringe. Esther, however, offered a wry smile. The side of a tooth near the front of her mouth was discoloured — it always had been and had seemed alluring when Tamar was a child. Now it struck her as an irreversible mark of decay and ill health, and she hated to see it.

In the hallway between her bedroom and Esther's, Tamar put the laundry basket down and turned to walk past Robert, who was hovering right behind her. "Where are you going?" he said, in his normal Canadian voice, the one he used when he wasn't joking, which was rarely; he joked even when angry or despondent.

"To the den. To sit." She stopped as he took hold of her upper arm. Not hard, but he was touching her, and she waited for him to stop.

"You've more than got your figure back," he told her. "You look better than ever. Do you know that?"

"Thank you." She stood perfectly still.

"Why are you so afraid of me?" He moved to embrace her, and she stiffened as he pulled her against him and smoothed her hair, kissing it. "I know it's difficult."

"You don't know me," said Tamar, surprising herself. She glanced toward the kitchen, assuring herself that Esther couldn't hear their voices.

"I know you." He kissed her gently, and she parted her lips

slightly as he pulled away, the taste of him making her head light. "I know you," said Robert. "I want to know you, Tamar. Just trust me. Show me everything."

Tamar pulled back and shook her head. "Wait." He must have been repeating something he'd heard in a Hollywood movie — and he thought people actually said things like that to each other. To trust him seemed as absurd a request as if he had asked her to open her rib cage and give him her heart.

"No more waiting." His face was in her hair, his hands fumbling with the buttons on her blouse as he tried to manoeuvre her toward her bedroom door.

"What are you doing?" Tamar's question came out irritated, disgusted; she was grateful that the panicked pounding in her chest was inaudible from the outside as Robert secured her around the waist with one arm and bent to grab her skirt with the other. She wedged her elbows between herself and his shoulders and tried to pry his hot, wiry frame off her, but he just sank lower, the side of his face below her breasts, now trying to reach up her skirt with both hands. "What are you doing?" Tamar said again, aware of the words' absurdity but unable to formulate any others.

"You're my wife." She could feel the heat of his breath through her blouse. "You are my wife, Tammy, my wife." It had been almost two years since he'd called her Tammy — back before Ginny was born. He had found the incongruity hilarious and romantic. Back then, he'd said it with such affection and optimism. Her skin felt damp; he was drooling. She thought he might be crying. "I miss you," he said, his voice rushed and muffled against her chest. "I want to kiss you again, I want you to feel me again. Remember how you used to love it? I want to kiss your legs, I want your cunt. Please. I want to give you pleasure, I want you to love it."

"My mother. Be quiet, please, Robert, please."

"Oh, God."

Tamar forced her knee into his abdomen and pushed hard with her leg and both arms. Robert staggered dramatically against the far wall, clutching himself, and Tamar started towards him, horrified, to see if he was hurt.

"I didn't think you had it in you," he gasped, his eyes wide, watery and bloodshot. He was shaking; she couldn't tell if he was laughing or crying, and it occurred to her that he was a remarkably good-looking man, a remarkably good man, and didn't deserve any of this. "I surrender," he said. "I give up." As Tamar left him where he stood, he called after her, "You win." She sat in the den with a magazine, staring fixedly at an enormous photograph of a woman with straight, centre-parted hair and a man's tie around her neck, waiting for her hands to stop shaking.

Was this the kind of story Dr. Manning wanted to hear? Such a story is better forced back out of the mind before it infects everything, makes every memory appalling. It was only a few days after Robert's attempted seduction that Tamar found, on her bed, a paperback copy of *Anne Frank: The Diary of a Young Girl*, and opened it to see the inscription, in Robert's handwriting: *Tamar, trust me — my ears and my heart are yours. R.* She turned it over to read the blurb on the back and was seized with anger, dismay and disgust. Robert's gesture was as menacing and as ingenuous as a cat leaving a mangled mouse on its master's pillow, a trail of muddy, bloody paw prints in its well-intentioned path. Tamar was tempted to destroy the book by ripping or burning, but instead she carried it out of her bedroom, out of the house, and disposed of it in a garbage bin across the street. She pictured Robert telling other doctors and nurses at the hospital, "My wife is a real-life Anne Frank." She imagined them all looking at her with pity and fascination at the next dinner party.

When Robert came home from work that night, Tamar could barely look at him. She dreaded the expectant, kind longing with which he was surely gazing across the table and was sure she would scream if he told her one more time that his own father had wanted him to enlist, caring "more about politics and honour than human life"; that his best friend was killed by "the krauts" in Dieppe; that his Irish ancestors had been quarantined in typhus-infested shacks in Montreal. She was aware of hating him, of wanting never to see him again. It was not malice but stupidity — bland, wide-eyed stupidity — that caused most of the suffering in the world. The kind of stupidity that had overcome her and caused this absurd, unrectifiable situation: an alien living in her home and understanding nothing.

Ginny was talking in a bored voice about a saint she found "kind of interesting" who had desired, more than anything, even as a child, to be martyred by Moors, and, half listening, Tamar wondered if Ginny had known how strange it was that her parents slept in separate rooms; did she know how Robert had irritated and repulsed her, how he had hounded her, invading her privacy in every possible way? Dr. Manning claimed that children perceive and understand all those sorts of things. Then Tamar remembered something more important: how Ginny, a year or two after she and Steven were married, had started phoning often, in a panic about the tiniest of discomforts, the nuances of interactions. Ginny was upset because she'd gone out to do errands and had asked Steven to finish the laundry. "He hadn't even remembered to do a single load of laundry. Not a single load. I just stood there watching him resolve to help me with the housework, and all I could think about was leaving. Going somewhere alone, like to a Mediterranean city, where I could walk around in markets all day wearing dresses, and sit on the beach, and just leave all the fucking dirty laundry and malls and playgroups behind. Isn't that awful? All I could think was that I could leave; I could. I could just lift myself out of this pile of . . . of crap."

And Tamar was speechless, because it had never occurred to her, at such moments with Robert, to imagine herself alone. To imagine herself without Esther, without Robert or Ginny, let alone desire it. "Hello, Mother? Don't you have anything to say? Any opinion at all?"

"Please don't yell at me," said Tamar. "I don't know what you want me to say. All this complaining you do."

Perhaps if Aga and Minnie weren't in the room, Tamar could have broached these things with Dr. Manning. Aga was slouching in a chair by the window, staring out at the parking lot through her absurd black-rimmed glasses, distressed, disgusted or bored, and Minnie was bent over a colouring book at her sister's feet. It was such an odd thing to do — to bring a fifteen-year-old and a five-year-old to these meetings. Steven claimed that the girls needed to feel involved, that Aga needed more than anything to understand the situation properly. The more she was kept in the dark, he was certain, the more anxious she would become.

"Can I ask a question?" Aga cut in, addressing Dr. Manning.

"Yes, Aga? A question for your mother?"

"A question for you," said Aga, and the doctor nodded. "Do you think my mother's a hysteric?"

"Where did you learn that term?" Steven asked.

"I read it in a book." Aga shrugged. She was always reading books. "A book about psychoanalytic theory."

"Isn't she clever," Tamar said.

"Yes," said Steven. "She is."

"Isn't she! Throwing words around that I can't even say." Tamar laughed lightly and looked at Dr. Manning for sympathy, only to realize he was noticing and assessing everything she said, studying her as though he had just figured something out — probably that she had single-handedly driven her daughter to insanity.

"Aga," Dr. Manning said, turning to the girl with a sympathetic, indulgent air. "We don't talk about hysteria anymore, but you're right that conversions like your mother's are very Freudian. She's converted psychological problems into physical pain."

"Hysteria," said Aga, eyeing Ginny. "Mama. You used to talk about hysteria, remember? You explained it to me — you said Oma Esther was a classic case. Dad, you used to accuse Mom of faking all the time. You always said she was suggestible. All her digestive problems? You said they were because of Oma Esther in the Holocaust, remember?"

Steven looked at the girl, surprised and hurt. You're not her father, Tamar thought.

"Your mother was a Holocaust survivor?" Dr. Manning asked Tamar.

"Hold on," said Steven. "What does that have to do with anything?"

"Why are you so afraid of talking about your wife's past?" Dr. Manning asked him. "You should consider that question seriously. This is the reality of the situation."

"The fucking reality of the situation," said Steven. The word sounded forced coming out of his mouth; Tamar had never heard him swear before. Aga looked at him with undisguised contempt. "The reality of the situation," he said again, as if he had never heard anything so sad or so stupid.

Aga looked back out at the parking lot, and Tamar almost envied her the adolescent entitlement to disdain, not to mention her apparent ability to understand what the doctor was talking about. Tamar thought of Asher — he had aspired to be a psychiatrist, hadn't he? Or something like it? He had aspired to sit in rooms like this one, leading patients to recall their least dignified moments. That's what he'd been trying to do all those years ago; he'd been practising on Tamar. She wondered what Asher would make of Ginny's condition; how odd that he was out there somewhere, doing things, with no idea what had transpired.

The last time they went to Dr. Manning's office as a family was on an uncommonly cold day in early spring. The doctor said Ginny had to re-establish her life in her own way, perhaps in a way that none of them had anticipated, and that she needed some breathing room. From then on Ginny went alone, or perhaps she stopped going at all. Soon Tamar would no longer know her daughter's schedule, and when Tamar went to visit, there was no telling if Ginny would even be home. Ginny had already changed so much. She was sleek and thin and strong, and so guarded.

It had already been growing dark when they left the hospital for the last time, and Tamar sat beside Steven in the front seat. The others squeezed into the back, Minnie in the middle. The sky was grey, streaked with clouds, and the hospital and the parking lot were grey, too, white showing through only where the last remnants of snow lay in filthy piles. Steven's hair, at the temples — Tamar had never noticed it before — was turning grey. Steven started the ignition and turned on the heat, which blew cold air from outside into the already uncomfortable car, and then he let his arm fall to his side.

"Just going to let the engine warm up a bit," he mumbled, then cleared his throat and said, "We're here for you, Ginny. Do you understand that? We are all sitting here, we all come to this hospital again and again, me, your mother and the girls, for no other reason than you. Do you understand that?" He turned to look, and Tamar couldn't help but do the same. Ginny was impassive in her ski jacket and track suit. She had removed her mitts and folded her bony fingers in her lap. The hapless air she'd adopted after the accident had given way entirely to straight-backed, patient tolerance. Minnie was leaning as far as she could into Aga, practically sitting on her lap to avoid contact with her mother. Aga turned from the window to watch Ginny as well; they were all staring at her, waiting, except for Minnie, who rested her face against Aga's collarbone and closed her eyes.

"Do you have something to say?" Tamar tried. "Please. This has gone far enough, don't you think. Surely you can tell us something — what do you think about what Dr. Manning said? Do you want us to stop coming with you? Do you think he's helping you?"

A family was crossing the parking lot, a couple pushing a young boy in a wheelchair, another boy walking alongside. "I always hated it when they put you in a wheelchair. Every time you were in the hospital, do you remember? They always made you leave in a wheelchair. Remember," said Tamar half-heartedly. She sounded absurd to herself. Remember, remember — Tamar was weary at the very word, the monotony of repeating it again and again, dredging up anecdotes. And now Dr. Manning was telling them to stop the stories, to stop hoping that one magical time, Ginny suddenly would remember. That something would remind her of herself, and she would blink, shake her head and say, exasperated, "Oh, Mother, that's not what happened at all. What planet are you living on?"

"Minnie," said Aga. "Don't. Stop that." Tamar opened her eyes to see Minnie with both booted feet against Ginny's arm, pushing hard, her back braced against Aga's side. Ginny wriggled, trying to get away, looking no more alarmed than someone struggling to find a comfortable position in an ill-made chair.

"Minnie," said Steven.

With the low, sustained whining sound she'd make when she'd fallen and was deciding whether to cry, Minnie twisted in Aga's arms to plant her feet more firmly against Ginny's side, kicking her quite hard with one foot. It wasn't clear from the way she held the child whether Aga was trying to stop or to bolster her. Ginny leaned back to escape the little boots, but, without flailing or losing control, Minnie kept up her attack, pushing and kicking and increasing the volume of her whine until it was almost a howl. Finally, she stopped to take a deep breath and then shrieked so loudly and despairingly that Tamar cringed, pressing her hands to her ears. Aga looked pained as well but kept her arms around her sister, who arched her back to push Ginny with all her might. Ginny moved quickly to open her door, step outside and slam the door closed again. She pulled her hood up over her tuque, shoving her hands into her pockets as she turned away to look off toward the highway.

Tamar inhaled deeply; she had been holding her breath.

"Minnie," said Steven. "Come here." The child was sobbing. "Come here. Come on." Minnie climbed between the front seats, Tamar and Aga both helping her, to sit on Steven's lap. "All right. All right, baby." He rocked the child in his arms, quieting her howls to a muffled weeping. As Minnie's sorrow gave way to silence, Tamar watched Ginny, who was still facing away from the car and had taken a few steps, futile, since there was nowhere to go. Her pants were enormous. It was a wonder they didn't fall down.

Oh, how Tamar longed to know what her daughter was thinking. She watched Ginny walk slowly away from the car and stop a hundred feet away to stand in the middle of the concrete expanse. Arms straight down at her sides like a child's, she looked around, sleeves ruffling in the wind. No one would have guessed that this wisp of a woman was the nick in an intricately woven fabric, that a world was unravelling around her. Tamar wondered if she'd have recognized Ginny, so thin and bundled into so many clothes, standing so still and quiet and looking so alone, from across a street, across a parking lot.

"We'll get out of this mess," Steven told Minnie, who was leaning against his chest, a few matted red curls sticking out from her tuque.

No, Tamar whispered, and then turned to Steven with a horrified sense of revelation. She dug her nails into her palms. "You want to be rid of her," she said. Steven put his head on Minnie's head, and Tamar said, "You want to be rid of us." He wanted the girls to himself, to make other plans, to move on. Ginny couldn't resume her old life; perhaps she sensed that the moment she seemed herself again, Steven would push her out the door. Tamar met Aga's eyes and saw the anguish on her face. He wasn't even her real father.

Without looking at Steven, Tamar opened her own door and stepped outside. It was so cold the wind blew through her cashmere hat, burning her ears. "Come back," she called. "Please come back." She walked over and pushed her arm through Ginny's. "Please come back now," she said again. She tugged gently. "Don't you know that men come and go? I hope this isn't about a man, *liefje*." It felt strange to use the old endearment; she was still pretending she was speaking to Ginny. "Those aren't the people to depend on." The thin woman's hood hid her face. "You've always asked too much of men."

She almost expected her daughter to sigh, "Oh, Mother. You don't understand anything." Why wouldn't she just say it? She would never say it; this woman would never say anything of the sort, this woman who was no longer Ginny. Minnie was right; Minnie knew, had known.

Tamar started at a knock on the door. She began to stand, but then exclaimed, "Oh," as Aga came into the room. She eased back into her chair. "Do you like it? What an improvement. The way it frames your face."

Aga touched her new bangs and ran her hand over the length of her hair. "I really like it, yeah."

"She didn't do your face, too?"

"I don't really want makeup, Tam-Tam," Aga said, standing just inside the doorway, hesitant to come further inside the room. "I don't wear makeup."

"Just some lipstick? I'll tell Cassandra."

"It doesn't suit me. Honestly, Tam-Tam. I really don't want it."

"Doesn't suit you." The familiarity of the argument, the comfort of it, gripped Tamar with the allure of a route walked many times, long ago. "You are your mother's daughter," she said. Aga stiffened at this, pressing her lips together.

Tamar remembered the photograph she held. "Come and see this. Don't you smell lovely," she added, as the girl leaned over. She turned and pushed Aga's bangs to one side experimentally, then smoothed them back down. "I love the layers," she said. "There's some wave in your hair, you know. It's not bone straight. We could even out the colour — it's so dark on top."

"That's you, Tam-Tam?"

Tamar looked back at the photograph in her hands. "Yes, can you believe it? That's me. We'd been having a picnic — see, that's the beach umbrella my father's holding. Look how tanned I was, brown like a little Indian."

"Tam-Tam."

"And my mother, your Oma Esther." She tapped the glass with her long, red nail. "And my father." She tapped the glass again. "My father's name was Jozef. Did you know that?"

"Yes," said Aga. "Mama told me. When I was little. I always used to look at this picture when I was here and wonder about him."

"You did?"

"What was he like?"

"He was — he was very tall. He had so many friends, always a house full of friends. And he was funny. Oh, he was such a funny man. He was like a child pretending to be grown up. That's what he was like."

Aga turned to lean against the desk, half sitting on a folder full of receipts. Her hands, Tamar saw, were trembling.

"When you were a tiny thing," said Tamar, "I thought, *there is a child with secrets*. Your mother never wanted secrets; she wanted to tell. Always to tell everything." Their legs were almost touching, and for a moment Tamar wished she was the kind of grandmother who held children in her lap to comfort them. What a thing to think about a grown, sixteen-year-old girl.

"Tam-Tam, what did you think of Dr. Manning? Was he doing

any good, do you think? Was he right that we shouldn't go any-more?"

Tamar ran the tip of her nail over her father's face. She almost laughed, suddenly imagining Jozef in a psychiatrist's office. "I don't know what good it does," she said finally, "to remember every little thing the way he wanted us to. It doesn't seem right to me. Never in my life. I wasn't brought up to confess things but to make the best, to make a good life. That's what my father would have said." Aga's father, her real father, had been the type to collect confessions like something rare and precious. To squeeze secrets from his subjects, despite the damage he might do.

Dr. Manning's story-telling sessions had done nothing at all to remind Ginny who she was supposed to be, but they had provoked in Tamar a distressing habit of focusing on the past, forever attempt-ing to reconstruct long-past scenes in all their detail. Shopping at the Bay, months after leaving Dr. Manning, Tamar found herself thinking of Asher Acker and struggling to recall, not just his manner, but the details of how she had let him into her life. Sheila and Fred, Steven's parents, had known Asher, too, at least a little; they had known him as Steven's friend. "He was a bright boy with a lot of misdirected energy," Sheila said one time, motherly, forgiving, "a confused kid." And how humiliating that it hadn't occurred to Tamar until so late that she was an adult and he a child. The first time she met him, at the makeup counter, surely she'd doubted she would see this odd young man ever again. It was incredible that this absurd person would go on to have such an impact on her life. Why had Ginny been holding that terrible letter when she fell? A twelve-year-old letter, its cheap ink already fading.

"But sometimes," said Aga, still leaning against the desk so Tamar had to look up to see her, "keeping a secret could drive you crazy." Tamar saw that Aga's face had grown pale as paper, pale to the lips, and she barely resisted saying no, preventing whatever words were about to bombard her. "I" — Aga addressed the back wall, looking at the door to the servants' staircase — "I argued with my mother the day of her accident." Aga's face contorted as she struggled not to cry.

Tamar reached up to brush a small clipping of hair from the child's cheek. "Daughters and mothers always argue," she said, and Aga sighed. It was such a familiar, disappointed sigh. Just as Ginny had sighed, always, after offering Tamar some anguished confession. Tamar looked back down at her young parents in the photograph. Even as a child, Tamar hadn't told her mother about any discomforts beyond the obvious scraped knees and sore throats. And as an adult, she could never have complained to Esther about her worries, about her anguish over Robert. She would never have thought to do so. She had protected her mother; she had tried; she had tried so hard.

"You were always Oma Esther's favourite," Tamar said.

"I know." Aga sighed again, deeply, resigning herself to disappointment in Tamar for changing the subject. "That's what Mama always said."

"Yes. She was right. Oma Esther used to feed you the strangest foods, did your mother tell you? It drove her mad."

Of course, Esther had loved Ginny from the moment of birth, but it was a subdued kind of caring, as though the sounds of a baby in the house might shatter her. As though she didn't want to get too attached, just in case. And why it was different with Aga was as much a mystery to Esther, Tamar suspected, as to anyone else. Esther was in her late sixties when Aga was born and hadn't seen it coming; she had watched Ginny's growing belly with noncommittal trepidation all through the pregnancy. But at the hospital, as Ginny lay limp and exhausted and radically, alarmingly depleted in size, just as Ginny told her nurse, "I don't know, there is no father" and agreed, finally, to move back home, Esther placed the tip of her index finger in the baby's tiny palm, and, as the fingers closed and held on tight, she fell in love.

It came as a shock, surely, to love someone new with such force after two and a half decades of directing her passion away from anyone still living. Convinced that Ginny was breastfeeding for too long, Esther eventually began sneaking the baby pureed chicken and vegetable concoctions. She continued to feed Aga as she saw fit, waving off Ginny's increasingly enraged protests. "She's a big, growing girl. She doesn't need your milk any longer, needs you to find a job, rather."

And Ginny did get a job. Tamar avoided most of the commotion because she was up in the salon, hiring, managing and waiting for the money coming in to balance that going out. But when she went downstairs during the days, she found Ginny teaching piano, bringing a stream of children into the living room to stab at the keys as Esther barricaded herself in the kitchen, writing cryptic messages to herself in her cookbooks, planning meals and blending utterly inappropriate ingredients into baby-food softness.

"I've missed my mother since she died," Tamar told Aga. "But I'm grateful she went so painlessly, after all she went through. That she isn't here to see your mother so ill. Do you remember Oma Esther's funeral? Your mother's speech? It was so lovely, the things she said."

"Yes. And Mama changed Minnie's first name to Esther. I'd better get home," Aga said. "Dad's probably making dinner. Thanks for getting Cassandra to cut my hair." If Esther had been there to see her great-granddaughter's anguish, she would have taken the girl's hands and kissed her wrists, would have reached up to hold the child's beloved face with both hands.

"Aga," Tamar said. "I argued with my husband the day he died." Aga looked at Tamar in astonishment. And Tamar was surprised herself. She had scarcely mentioned Robert in years; she had never before mentioned him to Aga. "Yes, and I've always felt terrible about it. That the last thing I said to him was nasty. I always felt that perhaps my words had somehow — well."

"What were you fighting about?"

Tamar hesitated and smoothed her top, then folded her hands in her lap. "Your grandfather and I used to argue about the newspaper. It irritated him that I didn't read it. That I wasn't interested in 'world events.' I was forever tidying loose pages; he left them lying around every room. Oh, that house was a mess. Robert read two or three newspapers every day. He was a very clever man, you know. That's where your mother gets it from." Tamar looked at Aga and added, "You're like your grandfather in that way too, Aga." *There's a difference between a confession and a confidence.* Tamar could hear Ginny's voice — was that what Ginny had said?

"When your grandfather died," she went on, "there was a trial happening in Jerusalem. The trial of Adolf Eichmann. He was in charge of deportations during the war in Europe. The Second World War. My parents," she added, "were among those deported. Oma Esther — did you know?"

Aga nodded. "I know," she said. "Mama told me." She knew, at least, something.

"I was terribly worried that Oma Esther would see these newspapers, the ones with Eichmann's picture, that they would upset her." Esther had never read the papers, and could barely read English at all, but Tamar was sure a photograph would catch her eye, or she would overhear Robert reading aloud. One day Robert read a quotation from the paper to Tamar: Eichmann had bragged that the millions of lives on his conscience gave him "extraordinary satisfaction."

Tamar had stepped closer to the television one evening, in order to see Eichmann clearly. "Isn't it true what the reporters say?" said Robert. "That he looks so ordinary?" Tamar hadn't thought Adolf Eichmann looked ordinary at all. Even in photographs, there was something wrong about him. The eyebrows and jaw were always distorted into an asymmetrical grimace; Tamar saw that this man had once possessed attractive features, but that, as he sat in his government office honing his infamous strategies, he had pursed and furrowed and winced until, as the television showed, his face never rested. Even as the eyes remained calm, the mouth and brow twitched with a gruesome, and suddenly world famous, tic.

"So you see," Tamar told Aga, "I asked Robert to stop leaving those papers lying about. The day he died was Yom H'Shoah. Holocaust Remembrance Day. We argued because he'd been reading those stories about Eichmann and was suddenly an expert about what happened in Europe. He insisted I ought to take my mother to a synagogue. Can you imagine me and Oma Esther? Oh, he just didn't understand us, and I was so angry. I'm not explaining this well."

"No," said Aga. "You are." Tamar was grateful that her granddaughter wasn't the sort to weep or profess some extreme emotional state, that she was unlikely to grasp Tamar suddenly in an embrace.

"Robert told me he'd been reading to Ginny from the coverage of that trial." Tamar shook her head. "I was so upset. An eleven-year-old girl. I was so upset with him."

"He did? Really? To Mama?"

"Yes. To your mama." Tamar hesitated. "I don't know quite what your mother told you about the war, what happened to me and Oma Esther, but sometimes people have the wrong idea about these kinds of things. Sometimes people — they come to believe strange things about each other. You see" — Tamar paused and found the words she needed; after all, she had practised this monologue in her head many times, though she had always imagined addressing it to Ginny — "You see, Aga, your grandfather had come to believe that Oma Esther and I were like those poor people whose stories he read in the papers. They were always printing little stories about Jewish immigrants to Canada as sidepieces to that trial, full of gruesome details. Robert believed that Oma Esther and I had each experienced a kind of world-class drama. What happened to the Jews in Europe during the war — it had become almost stylish to talk of it. It was the first people had heard about it here. I couldn't explain to him that, for me, those years had been terribly undramatic. I stayed with neighbours; they hid me in their house. My life was very strange. I felt as though I were dreaming. I was often alone in the house for many hours of the day, and do you know what I did with my time?" Aga shook her head slowly.

"I dedicated myself to erasing evidence of my day-to-day existence. My clothes were the same size as Femke's and were kept in her drawers and closet. But there were things most people would never think of — signs that could alert a careful inspector to an extra person in the house. After washing my hands, I wiped water droplets from the sink; after eating, I washed all the dishes I'd used, dried them and put them away. I was always on the lookout for long blond hairs, especially in the tub and the bed, because the van Daams were all dark haired. I was careful to have only one object out of place at any time: a book, for instance, or a deck of cards." Tamar turned her gaze from the piles of folders on her desk. Aga had removed her glasses — and the way she held her mouth. Tamar inhaled sharply.

"Are you all right, Tam-Tam?"

"My God. How you remind me sometimes of —" Tamar shook her head. She had only spoken to one other person of these things at such length.

"My mother."

"Yes," Tamar breathed. Asher. Sitting in Robert's old mustard-coloured chair, limbs stretched out casually, in the old apartment's living room. That room had seemed so dark always, with its walnut-stained mouldings and heavy burgundy rug. And she told Asher about the end of the war. How the city hadn't looked different in any obvious, impressive ways, but that when she tried to live with her mother in their old house, every familiar word crumbled. Everything, even their language, was contaminated at the core, rotten. A child of German sympathizers had been sleeping on her soft mattress all those nights while she had huddled at the edge of Femke's bed or in the crawl space above the ceiling, trying not to breathe.

Tamar had told Asher how Esther came back alone. That there was no joyful reunion, no frantic conversation, Tamar's parents holding each of her hands as they related what had happened, how they'd eluded harm. The Germans were gone, but then so were the van Daams — the only people Tamar had seen or talked to for two years. Her father was missing and her shy young aunt Anke was dead. Tamar had described to Asher how Esther had been shaken long and hard until she collapsed, and then, in the quiet afterward, was permanently greyed by settled dust.

"I was telling you about the day your grandfather died," Tamar said. Aga reached for her glasses and put them back on, crossed her arms as though she were cold. "I told him that he must stop obsessing. That my mother and I came to Canada to start a new life and forget about those bad years. To leave those terrible times behind. Robert and I fought, and we both said terrible things. He said that if it weren't for Ginny, he would regret ever laying eyes on me. He claimed that my mother was kind but I was cold hearted. He said he had come to know my mother more than I did. That I wouldn't listen to her. He said such cruel things. And I told him I could barely tolerate his presence. I said I found him repulsive . . .

"And then I watched through the window as he rode away on his bicycle. Your mother was sitting on the handlebars. They were almost at her school when it happened. The ambulance picked them up with schoolchildren watching from the other side of the fence, on the playground."

"And you felt like it was your fault."

"I wondered if I'd worn him down, treated him unjustly and driven him to recklessness, though I knew he could never have knowingly put your mother in danger. How he adored that child. I was sure I had tried, that I had tried so much to understand him. I wasn't, I suppose, clever or strong enough. What could I have done?" Tamar was suddenly very tired of speaking. Already the regret that follows any lengthy confession was creeping over her skin. "Oh," she said, making it worse, "but that was all so long ago." After a long silence, she stood, to indicate that she had finished speaking, but Aga didn't move. "I don't know how I'm to get this office in order," Tamar said.

"Thanks, Tam-Tam," said Aga. She stepped away from the desk. "Dad's probably made dinner." She was looking away, embarrassed, like a lover who wants to leave but doesn't know how.

"Let me get you that skin cream before you leave," Tamar said, and led the girl down the hall to the stock room. Tamar kissed Aga goodbye at the top of the stairs. Cassandra was leaving for the day as well, and Tamar asked her, though she didn't expect an answer, why Cassandra hadn't done Aga's makeup. "Just a bit of lipstick," she said.

"Maybe we'll convince her next time," Cassandra said, already on the stairs.

Everyone else had already left. Tamar was alone. She knew she ought to go home as well; there was leftover takeout in the fridge. She checked the aesthetics rooms; the girls had turned off all the lights and also the main light in the salon. It was always so strange to be alone in this room, with the empty chairs and so many mirrors. She stood in the centre and turned slowly, as she'd done fifteen years earlier, amazed that all this was hers, seeing her reflection from every angle. Unmistakably, she was an aging woman. Elegant, yes, but unmistakably middle-aged. At such an age, one ought to be past foolishness.

Tamar went back to the office, sat at her desk and stared at the picture of her own young face. Tamar and her parents standing on a cobblestone road, tramlines under her father's feet. They must have met someone who agreed to take the picture, but she'd always recalled only her parents' company, the three of them walking to catch their tram, alone in the quiet, windy late afternoon, without seeing another soul. Jozef had the folded beach umbrella over one shoulder and the picnic bag over the other. As always, he walked too quickly for Tamar and her mother to keep up. Every minute or so, he'd notice where he was and stop to wait for them. He'd put his free hand on Esther's shoulder or touch Tamar's hair until his mind wandered, and then he'd forget himself again and stride off ahead with the giant, gangling steps that came to him naturally. Tamar loved how he walked with a cigarette between his lips, and how, when he laughed or called out for them to hurry, a cloud of smoke formed in front of his face, making him squint as if surprised by sunlight through a window.

Tamar recalled viscerally the smell of the air at Noord Wijk, the beach outside Amsterdam, and the moment she had turned her head, shading her eyes with a hand, to realize she had unwittingly followed the sea so far that the day's picnickers were mere dots in the distance, separated from her by an expanse of dark, wet sand scattered with rocks and shells. Her parents were among the dots, but she didn't know which they were. She had wandered away to squeeze damp sand between her toes; the water hadn't been warm enough for swimming, and the day was breezy. As the tide receded, she had followed, edging further and further, step by step, daring the icy water, creeping back up, to lick her toes. Once she took a step forward, she wasn't allowed to step back again; that was the rule. "One, two, three, four, five." She practised her English. "Please pass the pepper. May I please be excused?" English, that year, had become her favourite subject in school; she must have been nine or ten, perhaps a little younger. "May," said Tamar, curling her toes into the sand as the water crept to a hair's breadth from her skin. "I please" — she edged another millimetre down the beach — "be excused."

When she looked back and saw how far the tide had led her, she wanted to run madly, to yell for her parents — the urge possessed her, pushing her bodily forward. She didn't move. Her body wanted to flee itself; she pictured herself flailing, moving so quickly her feet would sink into the sand, trip over each other and send her sprawling. She let it hold her body full in its grasp — the need to escape this wasteland of beached sea life and return to humanity, to find her parents. But still she didn't move. Instead, she let out a small, strange scream. She absorbed the terror of being alone, a tiny girl standing on ground that had so recently been under the sea and soon would be again, and then began a measured walk toward the skyline. Her head was foggy, heavy with salt, sun and the breeze, which seemed to keep changing direction.

When Tamar finally did find her parents, they were unconcerned, her father asleep and her mother reading a novel. She sat down between them without a word, as though she had never doubted they would be there, at that exact spot, waiting for her. Her mother, in a long, white dress made of some diaphanous fabric decorated with a pattern of tiny flowers, turned from her book to touch Tamar's hair with a soft, white hand. She had set up a beach umbrella to protect her skin; she hated it when her complexion darkened and usually wore a hat. Tamar lamented that she was clearly not fated to be as doll-like as her mother, who was surely the most feminine creature imaginable. Esther had fashionably bobbed hair, chunky from the salt air, with a fringe that framed her face. Tamar's father snored quietly, looking as relaxed as a long, angular man in bathing trunks stretched out on a towel could manage, and she touched one of his bony hips. Her parents were peaceful and relaxed, as though nothing had punctured the pleasantness of the day; Tamar was proud of herself.

The photograph had surely been taken that very day, the memory of which had always been painful, had always haunted her moments of fierce longing and regret. It was terrible to think how she hadn't detected anything ominous, that there was no foreboding of doom. Despite an amassing of potent, private tragedies, such as the ease with which her parents became unidentifiable dots below the horizon, life would always resume as usual; the three of them, it seemed certain, would continue indefinitely as they were.

Yet it had started that day on the beach — so many times since then, Tamar had held herself in check. She had stood still as a statue and watched from across the street as her parents were led from their house, and when she did move, she ran in the wrong direction: away. Yes, her choice had saved her life. Still as a statue she'd stood, still and silent as a plank she'd squeezed herself above the van Daams' ceiling during raids. Perhaps it was true that she couldn't have saved her parents, but all her life she had remained immobile; she had steadied herself, listening to her own heartbeat, while the world crushed Ginny's soul thin as tissue paper, crumpled her up and threw her away. Why hadn't Tamar tried harder? And now it was too late; it was the second-last day. In less than twenty-four hours, she would return from the Remembrance Day service at the war memorial and towel her hair dry before sitting at this very desk to sort through files, trying to convince herself she could still run the business by herself, and would answer a knock on her office door, expecting to see Cassandra or Marcy.

Ginny. In a new, tight hyacinth blue sweater and a black skirt, holding a shoebox to her chest with a freshly manicured hand. Between her fingers, an unlit cigarette. Her hair was cut and styled. A smart, contemporary look. Only a professional facial can give skin such a glow. She had gone to another salon. And her clothes — every slim curve of her body showed. "I hope you're not busy," Ginny said, stepping into the room. "May I?"

"My God," said Tamar. "Look at you."

"Yes. Listen. I thought I should tell you in person that I'm leaving tonight. I got rid of most of my old things, but I brought you these." She offered the shoebox, but Tamar didn't take it, so Ginny walked across the room and placed it on the desk, beside the ledger. "Oh," said Ginny, looking down at her own hand, following Tamar's gaze to the unlit cigarette. "Would you like one? You smoke, don't you?"

"No," Tamar said, truthfully. She hadn't touched a cigarette in over a year. "What is this, Ginny? You can't travel alone. You're not well."

Ginny laughed, not the hysterical, choking spasms of her illness, but briefly, cheerfully. "I'm well," she said. "I'm not going to be called Ginny anymore. I'm Virginia from now on. I'll be leaving tonight, so" — she clasped her hands and smiled apologetically — "so, goodbye, Tamar."

"Who will you travel with?" said Tamar. "Where will you be? How will I reach you?"

"I don't know," Ginny said. "I don't know what my plans will be."

It was Minnie's shriek in the stairwell, that piercing scream, a year and a week and four days earlier, that had straightened Tamar's spine along with her resolve, leaving no room for panic. She told Cassandra, at the reception desk, "Phone for an ambulance," and within seconds she was down the stairs and past her daughter's limp frame to sit by her head. She told the girls to wait outside.

Ginny's body had been slanted toward the Inner Beauty exit, and Tamar knew not to touch or move her, despite how awkward and uncomfortable she looked, lying head first that way. She carefully extracted the bundle of folded papers from Ginny's grasp and put them in the pocket of her trousers, then took the hand in hers. How horrible it was to see a loved and memorized face unconscious — and how entirely different from watching a sleeping face, which always looks childlike and vulnerable, open and terribly naïve. The face of someone unconscious is a thing with no personality, and Tamar realized what it meant that Ginny had witnessed her father's death, had seen his unnaturally bent body beside her on the sidewalk all those years ago; the girl had surely carried that image ever since.

But what startled Tamar the most, what haunted her and would have her lying awake staring at the ceiling all through the night while Ginny flew to Spain, and through many nights in the years that followed, was the sensation of Ginny's hand in her own. As Tamar sat on those stairs willing life back into her daughter's body, Ginny had squeezed back, then opened her eyes and stared. Tamar met her daughter's eyes — not a stranger's eyes and not the eyes of someone who has forgotten her own name. It was Ginny, faculties intact, with the same look she'd had before leaving with Asher fifteen years before, only calmer, more determined and without the edge of hysteria. It was as though Ginny had grown into herself, become mature, and made a decision that she knew, although she was sorry, was the right one.

Tamar was sure that during those precious, terrible moments in Inner Beauty's exit-way she had seen a glimpse of her daughter at her best, what she could have been if Tamar hadn't allowed her own parents to disappear, hadn't permitted the past to follow her across the ocean to paralyze her and leave her mute at all the most important moments. And when Ginny closed her eyes again, she looked more asleep than deathlike. Tamar felt a sharp stab of recognition. Fear. She was sure something had changed, that Ginny would awake to make accusations at last — to demand explanations. Tamar imagined herself explaining. *Sometimes, my love, a person is so sorry, it seems insulting to apologize. As though an apology, as though words, could begin to make up for the harm one has done. As though one has the right to ask for forgiveness.* With fear but also with relief, she anticipated admitting how many times she had rehearsed this conversation in her head — more times than Ginny would probably care to know.

"There are some things I've been waiting to tell you," Tamar told her daughter on the last day. "Sit down." She motioned toward the desk chair, but Ginny didn't move. "It's about your father. Aga was here yesterday, and I was telling her . . . about your father. The day he died . . ."

"Tamar. I'm sorry." Ginny glanced toward the door.

"I've been waiting to talk with you, though. It's about time we talked about it, don't you think so? There was an old letter. A very old letter. I found it in your hand."

Ginny touched Tamar's arm, her pained, pitying expression unable to disguise the joyful conviction that she was already on a plane, already gone. "Goodbye," she said.

"Virginia," Tamar said. "This is absurd. This is unbelievable."

"Please. You don't understand. It's good. Everything is fine." Ginny had her hand on the doorknob.

Tamar stood beside her desk, stood stock still. If she were more like Robert or Asher, she would long ago have thrown herself at the girl's feet to hold the fabric of Ginny's skirt in both fists and beg her for another chance. Sometimes the only reasonable course of action, Tamar saw, too late, is to howl and cling, to cry love and promise to change. When she heard the sirens outside, Tamar had held her daughter's limp hand tightly and told her that everything would be all right. Oh, but she had feared the wrong thing.

J. Virginia Morgan Workshops
    [jvm@willingamnesia.com]
To: jazwinter@furymail.ca;
    vlinderkind@eternalpresent.org

Thank you for registering for my Willing Amnesia™ workshop! Don't forget to stop at the door and pick up your registration package, which includes your copy of my latest book, Accidents.

"Willing amnesia" is the revolutionary life-practice I developed nine years ago after a head injury that left me with an enlightening episode of temporary memory loss. During the three hours we spend together, I will show you how willing amnesia changed my life and can change yours, too. Since I developed these techniques to take control of my life, my career has soared with three best-selling books; I have improved my self-image; and I never waste a moment. I want to share my discoveries so you, too, can harness your freedom and shape your future! Together, we will practise exercises to help you centre yourself in the present. Unlike psychotherapy, my methods are straightforward and don't involve years of talking about painful memories. And unlike a lot of the many self-help approaches available today, mine takes a holistic approach: whatever the problem areas in your life happen to be, my methods can — and will — help.

You will need to bring one object with you, so please carefully choose an item in advance. Go through your desk drawers and the back of that shelf at the top of your closet to excavate a "buried burden." Go through your drawers and find an object that's been in there for at least a year. Hold the object for one minute and then write down three words describing how it makes you feel. If those words are negative, if you want to shove the object quickly back down under your sweaters, then what you hold is a buried burden. If you cannot bring yourself to dispose of this item, but would never put it out on your coffee table for all to see, then you've found what we're looking for.

Together we will forget our troubles and forge ahead into a future where anything is possible — as long as you're willing!

J. Virginia Morgan

Six

Jasmine showered quickly under cold water, soaking her bathing suit, and passed several nude women before walking around the tiled corner. Everything about it was good: the smell that she felt in her sinuses and her eyes; the rough concrete under her feet after she abandoned her flip-flops by the wall to hurry, shivering, to the edge of the slow lane; even the bad radio music echoing against the water and up to the high, high ceiling. The room's colour scheme was brown, beige and yellow, maybe intended to remind you of the beach. Several people were circle-swimming just fast enough to stay afloat, and Jasmine pulled down her goggles to slip in for a couple of warm-up freestyle laps. One middle-aged lady jerked along with her legs way down in the water, resting her torso on a kickboard. Justin, Jasmine's old swimming coach, used to joke that those boards had two purposes — to improve kicking and to fool people into thinking they were actually swimming.

Besides the chlorine and the radio music and the occasional sound of a lifeguard's whistle, every pool was different. The height of the ceiling, the acoustics, the colour of the tiles and the walls. Jasmine usually swam at a public pool, and this one seemed even bigger than the one at Dad's university, though both were Olympic-size. The ceiling here was higher, and there was a second, smaller pool off to the side for old people and babies who didn't know how to swim. An aerobics class was flailing around in there. High over-head, in the wall above the balcony, was the long window of a room at street level where people could watch from the comfort of sofas. Agatha was up there, surveying the scene from behind glass so the chlorine wouldn't sting her eyes and frizz her hair. She was trying to be in charge again, as if the night before had never happened. As if she hadn't gotten Jasmine stoned, had never suggested they ride around on the subway, eating Thai food out of cardboard boxes and whispering about the other people on board, laughing until they cried.

It would have made sense to go swimming the day before while Agatha was working; the pool was only a few blocks from the bookstore, but Agatha didn't want to leave Jasmine alone even for a second. Jasmine had brought her swimming gear just in case and mentioned the pool again as her sister unlocked Eternal Present. "That's okay," Agatha said. The doorway was full of beads on strings that you had to push aside to get in. "We'll go together, tomorrow." As if Jasmine couldn't be trusted alone; as if she hadn't been going to the pool by herself after school since she was twelve. As if she hadn't taken the bus all the way to Toronto with no help from anyone, and taken the bus to Aylmer before that. What Agatha didn't know was that Jasmine had been drunk on peach schnapps a week earlier in Benna's house, dancing to hilarious disco music, making Benna laugh until she cried, no parents to be seen. But Jasmine knew she had to be a good guest — she didn't want Agatha calling Dad and ruining everything. So she put on her clothes and ate the cereal her sister put on the table, even though she never ate cereal because she hated how it was always soggy by the time you got to the bottom of the bowl. The apartment looked different in the daylight. Worse. It was just a big room with a lot of stuff thrown into it. The walls were too white, and the corners too blunt, and the ceiling was cardboard, with a big, brown water stain. While Jasmine did her eyeliner and finished drying her hair, Agatha stood at the door with her jacket on, repeating a million times that Jasmine was making her late.

Practising her bilateral breathing, Jasmine waited for all the events of the last thirty-six hours to fit together; she waited for a clear picture of what she was going to do next. Everything was all planned out, except the three words. Three perfect words. In the middle lane, she pushed off hard, streamlining her body, arms straight, hands clasped above her head. When both her ears were underwater, the sound was like the inside of a seashell. She counted more than two seconds before breakout and then slowly built speed, like Justin had taught her, and was surprised that her body felt normal, not even achy, and definitely not sick like after she drank the peach schnapps. Drugs were supposed to be so bad, but she felt completely fine, and no more addicted than before. When she rolled over for a length of backstroke, Jasmine tried to spot Agatha up above, but her goggles blurred everything. *Blurry* was a good word for how J. Virginia Morgan made Jasmine feel. As if she couldn't get a clear idea of anything.

Jasmine had spent most of the previous morning sitting in a big beanbag chair, flipping through magazines about tattoos and crystals and watching Agatha say hi to Eternal Present customers as they came through the beads, which wasn't very often. A couple of times, people asked Agatha to open the jewellery case, and one woman bought a T-shirt with a picture of a frog on it. Jasmine liked the chunky stainless steel rings and wished she had some extra money, but she couldn't spend anything because she only had just enough for a bus ticket back home, or to somewhere else. So as soon as she bought something, that was it. She was in Toronto for life, or until she figured out how to get more money.

Agatha's life was a lot different than Jasmine used to think. As they'd left the apartment and walked to the corner, Jasmine had looked up at her sister's windows. The building didn't even look like a place where someone would live. It was square and brick, with big, flat windows, and the rest of the street was stores instead of houses. She'd pictured Agatha living in one of a long row of brick town-houses, like in movies of London or New York. The kind of place where people sit on the front steps, talking to each other.

When they got off the streetcar, Agatha had explained that they were on College Street and then stopped in a café to buy herself a coffee. Jasmine said she wanted one, too, though she'd never drunk coffee in her life. Filled to the brim with cream and sugar, it was still as bitter as coffee ice cream, which Jasmine hated. But they walked down a street of old brick houses, and Agatha drank her coffee as if she needed it to live, so Jasmine forced down as much as she could.

She kept holding the cup for a couple of hours before dumping the rest in the toilet. The washroom was at the back of a storage space lined with boxes, just like the one at Tam-Tam's old salon. But this room wasn't clean and white-tiled; it had an old, fraying blue carpet and a red velour sofa that would surely release dust clouds if anyone sat on it. Jasmine wandered back past Agatha, behind the cash, over to the window, and returned to her beanbag chair. She sat down with a sigh, and Agatha looked up from her book to shrug sympathetically, as if she was bored, too. Agatha had always been that way. Even when Jasmine was little, when she spent weekends at Tam-Tam's and she and Agatha shared Tam-Tam's dead mother's bed. Agatha would just read and read, and maybe write something down in a notebook, and Jasmine wasn't even allowed to say anything for hours. One time, Jasmine had been so bored, sitting on the afghan-covered bed, colouring and trying to see patterns in the wallpaper, that she'd grabbed a fistful of Agatha's short, bleached-blond hair and bitten her as hard as she could, right on the side of the chin. She remembered Tam-Tam opening the door, horrified at the howl, Agatha leaning into her hand to hide tooth-marks. Tam-Tam held her chest as if she was trying not to have a heart attack. Then Jasmine sat on the counter in the bathroom while Agatha washed the germs out of her skin. At Tam-Tam's house, they weren't allowed to leave drops of water in the sink; they had to wipe it out with a tissue before leaving the room. It was a bit funny, afterwards, to see the marks on Agatha's face and how Tam-Tam pretended not to notice them, probably because she thought Agatha got them from a boy. Even Agatha thought it was funny.

Squirming with boredom in the beanbag chair, Jasmine felt like a six-year-old, her jaw and fists aching to break through the surface of something, to make something happen. "You're just like Tam-Tam," she said. "Working in a store where only women go."

Agatha nodded, without looking up. "I guess that's true," she said.

"Have you talked to Tam-Tam lately?"

"Not that long ago." She hadn't talked to Tam-Tam in weeks, at least. Maybe months. Jasmine knew it, because Tam-Tam was always saying that Agatha never called anymore.

"I just saw her a few days ago," Jasmine said. "She bought me this sweater."

Agatha put her book face-down, so the spine might crack. "It's tighter than you would normally wear," she said. Jasmine crossed her arms. "I mean, it's nice."

"Sure."

"It really is. Tam-Tam has good taste."

"She has a boyfriend, you know."

"No!" Agatha actually looked interested in something Jasmine was saying, for once. "No she doesn't."

"Yes she does! This man who owns a restaurant near her house. His wife used to get her hair cut at the salon before she died. Now he takes Tam-Tam out for dinner all the time."

"They must be friends," Agatha said.

"They go on dates." Jasmine felt like grabbing her sister around her skinny neck and shaking her. Agatha had left Jasmine all alone with their family for years and years and now acted as if she knew more about them than Jasmine did. "His name's Victor. He sleeps *over*." Jasmine had no evidence for these sleepovers, but she was sure it was true. "Oh yeah, and she's thinking about moving, now that she finally sold Cassandra the salon. She's going through all her stuff, getting rid of things. She gave me a bunch of old clothes, like from the sixties. And she's been sending boxes of junk to the Sally Ann."

"Wow. Huh."

"What?" said Jasmine. Agatha shook her head. "What?" said Jasmine again. "What were you thinking when I said that about Tam-Tam moving?" She pulled herself out of the chair, walked over to the jewellery case and tapped her fingers on it, smudging the glass. It drove her crazy how secretive her sister was. Jasmine told Agatha everything, and then Agatha just gazed off into space as if she were thinking a million things but couldn't be bothered to say them out loud.

"It's so frustrating," Jasmine started, and then noticed her sister looking worriedly at the store's back wall, behind Jasmine's back. "What?" Jasmine turned. It only took her a moment to understand. There on the bookshelf at Agatha's work were rows of books full of advice and ways to find your True Self, and right in the middle of the middle shelf were all three of J. Virginia Morgan's books, shiny and new, with the latest one, *Accidents*, placed face out. Below her eyes, Jasmine felt the familiar throb of dismay, the sick, slick ache in her throat. Agatha sat across from these bright red covers every day; she sold J. Virginia Morgan's books to people. She must have read them all, too, every word, the same words Jasmine had read. Jasmine and Agatha could have been talking about those words, all this time.

"Min?" said Agatha. Jasmine held her fingertips against her nostrils, breathed rapidly through her mouth and put her head back just as her sister said, "No!" Somehow, Agatha managed to bolt out from behind the counter, grab Jasmine by both shoulders and turn her away from the books just as she sneezed. Blood splattered the jewellery case. "Jesus!" said Agatha.

Hand over her face, Jasmine felt blood drip down her wrist, and she let out a loud laugh.

"Jasmine," said Agatha. She found a box of tissues behind the counter.

"Agatha," Jasmine imitated her sister's bossy tone. She held a wad of tissues under her nose, tossed it onto the soiled glass case and pulled some clean paper from the box.

"Jasmine," Agatha sighed again.

"What is your problem? It's not like I'm having a nosebleed on *purpose*."

"I didn't say it was on purpose," Agatha said.

"Then why do you keep saying my name like that?"

"Like what?"

Jasmine mimicked the condescending, exasperated tone perfectly and, from the silence that followed, knew she'd hit a nerve. Agatha went into the storage room, and Jasmine hoped a customer would come in and see the blood before it was cleaned up, but no one did, and her sister reappeared with a bucket full of soapy water. "You can clean that up," said Agatha.

"No way." Jasmine shook her head as Agatha went back and sat behind the counter. "I can't clean that up. Why don't you even care that I'm having a nosebleed?"

"You can go to the washroom until your nose stops bleeding, and then you can clean it up."

"There is no fucking way I'm cleaning that up," Jasmine said. "You think you're so grown up. You're being mature right now or something?" Agatha started to say Jasmine's name again and stopped herself. "I can't believe you didn't e-mail me back." When Jasmine raised her voice, it sounded absurdly nasal and made her nose bleed harder. "Those books are right there," she said, lowering her voice and pinching her septum harder. "You knew all about this and you wouldn't tell me anything. Why do you tell me stuff anymore? She's my mother, too." Agatha looked ghostly pale, the way she always did when nervous or upset, her eyes so intense they were scary. "Do you talk to her?" Jasmine said. "Do you know her?"

"No."

"You've never met her? She's never come here?"

"She's never come here. I've never met her, Jasmine."

Jasmine tossed her tissues aside for some clean ones, then went to the storage room and shut herself into the washroom. It took about five minutes for the blood to stop, and then she sat on the toilet to stare at the blue tiles and their filthy grout. It was so weird that Agatha worked in this store. A store that sold J. Virginia Morgan's books. It was so fucked up. Agatha could have warned her that morning, when she forced Jasmine to get out of bed and get ready to come to work with her. Jasmine had woken a few minutes earlier to the sound of Agatha showering, relieved because she realized she'd been dreaming about something other than Benna. Something about a library, about her sister. And it had been a full five or ten minutes before it occurred to her to wonder what Benna was doing. Whether Benna missed her. And what she'd said, which was the worst part, when she got back to school.

"Idiot," Jasmine said out loud, hoping this meant she didn't love Benna anymore.

Someone tapped her toes, so Jasmine finished her length and stopped at the lane's corner to let the faster swimmer, a muscular Asian guy, pass. She touched her nostrils, to check, out of habit. Only once had her nose started bleeding in a pool, when she jumped off the highest diving board to prove to Justin she wasn't scared. Usually she got nosebleeds when she was sitting around thinking about something awful. People seemed to think she made it happen just to be gross. But she didn't. She couldn't help it.

She had waited as long as she could before peering into the store to see that Agatha had already scrubbed the glass and the wall and was discussing the aromatherapy display with a beautiful hippie. The bucket was sitting inside the storage room's door, and Jasmine tipped the dirty water into the toilet, then stowed the bucket under the sink. She sat quietly on the beanbag chair for the rest of Agatha's shift, moving only when her sister went into the back. Then she slipped copies of J. Virginia Morgan's second and third books into her backpack and carefully reassembled the remaining books so no one could tell anything was missing.

It had been only two weeks since the last time, since she'd sneezed blood all over her clean white bed sheets and one of her bedroom walls. She'd missed her Audrey Hepburn poster by inches, and it took Lara a whole hour of scrubbing to clean the wall. Jasmine sat in the bathtub, recovering, waiting for her sheets to be changed.

"Do you realize," Lara said, coming into the room without knocking — luckily, Jasmine had closed the shower curtain — "that my mother is *deathly ill*?" Lara was really a lawyer, but she stayed home half the week because Bev was dying and they wanted to see each other a lot first. It didn't make much sense because Bev just wanted to watch TV all the time anyway, and she always made Lara upset. The really funny thing about it was that Lara's mother didn't even seem that sick. Besides being skinnier than before, which was an improvement, she seemed fine. It was like one of those illnesses in the movies, when you're supposed to live it up because one day soon, with a brief, fierce pain in the chest, you will drop dead.

"So?" said Jasmine indignantly. Dad always told Jasmine she looked *indignant*, another good word for how she felt about J. Virginia Morgan.

Waiting out the lap, Jasmine thought of how desperate Lara had sounded as she left the room, saying, "Next time you do this, you're cleaning it up yourself." She felt a strange twinge of remorse. Lara had still been mad, after all, about the fire and the resulting round, black scorch mark on the bottom of the tub. Jasmine realized she hated the scorch mark now, too, but only because it would always remind her of Benna. How Benna didn't care where Jasmine was, or why she was gone, or whether she would ever come back. It was weird not to exchange e-mails, not to read about Benna's day. It was so weird to go through with the plan Benna had helped her rehearse, knowing they would never even talk about it.

Benna had been sitting on Jasmine's bed, reading out loud. "Hold the object for one minute and then write down three words describing how it makes you feel."

Jasmine picked up the Teen Star calendar from her desk. "Retarded, retarded, retarded," she said.

"It makes you feel retarded?"

"Okay," said Jasmine, and thought about it for real. J. Virginia Morgan's pamphlet, which Jasmine had ordered from the website, recommended checking the backs of closets and drawers to find the perfect "buried burden." The calendar, which Hilary had given her for Christmas, was in a drawer, under all the socks. Jasmine thought hard. "Pissed off," she said. "Embarrassed. Disappointed." Benna said she was supposed to write them down, so Jasmine wrote her answers in black marker on the back of a crumpled geography assignment and held up the paper for Benna to see.

"Okay," Benna said. "Would you display this object on your mantel, your coffee table or your wall? No? Then you've . . . um . . . ex . . ."

"Excavated."

"Excavated a buried burden. What does that mean, anyways?"

"Excavated? It's like when you dig up dinosaur bones or old pots or something."

"Sure," said Benna, putting the pamphlet on the bed beside her and stretching out her legs. She rested her feet, in their black nylons, on Jasmine's pillow. "What's a burden?"

"It's something that weighs you down. Something you're stuck with, that you don't want." Jasmine liked explaining things, except that Benna always said "Oh," as if she was disappointed and bored with the lameness of the answer.

Whenever Dad was home, Jasmine hurried Benna past him and up to her room, not only because she was afraid he'd tell them some dorky joke, but because she didn't want to hear him describe Benna as *not the sharpest tool in the shed*, which he would surely do if he had a chance to talk with her. Benna might not know a lot of the things Dad thought were important, but she knew how to be cool. She knew how to dye her own hair the lightest colour of blond you could get, and how to wear clothes that were kind of punk, kind of skanky. She knew how to talk to guys, and Jasmine had noticed before they became friends that Benna wore shoes without socks in winter and her ankles didn't show any signs of being cold. Dad was so far from knowing how to be cool that he didn't even recognize it when he saw it.

"You should have something, too," Jasmine said, sitting on the bed beside Benna, Teen Star calendar in hand.

"But we're not at my place."

"Your bag's full of junk." Benna crawled past Jasmine to retrieve her backpack from the end of the bed. She unzipped it and dumped the contents, lint and dirt tumbling out right onto Jasmine's comforter. Benna looked blankly at the pile of books, paper and old lipsticks. She poked a couple of receipts and other crumpled papers and grimaced at a balled-up pair of nylons.

"Oh God," she said finally, holding a scrap of binder paper between her fingers.

"What's that?"

"Some phone number. The guy from the Ex. Remember, I told you? In the summer? The Ferris wheel guy?"

"Right," Jasmine said quickly, not wanting to hear the whole story again.

"As if he really believed I was sixteen," said Benna.

"Okay." Jasmine handed Benna a pen. "Write your three words on the back." Benna sat, thinking, and Jasmine waited, looking at her friend's black nail polish, which never seemed to chip. Jasmine imagined the high school guy from the summer kissing Benna up at the top of the Ferris wheel and maybe putting Benna's fingers in his mouth, one by one.

Benna handed Jasmine the scrap of paper, where she'd written, *Fuck! You! Asshole!*

"Now," Jasmine told Benna, "we set them on fire."

"Seriously?"

"Yeah. In the wastebasket. Let's do it in the bathroom." Jasmine emptied her metal wastebasket, put the calendar and her three words in it and held it out for Benna.

With the trash can and its contents set up in the middle of the tub, Jasmine had a moment of doubt. She'd read and reread the article that described one of Virginia's workshops, and now she read the important passage to Benna: *She sprays a generous amount of lighter fluid into the metal container and smiles at her audience. "You should probably do this outside," she cautions. "I can't be held responsible for burnt-down houses." The ten women and one man laugh, eyeing the bin warily. "You want to run up here and save these relics, don't you?" says Virginia, grinning. More nervous laughter. Virginia lights a match. "Bombs away," she says. The flames spread fast, then burn high and blue, the metal can and its contents looking like a giant flaming sambuca. "Forget it!" she exclaims, and her audience joins in tentatively. "Forget it!" she yells, and everyone yells along with her.*

Jasmine stared down at the printout in her hand and then looked at Benna. She didn't have any lighter fluid, but luckily Benna suggested dousing the calendar with Lara's facial toner. Still, the metal bin didn't fill with fire, didn't billow with flames like in the photographs of Virginia's workshops. Jasmine and Benna leaned over to watch the phone number disappear quickly, with a brief burst of real fire, and then waited as a small blue flame crept over the calendar, crumpling it, turning it black. Slowly, the edges crumbled into ash.

"Forget it," Jasmine said. *Forget it* was J. Virginia Morgan's "mantra," according to the magazine article. Benna echoed her, not even trying to sound as if she cared. Jasmine sat down on the edge of the tub to wait, and Benna lowered the lid to sit on the toilet.

Benna got bored first and wandered over to the mirror to put her own bleached hair in a bun and then take it down again. Jasmine checked the slow smouldering in the trash can; there was a faint smell of melting plastic.

"It fucking stinks in here, by the way," Benna said. Her hair was so, so blond, but not dried out at all.

"My sister tried to bleach her hair one time," Jasmine said. "When I was a kid. And ended up shaving it all off." Benna laughed. "Her hair was in the tub the next day. No one cleaned it up. Someone took a shower with it in there, too, so it turned into this wet clump. It was in there for*ever*." Agatha's bald head and the wet mass of multi-toned hair in the bathtub seemed to coincide with long conversations in the living room, Dad, Agatha and Tam-Tam all looking panic-stricken. Agatha took to wearing a tuque in the apartment, pulled down to the tops of her glasses. She even wore it to bed, and Jasmine remembered sleeping with her sister, pushing her hand under the hat and feeling Agatha's head, prickly in one direction and velvety in the other.

Pushing her goggles up to her forehead, Jasmine tried to see her sister again, up in the window. Just a smudge of blond hair and blue jacket. Agatha looked so different now, with her long, blond hair and no glasses. She still dressed cool, though, and looked awesome at the bus terminal in that Halloween dress with the A on it. Readjusting her goggles, Jasmine checked for the fast Asian guy and pushed off, rolled onto her back.

Jasmine had already loved swimming back when her real mother was around, and Agatha used to take her to the pool, which was far enough that they had to take the bus. When she swam, Jasmine would pretend to be a dolphin, far from any land, with miles of open blue water in every direction. A dolphin looks big and lumpy on solid ground but becomes sleek and fast in the middle of the ocean, where it belongs. She had seen tropical fish from inside a submarine when Grandma and Grandpa Winter took her to Barbados, and she loved the brightly coloured creatures around and below her, swimming alone and in schools. All quiet and watchful, purposeful and independent. She still thought of the sea sometimes when she swam, but more often she thought of space. She was training for the day she'd be tethered to a space shuttle, the earth huge and blue. Often she'd imagined unhooking the rope that bound her to the shuttle and pushing herself away. In space, there's no drag, no resistance, so once she pushed off, she'd keep moving forever, and quickly, away from all the people who didn't understand her anyway. She pictured their surprised faces framed by the shuttle's round windows as they watched her float away into the vastness, waving goodbye. All the people who treated her like a kid and got mad at her for things she kept accidentally doing wrong. Like skipping swimming, and then school, and running away.

And now stealing. Stealing not only from a store, but then from her own sister, which was probably considered even worse. Like how murdering a family member is worse than if the victim's just a normal person. According to the laws of every major religion and every country ever, stealing is wrong. It wasn't as if Jasmine didn't know that, or didn't feel bad about it. She didn't think stealing was a fun pastime like Benna did. Even at La Boutique, in the mall, where she knew all the staff, Benna often came out of the changing room with lacy underwear and skimpy dresses under her jeans and the sweatshirt she wore specifically for this purpose. Jasmine would never have done that; once she stole a lipstick from the drugstore to see if she could, but then she felt terrible and put it back the next day, before she opened it. According to J. Virginia Morgan herself, though, sometimes it's the right thing to put aside everyday rules. *For instance*, she told one interviewer, *honesty is certainly the best policy, but it isn't always the best practice.* This was a seriously hard sentence to understand, but after a long phone discussion with Grandpa Winter about the difference between policy and practice, Jasmine was pretty sure she got it. Anyway, the point was, sometimes there's something really important that has to happen, and you have to make it happen, even if it means doing something a bit illegal or weird, like stealing something that you really need or telling a lie to spare someone's feelings. Or leaving your husband and two daughters and never looking back.

Grandpa Winter was also the one who explained to Jasmine what *sophistry* meant. When someone seems really convincing but they're really tricking you by sounding all smart; when you know there's something wrong with what someone's saying, but you can't quite figure out what it is, that's sophistry. Jasmine tried to explain to Benna why she was pretty sure J. Virginia Morgan's writing fell into this category. "It's bullshit, you know?" Jasmine said. "That's basically what I mean. My real mother writes all this bullshit, but she's just an asshole. You know?" But Benna just lay back on her waterbed with her fishnetted legs up the wall and her hair all messy and looked kind of beautiful, kind of brain dead. The really crappy thing was that Mei would have understood everything, but Mei wasn't the one Jasmine wanted.

It still felt bad to have taken Agatha's prized possession, even if it was for her own good. It had only been the previous evening that Jasmine found out about the shoebox. After they took the streetcar home in silence, Agatha had put on a CD and then sat on the sofa with her eyes closed for the longest time. Jasmine sat beside her and watched. Agatha was really mad, Jasmine guessed, about the whole nosebleed thing, and maybe the whole running away thing, which was so unfair. Just as Jasmine was wondering if they were ever going to have dinner and was trying to decide whether to bring it up, Agatha leaned forward to reach under the couch. "Tam-Tam sent me this," she said. "I guess because she's getting rid of old stuff, like you said. She didn't tell me she was moving." Agatha put the shoebox on the cushion between them. Jasmine asked what was inside, and Agatha put her hand on the lid. Tam-Tam had offered Jasmine all those old clothes, but it was still annoying that Agatha got this secret box, obviously with something precious inside.

"It's one of Oma Esther's books. And" — Agatha held it closed with both hands — "something our mother gave Tam-Tam."

Jasmine couldn't believe it. Why did Tam-Tam give this to Agatha, who never even called her? She took a deep breath. "What do you mean? Stuff she didn't burn?"

"Yeah." Agatha must have known what it said in *The Willing Amnesiac*. That their mother had burnt everything. Agatha carefully put the lid aside. The box was full of folded, colourful paper, all different shades of red. "They're origami cranes." Agatha pulled one out and the others followed; they were tied together by a long piece of yarn. Agatha stood and held her arm over her head, to show Jasmine how long it was.

"That's it? They look so old."

"They're as old as I am. Our mother made them when she was pregnant with me. I heard about them a long time ago. I read about them in an old letter I found once, from my biological father to Dad. It's so strange to have them. I can't believe Mama kept them all that time."

It had been a long time since Jasmine heard Agatha talk about her "biological father." That's what she'd always called him, back when she lived with Tam-Tam and was suddenly obsessed with this person's existence and with the fact that she wasn't actually related to Dad or Lara. "How could I live with them?" Agatha said once. "I'd be like a foster child." She told Jasmine, back then, that her biological father had wanted to meet her, but Dad and their mother wouldn't let him. Jasmine hated him, this stupid biological father of Agatha's, out there somewhere, making Agatha special and not totally Jasmine's sister.

Jasmine touched one of the cranes. "Why were they the only thing she didn't burn? Why did she give them to Tam-Tam?"

"I've been wondering about that," Agatha said, sitting with the string looped over her hands. "When our mother made these, she thought they would protect her. Maybe she thought they would protect Tam-Tam, too."

"But Virginia doesn't believe in lucky things, like — superstition."

Agatha shrugged. "I don't know if anyone can really not believe in anything. You know, really not believe that anything is connected. Not even one moment to the next. In Virginia's second book, she says that continuity of the self through time is an illusion. An illusion that catches us, like a trap. Do you know what she means by that?"

"Not really. Do you?"

"I think so. But I don't think anyone could really believe that. Or, you know, that they could break free."

"What book is that?" Jasmine asked, looking in the box. Agatha put the cranes down. "It's one of Oma Esther's cookbooks. The one with the challah recipe, this bread I used to make with her. Look here." Agatha opened the book to a page in the middle, scrawled all over in pencil.

"She had nice handwriting," Jasmine said.

"I know. Look, she wrote my name there, and her sister's. Anke, that was her sister."

"What language is that?"

"I think it's Dutch. I should find out what it says. Maybe I will, sometime."

"Agatha," Jasmine said quickly, before she could change her mind. "Our mother has one of those workshops tomorrow. In Toronto. It says where on her website. Will you take me there?" Agatha stared at Jasmine and shook her head slowly. "Come on," Jasmine urged.

"That's a really terrible idea."

"Please. I have to see her."

"No way."

Jasmine hadn't really expected her to agree. She sat back and watched Agatha put the birds away, put the box under the couch. "I want to get rid of her," Jasmine said. "Don't you even care?"

Agatha stared at Jasmine and shook her head, then stood and went to her bookshelf. She pulled away a cardigan draped over some of the books. "There are all Virginia's books and others like them," she said. "I've read pretty much every self-help book and every memoir by a woman ever written. See these? They were written in the 1700s. And these? The 1800s. I've read *all* of them. Trying to understand. So yeah, I do care, actually."

Agatha sat in the big, upholstered chair by the books, crossed her arms and sighed. A flash of movement in the kitchen caught Jasmine's eye, and she jumped. A mouse stood in the middle of the floor, trembling with readiness to run. Agatha's eyes were closed; she looked so tired. Wondering if she should say anything, Jasmine leaned forward, and the mouse darted under the fridge. Agatha drew up her legs and put her forehead on her knees.

"What are they about?" Jasmine said. "The other women's books?"

"Mostly just the usual things." Agatha didn't open her eyes. "Love. God. Money. Some big solution for all your problems."

Love. On Bev's favourite show, people were always falling in and out of love. Falling in love with one person and then accidentally falling in love with someone else and leaving the first standing alone with a ring box in his hand, eyebrows twitching with humiliation and anger. Even though it kept happening, the square-jawed doctors and police officers were always surprised. Lara hated these shows but sometimes watched them anyway, just to spend time with Bev. Jasmine's real mother used to watch soaps, too; she remembered the almost painful boredom she'd felt when Agatha wasn't home, and instead of playing, her mother sat on the brown corduroy couch watching the television as if it was telling her something important. The concerned, patently grown-up expressions on all the characters' faces during their endless, intense conversations about the incomprehensible intricacies of daily life. It was so boring.

"Why don't you have a boyfriend?" Jasmine said.

"I just don't right now," Agatha said. "I was seeing someone for a few months, but we broke up."

"Did he dump you?"

"No. Well, no." Agatha leaned back, wrapping a green and brown crocheted shawl from the back of the chair around her shoulders. "I broke up with him, actually."

Jasmine recognized the shawl. It used to be at Tam-Tam's house, on Agatha's bed. Esther's old bed. Jasmine crawled over to sit at Agatha's feet and touched the fabric. "Why?"

"I just knew what would happen. He told me I was going to have an interesting life. We were lying on the bed" — she waved her hand toward the bed on the other side of the bookcases that she and Jasmine had been sharing — "and he sort of leaned over me and said, 'You're going to have a really interesting life.'"

Jasmine agreed; that was awful. "So you just dumped him?" She realized she'd started picking little bits of lint off Agatha's sock and pressing them together into a ball. She placed the lint-ball on her sister's knee and set to work on the other sock.

"Yup," Agatha said.

"Did you cry?"

Agatha shrugged. "I cried for about an hour. The next day, I felt better. I guess there's nothing worse than ending up with the wrong person, you know?" Jasmine asked where they met. "On the bus. The bus back from Ottawa in the spring."

"Did you love him?"

Agatha said she didn't, but then said, "Maybe. I could have, if he'd love me back, I guess. Oh, I guess I didn't. He claimed he loved me after about two weeks. But he didn't. Believe me." Agatha stopped and leaned her head to one side, narrowing her eyes like she was trying to see inside Jasmine's brain. "Do you love someone, Min?" Jasmine looked down at her hands and shook her head. "Someone you shouldn't, maybe?" Agatha prompted. "Sometimes it really hurts, I know. Loving the wrong person."

"Have you ever loved the wrong person?"

"I've liked people a lot, and felt like I loved them at the time. And it's always been the wrong person. Jasmine, you can tell me if you want. Is it someone at school? An older guy? Someone really — weird? Your teacher or something?"

"No!" Jasmine abandoned Agatha's sock. "God! Stop staring at me like that." There really were shadows under Agatha's eyes; along with her long blond hair and bright grey eyes, they had always made her look tired and mysterious, like she knew terrible things and was hardly able to stand it.

"Remember when you ran away?" Jasmine said. "Where did you go?"

"Oh God. That was so pathetic, Min." Agatha shook her head and fell silent. She always did that, as if she was thinking the rest of the story but forgetting to say it out loud. But then she went on, "To this guy's house. This grungy little apartment near the 7-Eleven on Beechwood. He looked completely baffled when I showed up at his house. I thought he was my boyfriend, but I guess that was news to him." Jasmine asked what it was like staying there, and Agatha shrugged. "Well, I was only there for two days. There wasn't any toilet paper."

"What did you use?"

"I used my underwear and then threw it in the garbage." She grinned.

"No way."

"Way!"

"Did you do drugs?"

Agatha looked at Jasmine oddly. "Why? Do you do drugs, ever?"

Jasmine shook her head. "I drank schnapps a bunch of times. A lot of it, like half a mickey. I *would* do drugs. I don't care. I want to. I just don't know where to get them." Agatha stood up and told her to wait, then went into the kitchen, Esther's shawl still around her shoulders, and came back with a skinny little cigarette.

"This," she said, "is a joint. If we smoke it together, will you promise not to do any other drugs? Anything other than pot?" Jasmine stared at her. "Well? Just have one or two tokes. Puffs." Jasmine made Agatha promise there was no tobacco in the joint before she smoked it. She hated tobacco, unless it was in Grandpa Winter's pipe. She knew it wasn't logical, but there was something pretty nice about Grandpa Winter's pipe, clenched between his teeth. It wasn't gross like Bev's cigarettes.

"Come sit on the sofa," Agatha said.

When Jasmine stopped coughing, she and Agatha both leaned back and sat in silence for about a million years. The sofa was unbelievably comfortable, like sitting in a huge teddy bear's lap. When Jasmine was little, she'd often fantasized about owning such a teddy bear chair. Wrapped in the crocheted shawl, Agatha looked like a little girl in an old-fashioned painting. She'd always looked as if she belonged in a dark library and seemed out of place playing in the park or riding a bike. Toronto suited her, even though it wasn't what Jasmine had expected. "Everything here grinds along like a dirty machine," Jasmine said, her voice echoing strangely through her head. It was true. The subway and the streetcar, the way everything rattled.

"Our parents used to smoke pot all the time, you know," Agatha said.

"How do you know? Your eyes are all shiny."

"Your eyes are like two big shiny balls." Agatha leaned close and grinned like a crazy person. "Where are you going?"

"To look in the mirror."

"No!" Agatha grabbed Jasmine's legs and wrestled her back onto the sofa, pinning her down. "Don't," Agatha said, her whole weight on Jasmine's back. "It'll freak you out." Jasmine laughed, Agatha's hair tickling the side of her face.

"How do you know?" Jasmine said.

"How do I know what?"

"How do you know, uh, that thing I was asking you about before."

"What?"

Jasmine laughed. "Would you get off me, you freak? Okay, how do you know, how do you know — oh yeah, how do you know our parents used to smoke pot?"

"They *did*?" Agatha sat back and opened her eyes wide. "No *way*." Jasmine put a hand to her forehead and shut her eyes tight, then curled into a fetal position, pressing her hands to her ears. She needed her brain to slow down. Benna said she'd smoked before, but Jasmine realized she didn't believe it anymore. She leaned back into the sofa. Benna probably wouldn't even have an interesting life. Virginia wrote that the opposite of love was indifference. Sud-denly, it no longer mattered. Probably that was what it felt like for Jasmine and Agatha's mother to stop loving her own husband and children. It was too bad Jasmine had confided in Benna about so much, but at least Benna hadn't seemed to understand the details of what Jasmine was saying, or its importance. Benna was stupid. That was the way life worked. You love the wrong person. You love an idiot.

Agatha stood up. "Let's go get Thai food."

As she always did while swimming, Jasmine took the time to ask herself some vital questions. Why had she run away? According to Dad, you don't always know why you did something until a long time later. That's what he said when Jasmine asked him, one time, why he married her real mother. The reasons Jasmine ran away were that she was mad because Bev was always smoking in the house and Dad let her, and also she wanted to find her real mother, who was the most selfish person on the planet. And because Benna took off after Jasmine kissed her, so going back to school would be a nightmare. Benna wouldn't be her friend anymore, and everyone would say Jasmine was a lezzie. Agatha was so lucky to be twenty-four years old and not fourteen, so she didn't have to go to school with Benna and a bunch of other faggots. Also, Jasmine told herself, she ran away because Agatha ran away, and their real mother ran away, and they both went to Toronto. So Jasmine went to Toronto, too. It's not that fucking hard to go to Toronto. Anyone can do that.

Agatha had always been like that, all of a sudden taking charge and making everything fun and crazy. Like when she made Helena microwave that grasshopper, or how she used to convince Jasmine that different places were haunted, like the wooden house in Aylmer and the stairs between Tam-Tam's office and the kitchen downstairs.

"I love riding around on the subway," Agatha had told Jasmine, after they bought food at a little Thai takeout restaurant near her place.

Jasmine loved doing that, too, on buses. This little similarity made her want to hug Agatha and maybe cry, but she pushed the feeling away. The subway was underground a lot, which meant you couldn't see anything out the window. Just darkness and your own reflection. Jasmine waited for the parts when the train went outside. But, Agatha said, it's the other people that are interesting. The kinds of people that ride around in the middle of the night. "Who are they?" Agatha whispered in a way that sent shivers through Jasmine's body. "Where are they going?" She pointed out a couple of girls, one dressed all in black with chains attached to her pants and the other wearing purple pants with a pink shirt. They were holding grocery bags. "I bet those are cousins," Agatha whispered, pointing with a chopstick. "They're both allergic to sunlight, so their parents send them out for groceries at night. But they can't stand each other."

"They're alone in the world except for each other," Jasmine added.

"You never know," said Agatha, "who you might see. Once I ran into an old friend from camp. Or, look, maybe that guy over there is your future husband. There might be someone you're supposed to see, so you have to go places where there are people and wait for the ones that're yours."

"That's crazy." Jasmine swallowed a mouthful of delicious, greasy pad thai. "Why is this so good? This is the best food I ever ate. Why are you laughing like that? What's so funny?" Jasmine laughed herself and almost choked, trying to swallow another bite. "Maybe that guy is your future *murderer*," she whispered, and Agatha giggled in horror.

"Hey there, ladies. Ladies." Jasmine looked around to see a man sitting on the long seat across from them. He wore a red baseball cap and had a large, bloody gauze bandage wrapped around his knee. "Ladies," he said. "You girls all alone?"

"Your knee's bleeding, sir," said Jasmine, and Agatha laughed out loud.

"My sister's right," Agatha said. "You should listen to her. You should go to a doctor, buddy."

"Ohh," he said. "Sisters. But what are two young sisters doing here? Where's your momma?" Agatha leaned around, so Jasmine could see her face but he couldn't. Her cheeks were red from laughing. "Where's your momma," he said again.

"She went crazy," Jasmine said. "She doesn't love us anymore."

Agatha leaned her forehead against Jasmine's shoulder, shaking her head.

"You tell her she should keep an eye on her two young girls. This world's a bad place."

"Okay," said Jasmine. "Thanks for the warning."

"This world's a bad place," the man said again. "You girls want to come with me? You need some help, a place to stay until your momma comes back?"

The subway pulled to a stop, and Agatha grabbed Jasmine's hand. "No thanks," Jasmine said, as Agatha dragged her off the train. "She's not coming back. We're wayward waifs," she yelled over her shoulder. Agatha pulled her, running, down the platform and into another car just before the doors closed.

"These seats are the colour of goulash," Jasmine said, as they sat down again. They were alone. "Like tomato sauce and sour cream mixed together. Our mother used to do that, remember? Oma Esther's goulash?" Agatha nodded slowly as the train gained speed. "Aga," Jasmine said. "Why wouldn't you write back to me? Why didn't you tell me about the books and the articles, that you already knew all this stuff? Why did you keep it a secret?"

"I don't know," Agatha said. Jasmine waited, but Agatha just shook her head. "I'm sorry, I don't know." She looked up as the train stopped. "This is the end of the line." But the train started again, eased into the pitch-black tunnel, and was filled with a low, moaning metallic wail that went on for so long that Jasmine covered her ears. She closed her eyes; the subway car was shaking. Finally, the sound stopped, and the train pulled into the station. The same station, Jasmine saw, but now they were on the other side of the platform and facing the other way. She hadn't felt the train turning around at all, and this fact struck her as horrible — that in the dark she couldn't even detect a hundred-and-eighty-degree turn. Agatha touched Jasmine's cheek with the tips of her fingers.

Jasmine lay awake for a long time after they got home. She used to sleep with Agatha all the time, first after their mother's accident and then at Tam-Tam's house. No matter how different Agatha looked, she was still the same, so skinny and warm. She smelled mildly like a combination of spaghetti sauce and flowers, and, Jasmine noticed, staring up close, the expression on her face said she would punch anyone who woke her up. She slept so soundly that it was pretty much impossible to wake her anyway. One morning, in Esther's old bed, Jasmine had sat on her sister's chest and pulled her eyes open by the lashes. In a split second, Agatha grabbed Jasmine under the arms to toss her aside with superhuman strength. And then she put her arm around Jasmine and just kept sleeping.

Everyone thought Jasmine didn't remember anything. But she did. She remembered the sprinklers in the tremble park, and Mama in her green bikini, sneezing all the way home. And lots of other things, too. She remembered sitting beside her mother in the back seat of the car, and the hospital where they kept taking her back to show the doctor that she wasn't fixed yet. And she remembered Inner Beauty's stairs, how she was thinking about the glory of a fireman's life and the injustice of not being allowed to watch Agatha get her hair dyed. Jasmine hadn't known back then that she wanted to be an astronaut; she thought she was going to be a fireman, ever since she went on a field trip with her kindergarten class to the fire station to see the men sliding down poles from the ceiling, dressing in their shiny outfits, and turning on all the trucks' sirens and lights in preparation to save the day.

She'd been pushing her fire truck up the paisley walls and along the orange banister, but then she remembered she had to stay alone until she calmed down. Leaning against the wall, she counted to twenty in her head and kept going to thirty. She let her body go so limp her mouth even hung open; that's how calm she was. But then Jasmine noticed one of her feet wiggling in its shiny red fireman's boot, as if it had a life of its own, and she thought maybe she hadn't calmed down after all. The fire truck had definitely been in her hand before she tried to be calm, which was probably when she put it down, and then the door at the bottom of the stairs opened, and beautiful Marcy, with her perfect lips and nails, came in with a cup in her hand. And some time later, Jasmine was sitting in Marcy's aesthetics chair, having red sparkles dabbed around her eyes.

Firemen didn't usually wear sparkles, but Marcy was right when she said there was no reason Jasmine shouldn't be the first.

She didn't even notice her fire truck was missing until she and Agatha had already hugged Tam-Tam goodbye and were standing at the top of the stairs, ready to go home. They were holding hands; Jasmine was trying not to look at her sister's face with its new red lips and scary eyelashes. Agatha's hair made her look too different, but her hand felt the same, and Jasmine held it tightly. Their mother walked down the stairs ahead of them, and that's when Jasmine saw the truck, sitting on a stair almost halfway down, not far from the wall. She just didn't want to have done something wrong again; she thought her mother would walk past it without noticing. She was always doing something wrong, always being sent somewhere to calm down, and though she wanted to be good, like Agatha, she couldn't sit still and quiet for hours with a book in her hand. Within minutes, Jasmine always thought of a new idea, and soon she'd have accidentally done something bad again, like drawn a map of her veins all over her body in permanent marker or wrapped each of Dad's ties in toilet paper so she could give them to him as gifts. It was an accident — but then Mama looked back to talk to Agatha. She wasn't watching where she stepped; her foot, in its dainty lady-shoe, was on the truck's roof, and Jasmine knew instantly that not only had she done something wrong, she had ruined everything, done the very worst thing.

Mama must have been really mad at Jasmine about the fire truck on the stairs because, a year after her accident, she told everyone else she was leaving, and then she was gone. It was Jasmine's fire truck on the stairs — that's why all Virginia's books were red and why she never told Jasmine goodbye; that's why she kept the red paper birds, as a secret message; that's why she was spiteful and cruel, and why it had to stop.

Jasmine looked up at the clock; it was almost time. Agatha was still up in the window; Jasmine couldn't see her clearly but knew she was there. It felt amazing to have a real plan, already set in motion. That whole thing with the pimps had been so stupid; she'd realized it even on the bus, before she entered the Toronto terminal. The terminal itself was plain and solid as a school cafeteria. She'd always known there were creatures that weren't quite solid, that exist past the tips of fingers, like celebrities, promising something beyond the mundane. But now she knew that when you see them for real, like that pimp in the mall or the God in Aunt Hilary's church, they fail to measure up. They become nothing. And J. Virginia Morgan was finally going to materialize, too. Hopefully Agatha would figure it out and show up in time to see Jasmine squash Virginia into the shit-stain she really was. Jasmine was doing it for Agatha as well, and for Tam-Tam, who was getting rid of all the stuff she didn't need anymore.

For Virginia's readers, the American magazine said, *this is a familiar story: the oppressive closeness of her household compelled her to move in with a boyfriend when she was very young; and her first daughter was born nine months later, but not before the boyfriend left the country, never to be seen again. Three years later, she married, and eventually her second daughter was born. During those years, the future guru taught piano lessons, read in her free time and, as Virginia writes in* The Willing Amnesiac, *"existed rather than lived, in a monotonous routine remarkable only for its lack of any distinguishing features."*

There was no one else in Jasmine's lane, so she swam to the middle of the pool and then sank into the water to pull down the bottom of her bathing suit. With her hands on her knees, Jasmine rolled forward and pushed her bare ass into the air. It was her patented synchronized swimming move, which she'd done at least once in every pool she'd ever swum in. It was all a trick; it was all bullshit, and Jasmine wanted to moon the world.

"What a lot of people really crave," Virginia says, "is to observe and contemplate suffering — like a child torturing an insect. Like a public execution. If people were really concerned about the Jewish Holocaust, they would be out in the world trying to stop the genocides that are happening today. Not rehashing the past. But anyway, I'm not interested in politics and history. That's really not my thing. I'm interested in people."

She finishes her cigarette in silence and says, "Why do people find the past so much more interesting than the present? The past is nothing. It's gone. Why do you think you need to know about my family to know something about me? I'll tell you something. These questions you're asking won't tell you a thing about my work, because I have nothing to do with all that crap. Let's talk about something else. Ask me something else."

In her latest book, the ironically titled Accidents, Virginia insists that most so-called accidents happen for a reason. "I think that when we feel cornered, we look for ways out. That's part of what I'm talking about in my book. We do whatever we can to make a change. Death is just the ultimate change." She nods seriously. "People who attempt suicide don't really want to die. They just don't know how else to change their lives."

"And your own accident?" I venture. "Your head injury?"

"Yes, well, I do think that happened because it was the only way I could change my life. But I don't remember the accident itself."

"You can't remember that day at all?" I ask, having read as much in her first book.
"That's right."

"Interview with the Amnesiac: J. Virginia Morgan Would Rather Not Remember," American Dreams Magazine

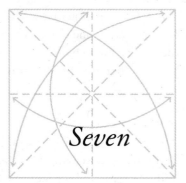

Seven

J. Virginia Morgan writes that everything can change in a single moment — a breaking point. All she remembers of the day her life changed, the day she ripped herself free, is every possible shade of red filling her eyes and nose. That's why the cover of her first book is cherry red, the cover of her second magenta, and the third a dark rose. On each, J. Virginia Morgan's name is printed in dark burgundy.

I was seventeen and still living with Tam-Tam when her first book came out. At the public library downtown, where I often went to do my homework, Mama's adopted name glared in red from a shelf of new Canadian books. At first I thought it must have been a coincidence, someone else, but when I saw the author photo, I was seized with dizziness, and the stabbing pain I'd come to recognize as panic, rather than a heart attack, gripped my chest. I sat in a soft, upholstered chair near the window and waited for the spots to clear from my eyes, and then I looked at Virginia's photo again. She was still almost as thin as when she left, her hair had grown long and sleek, and now her nose was different, too, small and straight. I opened *The Willing Amnesiac* to the first page and read the first line: *I woke into a white room full of cut flowers, and my whole life slipped away like some epic, complex dream that leaves a formless uneasiness in the wake of its details.* Virginia. I thought she'd left and was gone forever, but here she was, for anyone to find. I read the whole book, finishing it half an hour before the library closed for the night. Every word and every letter branded itself onto my brain.

It just takes one moment out of the ordinary, Virginia wrote, and then everything changes. One moment is the border between then and now, her and me, prehistory and real life.

"This is why she ran away," said Steven. He was standing beside my computer desk, reading the e-mail I'd found when I got home from losing Jasmine and sneaking glances around my home. Piles of books at his feet. "This is my fault, Agatha," he told me. "Not yours."

"No kidding."

"Well," he said, ignoring my regression to adolescence after five minutes in his company, "let's go to the" — he checked the printout — "Mylette Hotel. It's in Yorkville? How far is that?"

"It's far," I told him. "And it's rush hour."

Steven looked back at my building as we crossed the street, but he didn't say anything. I had never seen the car he was driving; it was shiny and new, a red sedan.

"After Jasmine left," said Steven, heading down Dundas Street, "I saw that she'd been reading about your mother online."

"J. Virginia Morgan," I corrected him. He looked at me. "She was reading about J. Virginia Morgan."

"Yes," he said. "Of course, yes. I see what you mean. I didn't know that you girls knew about those books."

"Of course we do, Steven." I didn't want to look at his face, didn't want him looking at me either. Already he had bruised my sanctuary by seeing my home, my apartment and my street. My city. He had his own life, a new lease. Jasmine had once told me that Steven and Lara jogged together and went to the gym and that they cooked with only organic food. "We didn't know if *you* knew about those books," I told him. "You could have said something."

He didn't answer, just eased through a green light in silence. As we approached the point where the road forked, I told him to take College Street, but he stayed on Dundas and drove two blocks. Then he said, "Agatha, I'm going to ask you to come back to Ottawa with me and Jasmine. Lara's mother has taken a turn for the worse."

"I have a job," I said. "I can't just leave."

"You work in a store." I leaned back in the seat and closed my eyes. I could feel the tension building in the back of my neck and my shoulders. "Are you working on applications for grad schools yet?"

"A few, yes. That wouldn't be for almost a year."

"Where are you applying?"

"Here and in the States. Why did you take Dundas? The traffic will be even worse closer to downtown. College is always better."

"Please think about it," said Steven. "Lara really needs her family right now."

It was an old, familiar argument, and I didn't need to speak for Steven to know what I was thinking. That I wasn't Lara's family, was only her stepdaughter because Steven had adopted me at the last second. Once when I first moved to Toronto for school I had introduced him to my roommates as my former stepfather. He hadn't visited me since. That was around the time I'd written to Asher Acker; according to my online search, he was practising psycho-analysis in Sacramento, California, and I found his office address. I described Mama's accident and everything that had followed; I told him that I'd read the letter he wrote to Steven, that he'd been right when he predicted his bond with Mama and me would come back to haunt us. But he never wrote back.

"Look at this." The street was getting more congested by the second.

"All right," Steven told me. "I'm upset, too, Agatha."

Jasmine was already in a room with J. Virginia Morgan; it was an uncanny thought, and my stomach clenched so painfully I had to open the window to get some air. It had never occurred to me to imagine or hope that Virginia would stop, to wish that loose thread unravelling from my family snipped and tied, its destructive path cut short. Her existence and the never-ending publication of her red books were my due, a reminder of what I'd done and even a reminder of how the world works, how it rebukes and conspires and torments us with cruel justice. For nine years, I'd tried to enumerate all that led up to the accident and all that followed, and each time I was less sure at what point things began to go wrong. Sometimes I'd find it, the answer — when I should have said something different, made a different choice; but then the precise clarity of remorse would slip away again, leaving me feeling, with a relieved hiatus from my burden of responsibility, that I couldn't have saved her, that it would have happened anyway.

But when Jasmine wished our mother dead, she said it with such vehemence, such determination. She stared at those books on the Eternal Present bookshelf and took bloody aim, and I leapt to protect them, as though she were poised to desecrate something holy. And as I watched her from above, slicing through the University of Toronto pool, I saw how the momentum of her convictions carried her. I would never have dared, at her age, to take the bus to a city I didn't know, alone. Jasmine looked so sleek and childlike from above, a tiny, buoyant creature carving a fearless, if reckless, path. There was nothing above or below for her to hold on to, nothing at either side. She was so different from me. How had I let go of her small hand so easily, turned and fled, barely thinking of her life without me?

I'd phoned Dad as I watched her and tried to persuade him to turn back. He said it was impossible. "She'd have to go to school," he said, as Jasmine backstroked. Although I was high above her, seated comfortably on a sofa, I was sure she was looking straight at me and my cell phone, suspicious and sad, knowing I was turning her in. "Think this through," he told me. "You'd have to cook for her. You're twenty-four years old."

"Maybe she could just stay for a while."

"I'm almost there," he said. "I'll see you in less than two hours, and we'll all talk."

"She'll hate me," I sighed. "More than she does already."

Steven turned off his cell phone after I called him from the pool, so when I realized Jasmine was missing, I had no way to reach him. I took the subway and streetcar all the way back to my apartment, where we'd planned to meet — where he was planning to ambush Jasmine and take her back home. And as he drove me down Dundas,

I knew he was right. I'd felt so competent and caring, watching her from above. I had already bought her a V8, just like I used to, for when she came out of the locker room clean and hungry. But she hadn't come to Toronto to live with me in a one-room apartment while I worked at Eternal Present and she started high school. She hadn't come for me at all; it was all about J. Virginia Morgan and her workshop, all about the one person who didn't care about her. It wouldn't have worked anyway. I couldn't make her get up in the mornings, punish her for skipping school and worry about what she chose to wear. I couldn't be the one to go to her parent-teacher interviews to discuss her problems, which promised to be many.

I looked at Steven carefully. His hair was slightly shaggy, and he was clean-shaven. I wondered why he'd kept his beard for so long; he had a strong jawline, a handsome face. He was only in his late forties, and I thought, not for the first time, of how his marriage to Mama must have seemed in retrospect. A youthful mess, a foolish misunderstanding. Now, with Lara, he was living his real life.

We shared the house in Aylmer for almost twelve years, Dad, Mama and I, and finally Jasmine, too, and during that time, our person-alities burrowed into all the small places no vacuum cleaner can reach. We trampled our birthday parties into the carpets and painted over our arguments, fusing them to the walls. And maybe it was when we moved downtown that we began to snip whatever ties held us together. Time shifts the contents of a house like the earth; what was topsoil when we moved in transformed slowly into the mulchy bottom layer of long unopened desk drawers, the far-back of closet shelves too high for even Dad to reach without standing on a chair. We turned up our comfortable mess all the way to its murky under-side. We cleaned out the whole place — emptied every cranny, excavated forgotten scraps of paper, gathering shoeboxes from their shadowy hiding places and exposing their contents to the light of day. Mama, Dad and I filled the hallways of our house with garbage bags. Even Minnie organized her drawings, put her crayons and coloured pencils away, sharpening each one before placing it carefully in its box. I examined and discarded outmoded clothes, old birthday cards, the sweater I'd planned to make in the sixth-grade "knitterbockers" club that had never progressed past a cuff hanging from a needle. I filled garbage bags with gifts from clueless relatives.

For all the garbage bags I filled haphazardly, I also packed two boxes with neatly stacked relics. Mama, I discovered much later, packed boxes of journals, photographs and old clothes, a collection of my childhood drawings, a string of red origami cranes. She put these boxes in the guest room closet at our new apartment, closed the door and didn't open it until after her accident. J. Virginia Morgan warns against clutter of any kind. Never shove something out of sight. Instead, get rid of it. If you want something out of mind, she writes, its continued and hidden existence can only do you harm. She writes that, in her house, she never places an object on top of another in such a way that one is hidden. All her cupboards are made of glass. *If you have anything to hide, dig it up. Not to polish it and admire it and show it off, but to get rid of it once and for all.*

Dad didn't have a big office in the new downtown apartment, so he took a carload of boxes to his office at the university. A year later, they were still unpacked in a corner, and one early October weekend when I was fifteen, he offered me a hundred dollars to organize his office. I had nothing to do, because Helena was away with the volleyball team, so I agreed. All day, while he was in the lab, I shelved books, organizing by subject before alphabetizing. Dad's office had floor-to-ceiling shelves on every wall. I wondered how it could be that I was more like Dad than Mama and resolved for the thousandth time that I would never get married or have children; I would never sit around chopping vegetables and doing laundry when I could be sitting in an office, surrounded by books, writing and publishing great insights.

Other than his books and neatly Duo-Tanged articles, Dad had packed one large shoebox, secured with a flimsy piece of tape. I came across it in the late morning, on top of a journal about narcolepsy. I could see from the logo that the box had once contained winter boots. I pulled up the lid and peered inside. And there it was, right on top. A thick, dilapidated envelope with Dad's name in the middle and another man's initials in the top left-hand corner: A.A. A.A's handwriting was heavy, in black ink on off-white paper. I closed the box and held it shut, then opened it again. Took out the envelope and held it in both hands. Pressing it to my face, I smelled only old paper that had been kept for years in a small space. I opened the envelope and looked inside, unfolded the old, plain beige stationery. I read and reread the signature.

A letter from my biological father to Dad. If only I'd had the self-help wisdom at my disposal, the foresight to do what Dad should have done twelve years earlier — to light a match and put an end to it. But I had to know. I wanted to see his handwriting, feel the way he formed sentences, to find something familiar that had made its way into my own blood. I put the letter in my bag and tucked the resealed box behind a row of books on one of Dad's shelves, where such boxes always go. I read the letter twice while eating eggplant curry in a café down the street. I was strangely calm when Dad drove me home that night, still calm at school on Monday. I reread the letter in the library at lunchtime, on the bus ride home, just as, long ago, Asher Acker read and reread Mama's covert postcard. And though I was calm, a virus had entered my bloodstream. I could feel it circulating, spreading, the symptoms beginning almost imperceptibly, like an itch in the back of my throat. I watched Mama standing in the apartment's stark white kitchen, yellow apron around her wide waist. All the appliances were shiny and science-fiction inspired, no wood anywhere; Mama was lumpy and larva-like, out of her element. Ballooning inside me, I felt a heady recklessness, a growing, giddy disregard for any consequences. I thought of the little girl who could set fire to things with her eyes, and I stared at my mama, waiting for the flames.

I had left my family for six years, and everything had changed while I was gone. Even Tam-Tam had stopped managing Inner Beauty, and now she was moving. Selling the salon, Jasmine said.

"Jasmine says Tam-Tam has a boyfriend."

"Oh," Dad said. "Victor? He's not her boyfriend, exactly."

"*What*? How do you know?"

"I phone Tamar once a month at least, to see how she's doing." He glanced over at me. "I always thought highly of her; I still do."

"Of Tam-Tam? I thought you never even liked her." I'd been sure he and Tam-Tam never spoke again after the day Mama left.

Steven kept his eyes on the road. "I always liked her. You know, my parents were always so normal; when I met Tamar, it was like seeing a whole different way of doing things. I liked it. I still do. She's an incredibly strong woman." I tried to recall a single instance during my childhood when Steven and Tam-Tam had seemed to connect. "She'd love to hear from you, Aga. I'm sure she'd be thrilled to tell you about the salon and Victor and everything else."

"Who *is* Victor?" We were passing Bathurst already, and my hands were starting to shake. It occurred to me that I could jump out of the car and run. I could change my identity and move to a different city; no one would ever find me. I didn't really have any friends who'd notice I was gone.

"Victor," Dad said. "It's a remarkable story, actually. He owns a restaurant in the Byward Market and his late wife used to have her hair done at the salon." Jasmine had already told me that much. "It turns out that he's from Amsterdam, the same neighbourhood as Tam-Tam. He came to Ottawa about ten years after her and Oma Esther. His family was friends with the people who hid Tamar during the war." I stared at him, and Steven nodded. "The parents have both died, but Tamar spoke with the daughter. Femke something — a different surname from the one Tamar remembered; she'd been married twice. They were living in Montreal all this time."

"No way," I said. "That's incredible. I mean, I remember Tam-Tam talking about her. That's just incredible. Did she tell you anything about it? What was it like talking to her?"

"It is incredible, you're right. She said they had a long talk. And she and Victor have become quite close friends. They spend a lot of time together. Dinner, plays. Your grandmother spent a lot of time alone, for a long time."

"But all her friends from the salon?"

"Those were clients and employees. They tend to come and go."

Suddenly, beside Dad in the car, I was desperate to see Tam-Tam, to see the salon again, at least once, before it was gone. Inner Beauty had always been a part of my life. In my earliest memories, I spun in the royal blue vinyl and chrome chairs, examined my head from every angle in the mirrors and leafed through the sample binders, colours and colours of dyes, polishes and shadows.

The Saturday two weeks after I found Asher Acker's letter, I wore my bright yellow rain slicker, prepared for the forecasted rain. It was Halloween. Since we'd moved downtown, it was only a ten-minute drive to Inner Beauty, and there was no longer any excuse to get out of occasional visits. As far as I was concerned, I'd grown up far past cute, but Tam-Tam's ladies still pressed their red lips onto my cheeks, then rubbed at the marks they'd left, long red nails leaving half-moon indentations in my skin. The morning was staticky and grey, thunder rumbling a long way off. I watched the dark clouds through the living room window of our eleventh-floor apartment and laced my newly bought army boots. I'd wanted them for months, but until a few days earlier, Helena had me convinced they would look stupid. They were polished black and steel-toed, indestructible enough to carry me fearlessly into my new, Helena-less life. Minnie had new boots, too, red rubber, with a matching rain hat. Four years old, she was chubby and wide-eyed, and everything made her laugh. The TV, the tone of jokes she couldn't possibly have understood. She laughed loudly with her mouth wide open, fell off chairs to roll around on the floor. Her round cheeks got the worst of it at Tam-Tam's, her effortless charm mercifully diverting attention away from me.

We took the elevator down to the lobby of our building, and Minnie was a fireman in her gumboots. For her Halloween costume, she'd have a plastic hose as well. "Firefighter," Mama tried to correct her. "You don't need a penis to fight a fire." But when she went to the rescue, Minnie was a man. Her name, she insisted, was Fireman Jeff. My mother was wearing a trench coat over her tucked-in grey blouse and a wrinkled black skirt that was too tight at the shin-length hem. She completed the ensemble with a blazer that wasn't the same fabric or quite the same shade of black as the skirt. Mama only put on makeup for Tam-Tam or if she was going to a university function with Dad. The lipstick and eyeliner didn't settle properly onto her face but sat like a slightly skewed superimposition. She went down to the parking lot to get the car, and I waited in the lobby with my sister. Red plastic fire engine in hand, Minnie saved me. We ran out of the building together, me leaning on her shoulder. "There!" she breathed. "You're okay now, lady. Try not to be scared. I'm going back in for the cat." She shaded her eyes against imaginary flames and puffed up with courage, but Mama pulled up and called out to us through the car window.

Languid in the front seat beside my mother, I turned to join my sister in a car song: "When you slide into first and you feel something burst . . ." My voice, I was sure, was lower than usual; there was something slower and softer about me. A constant, sleepy ache through my whole body. I had willed my life into the realm of the extraordinary, into the wiry arms of the pariah of grade ten history class. For the last month, when it was too cold to lie in the grass by the canal, we'd been meeting inside the school. Mr. Meyers always sighed and nodded, waving me away, when I asked to go to the washroom. My grades had been getting progressively worse this year, a drastic change from last year. More than a few minutes away from class would arouse suspicion, but each meeting under the gym-building stairs progressed from the last. Just the day before, Ingo Bachmann had pushed my back against the wall, his thigh between my legs. It was enough to last all weekend, all through Monday, until my next history class on Tuesday. I replayed every touch. The memory of his gangly long fingers pushed Helena's betrayal out of my head, overwhelmed even thoughts of two fathers. Ingo Bachmann and I kissed with mouths grotesquely open, gluttony and lust in one.

We crossed Mackenzie King Bridge along with all the buses. Mama glanced nervously at the hordes of Saturday shoppers entering and leaving the Bay, Minnie crooning, "When you slide into home and your pants are full of foam . . ."

"Please," Mama said, just as I joined my sister in the song's final uproarious cry, "Diarrhea!" Mama hated it when Minnie acted this way, twitching with an energy bigger than her body. Mama and Dad had explained to me that I mustn't get my sister too worked up; that we needed to keep her calm by maintaining an "atmosphere of serenity." I knew how Mama felt, but I didn't care. Minnie squirmed in her seatbelt, rubbing the back of her carefully combed head against vinyl. She'd have the makings of a large dreadlock by the time the car stopped. I grinned at her between the seats, and she pushed her fire truck back and forth on her lap, opened her mouth to start her siren noise, then glanced in Mama's direction and pressed her lips together with a superhuman effort to stay quiet.

"You're fifteen years old," Mama said. "Why do you encourage her?" I faced forward and crossed my arms.

We were all silent until we reached York Street, but just as Mama spotted a parking space, Minnie broke down. "WOOOooo-OOOOooo," she howled.

"Jasmine!" Mama jumped, her hands lifting right off the wheel. "You girls will be the death of me. Now I'm going to lose the space." But she didn't and pulled into it.

I started crossing the street, Minnie clinging to my hand, while Mama put money in the meter. She waited for a car to pass and speed-walked to catch us. "Wait up," she called, but I ignored her and didn't slow down until I reached Inner Beauty's orange door. Free hand on the doorknob, I watched my mother strut toward us in her pointy-toed high heels and unbuttoned trench coat. She was in one of her heavier phases, and her clothes were all too tight. She tucked in her shirts, then pulled them out in a puff at the top of her pants or skirt, presumably to hide the bulge of her stomach. According to Dad, her depression medication caused weight gain.

"Adults don't say *wait up*," I told her. "That's a kid thing to say."

"Jesus Christ Almighty, Agatha."

I opened the door and waited for her to go through, then nudged Minnie ahead so I could go up last. The stairwell's paisley wallpaper reminded me of the kitchen in our old house, Mama standing at the counter chopping at vegetables in that slapdash way of hers. That kitchen had matched her, seemed made for her, even complemented her skin tone. In autumn, the sun set around the time Mama cooked dinner, and we squinted across the long shadows of the fridge and table, walls aching with rust and brown. Minnie sat in the highchair with her back to the window, pumpkin-coloured baby mohawk a fiery slash across her skull, and I sat in a pool of sunlight on the counter, and Mama's wooden spoon stirred garlicky, spicy smells through the room to settle in our clothes and on our skin. Her hair and eyes had looked almost red in the dinner-cooking light, a fierce scarlet shining through from behind the brown.

That day at the salon, Mama was a blight on my existence, some-thing hateable and grotesque that I wanted to squash under my shoe. And just as Ingo Bachmann had been easily seduced, so my mother was proving easily squashed. The world was soft and pliable as rotten wood, yielding with alarmingly little resistance to my quiet, drawn-out tantrum. I watched from behind as Mama climbed the stairs, and I made a gun with my hand, aimed it at the back of her head. *Pow.*

Long before that day, Dad had stopped coming to Inner Beauty with us. He started again briefly when Minnie was first born, but everyone could see he didn't belong. With his beard and sweaters and his bulky height, he was incongruously male. It seemed right that my mother, my sister and I would venture manless into the land of bright blue swivel chairs, omnipresent mirrors, heavy odours of femininity in the making. Where beauty was applied with brushes and trimmed into shape with tiny, sharpened blades. Dustpans and garbage cans filled up over the course of the day with discarded bits, the fluffy no-good ends of smooth, bright coiffures. Old ladies sat in a row, chatting and reading magazines, their white hair in pink rollers; and Tam-Tam held court over the stylists, hair washers, eye-brow pluckers, leg waxers, manicurists, pedicurists and cosmeticians.

She invited them to treat me like a doll, a guinea pig. When business lagged, my cheeks were painted pink, my eyelids shadowed blue, my head covered in braids or curls.

I followed Mama and Minnie into the salon. Tam-Tam was at the reception desk, talking to a girl with short red hair while Cassandra arranged a display behind them. Mama and Tam-Tam kissed each other's faces carefully, to leave makeup intact.

"Isn't she gorgeous," Tam-Tam said, trying to rearrange Minnie's hair while kissing her forehead. In her early sixties, my grandmother looked like a young fifty. She reached out to grab my hand in a bone-crushing squeeze. "You're so tall," she exclaimed, standing close. She said the same thing the week before, and the week before that.

"You're taller."

"Only because of my heels," she stage-whispered.

Minnie ran her fire truck up Tam-Tam's black skirt. My grandmother glanced down at my sister, who was gazing up hopefully. "I'm a fireman," Minnie told her, a little uncertainly. Tam-Tam smiled and touched Minnie's tangled hair again.

Cassandra crouched so she was face to face with my sister and asked how many fires she'd put out. "About fifty million," Minnie told her, and everyone laughed except Mama, who stared past us into the bustling salon and sighed.

Cassandra had been working for Tam-Tam for about two years, and according to Mama, my grandmother liked her air of pretty helplessness, her willingness to accept any overbearing advice sent her way. Tam-Tam watched her playing with Minnie and said, "Cassandra, you need to get your eyebrows waxed. Never mind about refilling the bottles. Go to Marcy and get that taken care of."

Happy to escape Mama and Tam-Tam, I followed Cassandra into Marcy's small room, with Minnie in tow. We sat on stools while Cassandra arranged herself in what looked like a dentist's chair. Marcy was a voluptuous woman in a fake lab coat. Dad looked like a real scientist in his lab coat, but Marcy was a Bond girl. Her lipstick extended beyond her actual lips, encircled by dark, almost purple liner like a bruise. Her breasts pushed against the white coat, and her cleavage showed when she leaned forward. I tried not to look down at my own almost flat chest. I thought of Helena and her newly grown Bond-girl chest. Dad had readily invited Helena on our family car trips and called her "kiddo," but my mother always seemed suspicious, responding guardedly to Helena's posing-for-a-photograph smile. Maybe Mama sensed the mistake I'd made — that I was surprised to have caught and kept Helena's attention, not sure how I'd tricked her into noticing me and wanting my company. Mama had always been annoyed by Helena's faux-exotic prettiness, which got her the part of Snow White in our fourth-grade play, the chief's daughter in our fifth-grade Thanksgiving skit and finally Tiger Lily in the school production of *Peter Pan*. "She's a Disneyfied Indian princess," Mama complained, picking me up from rehearsal. "Why is she wearing war paint while rowing sedately down a stream?" I thought Helena looked beautiful with the feather sticking up at the back of her head. I'd wanted the part of Wendy but was in the chorus of lost boys instead.

Marcy stuck a tongue depressor in the wax and spread some on her own hand. I wondered if she, like Helena, had always had a Bond girl inside her, just waiting to bloom.

"Ready," she said. Fenced in by the chair's high arms, Cassandra looked vulnerable and small, trying to appear nonchalant before her eyebrows' impending fate. Marcy smoothed a piece of waxy fabric under Cassandra's eyebrow and ripped it off.

"So, Agatha," said Cassandra, pressing her finger above one watering eye. "Tamar says I'm supposed to cut your hair today." My hair was finally as long as I wanted it, halfway down my back. "Just those split ends."

I thought the slightly frayed ends were feral and sexy. I told her I needed my hair the way it was for my Halloween costume. I was going to wear a long red velvet dress that I found at the Salvation Army, with red wings I made out of pantyhose and coat hangers. "I even have red shoes," I said.

"What are you?" she asked. "A red angel? A devil?"

"A red bird," I told her.

"A cardinal?" Marcy said. She'd finished with Cassandra's eyebrows and was tidying her workspace.

"I guess," I agreed, not wanting to explain further.

"You should dye your hair red," Marcy said, before Minnie and I followed Cassandra out of the room, "and put black makeup around your eyes. It would be perfect." As soon as she said it, I knew I had to do it. Bright red hair would transform me; when Mama saw my Halloween costume, she'd realize I was inescapably smarter than she was, that she could never outwit me. Everything she'd done, all her conniving and cowardice. She'd see that nothing was hidden from me, even what happened before I was born.

It wasn't long before I found the perfect colour on Cassandra's chart, little bunches of different coloured hair attached to a laminated poster. "Scarlet," I said, pointing.

"That's not a hair colour," my mother argued. She slouched in the chair closest to Cassandra's station. "This is red hair." She pointed to her own head and Minnie's thoroughly tangled locks. "It would be kind of neat if your hair was the same colour as ours."

"No way. It's for my costume. Scarlet."

"You'll look like a freak. God, with those glasses, too." I pushed my heavy black-framed glasses up my nose with one finger and Mama shook her head. She'd begged me to wear an old, more feminine pair today, along with a different pair of shoes. The army boots, too, were part of my costume. An origami bird going into battle.

"Scarlet O'Hara." Mama shrugged. "O'*Hair*a," I almost yelled. "Get it?"

"Yes," my mother said. "Fine. Please lower your voice, Agatha. Your grandmother's customers need their serenity." A woman with foil in her hair and a leathery tan turned to glare.

"O'Hara," Minnie repeated. "O'Hara, O'Hara, O'Hara." She laughed and rolled onto her back at Mama's feet. "Ha!" she bellowed, an imitation of Grandpa Winter's staccato laugh. When no one joined her mirth, she went limp and silent, closed her eyes and pretended to be dead, tongue sticking out at the corner of her mouth.

Cassandra told my mother it was just semi-permanent dye, so the red would wash out within a couple of weeks. "Semi-permanent," my mother repeated. She stopped swivelling to help Minnie climb up into her lap. "Have you wondered why they don't just call it temporary?"

Cassandra smiled and shrugged, lifting a lock of my hair to examine it. I flicked a gooey blob of gel off the arm of my chair and it hit Mama's wrinkled skirt. She gaped at me.

"Sorry." I shrugged and looked away from her with a wave of aversion. Surely neither Asher Acker nor Dad had ever kissed her with the intensity of desire that Ingo Bachmann had for me.

I leaned forward to let Cassandra comb out the knots at the back of my head, shut my eyes and thought, *Ingo Bachmann*. Mama sat listless in her chair, hands clutched together around Minnie's belly. I caught her eye and thought, *Ingo Bachmann*. I watched my face in the long mirror as Cassandra paint-brushed dye onto my hair, scalp to tip, and held him in my head, a smug secret. Ingo Bachmann leaning towards me over the cafeteria table. Holding my hand behind the school. Crunching my glasses painfully against my nose with his face. Kissing me. Slobbery kisses that left my whole chin wet.

"Indigo Blackman is a freak," Helena said. The school cafeteria was pink with lime-green tables. We usually went somewhere else to eat, but Helena hadn't had time to leave the school because of volleyball practice. She was wearing her team T-shirt, which was straining over her breasts. Her hair was in a perky, high volleyball ponytail. "He's a pervert," she said. "He doesn't bathe."

"How do you know? What do you mean?"

"I know, Agatha," she said. "Everyone knows."

"He looks kind of interesting." I liked that he was tall, but not as tall as he seemed from a distance, and how he watched the ground when he walked, hair flopping into his eyes. His clothes were old and didn't fit him quite right, and his arms and legs were too long for his body. He'd already failed history twice and looked more than two years older than the rest of the class, with his awkward height and stretched-out limbs. He sat with his fingers spread on the desk, leaning forward and looking down. Sometimes a spit ball bounced off his back, and someone would snicker.

"Interesting?" said Helena. "Really? Why don't you go and talk to him?"

"Yeah," said Helena's friend, a blond, pig-tailed volleyball player who had pictures of shirtless body-builders in her locker. "Why don't you suck his interesting balls?"

Helena gave the girl a look of disdain. "Seriously, Agatha," she said. "Go talk to him and tell me what he says. It'll be so funny." He was eating a sandwich by himself, drinking chocolate milk from the carton and holding a book open. I stood up. The blond girl squealed as I walked away through a bunch of ninth graders to sit down across from Ingo Bachmann.

"What are you reading?" I asked after a few seconds, to get his attention. He held up the book. It was Kafka, in German. "Oh. My parents have that book. In English, though."

"Have you read it?" He still hadn't looked at me.

I shook my head. "My mother wanted to read it to me when I was a kid, but my father made her stop after the first page. He thought it might traumatize me."

His German accent drew out his words so his voice was like chanting. "I think you would like it." Ingo Bachmann stared at me with his too-moist blue eyes, squeezed them shut and then popped them open again, frog-like, as if he might start to cry. I imagined that his tongue might pop out, stick to me and suck me in, all so fast that no one would see, and no one would ever know what happened to me.

"Don't you usually read comic books?" I said, thinking of the volume I'd often seen tucked inside his history textbook. He didn't answer, and I felt my face turn red. "I'm sorry."

"Why are you sorry?"

"I don't know." He didn't respond, just smiled and tilted his head to one side. His hair wasn't greasy that day; he must have washed it the night before. It was fluffy, and one hair in the middle of his head stuck straight up. I tried desperately to think of something alluringly eccentric and intelligent to say. Something profound and dark to show that I appreciated the pain of being misunderstood and foreign. That I understood the metaphorical significance of waking up insectile, the edge of consciousness frayed by unsettling dreams. The sleeves of Ingo Bachmann's grey sweater were too short, the cuffs worn thin, and his fully visible wrists were obscenely lean and smooth.

"Do you like me?" I said.

He blinked hard, smiled and tilted his head even further to the side. "I think so," he said after some consideration. His lips were chapped and cherry red, and his lone vertical hair swayed gently. It didn't occur to him that I might be making fun of him. His skin was perfectly clear, his patchy stubble a white-blond glow. I followed him out of the cafeteria and out of the school.

"I was hiding in the library," I told Helena later. "Where did you think I was? Making out with Indigo Blackman somewhere?"

"Don't even say that. I didn't know what to think when you left with him."

"Yeah. Well, gotcha."

Ingo Bachmann was beautiful. He was so beautiful I wanted to kill him. I wanted to hold him down and take bites out of him. That's the kind of thing he would say, blinking hard. "That tree over there is so beautiful, I want to kill it. I want to chop it into pieces." Ingo Bachmann was all seventeen-year-old melodrama. Lying in the grass by the canal, he was tormented by the colourful leaves overhead, wrenching his floppy yellow bangs with a closed fist. The things he said would have made me blush if anyone else heard them. The thought of Helena hearing my conversations with him was unbearable. That first time, we left the cafeteria and crossed the street behind the school to stand under the trees. I pushed my forehead against the dent under his shoulder, closed my eyes to the smell of wool and deodorant and cigarettes. He rested his hand gently on top of my head. I looked up at his face, and Ingo Bachmann leaned down to meet my lips. We kissed open mouthed, breathing hard. His breath and saliva in my mouth and my nose, I wanted him to touch me everywhere, wanted to press myself against him, but he held me away, a tight handful of my shirt in his fist.

"WOOOoooOOOooo," Minnie's siren startled me, and I put my hands to my flushed cheeks. She sat on the floor, racing her truck back and forth with uncommon violence.

"Go and sit on the stairs until you calm down," Mama told her. "Minnie! Now." The front entranceway was Minnie's allocated time-out area. The only place where there was absolutely nothing to break, spill or move.

"Can I wait for Agatha?"

"No," Mama said. "You need a time out. By yourself." Minnie stood and looked ready to fight, but Mama's haggard stare defeated her. Walking away in a John Wayne-inspired swagger, bottom lip extended, Minnie looked down at the fire truck in her hand. Surely she expected Mama to confiscate it, but my mother was already leaning back, eyes closed, sighing her biggest sigh. Taking her chance, Minnie quickened her pace and held the toy in front of her body, where Mama wouldn't see it.

Tam-Tam came over to watch as Cassandra put the finishing touches on my hair. It looked as if it was soaked with ketchup. "It'll be very glamorous," Tam-Tam told me. I could tell she was pleased I was taking an interest in my appearance, even if it was a bit unruly. She turned to Mama. "You must take photos of this mysterious costume she's wearing tonight, Ginny." Mama didn't answer.

"Don't worry," Cassandra told my mother. "She's young." She leaned close, brushed dye behind my ear and whispered, "Be careful. You'll be a new person. Sometimes people do things they wouldn't normally do when they get a new hairstyle. I bet your boyfriend will love it."

"A boyfriend?" said Tam-Tam. I shook my head, caught Mama's suspicious eye in the mirror and looked away.

"Oh," said Cassandra, "I'm sure she has five boyfriends. Don't get into anything too serious," she told me. "You should just be having fun at your age. You'll get your heart broken sooner or later, might as well make it later." I nodded at my reflection in the mirror as Cassandra secured my hair inside a plastic cap. What she didn't know, I thought, was that love had already enveloped me, grown stale and started inexorably to slip away. Not the heady lust of Ingo Bachmann, but a love that had worked its slow way into my bones and then started to decay. Mama hadn't noticed either, and only a neglectful mother could fail to see this tragedy unfolding before her. Sometimes I suspected that she was happy about my loss.

When Helena moved across the river to Ontario to live with her deadbeat father, she'd insisted on going to my high school, even though it wasn't the one in her neighbourhood. Immediately, she'd joined the volleyball team and started spending time with the other gym girls. It was a bad sign. And then, a few days after I found Asher's letter, my slow disillusionment with Helena had accelerated. I had been lying under a tree with Ingo Bachmann, my head on his shoulder and my hand on his thigh. "Neither of my parents wanted me to be born," I was telling him. "I was an accident." His too-short blue cotton slacks were second only to track pants in their lack of style. Several trees, thick with autumn leaves, hid us from the walking path. Beyond another large maple, a black railing guarded the five-foot drop down to a walking path that ran alongside the canal. Four boys thundered past us, clumping through the leaves and mulch, and we both turned away, but they were too absorbed in their conversation to look at us through the branches. After climbing over the railing and jumping down, they apparently stopped at the bench directly below us. We could hear their voices clearly. The one who dominated the conversation had a loud British accent. His name, famously, was Swithin Barrington Sebastian Bennett, and he was in grade twelve, two years older than me. New to the school that year, he was the son of diplomats. His parents, the story went, had pulled him out of boarding school in England and brought him with them to Canada as punishment for shooting a purportedly gay classmate in the thigh during a hunting trip in the countryside. He had started this rumour himself. He seemed like the kind of person who could shoot a deer or an effeminate classmate without breaking a sweat, without removing the cigarette from his mouth.

I had turned with my back against Ingo's chest, and he had his arm around me. I felt his muscles tense. Ingo Bachmann wasn't the kind of person that liked to eavesdrop. I ran my hand along his arm, not wanting to move.

"She came home with me at lunch on Friday," Swithin was saying. "My parents were gone all weekend, and she came back on Saturday for more. Finally, on Sunday, I shagged her three times and told her to fuck off."

"Who is this chick?" someone said.

"You know, Helena Jacob. Swellena." The other three boys laughed, and I cringed, stunned to discover that the twelfth-grade boys knew who Helena was.

"Oh, yeah. Yeah, yeah. You fucked her? Swellena Jacob?"

"Three times, no joke. She was begging for it."

"Were her tits saggy when she took off her bra?" They all laughed.

"No," said Swithin. It was easy to imagine him torturing a small animal. "They were like melons. Big, sweet, round melons with these big hard nipples." He smacked his lips as if there was too much saliva in his mouth, and the other boys groaned in delight. "Melon-a Jacob," one of them said, and the others laughed at this stroke of poetic genius. "Swellena Melona."

"I highly recommend her," said Swithin. "A fine dish indeed." Somehow, he got away with saying things that rightfully should have seen him tied to a tree with his underwear on the outside of his pants.

Ingo turned me to face him. He knew that Helena was my friend, though we'd never talked about her. He stared at me and touched my face. "Let's go," he whispered. Perhaps Ingo Bachmann would have talked about me that way if he had friends to talk to. I couldn't picture it, but I knew people often did things I couldn't picture. I picked a yellow leaf out of Ingo Bachmann's yellow hair. "I'll go first," he said. He slipped the tip of his saliva-drenched tongue against mine and looked at me searchingly before standing and walking away without looking back. I wiped my mouth on my sleeve.

"The coup de grace," Swithin was saying, "was when I reached around and put my finger right in her arsehole. You should have seen her squirm." I crept to the edge of the railing and looked over. The top of Swithin's head was a dark, gel-shiny jumble, sticking out in carefully chaotic points. Two of his minions were leaning against the railing at the side of the canal, facing me, and one looked up to meet my eyes. I gave him the finger as I stood, then quickly turned away before he had a chance to react. I didn't have the courage to spit on Swithin's head, sure that he'd turn, and that eye contact with him would bore a hole straight through my brain.

Helena and I had made fun of Swithin as we marched across the frozen canal the previous winter, chanting his name in time with our steps, doing our best to imitate his accent. I had been feeling so guilty and superior keeping Ingo a secret, and now I discovered that Helena, too, had a secret lover from far away. And hers had been a real lover, with real sex.

I looked at Cassandra as she tucked a fresh towel around my shoulders. Even Cassandra had bigger breasts than mine. It was so unfair that I couldn't just inherit that one thing from my mother. "Okay, Agatha," Cassandra said. "It stays on for half an hour."

I couldn't put my glasses on without getting dye on them, so I stood and squinted across the blurry room. After reminding Mama to free Minnie from the stairs, I made my way back to Tam-Tam's private door and peeked in to see that her blue-carpeted office was empty. Somehow, the office always resisted the pungent odours of the salon; it was an oasis smelling faintly only of Tam-Tam herself. A hint of her lipstick, a scent that settled like a taste in the back of my throat. As always in Tam-Tam's office, I felt like a small child with dirty fingers in an art gallery. I folded my hands. Without my glasses, I couldn't make out any of the faces in Tam-Tam's photographs. I wished the red dye needed more than half an hour to take effect. I was dreading the ride home, which had always been Mama's favourite time for musing on the significance and tyranny of her mother's behaviour, past and present.

"I grew up in a haunted house," Mama informed me when I was eight. "My mother had ghosts hovering around her. Her father, her aunt. And Oma Esther, too. My grandmother was already dead before I was born, a living corpse. She died in the concentration camps." My mother didn't seem to think I needed any further explanation of these statements.

"My mother and grandmother have always been a bit like Norman and Mrs. Bates," Mama told me during another drive, forgetting that I was nine and far too young to have seen *Psycho*. She talked as though an invisible audience of hundreds were gathered on the hood of our car, hanging on her every word through the windshield.

"Mrs. Bates," Mama explained, "is a corpse. She's long dead, a skeleton wrapped in clothes. But Norman is a textbook Oedipal case. He can't let her go, so he pretends she's still alive. He dresses her up in clothes and murders people in her stead. Even speaks in her voice." Mama let go of the steering wheel to make arthritic claws with her hands. "This creepy old lady voice," Mama said in a creepy old lady voice, high and piercing. "Oh, don't be scared. I didn't mean that Oma Esther was actually dead. It was a metaphor, Agatha. I'm speaking metaphorically. Mothers and sons," she went on, "typically have relationships fraught with all sorts of sublimated desires, etcetera. Mothers and daughters aren't like that. It's *fathers* and daughters." She considered this statement. "Of course, I don't have a father and neither does my mother, so. And you have Steven, but he's not your biological father, and that must have an effect on a child. My mother's not a *lesbian*," she mused. "Though she might be; sometimes I've thought she might be. But usually I just think she's asexual."

"What's a lesbian, Mama?" Startled out of her monologue, Mama was quiet, chewing her lip and watching the highway. She was always disappointed when I acted like a child.

"What's a lesbian?"

"Well, when two women love each other and sleep in the same bed, then they're lesbians."

"Like when Helena sleeps over?"

"Well, no." Mama was clearly losing patience with the conversation. "Lesbians hold hands and kiss on the lips, that sort of thing. Of course," she went on, "according to some schools of feminism, any loving relationship between women can be lesbian, even if there's no sex."

"Helena and I hold hands."

"Yes. You do, don't you." She gave me a sideways glance.

"*We* hold hands, Mama," I added, grabbing her hand.

"True enough," she agreed absently, giving my hand a quick squeeze and then pulling away to change gears. She was silent for the rest of the ride home, deep in thought. Leaving me to contemplate my great-grandmother's status as living dead. My own possible lesbianism.

"Mama?"

"What?" She sighed.

"Nothing."

Dad and I passed Bay Street. We were almost there. Even my legs were starting to shake. I breathed deeply, reminding myself that Virginia was glad of the accident, glad she had changed. Even the doctors had implied that she somehow chose it. Jasmine was trying to force a resolution of some kind; I didn't know what she was planning to do, exactly, but I suspected that, once it was over, there would be no more J. Virginia Morgan just out of view in every subway station, no more late-night walks in random neighbourhoods as I dared her to step out of the shadows. Was I ready to lose her ghostly presence?

"Dad." I grabbed his upper arm as we approached the hotel on Avenue Road.

He felt surprisingly muscular; he must have been working out. I let go quickly. "We've been here before." He looked at the building as we drove past and then found a parking space less than half a block away. Maybe he didn't remember, but we'd all come to Toronto when Jasmine was three or four. Though we stayed with friends of Dad's, we went to one of these big hotels, this very one, I was sure, for lunch. The four of us had walked together, perhaps, past this very spot. We had been a family, and it hadn't felt fragile at all. Though

Steven wasn't my father until I was three, though Mama was always hurting herself, and even though they were always arguing over laundry and vegetarianism and Judaism and whether Mama had any ambition — despite all that, I had never suspected that we could break apart so easily, could bow out and make lives without each other.

"You don't want to see her, do you?" I said. "I mean, do you want to come with me?"

Dad shook his head. "She's your mother," he said. "I'll wait here." He squeezed my hand. "Unless you want me to come."

"No." She was only his ex-wife of long ago, but yes, she was my mother. *My mother.*

"Aga, wait." I looked at him; he was afraid. "What will you say to her?"

"I don't know."

I expected the world to crumble, expected everyone to turn and stare, my body glowing guilt-red. It was the kind of hotel lobby with high ceilings and well-dressed elderly people relaxing in burgundy plush chairs; a few people waited in line at the registration desk, luggage at their feet. I spotted a small placard announcing Virginia's "Willing Amnesia" workshop, directing participants to a conference room on the third floor. The elevators had dark mouldings; everything smelled like clean carpet.

I found the room down a third-floor hallway — a regular-sized door with a curtained window. It was clearly small; I'd expected a ballroom. I saw the participants list on the wall: only twelve names, all checked off except for two: Minnie Summer and Agatha Acker. At the sound of muffled voices through the door, I stepped back with a start and then walked quickly away, back toward the elevators, trying to figure out what to do. The carpet was navy blue, with gold stars and planets. I felt nothing but the urge to run. I reached the elevators and forced myself to turn around again.

"Agatha!"

I jumped, with a little scream. Past the last elevator, Jasmine was sitting in a large armchair, burgundy velour like the ones in the lobby.

"Shh," she said. "Be quiet."

I breathed hard, my heart pounding, and stared at her. "What are you doing?" I whispered back. "Let's get out of here."

"No way."

"What's that?" She was clutching a plastic shopping bag in her lap; her backpack was on the floor beside her.

"What took you so long to get here?" she said. I settled stiffly on the arm of her chair. "I was going to go in, but it's not like I expected. There were only a few people and in a small room. She would have seen me right away. I was supposed to surprise her at the end, when she sets fire to the stuff." Jasmine leaned close. "We have to show her. *She's* our burden. Virginia's our buried burden, don't you get it?"

"You weren't going to try to burn her, were you?"

Jasmine rolled her eyes and whispered, "*No!*" her voice cracking. "Why are we whispering, anyway?" she said, slightly louder, and I giggled. We were leaning close to each other, trying not to move suddenly, as if there was a hungry lion around the corner. "These are our burdens," she told me, holding up the plastic bag. "You still have to write the three words to go with yours. We'll go into the room at the end, when everyone else is coming out." She pulled a shoebox out of the bag and opened it. Tam-Tam's shoebox — my shoebox — with Mama's cranes inside.

I pulled it out of her hand, pushing the top back on. "I don't want to burn those!"

"Shh!" She glared at me and reverted to whispering. "Tam-Tam wanted to get rid of them. You should, too. We have to tell her. She's our fucking buried burden. We're right here. We can't just give up."

I looked at her helplessly. "How did you pay for this, anyway?"

"With your credit card."

I caught myself about to say her name in that way she hated and stopped myself, shaking my head. *Jasmine.* "Come on," I said. "It's almost over. Let's go to the conference room. That way we won't chicken out."

Jasmine stood to follow me down the hall. "Thanks, Agatha," she said.

We stopped outside the door, and I pushed my ear close to the crack, jerking away when I heard a woman's voice inside. I forced myself to move close again, and Jasmine did the same. I could barely breathe. Jasmine clutched my arm, hard.

"Okay," Virginia was saying, in a loud, clear voice. "Now we're going to say goodbye to all the things that hold us back, all those deeply buried anchors we've been talking about — those Christmas dinners with your in-laws, that extra ten pounds." A few women laughed, and someone clapped. "We're cutting them loose."

Jasmine tugged at my sleeve, and I squeezed her shoulder. We listened to the scuffle of chairs against the floor as all the women moved around. From what Virginia was saying, it was clear that they were all depositing their buried burdens in her infamous metal trash can.

"I need a volunteer," Virginia said. "Um. Yes, you."

I stepped back, and Jasmine pressed her hand, palm flat, against the door.

"Now?" I said.

"No," she whispered. "No, Agatha. Wait till after."

She grabbed both my wrists as I reached for the knob, and I twisted in her grip, trying to bend her arms the wrong way. She was too strong.

"I surrender, I surrender," I gasped. "You win." She let go, and I caught my breath, pushing my hair out of my face, looking down at the starry blue carpet. Jasmine grabbed for me as I lunged forward and caught one of my arms.

"Bombs away!" cried J. Virginia Morgan.

I threw the door open with my other hand, just as a chorus of women hollered, "Forget it!" They were sitting around a large table, and a huge blue flame exploded high from the metal can at the end of the table furthest from the door, obscuring the two women standing behind it. Jasmine yanked me back into the hallway and slammed the door shut.

"Holy shit!" she said, and I laughed loudly, then covered my mouth with both hands. We stared at each other for a moment, then turned and ran down the hallway as fast as we could, Jasmine a few steps ahead of me. I stumbled slightly, trying to keep up with her, and regained my balance as we reached the elevators. Sure that something monstrous was right at my heels, I ran past the elevators and into the stairwell, holding the door open for Jasmine to follow me. We sat on the top step to catch our breath.

"Jesus," I said.

"Did anyone see us?"

"I don't know. Maybe they heard us." We sat in silence, breathing hard. No one came. "Don't you think she must have been expecting us, Min? When she saw those names on the list?"

"Unless she's retarded," Jasmine agreed.

We sat in silence, and gradually the possibility of leaving receded. We were so close. She existed; she was right there.

I remembered what I was thinking that Halloween, as I wandered across Tam-Tam's office to the slim, pink door. I'd imagined myself taking the stairs down into the apartment to hide in Tam-Tam's bathroom. They'd find me lying in a bathtub full of bright red water. Mama would scream, seeing blood, not realizing that it was only dye from my hair. I'd sit up slowly, red streaks dripping down my body. "It's my Halloween costume," I'd say. "I'm a fetus, miscarried by a woman smoking in the bathtub."

I'd leaned close to the door that led to the servants' stairwell, careful not to get hair dye on the pink-painted wood. I was sure I could smell cigarette smoke, faint but definite. After Minnie was born and Oma Esther died, I had stopped using the servants' stairs and stopped writing letters to my great-grandfather's ghost. The phantom cigarette pack I remembered checking each week as I descended to visit Oma Esther in the kitchen was still a mystery; I used to tell myself so many stories, I often found myself remembering things that couldn't possibly have happened. And yet, recalling Jozef's role in my life, he seemed as real as Helena, as real as my Oma Esther. More real, I contemplated, than Asher Acker, who existed only as twelve-year-old words on a creased bundle of paper. I leaned against the door, smelling smoke, and I pictured Jozef's spirit relaxing in the stairwell. I wondered what he would think about my romance with Ingo Bachmann.

A prickling sensation in the back of my neck sent a shiver down my spine, and I turned. My scream scared Mama, and she screamed, too, stepping back. "Calm down," she breathed, wrapping her arms around her chest.

"How long have you been standing there? Why are you spying on me?" Mama always had an eerie habit of approaching me from behind, standing quietly and watching until I realized with a start that I wasn't alone. Asher wrote that Mama had all the habits that bothered her about Oma Esther. I'd never put it together that way before, but since reading Asher's words, I could clearly see what a hypocrite she was.

"What's that smell?" She looked around. "Were you smoking in here, Agatha?"

"No! Do you think I'm an idiot?"

"Well, where's that smell coming from?"

"You can smell smoke?"

She tried to reach around me to open the narrow door. "If you weren't smoking," she said, "why don't you want me to look?"

"Okay," I pleaded, struggling to block her, "just don't." Shoving me aside, she wrenched the door open. My hands were over my eyes, but when Mama gasped, I looked down just in time to see the downstairs door ease shut.

A group of women came down the hall, and as they waited for the elevators, Jasmine stood to peek through the door and sat down beside me again. She rested her forehead on her knees, and I put my hand on her back. "You okay?"

"Oh no," she said. "They all have copies of her books."

"Yeah," I said. "She was probably signing them. So?"

Jasmine slumped lower, hugging her legs. I waited, rubbing her shoulders. She had a huge knot near her neck, and I massaged. "Ouch." She pulled away from my hand. "This is a joke. I thought it would be — different. This isn't working at all. Let's just go. I can't do this; it's a total fucking joke."

"No way," I said. "We've come this far. Come on." The commotion by the elevators had stopped; the women were gone. I grabbed her hand and stood up. "Come *on*."

We walked back down the hall, toward the open conference-room door. I held Jasmine's hand tightly, practically dragging her the last few steps. I pushed her ahead of me through the door, just as I felt my head clear. I was ready for anything. White walls; polished pine conference table; curved, solid wood chairs. We stood and stared.

"I knew it," said Jasmine. "She's gone."

"Come on," I told her. "Where's your buried burden?" She pulled all three of Virginia's books out of the plastic bag, and I led her past the table to the metal trash can that was still sitting there. We both bent over to see inside and stared at the pile of intact knickknacks and T-shirts and one teddy bear with faint scorch marks, until Jasmine finally kicked the can as hard as she could.

"Fucking sophistry!" she yelled. She slammed her three books, one old and worn, two brand new, onto the table, and a small piece of paper drifted out onto the floor. We both bent to pick it up, and she grabbed it, just as I saw her handwriting in thick, black permanent marker: *Please Forgive Me*. She shoved it in her pocket, and I touched her arm.

"Those were your three words? *Why?*"

"Forget it." Jasmine reached for her books, and I pushed my arm through hers, pulling her toward me despite her resistance. Halfway down the hall, she wrenched herself free and walked a few steps ahead of me.

"Jasmine?" I said, as we stepped into the elevator.

She looked at me.

"Dad's outside in the car."

I was the one who needed forgiveness; I should have confessed long ago. But who could I tell? Who would have understood my anger with Mama for opening that pink door, for forcing me to realize those cigarette packs had belonged to Tam-Tam all along? How could I confess something so absurd? Mama had looked at me helplessly, arms hanging limply at her sides. We stared at each other until her eyes darted to the side like they always did when she was thinking hard. "What a sneak." She sounded intrigued and triumphant, like a sleuth smacking her lips over a long-hidden clue. "Do you know how guilty she used to make me feel? How long do you think . . . Agatha, why are you crying?"

"You stupid, fat cow." I choked on tears to get the words out, and then I was yelling. "You don't understand anything. You ruin everything. You always have to ruin everything I care about."

"I don't understand what you're talking about." Mama stepped away from me as if she was afraid I might explode. "What on earth is wrong with you?"

"Everything! Everything is wrong with me, and you just have no idea. You're so stupid. You're a big blundering disaster that ruins everything and doesn't even notice!"

Her utter confusion only made me angrier; I wanted to slap her, punch her, make her suffer. She said, "But what does Tamar's smoking have to do with you?"

"What does anything have to do with me?" Mama shook her head. There was a smudge of mascara high on her left eyelid. "I have to know everything, because you're too dense to know it yourself!"

Mama crossed her arms. "Oh, I know more than you think I do," she said. "I know you're sexually active, if that's what you mean. I wash your underwear, young lady. I know what it means when a girl trades in her sports bras for black lace ones."

"Asher!" I said, not caring how loudly. "Asher, my biological father. He didn't take off to you-didn't-know-where. He went to Israel and then California. You smoked while you were pregnant with me. You only married Steven so you wouldn't have to live with Tam-Tam and Oma Esther." I didn't look at my mother. Keeping my eyes focused on the door to the stairs, I told her, "I know you and my real father didn't want me. You both hated me. And I know he died when I was ten. I was in your closet when you and Dad were talking about it. I kept waiting for you to tell me, but you never did.

Because you're a coward!" I finally looked at Mama's face, and I reached for her arm, sure she was about to faint.

Putting out her own hand to stop mine, she said quietly, "Asher's not dead."

"But I heard you say so."

"No, we never said that. When you were ten? He came to Ottawa for some shrink conference and wanted to visit us. He wanted to meet you, and we said no. That must have been the conversation you heard." I felt as disoriented as my mother looked. Jozef killed off once and for all, and Asher resuscitated after being dead and buried for almost six years.

"Your father used to sleep with prostitutes," I said. "Tam-Tam told Asher, and Asher told Steven. They all kept that from you. Like you're some delicate flower that can't handle the truth. And meanwhile, you don't bother to protect me from one solitary thing. And you want to know what else I know about?" Mama shook her head. "Asher used to visit Tam-Tam when you weren't home, and he wanted to have sex with her. When she said no, he went for you." I said to the pink door, "You're all assholes. Everyone." Meeting Mama's expressionless face, I went on, "Helena slept with Swithin Bennett and didn't tell me. The boarding school guy. And he makes fun of her for it to his friends."

Unmistakable sympathy flashed across Mama's face. "Pumpkin," she started, reaching for my arm. "I know — "

"No." I pulled back. "You don't care. I wish I had a different mother. You're the worst mother in the world."

"Ag?" I turned to see Minnie standing just inside the door. Someone had painted red sparkles around her eyes. Crossing her arms inside her cardigan and leaning her weight on one foot, she told me, "Cassandra says come get your hair washed out."

Before grabbing my sister's hand on the way out of the room, I turned back to Mama, took Asher Acker's folded letter out of my back pocket and shoved it into her hand. "Agatha," she started. I left the room before she had a chance to finish.

"So you didn't see her at all?" Steven said.

"I just want to be able to forget about her." Jasmine was crying in the front seat, Steven's arm around her shoulders. He'd been standing, pacing beside his car when we left the hotel, and he hurried to meet us, checking around and behind us for ghostly figures of ex-wives. "I guess it was a fucking stupid plan," Jasmine said. "Nothing I do ever works." The sun was already setting and it was chilly; a brisk wind lifted dry brown leaves from the gutter. In the back seat, I buttoned my jacket and wrapped my scarf around my neck, up to my chin. Jasmine just groaned into Steven's shoulder. "Why do I have to be related to that freak?" she said. "And her fucking sophistry bullshit books."

"But why did you ask for her forgiveness?" I said.

Jasmine ignored me. She was still angry about Steven, despite how obviously relieved she was to see him.

"You know why," she said, finally, her voice muffled by Steven's sweater. I shook my head, and Steven said he didn't know why either.

"The accident. The fire truck."

"No," I said. "No, no."

"Agatha," said Steven. He handed me a box of tissues from the front seat, and my hands were shaking so badly, it was hard to hold them. "Sweetheart," he said.

I choked on a sob as I tried to speak and broke into a coughing fit, still crying. Breathing hard, I waited until I was calm enough to speak. "It was my fault," I said. "I was so mean to her that day. Right before she fell. Dad, I stole your letter from Asher Acker. The one that said all that stuff about Tam-Tam." My voice was still shaking.

"Oh, Jesus," said Dad. "That letter? I thought I lost that damn thing years ago. You read that?"

"I gave it to Mama," I said. "Right before she fell."

"What letter?" said Jasmine. "What stuff about Tam-Tam?"

"It was this horrible letter," I said, blowing my nose. "From my other father to Dad. It said things about Mama and Tam-Tam that were" — my voice cracked — "so, so mean. If I hadn't given her that letter, Mama and Steven would probably still be together."

Jasmine turned around and stared at me, her face twitching almost comically. Then she lunged between the front seats and grabbed me by the hair on top of my head, pulling me towards her. I screamed in pain, trying to pry her fingers open. "Why didn't you tell me," she howled, shaking me with each word. "This will never be over. You fucking psychopath! Why do you think you're too good to tell anyone anything? Why don't you love us anymore?"

Jasmine let go abruptly, crying out in pain herself, and then sat back, her eyes tearing, holding her wrist where Steven had grabbed it.

"Girls, that's enough." Steven put his arm across the seat between us. "Please!" he said, as Jasmine moved toward me again, fists clenched.

"But Dad," said Jasmine. "She made me smoke drugs."

I gaped at this non sequitur of a betrayal, too shocked to keep crying, but Dad said, "Jasmine, please. Your sister's been doing her best. Ginny and I weren't going to stay together, Agatha, even if there was no accident."

I sat back. "I know," I said. And I did know. I felt my body go limp. "Why didn't you ever say that before?"

"I could have. I should have. I didn't know if it would make things better or worse. You should have told me you saw that idiot's letter. I should never have kept it. It was a piece of garbage, you know. But Agatha, there's no way anything in that letter came as a shock to your mother or changed anything for her. It couldn't have. We'd already grown apart. It was all ancient history."

"But Tam-Tam?"

"That's right," said Dad. "He claimed — I just don't know. I don't know if any of that was true. What he wrote — I'm sorry, Agatha, but he was the kind of person who said things just to get a reaction. You're nothing like him. Nothing."

Jasmine leaned forward to rest her forehead against the dashboard. I smoothed my hair where my scalp was stinging.

"Agatha," Jasmine said. "I'm sorry I pulled your hair."

"That's okay, Jas." I wedged myself between the seats to put my arm around her back.

"And I'm sorry I ran away when Bev's dying. Poor Lara. Does Lara hate me now?" I held her arm tightly. She had a home to go back to; my story was slipping away, everything I'd told myself for nine years.

Dad put his arm around her, too. "No. We both love you girls."

I met his eyes in the mirror.

"Oh my God," I said. "Look. Look! There she is." My sister shook the hair out of her face, Dad and I each with an arm still on her back. We watched J. Virginia Morgan walk down the sidewalk from the front of the hotel, hands in the pockets of her brown leather jacket. She approached quickly, with a straight-backed, even pace, pulling out keys.

Ingo Bachmann once said that after a moment has happened, nothing can take it away again. "It'll always be true," he said, "that we lay here under this tree on this day, and your hand was absent-mindedly pulling at the back of my shirt — no, don't stop. Agatha Winter and Ingo Bachmann. We don't need to engrave our names on any tree, because this moment is permanently engraved on every other moment that ever passed or that will ever come to be."

"Yes," I agreed, caught up in the Ingo Bachmann-ness of Ingo Bachmann. "Even if I saw you on the street ten years from now, and you didn't recognize me, or pretended not to see me, that couldn't undo this moment. But that means we can never take anything back, either."

"Of course we can't," said Ingo Bachmann.

And Virginia stepped past us. The setting sun shone on her face, making her squint. Her hair, long and slightly frizzy at the tips, shone a fake, shiny mahogany. I stared at her face as she went by. She looked like Jasmine, like my mama, as much as a cousin would. Her skin was smooth, her lips full. And she was tanned. Mama had always worn sunscreen and big, floppy hats; she'd burnt badly as a child and said it was impossible for her skin to get darker.

"Goodbye, strange lady," Jasmine said as Virginia passed her window. She yelled, "It was an accident."

Dad cowered, afraid this slender, tanned spectre might come too close, somehow touch him.

"Goodbye," said Jasmine. "Goodbye."

Dad stared at Virginia, and I watched his face in the mirror. "That's her," he said, shaking his head. "Jesus. *Jesus*. That's all? I never knew that woman."

As Virginia opened the door of a new-looking black Saab, she turned and looked in our direction, and the wind blew her hair forward, over her shoulders. Her eyes were bright, reddish brown, and just for a moment, I thought I saw Mama turning from the stove, framed by paisley wallpaper, with a wooden spoon in her hand. *Agatha*, I heard her say. *Get off the counter. Get down from there.* I wondered if Dad was remembering Mama, too, maybe when they first met — back when she was the life of the party, his voluptuous young student, obsessed with Nietzsche and Spinoza, writing papers about parts of the brain and handing them in for him to grade.

Inside her car, Virginia fiddled with the mirror and put on glasses; Mama never had glasses. I'd met Virginia once before, eight years earlier. She'd already taken everything she wanted from the house before she told anyone she was planning to leave. I was the only one who'd watched her go; eleven floors up, I stood with a hand on my newly shaven head and watched her taxi drive off. Now we all watched together as Virginia reversed out of her parking space too quickly and stopped with a bit of a jolt before driving away.

I looked down at the shoebox in my hand. I opened it and pulled out the brightest of the faded red cranes, the others following. They dangled from the mustard yellow yarn like a mobile. It took Dad a moment to recognize them, and then he leaned to look closer. "Are those . . ."

I nodded.

"Ginny used to make — do you girls know what those are?"

I opened my door and got out of the car. I hurried around to the back; the wind was blowing harder, and I pushed a strand of hair out of my mouth. After tying one end of the yarn securely to the car's antenna, I tested my knot; the yarn was still strong, after a quarter of a century. I climbed back in the car.

"We know what they are," I said.

"Yeah," Jasmine said. "That's so cool."

"Let's go," I said. "You can both stay at my place, and we'll leave for Ottawa in the morning."

"But your job?" said Dad.

"I'll tell them it's a family emergency. If they don't understand, I guess I'll have to find a new job." I felt far less confident about this decision than I tried to sound. "I'm sure they'll understand. Okay, Dad?"

"Good girl," he said. Jasmine and I turned to watch Mama's cranes out the back window as he pulled out onto Avenue Road. "We'll see if they hold together all the way home," Dad said. "They're just paper, and this is a real wind." We watched the red birds lift and flutter like a kite's tail in the sun's quickly fading crimson glow.

Eyes closed, I couldn't see or hear anything but the water against my head. If it weren't for the unforgiving porcelain behind my neck and the already cold drop of water sliding down behind my ear, I would have been perfectly comfortable. Cassandra rubbed my scalp, and I opened my eyes to see the underside of her chin, a line where beige face collided with white neck. I saw the backing of her nose ring inside her nostril. When Cassandra lifted her hands off my head, I saw that she was wearing latex gloves. She pulled them off and helped me sit up, then combed out my hair and blow-dried it before I followed her back to her station.

"Wow," said Cassandra, and we both looked at me in the mirror. My hair was red as a crayon. In contrast, my eyebrows were almost white and my eyes bright grey, even through my glasses. "Wait right here," Cassandra said. She came back with a box of makeup. "Take off those glasses and close your eyes."

I hardly recognized my reflection when she was through, and not only because my glasses were off. Cassandra had given me red false eyelashes that curled up like the spokes of a rake. Silvery-black liner surrounded my eyes, and my eyebrows were shaded a light reddish brown. My lips were as red as my hair. "You're going to look amazing tonight."

I put on my glasses, and the lashes bumped them when I blinked. The costume was ruined now that I'd spilled my guts to Mama. It had lost all power, gone slack. I stared, deflated, at my absurdly brilliant head. I didn't even feel like dressing up and going to the dance anymore. Helena would be there with her volleyball friends, and I'd have to watch her glancing at Swithin while he ignored her. Ingo Bachmann would never go to a school dance. I only wanted to sit down with Mama and hear her explain herself. My anger had faded, and I was eager for the earnest discussion that comes after a fight.

"Enjoy it, babe," said Cassandra. "That colour will start fading as soon as you shampoo."

She'd turned me into someone else.

Mama was already in her coat when I got to the door, and Minnie wiggled her bum as I readjusted her in my arms. "You're getting heavy, Fireman Jeffrey," I told her, making her giggle crazily. With a bit of a struggle, I disentangled her limbs from my body and set her on the floor, and she grabbed my hand. Mama kissed Tam-Tam's cheeks, and I watched for any sign of change. Any indication that her mother had changed for her today, the way Mama changed for me when I read Asher Acker's letter. Instead of the usual air kiss, Mama's lips made unabashed contact with Tam-Tam's cheek, and she leaned forward to hold her mother in a close, weary hug. Surprised, Tam-Tam patted the middle of my mother's trench-coated back.

Mama stood at the top of the stairs, holding the door open, waiting for me and Minnie to go through. "Go ahead," I said. Mama sighed and started down the staircase. I watched her back, her harried gait. Mama click-click-clicked on her high heels. Still walking, she turned to look back at us. Minnie's fire truck was on the next stair, and I realized Mama hadn't noticed it, that she was on a collision course. "He was right, in a way," she called up to me.

I was paralyzed on the top step, Minnie's hand in mine. "But," Mama added.

"Watch out!" I said.

I did say that, but was it before or after Mama's foot was on the truck? Before or after the audible crack of ankle bone? Her leg flew up, hand grabbing for the orange rail, and her body jerked in a strange, whiplash turn so she was facing us. The fire truck clattered down the stairs as Minnie screamed. Mama's eyes and mouth were wide open. She seemed to pause, to look straight at me before flailing into a back dive. I yelled, absurdly, "Wait!" and there was a thud, a crack louder than any human head should ever make. Dad would draw diagrams, trying to figure it out. He sketched Mama's brain inside a stick-figure body flying backwards down a staircase, lines and equations indicating the velocity of the fall, the force of impact. He drew an arrow pointing at the front right of her forehead, sketched it over and over, perplexed.

Minnie stopped screaming, and it was strangely quiet. I was aware of rain against the door. On the bottom step, the plastic fire truck had landed upright and unharmed, and Mama's high heels pointed up the stairs at me, her left foot twisted at an unnatural angle. Usually, after an accident, Mama would swear at the top of her lungs, but this time she didn't make a sound. Her body slid backwards down the stairs as slowly and peacefully as a bag of sand.

Acknowledgements

I developed these characters and ideas throughout my master's degree at the University of New Brunswick, and I'm grateful to my mentors there, especially to John Ball for his guidance and for pushing me to send that first attempt out into the world. "The Guiding Light," a story from a previous draft of this work, won the 2007 Fiddlehead fiction contest and appeared in the Spring 2007 issue of the magazine. The Social Sciences and Humanities Research Council and the Canada Council for the Arts provided financial assistance during stages of writing this book. Laurel Boone, my editor, gently and expertly showed me how to turn a collection of ideas into a novel. I thank everyone at Goose Lane Editions for making me feel in such capable hands, especially Dawn Louwen, proofreader extraordinaire.

I am grateful to all the people who wittingly or unwittingly sparked ideas, those who provided essential details, and those who critiqued bits and pieces along the way. I owe a special debt to my constant first reader, Barbara Romanik, who read every word between these covers, along with many other words she wisely advised me to delete; my parents, David and Christina Lewis, and my sister, Chloe Lewis, for always telling me to write and never suggesting I do something more practical; my Oma, Mary van Embden, for many hours-long talks about everything from Dutch phrases to the depth of the ocean at a particular beach; and all my family for teaching me, from a young age, that the world is full of eccentric, loveable characters with mysterious pasts. Everything is easier with the love and support of Melissa Kehoe, Nomi Claire Lazar and Sarah Steele. And thanks to Jason Markusoff, for every little thing.

Achevé d'imprimer au Canada en janvier 2008
sur les presses de Quebecor World Saint-Romuald